D0925479

TWO AND TWENTY DARK TALES:
DARK RETELLINGS OF MOTHER GOOSE RHYMES

TWO AND TWENTY DARK TALES:
DARK RETELLINGS OF MOTHER GOOSE RHYMES

By

Nina Berry, Sarwat Chadda, Leah Cypess, Sayantani DasGupta, Shannon Delany with Max Scialdone, Leigh Fallon, Angie Frazier, Jessie Harrell, Nancy Holder, Heidi R. Kling, Suzanne Lazear, Karen Mahoney, Lisa Mantchev, Georgia McBride, C. Lee McKenzie, Gretchen McNeil, Pamela van Hylckama Vlieg, K.M. Walton, Suzanne Young, Michelle Zink.

Foreword by Francisco X. Stork

Month9Books

Copyright © 2012 by Nina Berry, Sarwat Chadda, Leah Cypess, Sayantani DasGupta, Shannon Delany with Max Scialdone, Leigh Fallon, Angie Frazier, Jessie Harrell, Nancy Holder, Heidi R. Kling, Suzanne Lazear, Karen Mahoney, Lisa Mantchev, Georgia McBride, C. Lee McKenzie, Gretchen McNeil, Pamela van Hylckama Vlieg, K.M. Walton, Suzanne Young, Michelle Zink, and Month9Books, LLC.

Two and Twenty Dark Tales: Dark Retellings of Mother Goose Rhymes

ISBN 978-0-9850294-1-8 (tr. pbk)
ISBN 978-0-9850294-0-1 (e-book)

Month9Books, LLC, PO BOX 1892 Fuquay-Varina, NC 27526.

Visit us online at: http://month9books.com

Cover design by Heather Howland and Alicia "Kat" Dillman
Edited by Georgia McBride and Michelle Zink

For Tia and Jake, always.

Publisher Acknowledgements

This anthology would not be possible without the devastatingly creative minds who have contributed stories, including: Nina Berry, Sarwat Chadda, Leah Cypess, Sayantani DasGupta, Shannon Delany with Max Scialdone, Leigh Fallon, Angie Frazier, Jessie Harrell, Nancy Holder, Heidi R. Kling, Suzanne Lazear, Karen Mahoney, Lisa Mantchev, C. Lee McKenzie, Gretchen McNeil, Pamela van Hylckama Vlieg, K.M. Walton, Suzanne Young, and Michelle Zink.

Special thanks to Michelle Zink, who also served as an editor, making the stories rock even harder. Thanks to Pamela van Hylckama Vlieg, who also helped with blog promotion. Next, a special thanks to Month9Books staffers: Jennifer Million, Mandy Schoen, Kelly P. Simmon, Linda Covella, Cameron Yeager, and Rachel Bateman.

To Tracey and Karen at Media Masters Publicity and Deborah Sloan at KidsBuzz and Deborah Sloan and Company: without your generosity of time and service, we'd be just another book released into the world without anyone aware of its existence.

Francisco X. Stork. I could not be more appreciative of the person you are, or the level to which your contribution has elevated the value of this anthology. Thank you for indulging our darkness.

Dana Borowitz, you came in like a whirlwind, and made me feel not so crazy after all.

Tamar Rydzinski, my agent, confidant, and friend. Thank you for supporting my crazy ideas, and pushing me to do my best.

Finally, to Super 8 and Fantastic 4, you are my loves and my life. Without you, I am nothing.

Table of Contents

Introduction
Georgia McBride

This anthology is the first in a series of annual charity anthologies from Month9Books, in which proceeds from the sale of the first five thousand books will be donated to a deserving charity. In 2012, TWO AND TWENTY DARK TALES proceeds will be donated to YALITCHAT.ORG, a literary organization that fosters the advancement of young adult literature around the world. For more information on YALITCHAT.ORG, please visit http://yalitchat.com. Contributing authors donate their advances to the charity of their choosing. Please join us in the celebration of young adult literature with TWO AND TWENTY DARK TALES: Dark Retellings of Mother Goose Rhymes.

Foreword
Francisco X. Stork

The question that kept coming up as I read the stories in this volume was why would anyone want to transform innocent nursery rhymes into dark and scary fairy tales? What kind of perverse minds would twist words meant to put us to sleep into colorful and sometimes fun, but nevertheless scary, nightmares? The only answer I could come up with is that there is something about the collection of rhymes we call "Mother Goose" that requires additional work for these glimpses of childhood reality to make sense to us as we grow into adulthood.

The dark tales in this volume immerse us into the childhood world of innocence and heroism, but they also add something to the original telling. The tales now contain the other side of reality, the darker side of fear. Wishes are not always fulfilled, and the security and permanence of our parents' love is no longer a sure thing. There is something in us that demands this kind of wholeness from our stories as we grow older. It is as if in order for us to give our hearts to the good, we must also believe in the bad. In order for us to live in the light, we must be aware of the darkness.

I am accustomed to creating characters that are good and characters that are bad, and most of all, characters that are both. I am accustomed to creating a reality that has evil and suffering and therefore, hopefully, believability. That is the only reason I can think of to explain why I was asked to write this foreword. But even as I figured this out, I still needed to ask myself about the need to complicate the simple and the comforting into tales that are decidedly discomforting and scary, even as they delight. Why take something meant to lull us into peaceful sleep, and convert it into something that will scare us into wakefulness?

One simple answer is that this is what authors do. Their restless imaginations take the seed of an image or a word and transform it, or rather, discover in that small nugget a hidden and potential conflict. And conflict is what makes a story a story. In other words, this book is a microcosm of how all stories are made. We elaborate on the hints given to us by our own lives, and the new reality that is hinted at is always complicated, a mixture of the good and the bad. But what exactly attracts these authors to terror, toward an exaggeration of the bad?

This book is meant for young adults, so the tendency toward the more complex is an attempt to respond to the more complex mind of the young adult person. Life gets messy in adolescence, and the simple answers of childhood are no longer sufficient. The new-found complexity of the world comes with perplexing, seemingly unanswerable questions, the most important of which is this: what is the meaning of life?

I am willing to bet that the authors of these stories have not forgotten the terrors that surround this single question. In fact, I am certain that for many of them, this single question still terrifies the living daylights out of them. The reason why the question of life's meaning is still so full of terror is because they have remained young enough to see all those things in our world that seem to deny our lives meaning. They remember the darkness of their young lives, that period when meaning seemed obliterated by overwhelming forces, and they still see this darkness as a force hell-bent on destroying all vestiges of hope.

There are times in our lives when there are more questions than answers, when darkness is more pervasive than light. The writers of these dark tales have suffered enough to discover that the only way out of darkness is to confront it head-on. This confrontation is never easy, and it doesn't always have what the world considers a happy ending. But what the confrontation with darkness does have is a sense of celebration, a sense that we are supposed to face darkness, regardless of the outcome. We are meant to be heroes. We are meant to fight witches and monsters and evil spirits, even if it appears that we will not survive the encounter. In short, we are meant to hope and to believe in the impossible. The meaning comes from the fight itself, from fighting against such great odds and such great powers, regardless of whether there is a great victory at the end, or not. Our victory is in the trying.

The writers in this book understand that the happiness of the nursery rhyme is not a lasting happiness. There is something about nursery rhymes that is at worst, deceiving, and at best, incomplete. There is something unsatisfying about the innocence presented. There are too many questions left unanswered. Why do the witches call the children out to play? Why did Jill come tumbling after? Why couldn't all the king's men put poor Humpty Dumpty together again? The authors of these dark retellings shine the light of their imaginations on the disturbing questions contained in nursery rhymes and, in doing so, give the rhymes new life.

I guarantee these tales will delight you and scare you, just like you are often scared by the overwhelming darkness that surrounds your familiar ways. But, in the end, you will be grateful for your fear, for it is only in the darkness of fear that you will discover the light.

TAFFY WAS A WELSHMAN

Taffy was a Welshman,
Taffy was a thief;
Taffy came to my house
And stole a piece of beef.

I went to Taffy's house,
Taffy was not home;
Taffy came to my house
And stole a mutton bone.

I went to Taffy's house,
Taffy was not in;
Taffy came to my house
And stole a silver pin.

I went to Taffy's house,
Taffy was in bed;
I took up a poker
And threw it at his head.

– Mother Goose

AS BLUE AS THE SKY AND JUST AS OLD
Nina Berry

When the girl sneaked in at midnight, he used his penlight to make a note. His handwriting was small and neat, like the tidy little mustache under his pointy nose and the thin strands of hair glued precisely to his clean skull.

Henderson, for that was the name he used (though it was not the one he'd been born with), liked keeping fastidious notes in tidy lines. He enjoyed impressing his clients with precision.

He would need to stay sharp in order to keep his latest customer happy. The customer, who went by the odd name of Arawn, hadn't struck Henderson as someone easily pleased. Those heavy restless hands and turbulent gray eyes were looking for a reason to batter and strike.

Arawn's instructions had been clear-cut. Find a girl. Here, Arawn had handed Henderson an address scribbled in a jagged hand and a blurry black and white photo of a female of troubling beauty, about seventeen, with shiny black hair teased into a bouffant from forty years ago. Her wide, dark eyes glanced over her shoulder with a haunted look.

"Is this a recent photo?" Henderson had asked. The heavy paper was creased and faded.

Arawn didn't like questions. "It will do," he said.

Henderson had found the girl, residing in a county group home for orphans. From there, his instructions were clear. He was to wait outside the home, then follow the girl to school in the morning and wait some more. If at some point she departed in the company of a young man with golden hair and a black vehicle, he was to follow her. If she left the school without the golden-haired young man, the case was over.

Henderson took note of Arawn's exact words: "in the company of a young man with golden hair." Not many many big-fisted, murderously-minded clients like Arawn described another man's hair as golden.

Arawn had said that the young blond man would take the girl, Aderyn, in his black vehicle to a place where they could be alone. Arawn did not know exactly where, but Henderson was to follow and find out.

As soon as the two went to this place and were alone, Henderson was to call Arawn, not a moment earlier, and certainly not a moment later. Arawn hadn't said why, but Henderson got the distinct impression he didn't want the golden-haired young man to get to know the girl Aderyn too intimately.

"Perhaps I should call you as soon as they leave the school?" he had asked. "Why wait?"

Arawn had scowled. "So many girls it could be, so little time. The young man with the golden hair will discover if she is the one I want," he had said. "If she is, he will take her somewhere to be alone. Only then should I be called, for I may not stay in this cold land for long."

Henderson wanted to ask him what he meant by that, since this land was Los Angeles in the summer and hardly cold. But he refrained. Arawn didn't like questions.

Arawn had reached into his enormous wool coat and pulled out a heavy velvet bag full of something that clicked. "She is the first of three. If you succeed in helping me with her, there will be two more jobs, and two more payments like this."

Then, in the most startling moment of all, Arawn had opened the velvet bag, tilted it, and spilled a half dozen gems, sparkling white, red, green, and blue, onto the palm of his hand.

Henderson's cold little heart had hugged itself at the sight, and Arawn had tossed the gems like jacks onto the desk. Then he turned in a swirl of long embroidered scarf, and vanished through the door. The desk lamp brightened with his exit, as if a scrim of darkness had lifted.

The gems, it turned out, were authentic and of the finest quality. Rubies, sapphires, emeralds, and diamonds worth more than everything else Henderson owned. He'd resolved then to complete this task in good order for Arawn, not only because the man was the type he preferred not to cross, but in hope of the other two jobs and two more payments of gems.

Or perhaps an opportunity would come along, allowing Henderson unrestricted access to that velvet pouch. Arawn was someone accustomed to being obeyed, and men like that were better complied with as far as prudence dictated. Henderson might not be a particularly obedient man, but he was prudent, so he gathered up his binoculars, his notepad and pen, his granola bars, a six-pack of Diet Dr. Pepper, an empty bottle for pissing in, and set out for the group home.

He parked across the street and was on his second soda when Aderyn showed up after midnight. Her heavy black hair was scraped back in a ponytail instead of a bouffant, her cheeks dangerously thin, but there was no mistaking the sad dark eyes from the photograph. He made a note of the time: 12:05 a.m. precisely, and of her attire. Her stick-thin legs were clad in white jeans tighter than he thought proper, topped with a baggy black shirt and oversized leather jacket, her feet shod in soft black boots.

She paused at the foot of the jacaranda tree flowering in the side yard and pulled a long, shiny knife out of her backpack. She touched one finger to the edge of the blade, as if making sure it was sharp.

Henderson tut-tutted as he made a note. Were county group homes really so dangerous that a tiny girl like her would need a knife like that? That was a shame. A shame indeed.

She tucked the knife away. Then she looked up at the moon through the branches of the jacaranda tree, opened her mouth, and sang melancholy words he did not understand. The mournful melody sidled into Henderson's soul and pierced his heart. The pain was so exquisite that when he blinked to find the refrain was over, he found her already perched high up in the jacaranda tree. If he didn't know better, he would have sworn she flew there. She balanced easily on the stout branch, looking uncommonly comfortable, and climbed into the third story window of the home.

During the hours he waited for the sun to rise, Henderson tried to hum the tune she'd sung. But no matter how many times he tried, he was always at least one note off, here or there.

***

There was a man in a car outside the group home, watching her and taking notes. Aderyn had seen him the night before as she slipped into the window of the hell-home. She saw him again the next morning. He'd moved his rusty yellow sedan down the block, but he had the same old-timey Clark Gable mustache and was still wearing the same maroon tracksuit, peering at her through mini-binoculars.

Well, the world was full of weirdos, as more than one occasion had taught her. Cop or stalker, it didn't matter. Nothing was going to get in the way of her plans.

She sped up her pace, hoping to leave the little man in the tracksuit behind, and felt in her backpack for the knife. It was still there, better than money in her hand. Soon she'd be where no one could follow her.

She would have done it last night, but she needed to return the books to Mrs. Davis. The tiny old woman with her dyed blond pile of hair and her black-rimmed glasses would make her tea and ask her how her day was going, and for that forty-five minutes Aderyn would feel that she mattered. She wouldn't say goodbye, but she could leave the books behind, and Mrs. Davis would understand she was grateful.

The battered yellow sedan followed her all the way to school, sneaking in and out of traffic, disappearing for a few minutes, only to reappear, waiting for her at the drop off. She flipped him off then darted into the school.

She'd reported the abuses at the group home, but had no illusions that he was sent to investigate that. She'd long ago given up the fantasy someone would come and save her. No. The cycle of group home /

foster home / new school / rejection / group home would continue on and on, unless she put a stop to it.

Her appointment to see Mrs. Davis was the only thing she looked forward to, today or any day. And even kind old Mrs. Davis couldn't save her. Aderyn felt her backpack for the outline of the knife and was reassured to find it there.

As she walked up to her locker, a lady jock in the hallway gasped, "Have you heard? Did you hear?" and ran over to shout to her soccer teammates that Mrs. Davis had been killed that morning on her way to school.

A car accident, she said. A hit-and-run.

***

Mrs. Davis's office had smelled vaguely of chamomile and tar. Aderyn liked to think that, in between counseling sessions, Mrs. Davis cracked the window overlooking the street and secretly had a cigarette, exhaling the smoke through the gap to mix with the traffic below.

Aderyn had said nothing to the old lady for the first two sessions, of course. She was there because some bureaucrat had labeled her "at risk." She didn't understand how talking to a little old lady was going to change that. Mrs. Davis had asked questions and cracked quaint jokes. She'd pinned and re-pinned her unlikely pile of blond hair and made endless cups of tea.

The third session, Mrs. Davis had pulled out a book and read aloud from it. Aderyn hadn't really understood what was going on at first, but as the words rolled out of Mrs. Davis like waves on a beach, pictures formed in Aderyn's head. They were images she'd never seen anywhere else—of horses flashing in the dark, of hay as high as houses, of owls and the moon, and fire as green as grass. She flew over the sunrise with black and white wings, and when Mrs. Davis finished speaking, she came to rest gently on the earth again, tears on her cheeks.

"It's by Dylan Thomas, a Welsh poet," Mrs. Davis had said, holding the book out. "Would you like to borrow it?"

She'd eaten that book whole and moved on to more poetry, history, and mythology. She'd discovered that her name meant "bird" in Welsh, and that the old Welsh myths were like dangerous bedtime stories left unfinished, to loom over her dreams at night.

She never remembered her dreams before, but now she started to write them down. Dreams of black and white wings flying over green hills. Most of the time she flew only to be caught in a net and held in a silver cage. But a few joyous times she took someone by the hand and taught her to fly too. That was the best dream.

She still had two of the books. One contained old nursery rhymes, the other Welsh history and myth. The subjects often seemed to intertwine. Mrs. Davis had loaned them to her after Aderyn had come to a session sporting a black eye, still smarting after a girl in the group home punched her in her sleep. When asked why, the puncher—who sported a black eye herself—said it was Aderyn's turn. Aderyn hadn't really understood that, since she barely knew the girl.

Mrs. Davis had a long silver stickpin in the shape of a bird she always wore on the neck of her favorite pink cardigan, the one starting to pill at the elbows. She'd run her fingers over the pin thoughtfully and let Aderyn cry and talk and yell. Then she'd looked over her black-rimmed glasses and said, "Bad things cycle round and round. Those who were harmed seek to harm. Those who were blamed seek to blame. If we all choose to do otherwise, maybe someday it will stop."

Aderyn had found strange comfort in those words. It was then she'd started planning how to stop the cycle without blaming or harming anyone but herself.

***

Now Mrs. Davis was dead, killed in a hit-and-run. There was no one left to speak to. No one to give the books to. No one to make smelly tea and read her words that sent the world reeling.

Aderyn did not cry, but she stood there staring at nothing for a long time. Then she opened up her backpack. Mrs. Davis's books lay next to the stolen knife. It was ready.

She didn't see the boy approach at first, so focused was she. He made no sound as he got near; no shadow loomed. He was suddenly very solidly *there*, standing by her locker, smiling. He had to be new. She would have remembered him otherwise.

His hair was the gold of sunshine on a wheat field. His skin was smooth and young, but his eyes were as blue as the sky and just as old. They pierced her, and an ache began in her bones that made her want to fly, fly into those eyes.

He looked at her and took her hand away from the stolen knife to kiss. His lips were soft and warm. His shoulders were broad and strong. In his ancient blue eyes she saw herself reflected, beautiful and desired.

"Aderyn," he said. "I'm Matthew, and I'd like to take you out."

"Hi," she said, for she was only seventeen, and life in a series of foster homes had not prepared her for his formal tone, his firm touch, his bemused gaze. "How did you know my name?"

"I saw a girl, delicate, clever, and kind. So I asked around." Self-assurance emanated from him like cologne. She envisioned herself pressing against him and some of that warm scent rubbing off on her. "Let's sneak out now," he said. "I'll drive."

She said, "Yes," and he didn't let go of her hand as they walked down the corridor. She hoisted her backpack over her shoulder. The knife could wait.

***

His car was big and black with opaque windows, like something going to a funeral. He opened her door and saw that she was safely bestowed on the shiny leather seat before shutting it with a gentle thump.

As he settled in next to her, she asked, "Did your parents give you this car?"

"I stole it," he said, and turned the key so that the engine revved. "I'm a thief."

She asked, "Are you stealing me?"

His laugh was a delighted shout. "Yes," he said, and peeled out into the street.

She was too captivated to see the mustachioed man in the tracksuit turn his yellow car to follow them.

At the drive-thru, Matthew bought her a chocolate shake and French fries without asking, just as she always did for herself. All the while he blasted a song she loved on the car stereo. He listed off her favorite colors (black and white), her sign (Aquarius), and her dreams (of flying). He seemed to understand what she meant before the words left her lips. And each time she confirmed these things, he drew closer to her, as if she had passed some kind of test. When he again intertwined his fingers with hers and took her photo with his phone, a warmth she had never felt before was kindling in the center of her chest.

The car purred down the boulevards toward the ocean. He rolled aside the moonroof so she could stick her head and shoulders out and pretend she was flying.

When he pulled up to the motel near the beach, she saw the rolling silver ocean first, and the dreary neon motel sign second. Disappointment tugged at her as he, still in the driver's seat, grabbed her legs and pulled her back down where he could run his hands up into her hair, freeing it to pour like black water around her face.

"Always so beautiful," he said, his blue eyes gazing on her as if remembering another time. "That's why I stole you. That and because he loved your song so."

"He?" she said, pushing away from him a little. His nearness made her heart beat fast as a baby bird's.

He cocked a smile at her, the way a cowboy cocks a gun. "Come inside, and I'll tell you what I mean."

"A motel?" she asked, and shook her head. "If you knew me as well as you claim, you'd know better than that."

"Aderyn Adain?" He leaned in close and touched his nose to hers. "I'd know that beak anywhere. For I have known you over many lifetimes. And if my luck goes badly, I will know you for many more. Here." He pulled from his coat pocket a bundle of papers tied with a string. He tugged the string free, and photos spilled onto the seat.

"But that's me!" She picked up a square black and white photo with a thick white border around the edges. Her own dark eyes looked back at her from under the brim of a black cloche hat with a white ribbon around the brim, her thick black hair in a bob with bangs cut straight across. "It can't be me."

"Neither can this," Matthew said, pointing to a photo of Aderyn in a black poodle skirt and white sweater, books tucked under arm. "Or this."

Aderyn stared at herself, this time with her hair in a teased black bouffant, eyes limned in winged eyeliner. Strange recognition stirred, and with it, hazy alarm. Aderyn had never known her parents. A homeless man had found her, newly born, in a Dumpster. No one looked like her. No one till this, till now.

"How'd you get these?" she asked. There were other unlikely photos of her, and of two other girls that looked familiar: a redhead and a blonde. There were drawings too, in colored pencil, of a black and white bird in a blue sky, of a white hound with red ears, and of a great white stag emerging from the forest, antlers pointed like daggers at the sky. Something about them nudged her memory too. "Do you know my mother or grandmother or something?"

Matthew gathered up the photos, tying them together again. As he tucked them into his pocket, the lapel of his coat slid aside to show a flash of silver in a winged shape. She leaned in, trying to see more, but he turned and opened his car door. "Come inside," he said. "I'll tell you about yourself."

Then he was up and striding toward the motel room door, the last rays of sunset gracing his head like a gold crown.

She watched him go, the photos an itch behind her eyes. She reached for her backpack and felt for the outline of the knife it held. Maybe now it could serve another purpose.

In the distance, Matthew opened the scuffed door to the motel room and bowed low to her. His arm swept in a wide arc toward the blackness of the room beyond.

She hadn't wanted to know anything in so long.

Weariness had weighed too much upon her. But now she remembered how it felt to want something. She had to know what he and those photographs could tell her. She hopped out of the car, hefting the backpack, and swept over the asphalt and past him into the motel room. The door clicked shut. Neither of them saw the man in the yellow car pull into the parking lot.

***

"We don't have long," Matthew said, taking off his coat and throwing it onto the bed. "I must have you before he gets here."

The words jarred her, but she was sadly not surprised. She swung the backpack around, unzipped the top, and laid her hand on the hilt of the knife inside. "He?"

"Your master." Matthew smiled. The old blue eyes in that handsome young face were not kind. "The one I stole you from."

"Stole me?" she repeated. She wanted to keep him talking as long as she could before she had to use the knife. "I don't belong to anyone."

"Well, he stole you first." Matthew undid the buckle on his belt. "From the earth. He took the three of you, and you lived many long years with him. Then I stole you back."

"The three of us—do you mean me and the other girls in those photos?" It still made no sense.

He undid a button of his shirt. Silver winked there again. "But he keeps tracking me down, before I can make you completely mine. Don't you see? I brought you back up to this world, but he came after us. In the battle that followed, the three of you fled. So we continue to hunt you."

He took a step toward her and she didn't back up, hoping the light would fall upon the silver near his collar. He said, "Each time I come closer to total possession. If you just let me have you here and now, this endless dance around the maypole can stop."

He undid another button. "I'd rather have you willing." Another step closer. "But it's not required."

At last, she saw the silver thing on his shirt in full. The dusty light from the bedside lamp gleamed briefly on a long silver stickpin decorated with the form of a bird in flight.

Her heart stopped beating and a small, mournful sound came from her throat.

"What?" He followed her gaze to the pin on his shirt. "Oh, this? Yes."

He lifted a hand to stroke the wings of the bird, then drew the fingers away fast, as if the touch burned. "I'm a thief, you know. After I hit her on the street, I couldn't just go without taking something, even though it was silver. It reminded me of you."

"Why?" Aderyn never cried, but her throat was almost too tight to speak. She never trembled, but her fingers on the knife hilt shook. "Why would you kill Mrs. Davis?"

"Because you mattered to her, of course." He undid the remaining buttons on his shirt and let it slide down his arms to the floor. His torso was lean and supple with muscle. Several deep scars marked his chest. "If I can't have you, I've got to be sure he doesn't either, and your Mrs. Davis would have gone looking for you. She might have caused trouble."

"He . . ." She shook her head to make herself think. "Who is *he*?"

"Arawn, of course." He unbuttoned the top of his pants, stepping very near her now. "King of the

Otherworld, master of the hounds of Annwn, he who lost the *Cad Goddeau* and his precious beasts to me."

Arawn. The word and his descriptions stirred in her memory. It could only be nonsense, yet she knew somehow it was not. Next to the knife lay the books of myth and nursery rhymes Mrs. Davis had loaned her. Aderyn felt sure she had read the name Arawn in one of them.

"And who are you?" she asked, gripping the knife hilt.

"What have you got there?" he said, and moved like quicksilver, lashing toward the backpack. Her hold on the knife was tight, so she kept it as he jerked the pack away.

He looked down at her holding the long, sharp blade, his gaze a dismissal. "Is that your plan?"

He emptied her backpack onto the bed. Everything spilled out—the books, her precious iPod, sheet music, dream journal, spare change.

He pounced on the books. "We're both in here. Do you remember yet? They even wrote a silly rhyme about us."

He sat down on the bed, leafing rapidly through the book of nursery rhymes, unconcerned that she was standing there with a large knife. "Here it is. Everyone gets the name wrong:

"Taffy was a Welshman, Taffy was a thief,
Taffy came to my house and stole a piece of beef;

"Should be venison, but that doesn't rhyme with 'thief.' They mean the roebuck, of course. I stole her first."

And he continued:

"I went to Taffy's house, Taffy was not home;
Taffy came to my house and stole a marrow-bone.

"Arawn used to give the hound a meaty marrowbone after a good day's hunt, so I stole one for her the same time I stole her. Oh, but here you are, my dear girl."

"I went to Taffy's house, Taffy was not in;
Taffy came to my house and stole a silver pin;"

He closed his eyes, picturing something from long ago. "You were in a silver cage. Over the years, somehow that became a pin in the rhyme. Which is why I had to take your friend's pin when I saw it, even though it burned my hand. Arawn thought the silver cage would deter me from taking you. He had no idea what I was willing to endure. For he loved you best. He hasn't slept since I took you."

He read on.

"I went to Taffy's house, Taffy was in bed,
I took up the marrow-bone and flung it at his head."

He slammed the book shut and gave her a wolfish smile. "That might work for the hound, but it won't work for you."

A bird, a roebuck (that was a kind of deer, wasn't it?), and a hound. The book of Welsh myths held a vague tale about a hero stealing those same three prized possessions from the King of the Otherworld in order to start a war. The humans had won, ending the King's rule over this world and banishing him forever to the Otherworld.

"But the name of the thief wasn't Taffy," she said aloud. "And it wasn't Matthew."

He shrugged, tossing the books back onto the bed. "They called me Amaethon then, one of the Children of

Don, brother to Gwydion the magician, cleverest of thieves who stole the secrets of the King of the Otherworld."

He stood up and paced away, then restlessly back again, as if the memory had bloodied an old wound. "I had to get him to fight a war with us somehow, didn't I? I saw how your songs lulled him to sleep, how possessively he stroked the red ears of his best hound, how he delighted in hunting the great white stag. If I hadn't taken what he loved, he never would have thought us worthy of battle. He never would have left his own world to array his forces against us. And he never would have lost. I won this world away from him! I saved humanity from enslavement and what thanks do I get? My own enslavement—to hunt the three of you over and over, dying only to be reborn to the chase again. It's as if I never left the Otherworld. Do you remember how it was? No one dies or ages there, and you would have stayed forever singing mournful songs in that cage had I not stolen you back."

Like a dragon in its cave, a memory stirred within her. Of a bright silver cage, of an angry man sent into peaceful slumber by her songs, of a blond head and blue eyes peering at her with a covetous smile. A flurry of movement in the dark, a dog's bark, the hooves of a stag brushing through the grass.

"He kept us for so very long to serve him," she said, unsure where that thought had come from. "You promised us freedom if we came with you."

"You would have roused the guards if I hadn't." He ceased pacing and returned his gaze, still angry and affronted, back to her. "After Gwydion changed you all into girls, the only way to keep you out of Arawn's hands forever is for a human man to taste you." He reached for her. "As I will taste you now."

She backed up toward the door and nearly tripped

over the shirt he'd left on the floor, but righted herself just in time. "Where are the other two?" she asked. "The hound and the deer?"

He shrugged. "Helgi's down in Lima, and Cara's somewhere in Bengal. I'll get them next. Your locations change every time. That and the fashions are the only things that do."

Helgi and Cara, she thought. *Lima and Bengal.* There were two others, like her yet not alike. Helgi and Cara. Lima and Bengal. "You are going to rape us."

"Only if you say no. Don't you see?" He opened his arms wide, as if making her the most generous offer in the world. "One time with me and you can never be his again. One time with me and this endless cycle of hunting and dying will end. I told you all as much that very first night, my sweet lapwing, hound, and deer. One time with me and then you will be free."

He dropped his hands and shook his head. "Yet each hunt is like the first. Arawn finds us too soon."

"We got away that first time." She looked up and up at him. She was so small, and there was no silver cage between them. Another memory stirred. Of his hands fumbling with the catch on the cage, the skin burning and falling off his fingers from touching the silver. The scars on his chest . . . "He killed you with a silver sword."

"Damn him," Matthew said without heat. "We know each other's weaknesses too well. He can't stay in this world for long, lest he freeze. But each time he stays long enough to kill me. And so I am reborn. And so we hunt. He from the Otherworld, me from this, until we find you again."

"We three are reborn, too," she said, remembering Mrs. Davis's words. "Over and over. Bad things cycle round and round."

"This time it can be different," he said brightly, and reached for her. "If you just let me have you . . . ."

She stabbed him with the knife.

Or she tried. The blade slid right off him as if his skin was made of stone.

He tweaked it right out of her hand. "Silly bird," he said. "Pretty lapwing, sing to me now."

A fist slammed into the door from the outside, startling them both.

"Arawn!" Fury took Matthew. He threw the knife at the door. It thunked point first into the wood. "Always he comes too soon!"

"Always you talk too much," she said. Under the soft sole of her boot, she felt something small and hard. A quick glance down showed her Mrs. Davis's long silver pin.

Matthew's blue eyes were glacier cold. "Always I must kill you."

The door shuddered under another blow, then another, and another. Wood cracked, and the frame around the door split from the wall.

"Just let me go," she said.

"Oh no," said he. "For if he gets you first, then he gets me too. I'll be singing next to you in that cage, or hunting with his hounds . . . or fleeing them, at his pleasure." He eyed her neck and flexed his hands. "It won't hurt. I'm quite good at snapping your neck by now. If you just stand still. You know you don't want to live anyway . . . ."

But she did. The driving need to live now flashed through her like lightning in a thunderstorm. Mrs. Davis's death could not go unavenged, and now she knew: there were two other girls out there, somewhere, lost like her.

She had thought there was no one. But there was,

and had been, and would be. Maybe the warmth that kindled inside her earlier hadn't been for nothing.

Another thunderous blow on the door shook the room. Then a fist splintered through the door, blood streaming from the knuckles.

Matthew grabbed for her, but she had already dropped to the floor. He fumbled with the air where she had been, then looked down to see her rip the silver stickpin from his abandoned shirt.

"Wait, no!" He tried to step back. But not fast enough, for she stabbed the pin into his foot. It slid easily through the leather of his boot and between the bones beneath.

He cried out in pain. His foot hissed and smoked. She ignored the flying bits of wood coming from the door behind her, yanked the pin out, and stood up.

His old blue eyes were wide with fear. "No, I'm supposed to kill you," he said. "That's how it's always been."

"Well, it's like *this* now," she said, and pierced his blue left eye with the pin. It sank deep, up to the outstretched wings of the bird in flight, and into his brain. Flesh sizzled. Blood and viscous jelly oozed out. She wrenched the pin out, and Matthew toppled to the floor.

The door blew inward. She turned to see a hulking figure in a long scarf and cape-like coat looming there. His long dark hair was wild around his face, his gray eyes alight with fury. She knew him now.

"Your Majesty," she said.

He halted in mid-stride, for what he saw made him pause. He took in the form of the golden-haired young man lying motionless on the floor, the left side of his head a mass of burning crimson gore, and did not know what to make of it.

"Hir yw'r dydd a hir yw'r nos, a hir yw aros Arawn," he said.

She understood what she heard, for he had said it countless times before. *Long is the day and long is the night, and long is the waiting of Arawn.* "You will wait no longer," she said. "For this time I have killed him. Instead of, you know, the other way around."

His eyes ran over her, realizing, and though they were gray, they held the same covetous look she had seen in Matthew's face. "At last. I will take you back to my world, out of this cold. Six thousand years it is since I slept, since I last heard you sing. Now you will be my sweet songbird forever."

"No," she said. "I will sing to you only once more."

"Wait!" His face grew pale. "Not yet, not here . . . " He strode toward her, hand outstretched to cover her mouth.

But she had already begun to sing the words of the old lullaby he had taught her long ago.

*"Holl amrantau'r sêr ddywedant
Ar hyd y nos."*

The furious gray eyes fluttered. He halted mere inches away. "Six thousand years since . . . " he said, trailing off as her voice hushed low, soft, drowsy, irresistible, whether in Welsh or English.

*"This is the way to the realm of glory,
All through the night."*

He swayed and shivered. "So cold," he said. Then his eyes closed. He would have fallen if she had not helped him to the bed, where he curled on his side like a baby and slept.

She touched his cheek. It felt like ice.

"Darkness is a different light,
That exposes true beauty."

A scuffling sound made her turn her head. The mustachioed man in the tracksuit was stealing toward her, ignoring the body on the floor. His tiny eyes were narrowed as if against a gale force wind, and she understood it took all of his will to resist the power of her song.

"I . . . mean you no harm," he said, wincing at every note. "The bag he has. The velvet bag."

Still singing, she stepped back, allowing him to move past the body of Matthew to get closer to Arawn. His fingers wiggled into the big man's coat, now cracked with frost, and drew forth a heavy velvet bag full of something that clicked.

"Teulu'r nefoedd mewn tawelwch
Ar hyd y nos."

Henderson focused all his thought on the bag, forcing himself not to see the rim of ice now gleaming where Arawn's skin had been. He could not be bothered with impossible twaddle like that now. One slip and the girl's song would take him too. Only the siren call of the gems was stronger, so he laid all his thoughts upon them. They winked as he poured them into his palm, whispering their promises.

A small hand reached over and scooped up half the gems. He dared glance at her face with its white skin and black eyes, nose like a beak, sharp over her mouth as she sang. The sleek black hair on her head resembled nothing so much as feathers now.

The song came to an end, and the silence was like a death.

On the bed lay a man made entirely of ice, sleeping as if he would never wake.

Aderyn slipped the gems into her pocket and made her way to the wreckage of the door. Henderson tried to hum the melody she had sung, longing to hear it again. But he was off by a note here or there. He knew he always would be.

"Have you ever been to Peru?" she asked, but not as if she was expecting an answer. "I bet Bengal is a beautiful place. There are two books on the bed you might find interesting. I leave them to you."

She fixed the silver pin to her t-shirt and stood in the doorway, her silhouette black against the sunset sky. "Now I really must fly," she said.

And she did.

– The End –

SING A SONG OF SIX-PENCE

Sing a song of sixpence,
A pocket full of rye;
Four and twenty blackbirds
Baked in a pie.
When the pie was opened,
They all began to sing.
Now, wasn't that a dainty dish
To set before the King?

The King was in his counting house,
Counting out his money;
The Queen was in the parlor
Eating bread and honey.
The maid was in the garden,
Hanging out the clothes.
Along there came a big black bird
And snipped off her nose!

— Mother Goose

SING A SONG OF SIX-PENCE
Sarwat Chadda

Blackbird watched the maid enter the Six-Pence. He sat farthest from the light, comfortable in the darkness. The other patrons, here in the lowest levels of the city, turned to watch her with eyes made of scales and desire, measuring the worth of what they saw, wondering whether to tempt and seduce, or to terrorize and devour. A few muttered then turned their backs, seeing her of little value. A poor, sad creature with few prospects in her short life. Neither looks—that much was obvious— nor intelligence. If she had possessed an ounce of the latter, she would not have come here.

To sell her soul.

What fools these mortal are.

She searched the gloomy tavern, peering into the shadowy hoods of the djinn, the demons, and the ghouls that frequented the Six-Pence. The tavern had earned its name because a mortal had once sold his soul for that meager sum, so driven by hunger that he'd given it up for the price of a single meal. Blackbird hoped it had been the most divine supper in all of existence, as he'd been collected the following night. The man's screams now joined the choir of the damned that wailed beyond the city's walls.

Blackbird clicked his talons on the tabletop, chipping slivers of wood from the surface. He peered at her, watching the flare of her soul shimmer and shift through his lens.

He groaned. He'd hoped she would be worth the effort, but no; it was a pale, flickering thing of little warmth. Despair dampened its colors, while her selfish desires and her small ambitions shrunk it. Envy and malice drained whatever taste there once might have been. It was a soul in name only. She was not evil, but she was petty.

A ghoul stalked across the room, bent so low he was almost on all fours. He sniffed at the ground, his eyes stitched shut for some past transgression, tongue clipped short, yet still slavering in a mouth of yellow teeth. The hairless demon was little more than a carrion creature—rarely taking a fresh soul but devouring whatever spirit might be left by the stronger demons once they'd finished with their meal. The ghoul's body was pasty and sick with disease; large pustules oozed across his crooked back, seeping green ichor along his gnarly spine and down his ribs. The girl backed away as he smelt at her feet.

Blackbird stood up. A deal was a deal.

Sable wings unruffled across his back and shadows stirred as the darkness within his feathers deepened. Other demons grimaced and snarled at him, wary of one of the fallen within the Six-Pence.

Like his brothers he was no longer bright and shining, but a beast with talons and twisted limbs, his head narrow and feathered, his thin jaw both a mouth and a beak. The rustle of feathers sounded like the scales of armor shifting before battle, the melody metallic and somber. The ghoul twitched, his sharp ears picking up the threat in those fluttering wings. He clicked his teeth and hissed, then scurried off, head near the ground.

The girl stared at him. If she was looking for some golden hero, she was sorely disappointed.

This was not a place for heroes. This was a place for deals and betrayals and terror. All these things, Blackbird excelled in. That he was cast down to live amongst the other demons who had never known what it was to soar, well, that was what made him cheap. Once, he would have traded the souls of a thousand newborn babies. Now, a tainted, washed-up girl was all he was worth.

And now that she had seen him, she was afraid. What had she expected? Her mother's tales of the host flying over the city, clad in bright silver and on eagles' wings? How the winds howled at their passing and the terrible radiance of their eyes, too intense, too noble, for mortals to look upon?

He wore no shimmering armor nor carried a flaming sword. No, she saw something wretched and miserable. Perhaps that was why he hated her. He was no less petty than she.

"Sit," he said.

The maid brushed her hand through her hair and, despite the fear radiating from every pore, smiled as she put herself on the stool opposite. Her clothes were clean and good quality, cast off from the princesses of the Counting House to be sure, but she or someone skillful with a needle had re-stitched them to fit her. To a mortal, was she pretty? Blackbird could not tell, nor did he care. They all looked the same to him, fragile and ill-formed, a mockery of what had been intended.

"I am from the Counting House," she said.

Blackbird nodded once. "What is it that you want?"

"What else? But to be worth more than this." She pulled at the thin sleeve of her dress. "A better life."

"Then you should get up and leave here. If there is one thing I can guarantee, it is that your life will be all the worse for coming to the Six-Pence. For meeting me."

"I have dealt with demons before. The King summons you and you come flocking and bowing and scraping."

"If you mistake me for one of those pitiful beasts, then you are a fool."

"Perhaps you are right. None of the King's servants would be seen dead here."

Blackbird bristled. How dare she? His talons twitched, carving a groove into the wood. He was of half a mind to get up and leave when he saw the wry smile on the girl's lips. Whatever else she may be, she was brave. He clicked his tongue. "What is it you want? Beauty?"

"Am I not already beautiful?" There was a mocking tone in her question.

"You mortals all look the same." Blackbird peered at her. Her skin still retained a freshness uncommon to the city, and perhaps there was color and life and desire in her flush, taut flesh and those glistening eyes. Beauty. Why did they all want it so desperately? How many souls had he swallowed just to make the mortal that much taller, that much slimmer, or fatter, or straighter, or rounder? Just to catch the eye of the King or one of the other demon lords. The rules changed so often he had concluded everything and nothing was beautiful.

"Beauty does not interest me," she replied. "I had it once and found it of little benefit."

"If not beauty, then what? Wealth? Riches beyond your wildest dreams?"

"Freedom." The answer was bold and aggressive. "I want you to take me beyond the wall."

"Impossible. Your soul is not worth so much."

The girl stiffened and her face paled. Then her gaze hardened and her thin lips drew a grim line. "I am not offering my soul."

Blackbird laughed. "What else do you have? I care not for money and your form—attractive as it may be to some beardless virgin of a boy—raises neither my hunger nor my passions." He stood up to leave. "I see I have wasted my time."

"I can get you the King's dish."

Blackbird stopped dead. His heart hummed with excitement and the feathers along his wings rustled wildly. It took him a few moments to gather himself but eventually, slowly, he sat back down.

The King's dish. A dainty thing, but powerful beyond all his other treasures. Blackbird shivered at the thought of it. He had glimpsed it once. Rusty and round, the dish was as old as the kingdom, older perhaps, and with it, the King ruled. To get his hands on it . . .

No. She was lying. He swept across the table, leaning close enough to see his reflection in her petrified eyes, and hissed, "Do not play games with me. The dish is guarded by one of the lords of flame, a djinn."

"That is why I stole this." She drew out a small object from a hidden pocket and opened her trembling palm.

Golden light shone within a delicate crystal vial. "The Queen's own honey," she said. "I serve food to many of the guards, including the djinn. With this . . ."

Blackbird nodded, wary of the poison within the crystal. He knew what happened when any immortal spirit consumed even a drop of the honey. Perhaps the maid could get the dish after all.

"He trapped my brothers within the reflection of that plate."

"Four and twenty. I know the story well. Of how you and your kin rebelled against the king. Of how all, all but you, were imprisoned. They say you bought your freedom through betrayal."

Blackbird scowled, ill at ease at being reminded of sins from long ago. "How will you get it?"

The maid sighed and sipped from his mug. She wrinkled her nose at the smell. "The Queen never leaves the Parlor now. She has the keys to where the dish is kept. After dinner she falls into a stupor which lasts for hours. A child could take the key from her then. I will collect the dish and return the keys to her chubby hands before she stirs."

"Where will you be? The Counting House is all but impregnable."

"The garden. No one uses it now. Meet me there. If I do not have the dish, you may fly off. If I have it, you will carry me beyond the wall."

"Do you know what lies outside?" asked Blackbird.

The girl lowered her head. "It must be better than this."

Her misery was palpable. Blackbird said nothing as he pondered the deal. Even if she could do it, they had many miles to fly to reach the wall, and the others of the Counting House and the Parlor would be after them. If they were caught, he'd be lucky to merely have his wings torn off. If unlucky, he would spend eternity inside the dish. He had seen the dish's effects; it broke the spirits of the greatest fiends. Whether lowly imp or great lord, the dish was a nightmare realm for those who considered themselves masters of Hell.

Could he fly her beyond the wall? To the endless

desert of wailing, lost souls and mortals too degenerate and twisted to belong within the city? They were outcasts who preyed on each other. And this was what the girl wanted? No, there was more. Someone out there she wanted to rejoin, perhaps? A lover? A parent?

"My child," she whispered, sensing his question. "He is out there."

"No. He cannot be. No child could survive beyond the wall." Was it pity, a faint flicker of compassion in his shriveled soul that made him say it? "Forget this and go back to the Counting House."

She shook her head. "You do not understand. Not knowing is worse than anything beyond the black gates. I don't care what happens to me, but if he is out there, he needs me. If he is not, then I will know." She raised her face and stared hard at him. "What difference does it make to you? Just take me beyond the walls."

"What is a child doing beyond the wall?"

"It is the fate of all of the King's bastards."

Ah. The King had passions beyond his treasure and the Queen was no longer able to accommodate them. If allowed to stay, the Counting House would overflow with his illegitimate offspring. Too cowardly to kill them cleanly, he made them suffer an even worse fate: exile.

Blackbird held out his taloned hand. "Be in the garden at twelfth bell."

The girl shook it.

***

Blackbird left the Six-Pence and wandered along the narrow, ramshackle streets. The streets emptied as the sky darkened from slate grey to charcoal, and the mortals took shelter before the bells chimed. The clouds rumbled. The rain fell hard, and large, swampy puddles swelled about him. The mud thickened and great, dirty torrents tumbled from the roofs, walls of water covering the crooked doorways and narrow alleys. He needed to return to his nest and prepare. His wings shook free, glossy black and so wide they almost touched the walls. Blackbird bristled with anticipation, his feathers rolling like waves. The buildings above him bent and twisted, all but obscuring the sky. Beyond them were stabbing spires of flint and glass and buttresses made of razor shard iron and spikes upon which writhed ghostly spirits, their lambent bodies haunting the narrow paths skyward.

With a single sweep, Blackbird rose a dozen feet. The second beat lifted him that height again, but twice as fast. The wind howled and screamed as he swept his sable pinions back, reveling in the way his muscles flexed across his back, the sharp joy shining from the feather tips as the smoke and the phantoms swirled and danced in his passing.

***

Blackbird hunched in a petrified tree, his hand around the hilt of his narrow blade. The copper-colored leaves shivered and sang in the soft, cold wind. He watched with a thief's eyes, wary of traps, guards, and the beast that prowled the garden of the Counting House. Even from high up in the tree, the crunch of bones was sharp and clear and the creature's deep chest growled with satisfaction as it sucked out the marrow.

Blackbird's slim fingers drew out a sharp needle. His gaze did not shift as he dipped the long point in poison from one of the small bottles that dangled from his belt. He shifted his weight forward. The bough creaked, rustling the leaves. The beast snorted and looked up.

Big mistake.

Blackbird flicked the needle and the shard of silver pierced the dog-demon's right eye. It blinked and twitched its head as a small bead of red and black blood seeped from the wound. Then it lowered its head, and died.

Nothing but the breeze stirred amongst the wild forest of thorns and black roses. Barbed wire wrapped the mutilated bodies of crumbled fountains, their bowls filled with rustling leaves. Nothing beautiful could dwell here. The long grass swayed while the trees— twisted, decrepit, and sickly grey—groaned in the poisonous earth, as if their roots were in pain.

The bells chimed twelve.

A door opened and a figure pushed through the wall of brambles.

The maid glanced around, her face pale and clear in the ghost-light. She held a cloth-bound object against her chest.

The dish. She had done it.

Blackbird leapt. He held the wings close to his body, managing his direction with a subtle shift of weight and re-angling of his feather-tips. The wind roared as he sped downward, his gaze unblinking upon the maid who looked around in fear. Then figures dressed in silver and gold poured from hidden doorways, brandishing bright swords and shining axes. Two ran with devil-dogs, the litter brothers of the creature Blackbird had just killed. They strained against their leashes and howled with blood-freezing lust. The maid screamed as the huntsmen released their beasts and the dogs raced toward her, their red tongues slobbering and huge, oily limbs beating hard upon the earth. Within a few strides the first was upon her, leaping high, its massive, fang-filled jaws widening to consume her head whole.

Blackbird rammed into the dog's chest, hurling it into a spiny tree trunk. It howled and thrashed as the long, slim thorns passed through its body.

Blackbird slashed wildly with his dagger as he sought out the maid's hand. The steel carved wounds into the demon-flesh and the air stank of putrescence and the garden filled with a mist of black blood as arteries opened and monsters died.

He darted and swooped amongst the melee. The guards were clumsy, earth-bound things with their heavy armor and wingless bodies. But they had numbers and sooner or later one would sheer off a wing, and then he would die. But for a moment, Blackbird exalted in his element as feathers and blood covered him.

He felt a hand grab his wrist and swung around, dagger raised and heart singing with bloodlust.

"No!" screamed the maid. He halted his blow, the wicked edge of his blade just touching her nose. He'd almost sliced it off. Then Blackbird pulled her against him. His wings pounded the air, and they were sky-born. Within moments, the frustrated cries of the Counting House guards vanished in the song of the wind.

***

Blackbird flew as fast as he dared and then faster still, the maid pressed close against him. They weaved through the tall spires and under the ancient arches and through the web of walkways and gantries that filled the spaces between the towers. They kept low to avoid the others, but every now and then he'd see a mighty-winged shadow pass over them as the kings of the eyrie sent their own hunters after them. Raptor cries echoed in the shadowy canyons.

She trembled in his close grasp and her heart pounded against his chest. She held herself rigid and straight, understanding his need to cut out resistance, and closed her eyes. Blackbird wanted to laugh. Why miss all of this? He swooped beneath a spike-encrusted buttress, his feathers stroking the razor-edged iron before he rose with a single flap.

Then he saw it: a thousand feet high, its skin covered with wire and spikes and guard towers. The wall.

Men armed with torches and crossbows ran along the top, preparing to prevent their escape. But he was too fast, too beautiful to be stopped, and the bolts flew and hissed around him. He was a streak of black lightning, a dark meteor, and the hurled spears were slow and he swept them aside.

Oh, the joy of such freedom! The maid stiffened as they spun between the flying darts and bolts.

Then he drew his wings to him like a cloak, and they descended. The ash-covered earth rushed past them as Blackbird searched for a place to settle. There, a cluster of old buildings. Talons extended, he settled them onto the desert beyond the wall.

"You are free," he said.

The maid, pale and gleaming with sweat, stumbled back and gave a nod. She handed him the object. "You have done all I asked."

Then she fell.

Blackbird, more out of instinct than compassion, caught her and felt the dampness between her shoulder blades and the feathered end of the bolt lodged between them.

"Can you see anyone?" she asked.

Blackbird looked about them. His heart, a dark thing for millennia, stirred as he saw where he'd brought them. A graveyard. Small bones lay, cold and white, scattered and picked at by the ghouls.

"Is he there? Do you see him?"

"I see him," said Blackbird. How was it that he knew? By the corroded gate stood a small boy, perhaps six, his hair flaxen and his skin grey, watching them with hollow eyes. He stared, his skinny limbs wrapped within the tattered remains of his burial shroud. "He is very beautiful."

"I told you," said the maid.

"Yes. You will be with him shortly."

She smiled then—an expression that was not common here—and closed her eyes.

Blackbird stood up, looking down at the mortal. What had she hoped for? The lands beyond the wall belonged to the dead. She had known and still gone. His attention shifted to the boy, slowly, cautiously approaching. Then the dead thing knelt down and took his mother's hand. He looked up at Blackbird. "She promised she would come for me." His voice was brittle, dry, and little more than a rasp but even within the still heart of the dead some faint emotion stirred. The boy pressed his cold, white lips to his mother's forehead. "Mother."

The maid's eyes opened. She did not gasp for the dead no longer draw breath, but exhaled, and Blackbird watched the silver cloud of her soul rise. He could have grabbed it, could have held it, squeezed it for what nourishment remained. He held out his hands but did not close them, and so the soul slipped like smoke through his talons. He had payment enough.

The maid stood, hands tightly around her son. "Thank you."

"You thank me for this? For losing you your life?" She looked back toward the city with its dark walls. "I lost that many years ago." Then she handed him the box.

Blackbird opened it.

A dainty dish, made of thin metal that reflected gloomy colors from another place.

He put the dish on the ground and it shook of its own accord. Cries rose from the metal. Light burst from within, throwing winged shapes across the looming clouds. Then, one after another, figures leapt from their prison and into the sky.

He knew them all. His brothers and sisters. Though not radiant as they had once been, they were his own. Four and twenty blackbirds, crying with the joy of freedom, beat their wings and turned back toward the city. His heart burned for the first time in centuries as Blackbird threw back his head and screamed, dagger aloft.

They were coming. Coming for the Queen in her Parlor and the King in his Counting House.

And the other blackbirds, they began to sing.

– The End –

HICKORY, DICKORY, DOCK

Hickory, dickory, dock,
The mouse ran up the clock.
The clock struck one,
The mouse ran down!
Hickory, dickory, dock.

– Mother Goose

CLOCKWORK
Leah Cypess

When the clock struck one, the mouse turned away from a mold-encrusted scrap of cheese and sat on its haunches, whiskers trembling.

The enchantment was not quite broken. It had been a mouse for a very long time, and human thoughts couldn't fit into its mouse brain. But through the pungent smell of the cheese and the hunger in its belly and the fear of cats came a tendril of something else: a desire to go toward those chimes. Toward the clock.

Because it was a mouse, it didn't question the desire. It scuttled along the walls until it was as close to the clock as possible. A hint of memory wisped through its mind, a memory of being tall and clothed and afraid, next to that very clock. For a moment it recalled being a girl, a girl with a knife hilt clenched in her trembling hand, grief and terror ripping through her. But the memory was vast and incomprehensible, and it swiftly vanished.

The mouse hesitated for a moment, torn between the compulsion and a wariness of open spaces. The clock's pendulum swung back and forth. The mouse blinked, then gathered itself and dashed forward across the hardwood floor.

That was when the cat pounced.

It streaked from its hiding spot beneath the couch, and a heavy paw knocked the mouse sideways. The mouse skidded across the floor, rolled to its feet, and ran. A shadow passed over it, and two paws came down on either side of it. The cat batted it across the floor, slamming it into something hard and slick. The base of the clock.

The mouse scrabbled to its feet, too slow and too late, as the cat leapt.

The echo of the clock faded away, the mouse's body blurred and shimmered, and the cat's snarl of victory turned into a shrill meow.

A girl crouched where the mouse had been. Her fingers twitched against the floor, and she let out an inhuman squeal.

The cat spat, whirled, and raced out the library doors.

***

Amarind got slowly to her feet, gasping and shivering, the clock silent behind her. When she looked up, the hands on the clock had moved five minutes ahead. She stepped toward it, drawn as the mouse had been, but this time knowing what she was drawn to: power. There was magic in that clock, in the swing of its pendulum and the ticking of its hands, the power of Time itself. She had known how to use that power, once . . . .

The door to the library swung open, and she caught her breath as she whirled, expecting the cat. It took her a moment to remember she didn't have to fear cats anymore. Another moment, once she saw the man standing in the doorway, to remember she still did have to fear humans.

She looked down swiftly, and was relieved to see she was dressed in a green, floor-length dress. A vague memory filtered through her confusion, of a woman's cold, amused voice: *The spell transforms everything that's on you. Do you think your dead hair and fingernails are more a part of you than the silk on your skin?*

"Where did you come from?" the man at the door demanded. He was tall and lean, wearing black silk clothes and a purple velvet cape.

"I don't know," Amarind said. "I was . . . until a moment ago . . ." She shuddered without meaning to. She could still feel the cat's breath, the brush of air against her whiskers, the terror of knowing she was about to die. "I think I was a mouse."

She stepped toward him, and had to balance herself to compensate for the lack of her front paws. The effort made her aware, for the first time, that there was something heavy and elongated strapped to her right leg, invisible beneath the layers of her skirts. She knew at once that it was a knife. Memory ripped through her again, of that knife in her hand, of an unconscious man on the floor . . . there, by the couch . . . and someone else dead behind her, someone who shouldn't, *couldn't* be dead . . . .

Tears stung at her eyes, and she pushed them down ruthlessly. She had no time, right now, to pursue memory. The man was staring at her with narrowed blue eyes. "You were enchanted? How?"

It requires the deathblood of a virgin princess, a knife forged by moonlight, and a clock made of cedar wood. She clasped her hands together and made her eyes wide. "I don't know, my . . . lord?"

"Majesty," he corrected her. "I am King Cedric of Hickere."

She dropped into a curtsy, not just because he obviously expected it, but to hide the expression on her face.

He started toward her, and she wondered why he didn't seem more surprised. Her entire body tensed, but she didn't know what to do. Run? Hide? Draw the knife?

Then someone said, "Your Majesty?" and a noblewoman came into the library, giggling behind her handkerchief. She stopped giggling, stood in the doorway, and stared.

King Cedric stopped short. After a long moment, he said, "Summon the guards, please. It seems we have a problem."

***

The guards recognized her at once. She saw it in their faces, in the way they hesitated before taking her by the arms, in the gentle way they escorted her through the halls. By the uncertain glances they exchanged when she said, "Take me to the throne room."

Kind Cedric looked at her over his shoulder, nothing uncertain in *his* glance. She glared back. Much as her instincts screamed for someplace small and secluded and alone, her human self saw where the true danger lay. If he thought he was going to question her alone, or get rid of her before too many people saw her, his memory was even worse than hers.

The king's lips thinned, but he nodded once before turning and striding on ahead. Amarind followed passively. By the time they reached the throne room, the memories of being a mouse were starting to fade, and she remembered who she was.

But she still didn't know what to do about it.

By the time they entered the throne room, Cedric was sitting on the throne where her father had once sat, wearing a purple cape her father had once worn. She remembered him as a plump and unimpressive boy, but sitting straight on the throne, with his chin up and the entrapments of regality around him, he looked like a king.

"Lady Amarind," the king said, and the girl who had been a mouse clenched her fists at her sides. She had meant to be silent until she got her bearings, but a sudden surge of rage and betrayal made her forget her plans.

"*Your Highness*," she corrected him, and his lips tightened until they were white.

"I am sorry, my lady. But you were believed dead. The throne was passed on."

"I was not dead," she said. "I was enchanted."

A murmur ran through the court. Amarind looked away from the king—who had once been merely her second cousin, and not one she particularly liked—to glance swiftly at the courtiers. Their faces were stiff, or suspicious, or calculating.

So that, at least, had not changed.

"Did you suspect what had happened to me?" Amarind demanded. She could not quite keep the raw edge from her voice, and the courtiers murmured again, even more uneasily this time.

"Of course not," King Cedric said.

Amarind bit down on her next question: *Where are my parents?* If Cousin Cedric was on the throne, there was only one place they could be.

And it occurred to her, then, that there was no

woman at the king's side. Even though if he really wanted the throne, there was someone he should have married . . . .

Panic rose in her throat. A sudden, vague memory growled at the back of her brain: brown hair covering a still face. Blood. A knife. Her own hand, taking that knife . . .

The deathblood of a virgin princess.

"Where," she asked, and the shrillness of her voice made the courtiers go silent, "is my sister?"

The silence stretched on. Then Cedric got off the throne and walked down the aisle toward her. He took both her hands in his, and she let him. Suddenly, it didn't seem to matter.

"I'm sorry, Cousin," he said.

Bile rose in Amarind's throat. She felt only a vague regret for the death of her parents, who had been rare and distant figures in her life. But her sister . . . Lily had been so sweet, so innocent, so unaware of danger.

Amarind hoped Lily had remained unaware. That death had come swiftly, and her sister had never known fear or betrayal.

Cedric lifted a hand to touch her cheek. Amarind almost shrank away—sideways, a mouse's movement—and controlled herself just in time, holding herself still, staring at her own hands to remind herself that she was in a human body now.

"Your family was betrayed," Cedric said. She stood rigid, staring at him, and he took his hand back. She could still feel the indentation of his fingers, right below her eye. "The assassins were hired by Lord Ofil, who has of course been executed. The kingdom was in chaos. Someone had to restore order."

How noble of you. "How do you know it was Ofil?" Amarind demanded.

Cedric's mouth went grim. "What are you implying, Lady Amarind?"

Princess Amarind. But she had pressed him far enough for one morning. If she presented herself as too much of a threat, he would probably kill her and get away with it.

A tremor of fear ran through her, subdued and familiar. She knew what it was to be prey. She knew she could survive like that, day after endless day, that the fear could sink in and become just another part of her. But she didn't want to be constantly afraid anymore, not now that she was human.

Yet no one at court would care more about a stray princess's rights than about maintaining the kingdom's stability. She didn't even blame them. Cedric's position was a lot stronger than hers.

Nothing less than magic would enable her to gain the upper hand.

Luckily, she knew where to find that.

***

It took her three days to get away. She took advantage of that time, getting used to being human again, to walking on two legs, to her lack of a tail. She got used to the heavy tightness of silk covering her body, to the heaviness of her hair when it was twisted above her head, to the endless variety of food she could eat. To the fact that she could eat it as slowly as she liked, and that no one was going to snatch it away or come up on her from behind.

She insisted on dressing herself, which fortunately had been a quirk of hers back before her transformation. Then, it had been because she didn't want maids to see the strange dyes on her hands, the unattractively bulging muscles of her upper arms, the occasional cuts when she had needed to use her own blood. There had been rumors about her back then, of course, whispers that she snuck out at night to practice witchcraft, that she was apprenticed to a powerful and evil witch. But there was a large difference between whispered rumors and confirmed rumors.

Now that she had been a mouse, none of that mattered. But she still refused to let her maid dress her, even though the endless buttons and ties of her gowns were difficult to master. Because she still carried a knife strapped to her leg, and she certainly didn't want the maids seeing that.

It was a simple knife with a short handle and a straight blade, nothing ornate or valuable marring its simplicity. Here in her room, she couldn't tell whether it had been forged by moonlight. But she knew that just touching it made her hands tingle—with memory or magic, she couldn't tell—and that staring at the shiny blade made her head hurt. She kept it strapped to her leg, hidden beneath voluminous skirts, and waited for her chance to learn more.

She managed to sneak back into the library only once. It required a glamour—a small spell, needing no more than a prick of her own blood and proximity to an hourglass—and then, while her evening maid was distracted by a handsome footman, Amarind slipped invisibly out of her room, down the hall, and into the library.

The grandfather clock chimed slowly as she entered. Amarind waited for the chimes to die, then approached it hesitantly, not sure what exactly she wanted. It was an old, stately, and powerful clock; she was not yet skilled enough to touch her blood to it and control the outcome. But maybe she didn't need magic that strong to find out what had happened to her.

She dragged over a small, ornate chair, climbed onto it, and touched one hand to the hour hand of the clock.

Time whirled around her, flinging her mind back, into a memory so real it enveloped her. She was lounging on the white couch, playing with the folds of her dress. It was short and stiff, a child's dress, and her body was a child's body.

"I saw you do it!" An even younger child was hanging over the back of the couch, all spindly arms and wild brown hair. "You turned Cousin Cedric into a frog. Tell me how you did it!"

"I did no such thing," Amarind said loftily, though her whole being hummed with secret knowledge. "You have quite an imagination, Lily."

"Why won't you tell me?" The younger girl pulled herself over the back of the couch and sprawled into Amarind's lap. Amarind laughed and pulled her close, hugging her while Lily squirmed to get free.

"I will tell you," Amarind promised. "I'll tell you about the magic, and the clocks, and the Witch. When you're old enough."

Lily snorted, got free, and stomped away. Amarind laughed and stretched ... and time hurtled forward. She stood in front of the clock, balanced on the tiny chair, eyes blurred with tears.

Lily had never gotten old enough.

She could have asked the clock to show her *that*. But her glamour was probably about to wear out. Besides, she wasn't sure she wanted to see her sister die.

She made it back to her room just as the glamour began to fade. Her maid didn't bother to ask why she was crying.

***

On the third day, Cedric left the castle for a day-long hunting expedition. It was foolish of him, but as Amarind recalled, he had never been one to forgo his pleasures. And maybe he thought she was harmless, now that she had spent the past three days wandering about court in soft-colored gowns.

She worked the glamour again, making it stronger this time. No one stopped her when she left the castle, or when she stepped out of the formal gardens and into the woods. She checked, but no one followed her as she walked along the narrow path lined with dead leaves and mud.

A mouse would never have walked like this, in a straight line, out in the open. Amarind had to force herself to keep putting one foot in front of another, to not dash sideways into the shadows of the trees. Above her, the tree branches crisscrossed the sky, letting in only the occasional, sharp shimmer of white sunlight.

This path, she had learned early, was there for her but not for anyone else. It had been that way since she'd first found it, at the age of twelve, and followed it to the cottage where the Witch was waiting for her.

She didn't need the clock, this time, for the memory. She would never forget the first time she had walked down this path. It had been more obviously magical then, fairly shimmering with enchantment and wildness and the possibility of escape. She had run down it without a second thought, desperate to get away from the stifling trap that was her life, to find anything—*anything*—that could breathe some magic into her endless, dreary days.

Today she walked slowly, stepping over a fallen

sapling, aware that there were worse traps than the constricted life of a princess. At least a princess could dream of something different. A mouse could not dream at all, could not even think past the next bite of food or the next place of safety or the next burst of terror. Every single second of its life was a cage.

Amarind shuddered all over, then set her chin and kept walking. She turned around a bend in the path, and there it was.

Today it wasn't a cottage. It was a house, tall and stately, made of yellow bricks with crystal windows. The Witch's home was never at exactly the same place on the path, and it never looked exactly the same either.

Amarind left the path, tramping through ferns. There was no sign of the Witch, and that was also the same. The Witch couldn't leave the house. Someone had trapped her there long ago.

The door swung open as she raised her hand to knock. Amarind took a deep breath and walked into the empty front room.

It was the only room in the Witch's home she had ever been allowed into, and it never changed. The wooden floor lined with rushes, the long table and elaborate brocade chairs, the pot in the corner where she had spent so much time stirring and stirring. Amarind's upper arms ached just looking at that pot.

And at the far end of the room, so immense it should not have fit, a grandfather clock of wood and gold and diamonds. Its base and sides were carved with runes that, Amarind knew from experience, made your vision blur if you stared at them too long. The clockface was carved of diamond, but had no arms. The pendulum and weights were solid gold, and despite the glass covering, the power leaking out of the clock was enough to make Amarind shiver.

"Stepmother?" she said carefully.

"I'm here," the Witch said. And she was, sitting in the chair at the head of the table.

Amarind dropped into a curtsy. Her heart was pounding, but that, too, was nothing new. Despite all her years of tutelage, the Witch still terrified Amarind. As a child, she had secretly liked that rush of fear, that sense that anything could happen to her at any moment. It was part of why the Witch's home was the only place she had ever felt truly alive, away from the sameness and boredom of every day at court, where it felt like nothing new could ever happen.

That had been before she learned what true fear was. Before it was driven into her that anything really *could* happen, including unthinkably terrible things.

When Amarind rose from her curtsy, the Witch was staring right at her, eyes large and dark against her unnaturally white skin. She was as cold and beautiful as ever, and as unmoved by whatever she saw on Amarind's face. Aside from insisting she be called Stepmother—for whatever reason, that amused her—the Witch had never acted as if she cared what Amarind did, or who she was, or why a princess was willing to stir her cauldron and run her errands in return for a few scraps of spells.

Right now, though, there was anger on her face, vast and terrifying. She looked Amarind up and down and said, "You bring a weapon into my home?"

Amarind's hand flew to her leg, to the hardness of the knife hilt beneath her skirts. "No. I don't even know how to use it. I'm just keeping it because it was here when I . . . when it . . ." And then the question flew up her throat and out. "Did you turn me?"

"No," the Witch said.

But she didn't bother to ask what Amarind meant.

There were no hands on the clockface, and that always meant a spell had been cast, a spell so powerful that the Witch had drawn on the power of Time itself. Transformations were powerful spells. The Witch had taught Amarind how to do them, and Amarind had spent many days turning cats into birds and dogs into cats. Once, in a fit of spite, she had turned Cedric into a frog.

But none of those enchantments had lasted more than a minute or two. Time ruled the spells it lent its power to, always. Only the Witch had ever been able to make any spells last. Only her castings had ever wiped the hands off the face of the great clock.

"If you didn't turn me," Amarind said, almost steadily, "who did? Who else has that kind of power?"

"I am hardly the most powerful of my kind," the Witch said. "Someone trapped me *here*, after all."

"Who?" Amarind asked.

The Witch's mouth went flat, and the small, hunted creature in Amarind cringed back, recognizing a powerful predator when it saw one.

But Amarind wasn't a mouse anymore. She could be a predator too, even if her strength was only a fraction of the Witch's. And she still had a knife strapped to her leg. She forced herself to meet the Witch's eyes, and hold herself still.

She had never before defied the Witch in even the smallest of ways. Just the touch of anger in those black eyes made her feel she was about to die. But by now she was used to that feeling.

At last, the Witch looked away, and Amarind found that she could breathe again.

"I cannot speak of that one," the Witch said flatly. "Nor should you. You were a mouse; now you are human again. You need to regain your place in the castle, do you not? I have spells that can help you with that."

That was why Amarind was here. But it made her suspicious, that what she wanted should come to her so easily. Slowly, she shook her head.

"I need to know who did this to me," she said.

"Why?"

Because someone had made her small and afraid and helpless, and she needed to do the same to whomever that person had been. Someone had killed her parents, had ended forever her sister's laughter, and that someone must be punished.

None of which the Witch would understand. So Amarind said, "Because they might try again."

The Witch was silent for a moment. "You don't remember any of it?"

"No," Amarind said.

"That can happen, with transformations." The Witch's voice was smooth and ice-sharp. "I could restore your memory. But it would require much power."

And I would have to pay for it. Amarind didn't know what the Witch would want, but she knew enough to shudder. "No."

"You cannot do it yourself, you know. Enchantments cannot be broken from the inside."

There was a hint of bitterness in the Witch's voice, and Amarind didn't dare look at her. She turned and started for the door.

"As you wish." The Witch's tone didn't change. "Leave the knife here, and I will use it to find out who changed you."

On the threshold, Amarind stopped and turned around. The Witch was still smiling.

In the ten years she had labored here, the Witch had

never offered her any sort of aid. And there was something . . . hungry . . . in her eyes.

She wanted the knife.

Where had the knife come from? Amarind was a princess, not trained in knives; she could as soon have wielded it effectively as shot an arrow. So it must have been used that night, by her attackers. Somehow—with magic, no doubt—she had taken it from them.

By her attackers . . .

Who hadn't attacked only her.

Amarind's stomach heaved. *The deathblood of a virgin princess.* Lily, so young and trusting. And the blade that had soaked up her blood was only a leather sheath away from Amarind's calf.

She wanted to unstrap it and fling it away. But she met the Witch's eyes, so vast and hungry, and felt like prey. The feeling was familiar; she had sensed it every time the Witch looked at her in this vast room with its silent clock. But until now, she had not recognized the feeling for what it was.

She remembered the cat's breath wafting hotly over her body, and with the greatest effort, managed to meet the Witch's eyes instead of turning and scrabbling away.

"No," she said.

The Witch stood.

Physically, that was all she did, but suddenly Amarind felt smaller than when she had been a mouse. It was as if a vast darkness spread around the Witch, filling the room, squeezing against Amarind's skin and snaking into her body. That darkness seeped around her heart, and suddenly, it was hard to breathe.

The Witch smiled, and Amarind knew that with one twitch of her finger, that darkness would squeeze her heart into a pulp. The Witch wouldn't change expression, either, while she did it. She wouldn't even blink as she watched Amarind die.

"No," Amarind said. Barely a whisper, but the Witch heard.

After what seemed like forever, the darkness faded away, and the Witch sat down. She looked at Amarind, a single crease marring her forehead.

"How did you know?" she said.

Amarind shook her head, unable to speak.

The Witch blinked. "You didn't know that I can't take the knife?"

Amarind shook her head again.

The Witch's eyes narrowed. "The terms of my confinement are . . . subtle. I cannot take, and I cannot call. In the hundreds of years I have been in this house, you are the only person who has ever managed to find me. I used to wonder why. I used to think that if you could do it, someone else could, and would. But now I wonder." The tip of her tongue flicked out, quickly, to lick her lips. "That makes you important, my child, to those who wish to keep me caged."

Amarind suspected that wasn't a good thing.

"I'll give you the knife," she said. "But I have to bring it back to the castle first. I have to use it to find out who betrayed my family. Once I've done that, I'll bring it back to you."

The Witch sat perfectly still for a moment. Then she said, "Go, then."

Amarind went.

***

Upon her return to the castle, Amarind went straight to the library and stood in front of the clock, her heart pounding.

How had the Witch known about the knife?

No, that was the wrong question. She had to ask another question first, a question she should have asked long ago: why did *she* know about the Witch? What did the Witch have to gain by teaching a princess magic?

The deathblood of a virgin princess.

Powerful enough to transform a human being into a mouse. Or to break a powerful enchantment and set a witch free?

Enchantments cannot be broken from the inside.

Amarind reached under her skirt and drew the knife. She held it up and looked at it, just as the door slammed open and the king strode in.

Amarind whirled, but made no effort to hide the knife. Cedric was wearing hunting clothes, brown and green, and a short brown cape. Clearly, her disappearance had worried the staff enough that they had called him in from the hunt.

Equally clearly, Cedric was not happy about that.

"Where have you been?" he snarled, after only a quick glance at the blade in her hand.

Amarind lowered the knife to her side, the way she had seen men do when they were about to fight. Cedric didn't look the slightest bit wary, which was wise of him. Amarind had no idea how to use a knife in a fight. She suspected she wasn't even holding it right.

Cedric scowled at her with a malicious arrogance meant to remind her where the power lay. She should have been frightened, perhaps. But the visit to the Witch had accomplished what those visits always did: to remind her how much greater and vaster the world was, how petty the powers and concerns wrapped around this mundane court.

Not that disdain would help her if Cedric decided to imprison or execute her. But it would make her feel better while he was yelling at her.

"I think," she said, "you know where I've been."

Cedric was silent for a moment. Then he reached behind him and pulled the library door shut.

"Now why," he asked, "would you think that?"

"Because someone killed my sister and anointed this blade with her blood." Amarind was gripping the knife hilt so hard her fingers hurt. "What did the Witch offer you, in exchange for her life? The kingship?"

"Of course," Cedric said.

In the silence that followed, Amarind realized he never intended her to leave this room alive.

"She gave you what you needed to engineer the coup," Amarind said steadily. "She probably told you how to arrange it. And in return . . ." She wouldn't have thought it possible, but her fingers clenched even more tightly around the hilt.

"Yes. All that, and more." He stepped toward her. "And all I had to do in return was bring her this knife."

"Not quite all." Amarind was amazed at how calm her voice emerged, when she felt like she was drowning in rage. "You had to make the knife first, didn't you? Forge it by moonlight." Her voice was not so calm anymore. "Anoint it with my sister's blood."

"It would have been your blood," he said flatly, "if you had been where you were supposed to be."

"You can't bring her the knife," Amarind said. "She'll use it to set herself free. This is what she's been after, all along . . . ." And not just, she realized suddenly, since the coup. It was why she had allowed Amarind to find her, years ago. She had probably meant to make the knife herself, to kill Amarind when the time came and use her blood.

Enchantments cannot be broken from the inside.

In the hundreds of years I have been in this house,

you are the only person who has ever managed to find me.

Amarind didn't doubt the Witch was capable of doing anything to seize this chance. Even depending upon a powerless boy-king.

"You can't," Amarind said again, wildly. The king laughed at her silently, and she knew it would do no good, but she went on talking. "You don't know what she is!"

"Yet you went to her, didn't you? How many times have you done her bidding, in exchange for some magic in your pathetic little life? I would never have found her cottage on my own if I hadn't followed you there, when you were too eager to be careful. Don't dare judge *me*, Cousin."

"I didn't know what she would do," Amarind whispered.

"And you still don't know." Cedric shrugged. "Besides, if I *don't* give her that knife, my bargain with her will be forfeit. I'd imagine the consequences of that would be . . . unpleasant. So I'll be taking it now."

He advanced toward her. Amarind stepped back despite her best intentions, until her back was against the clock. She put her free hand to her side so that her fingers were brushing the polished wood. He didn't look wary at *that*, either, which meant the Witch had told him little.

The knife trembled in her hand as she lifted it. Cedric laughed.

"You don't have to worry," he said. "She was quite annoyed when we couldn't find the knife. I'm sure she'll just kill you this time, rather than turn you into a rodent."

"That would be preferable," Amarind said sincerely. The memories swept over her again, the fear and the hunger and the constant, scrambling desperation. "But she didn't turn me."

Cedric lifted an eyebrow. "Then who did?"

Amarind stared at him steadily, and he actually stopped for a moment.

"*Me?*" Cedric's lips twisted. "Don't be ridiculous. I don't have that kind of power."

"I know."

He looked confused, and Amarind drew in her breath. No point in continuing to put off the inevitable. If it hadn't been the Witch, and it hadn't been Cedric, there was only one possibility left.

"But I do," she said, and slashed the knife across her palm.

The pain was instant and terrible, but not bad enough to stop her. The hands on the grandfather clock began to move faster. She turned and slammed her hand against the clock, smearing her blood on the polished wood, crying out this time from the pain.

Her cry lasted only a moment before it contracted into a squeak.

She hadn't been sure it would work, but suddenly she was small and fur-covered again, and the clock loomed over her. With the spell already set, a few drops of blood had been all it took to get it started again.

Cedric's face towered far, far above her, distant and colorless. He said something, but she couldn't understand it. The hands on the clockface were blurred and fading. But they were not gone, not yet; just as Cedric leaned down, the minute hand touched twelve. The chimes rang out, clear and cold.

The mouse turned and ran.

By the time Cedric's hand swooped down on the spot where she had been, Amarind was already inside the clock, through a crack between the glass and the wooden frame. It was a little tight, but once her head was through, the rest of her body flattened and slid in effortlessly. Something huge and shiny came swinging at her, and she gathered herself and leapt.

Fortunately, the golden pendulum was scored with elegant designs, practically roads for a creature as tiny as she. Her tail lashed as she clung to one raised design while the pendulum swung across the clock, hung for one moment, then swung the other way. This time, she waited until the height of the swing, then dashed up and across the pendulum.

It swung down more sharply than she had expected and she almost fell, claws scrabbling and slipping. Then, with a final surge of effort, she reached the top. Her claws scraped wood, and she squirmed upward through another crack, into a mass of sharp, turning gears. She dashed through them, twisting and dodging, and emerged up onto the clockface.

She leapt and clung to the engraved number six, not seeing the second hand until it swept toward her like a knife. She leapt upward again, scrabbling at the designs at the interior of the clockface, feeling the magic pulsate all around her. The second hand touched her fur, and she inched backward, but there was nowhere to go.

The fifth chime rang. The hand slicing toward her vanished, a moment before it would have swept her off her precarious perch, and Time whirled around her.

Her memory was flung back to a time when she had been human, wearing her green gown, kneeling over her sister's body. Lily's face was turned away, her mass of light brown hair covering her face, and Amarind was glad of that.

She looked up at Cedric. He stood several yards

away from her, his face white, holding the knife in his hand. In his shaking hand. He had probably never killed anyone before.

The deathblood of a royal virgin.

Impossible to tell how much Amarind had known, back then, of what the later Amarind had figured out. The Amarind in the green gown hadn't been capable of figuring out much of anything, with her sister's scream still ringing in her ears, her legs sore from running, her mind reeling from the horrors she had run through. She knew about the coup. She knew the knife in her cousin's hand was covered with her sister's blood.

That was all she needed to know.

She called upon the power of the clock. It wasn't difficult. The Witch hadn't told Cedric everything, and he was expecting a helpless princess. He didn't even dodge the blast of wind from her outstretched hand, and he went down with a thud, hitting the end of the couch and then lying still on the floor.

Amarind was glad of an excuse to step away from her sister's corpse. She pried the knife from Cedric's hand, which took a surprising amount of effort. It wasn't until she was holding it that she realized.

There was no blood on the blade. It shone clean and bright.

She looked down instinctively, but there was no blood on the floor, or on Cedric's sleeve. There was no blood anywhere.

It had soaked into the blade.

She held it up, noticing suddenly the runes carved into its hilt, the glimmer on its blade. She was so stricken that she didn't hear the footsteps outside until they began battering at the door.

Soldiers. But now she knew the coup had been arranged as a cover for *this*.

She wanted the knife.

The Witch had engineered all of this. The Witch, who held the power of Time. Perhaps the knife had to be given to her freely . . . but that would be easy enough to arrange. Now that the knife existed, there was no place on earth where she wouldn't find it.

Except . . .

The door shuddered. The frame splintered. Amarind reached for the power of the clock and drew the knife sharply down her palm, right below the flared green edge of her sleeve.

It hurt, but the blood didn't make it past the blade. The steel soaked it in almost before it welled up past her skin.

She scrambled for Cedric's body as the room began to tilt around her, yanking up the legs of his breeches. He actually had two knife-sheaths strapped to his left leg, each holding its own blade. She tugged one off and managed, with only seconds to spare, to tie it around her own leg and slide the knife in.

The door slammed open, but it was too late. There was nothing in the library but a dead princess, an unconscious man, and a mouse they couldn't see, trembling behind a bookshelf.

And a clock without any hands.

***

Time shifted and tilted. The clock still had no hands— or had no hands again, it was hard to tell the difference—and the mouse was trembling, but that was different, because now it was trembling so hard it could barely cling to the clock.

The library door slammed. Cedric was gone. To the Witch? Probably, Amarind thought. If she emerged human from this clock, with this power still strumming through her, there was no telling what she could do to Cedric.

But she wasn't fool enough to think she could do anything to the Witch. The Witch who had killed her sister for the sake of a knife. A knife that didn't exist as long as Amarind was a mouse. That would never exist again, if she died as a mouse.

She hesitated for a moment. She still remembered what it was to be a mouse, small and helpless and afraid. And with that memory came a similar one, of how she had felt in that house in the woods, staring up at the Witch's predatory smile.

If the Witch was freed, everyone in the world would know what it felt like to be prey.

The mouse turned and ran down past the number six, through the gears, and, half-sliding, down the pendulum. When it reached the floor, it turned and looked up at the faceless clock a great distance above it.

It knew that if it touched that clock again, while it struck the hour, the mouse would be human again. But before long its human memories would shrink away, too large and vast for the tiny thing it was now. It wouldn't remember that it had ever been anything else. The mouse hesitated for a second, paws tensed, body coiled.

Then it scuttled across the floor and was gone through a crack in the wall.

– The End –

LITTLE BOY BLUE

Little Boy Blue, come blow your horn,
The sheep's in the meadow, the cow's in the corn.
Where is the boy who looks after the sheep?
He's under a haycock, fast asleep.
Will you wake him? No, not I,
For if I do, he's sure to cry.

– Mother Goose

BLUE
Sayantani DasGupta

I am inking ancient fables upon the dying woman's brow when I hear the Boy call to me, loud and clear as a shepherd's horn.

My story-needle stops short in the middle of a rhyming lullaby, splashing my fingers with a deep indigo. It is the color of a young night, the color of sleep in the early dawn.

"Maiden! Maiden!"

He does not know my name, of course. I would have none to give him, at any rate, for my people lost that right long ago.

We who are called the Children of Ink hold memories for others that they would not keep safe themselves. We who travel only under cloaks of darkness have nothing to call our own, save the story-needles clutched like talismans in our ageless hands. We who are nothing in our own right are called only by the duty to tell, tell, tell, until our fingers and tongues bleed from the telling.

We watch over the memories of the living like shepherds watch over their sheep. But we are exempt from public haunt ourselves. We are non-persons, no one, nobodies, no bodied. We do not walk, but float, like wisps of breathy yearning escaping a lover's lips. We do not touch, except in our ancient ways—and only then, under cover of darkest sleep. The living have long lost their songs, their rhymes and lullabies; and so it has fallen upon us, the damned and nameless, the foot servants of time, to keep the story ink streaming beneath their skin, even if they cannot see it anymore.

But every now and then, a century, a day, a second, an aeon, there is one who awakens to us, one who can see our markings, and sometimes even our faces as we visit them or their loved ones, sewing our stories into flesh and bone.

Never me. I am too swift to be seen. My etchings twist and curve along the seashore, stain the sand and stone, swirl about the bark of the telling trees—more runes than letters, sometimes. When I am called to mark a newborn on her mother's breast, a bride or groom on their wedding eve, or an old man on his fever couch, I mark their body-stories swiftly, my needle moving with the speed and ferocity of a hundred moths' wings. These are the only touches I have known. But they have never known me.

But now, the Boy calls. He has seen me, as I mark his grandmother, and he searches with the desperation of one who has lost something most precious in his keep.

I close my mind to him, bidding him away, as I know I should. But the longing to be seen is fierce, and it frightens me.

Although the lighthouse of my presence is dark, that longing makes a tiny firefly's glow, a spark that the Boy follows, and follows, until at last he finds my telling tree deep in the mossy wood.

He comes with his animals and his bow, a horn at

his belt and a quiver on his back. He sings to keep the lambs calm as they pick their way through the shadows of haunted woods.

He is beautiful and dark and I take great pleasure in his form.

But when he sees me, the Boy's song chokes in his throat. I feel the silencing of his music like the thrust from a knife. For a moment, I had been lost in those warm sounds. Bathed in his voice and words, I had become something other than what I was. Now, I must again remember.

Whoever made that song-mark on him had great skill, I think. And suddenly, I am aching with jealousy at this other of my kind who has touched him, changed him, kept his people's memories alive on and through his very body.

"Are you real or am I dreaming?" His voice makes the leaves rustle and the buds green.

The animals bleat and stamp but I take no heed. As if looking in a mirror, I see my own hazy face in his eyes, and the feeling makes me want to weep.

I flee on the fog, of course. What else can I do? But I hear him calling behind me, "Maiden! Maiden!"

I do not come back to the wood until nightfall, and only then following the footsteps of the fox and badger, keeping well to the shadows. The Boy will have gone by now, I think, gone to a fire and a home, a bed and a dinner, the comforts and rituals of the living.

But I am wrong, for here he sits, asleep beneath my telling tree, his animals scattered far and wide like all my proprieties. If I remembered my duty, I should worry about him. Is there a mother or sister weeping for his safety? A father with a lantern even now searching for his lost boy in the darkness?

His breast rises and falls with an easy sleep, and I

can see that he is as near a Man as a Boy. His arms, even in their relaxation, are strong, and his back broad as if used to carrying the sun. Though I have not been called to mark him, I want to touch him more than I—for all my stories—can say. And for the first time in my many years, I realize there is something stronger than words, something beyond even my deft needle's abilities to darn images and memories.

As if hearing my desires, he opens his eyes. "You!"

I shake my wordless head, opening and closing my lips to show him that there are no sounds for my spending.

But he does not need them, he has enough in his own pockets for us both. "You are the one who came to my grandmother as she breathed her last; you covered her skin with letters that faded in the morning sun."

I nod. Yes, I think, studying his dark locks, the old woman was so like him. Yet I—who remember every tale I traced on every root and heart—cannot recall the stories I sewed into his foremother's skin, nor if my visit to his house was yesterday or a thousand yesterdays ago. It is as if I have caught the forgetting sickness of the living in my desire for this one of them.

"I have been searching for you ever since."

I nod again, but pull myself from his gaze enough to look around the sleeping forest. I should not be letting him talk to me. I am no temptress Calypso, no Circe of the sun and sea. But like those enchantresses of another time, my wanting is so great. My wanting to be seen. My wanting to be heard. My wanting to keep him here with me, in the forest of storied trees.

"What is your name?" he asks, and this seals his fate. No one has ever asked me this question.

I flap my lips again and again, willing something to come, from where I know not—that infinite stream of stories begun on mountain high? But my tongue cannot work without my needle and I feel myself wither and fade in frustration.

"Wait!" He reaches for me but I evade his grasp. There is nothing here for him to touch, and I cannot bear it.

I wrap myself in the thick fog, cloaking myself from the Boy's attention.

"Wait." He thrusts his arm—bared now, his shirt high over amber skin—through the mist.

"Can you mark me as you marked her?"

What does he say?

No. No. No. This is not the ancient way. We come to the living as they sleep.

What is he asking of me? The trees whisper and moan, and I feel my essence shiver, as if I, too, was mortal-made.

"Can you mark me, Maiden? Can you?"

He is so near now that I can smell his flesh. That pungent smell of living warmth; skin and bone, muscle, hair, sinew. There is blood pumping, an ocean of life-waters beneath that placid surface.

He is not mine, to touch and to mark. He is only Boy, Boy with his arrows and horn, his runaway charges, his forgotten home and duty.

"Please."

The word, a doorway, hangs between us. There is something like a snaking arm of fire that pulls me through, out of the darkness and toward him.

My needle, of its own accord, quivers. It wants to sing its song on his flesh.

But awake? With eyes of coal boring into mine?

I grasp my story-needle and feel myself become more real, more present in time and space. I am in the story forest, I think, with a Boy who has lost his charges even as I have lost my way.

I begin. The first pierce makes him wince and his eyes widen, a bride on her wedding night.

This thought makes me laugh, and it is the first sound he hears of me, and for this I am glad. My tongue is loose now that my needle flows, fast and fierce with its blue-black tales. His skin is warm and firm beneath my touch and I am drunk with the story-making. I sing him the ancient songs that run deep within me and now, through him.

"I want," he says, his voice faint at first.

"You want?" The moss and stones prompt him.

I dare say nothing, but wait. I am a clock with frozen hands. A whisper out of time.

"I want to hear your story," he finally says. "I want to hear you sing your name."

A beat. A pause. A breath. A cry. Then, with his witness, I name myself, crying out like a new mother as I give birth to she that I am.

"Blue," I weep and sing. "My name is Blue and I am the world's seamstress."

There is blood and ink flowing between us now, and I cannot stop the telling. We are Blue and Boy, we are the marker and the marked, we are the shepherd and the sheep, we are the story and the song.

My markings change, new runes I have not made before rush like rivers. I tell of my duties, and of my loneliness. I tell of my home in the trees, of the stone that is my magic place. I tell him of the secrets and the darkness.

I tell him of all those I have touched. I tell him of the stories I have sung into their skin. I tell him how I mourn when the ink fades and becomes forgotten.

The Boy smiles as I mark his flesh, now one arm, and then another. Without embarrassment, he removes his shirt, and I fill his body with ink and desire.

It is frenzied, tiring work, and as I mark him, he tells me his name. I say it, over and over, my tongue free to sing and speak.

Emboldened, I stitch our names together on his skin. First a bold outline, then a filling-in of color.

As I work, a story appears that has always been there within me. An ancient tale beneath the flesh. A tale of desire and discovery, of seeing and being seen. It is a tale that lives beyond the telling.

That is when I know for sure that the living may forget, but I am the one who must seek my way. I am the one who is lost. And this Boy—this Man, he is the one who has come to find me, to collect me home.

I know what to do.

I hand him my story-needle, and show him how to mark my being. He is nervous, at first, but soon the ink flows like fire, like rivers, like memory, like the endless, endless sea.

I wince, then cry, then laugh with the new sensation. I, too, am now marked, and this body thrumming with tales and time is now mine. As if awakened from an infinite slumber, I finally am. I can finally be.

This is the story I was waiting for all along. This is the story that will change everything.

– The End –

SLEEP, BABY, SLEEP

Sleep, baby, sleep,
Thy papa guards the sheep;
Thy mama shakes the dreamland tree,
And from it fall sweet dreams for thee,
Sleep, baby, sleep,

Sleep, baby, sleep,
Our cottage vale is deep;
The little lamb is on the green,
With woolly fleece so soft and clean,
Sleep, baby, sleep,

Sleep, baby, sleep,
Down where the woodbines creep;
Be always like the lamb so mild,
A kind and sweet and gentle child,
Sleep, baby, sleep . . .

– Mother Goose

PIECES OF EIGHT
Shannon Delany with Max Scialdone

He jumped at the sound of someone knocking on a nearby door. Outside, a man bellowed, and from his place in the dim room, Marnum could make out the noise of a scuffle before that door slammed shut and another—even closer—was pounded on.

Dust motes spiraled down in the slender light seeping between curtains drawn tight to hide their impromptu rendezvous, and Marnum looked at the woman whom the barracks boys claimed was his mother—the same woman whose jingling belt held a key that matched the shape of the scar on his cheek. The words of the prophecy came back to him, singing through his head like only the last allowable song could: *"Some are born for sacrifice, both catalyst and key . . ."*

"It can't be me," he whispered. "I can't be the sacrifice. The prophecy says," his voice softened, richened, as he sang, *"one unscarred, unmaimed, untrue, the opening shall be."* He shook his head, blond hair tumbling into his mismatched eyes. "I'm maimed," he said. "Scarred," he added, his lip curled just enough so she'd know he meant in more than a physical way. "I'm . . ."

"*Perfect*, except for the searing touch of a misguided mother's love." Her hand darted out, fingers brushing the raised, white shape that ran from the corner of his blue eye to the lobe of his left ear.

He slapped her away.

"I kept you alive," she whispered, "and I'll manage it one more time. Take this." She tugged a worn and wrinkled piece of parchment from her belt pouch, and pressed it into his hand. "This is how I'll shake the Dreamland Tree. Find the Pieces of Eight. *There was an old woman lived under a hill* . . . Find the woman as old as time. She is a soothsayer—a prophetess. By grace, you'll be placed on the right path."

The next door they pounded on was so close it rattled the walls and flexed the cobwebs hanging in the slender beams above.

"Out the back," the woman said.

He slipped outside and was in an alley.

"Remember the lullaby," she urged. Then she eased the door shut, and a lock slid into place.

How could he forget the lullaby? Every time he fell into a fever dream, he heard that forbidden string of notes and words—that *song*—calling him back:

Sleep, baby, sleep,
Thy papa guards the sheep;
Thy mama shakes the Dreamland Tree,
And from it fall sweet dreams for thee,
Sleep, baby, sleep.

Sleep, baby, sleep,
Our cottage vale is deep;
The little lamb is on the green,
With woolly fleece so soft and clean,
Sleep, baby, sleep.

Always it was her voice, the strange woman's voice, that sang the words as if she had no understanding that singing anything but the prophecy was taboo. He sighed, and, hugging the building, crept along, keeping an eye out for movement.

He froze when he saw the guards. Three tall men with bodies like tree trunks, clothed all in black, kicked in the front door of the building he'd just left. The emblem on their backs denoted their rank within the government's hierarchy. Huntsmen. He heard the startled shout of the woman whom everyone called Abby, but called herself Abbadon.

His mother? If she was shaking the Dreamland Tree . . . then his father guarded the sheep? He shook his head. He'd never had a mother or a father that he'd known.

Marnum swallowed a deep breath and pushed away from the building, hurling himself behind a wagon stopped across the street. Slipping into the shadows beneath it, he crouched, watching the roadway from a dog's eye view.

More Huntsmen wearing glossy black boots stomped past.

Somehow, he had to get out of the workhouse commune. The horse hitched to the wagon stomped a hoof, snorting as someone shifted in the seat above him. Tucking Abbadon's parchment into his shirt, he grabbed the rigging of the wagon and pulled himself into its gut, wrapping his arms and legs around its skeleton as it pulled out.

He hung beneath the wagon until his hands and arms were rubbed raw against the wood and metal. Spattered with mud—and worse, since the horse was not far ahead—he hung, the steady rhythm of the horse's hooves laying down the beat of something that wanted to grow in his head and become more. He pressed one ear against his shoulder, trying to muffle the sound. He was grateful to escape the place he'd grown up and worked in—now, the place he was a wanted man. Wanted for sacrifice because the Elders believed his death could connect the mysterious Pieces of Eight and reunite their people with Infinity itself.

When the wagon stopped at the edge of a small town, he dropped to the ground, knees bruising against stones in the roadbed, pants soaking up mud. He waited until the driver unhitched the horse and walked away. Checking that the road was empty, he slipped out from underneath cover, stood, and stretched. In the light of a nearby lantern, he read the parchment:

Infinite ways to test your fate,
O'er the mountains and hills she waits.

He paused. "*Find the woman as old as time,* she'd said. *An old woman who lived under a hill.* Ridiculous." He shoved the parchment back into his shirt. He was no sacrifice or savior—he was little more than a slave. He sniffed—and a foul-smelling slave, as well. "There is no Dreamland Tree. Just a children's fairy tale. Like believing in magic," he whispered to himself.

Two men stumbled out of a nearby building. Raucous laughter and the smell of ale and urine followed, mixed and strong. Slapping each other's backs, they suddenly drew up short, focusing on something beyond the road's edge. "Aye . . . eerie, is it not?" one asked, pointing a wobbling finger at lights that flickered in the distance.

The other murmured his agreement.

"They say thems will-o-wisps lighting that hill.

That there's an old woman, lives there still."

"Will-o-wisps? Magic?" His friend snorted. "Next you'll tell me they sing lullabies."

"No one sings lullabies no more," the other lamented. "Music . . . I miss it." He opened his mouth to croon some wavering sound, but his friend clapped a hand over his face.

"Don't you dare. S'enough yer drunk, but if they hear ya singin' . . ."

"I remember music . . ."

"Aye, aye. Ye remember the location of yer house? Let's get ye home. Enough about music and magic. Ridiculous ideas, both of 'em. Nothin' good ever came of thinkin' on either."

After they ambled away, Marnum crept to the spot they'd stood and peered between two ramshackle houses to the fields beyond, and a strange and sudden hill that rose up to be ringed by bobbing lights. He frowned.

The bobbing lights rearranged themselves, zipping to positions before the hill and lining up—tiny, fluttering, pinpricks of light, marking a path.

He gulped. It was the wind. Nothing more. The wind and the reflection of stars hanging far above. He looked up at a cloud-covered sky that only the moon dared pierce. If not the reflection of stars, then it was surely swamp gas.

He was hunted. Told by his mother he was the one to change everything. He'd always been different, he knew.

He froze at the edge of the road. *Don't step off the road*, was the warning from many a childhood tale. Strange things lurked in the wild. But the path to the odd hill was marked and clear. And strange things lurked everywhere—strange as that creature that had barreled into the barracks and mauled Jaxson before they could kill it. No wonder the other workers whispered it was like something straight from a nightmare. He swallowed again, but his feet kept him moving forward. If danger was everywhere, on and off the road, why not take the risk?

Still, he sprinted from the road's edge, running pell-mell between the shifting lights, all the way to the hill's base and across ground that was not at all swampy.

He bent over to catch his breath. When he straightened, he laughed at his own foolishness. He was nineteen. No need to be scared of things he couldn't see—especially when what he could see was frightening enough. When the hill tore open, the ground shuddering beneath his feet and hurling him into the hillside's waiting and rock-lined maw, he reconsidered just what he should be afraid of.

Pitching forward, he landed hard on his knees. His eyes adjusted to the glow oozing up from a brazier in the middle of a strange room. Smoke filled his nostrils and made his eyes tear and blink at its sweet, acrid scent. The place was dark and littered with reflections and shadows in odd shapes and sizes. He felt, more than saw, walls around him—walls that curved up toward a close but vaulted ceiling.

A shadow shifted right in front of him, and he stumbled back. *"Woman as old as time . . ."* he mumbled.

A candle stuttered to life, lit from the brazier, and he gasped when it illuminated the face and slender form of a young woman seated cross-legged on the floor. She could have been as much as twelve years his senior or two years his junior, but old as time? Hardly. Yet there was such a slow and steady gravity to her voice, such depth to her dark eyes, that he wondered if the hill had existed before her or had grown up over centuries *around* her.

"Speak of what it is you seek," she said, her gaze slowly taking him in.

"The Pieces of Eight." Even as the words came out, he felt fire rise in his face. Ridiculous.

Her eyes burned with sudden intensity. "Why now?"

"The Dreamland Tree . . ." He sighed. "Weird things are happening. Strange creatures coming into the towns and cities, diseases we've never suffered before. Things out of nightmares. It's said this Dreamland Tree needs to be . . . shaken?"

Her lips turned up at their ends.

"It sounds crazy."

"Not to one such as I. To shake the Dreamland Tree, you must connect the Pieces of Eight and find the arrangement to reorder your world."

Marnum blinked at her. *Ridiculous.* "You speak as if the tree is tangible—*real.*"

"I have slept in the shade of that tree. It is as real as I am," the soothsayer said.

He glanced around the room, little more than an odd hole in the hill, lit only by flame and whatever cooked and spit scent from the glowing brazier, and pulled out the parchment. "I have this."

"Ah," she said, reading the script. "But are these the words that begin a journey, or end it? It seems so familiar—like the ghost of a long-forgotten song."

"It's a song?" Marnum shook his head.

She nodded, and her hands swept some things off the floor before her, and she shook them like the barracks boys shook dice. She threw the rattling pieces down, and Marnum stooped to see.

With a slender finger, she prodded a set of tiny bird bones.

Marnum swallowed hard.

"Wise is he, so clever and strong, fell from grace, all for a song. He will give you more of what you seek. But do not stray from your duty, Marnum. Time is slipping away."

A breeze blew in and the lights guttered out, leaving the room silent, dark, and oddly empty.

"The tree is as real as I am."

Marnum turned and raced back to the road.

***

The road felt even wilder walking it at night, and Marnum kept his arms wrapped tight around him, his gaze sharp and wary. Dawn set fire to the sky at his back and still he walked, searching for his next turn. It was midmorning when he heard men on the road behind him. He glanced over his shoulder and felt the sun light his scar. Three men dressed in black pressed forward in a run, laughing as they recognized their quarry. Fast as a spooked buck, he vaulted away, racing down the road, until the only noise he heard was his own breath pounding out of his body in gasps, and the thrumming of his own blood in his ears as his heart raced to keep up with his flying feet. He no longer heard them—there was no sound of feet pounding the packed dirt, no shouts.

He spun to look, to see how far behind . . .

Someone joined them—a flash of a royal guard's crimson-colored suit and . . . a wolf mask?

He jerked backward, seeing a third man emerge from his blind spot, his hand nearly on Marnum as he closed the last bit of distance between predator and prey, just a moment before the one in the wolf mask pummeled the first Huntsman, taking him to the ground with an efficiency that made Marnum's eyes widen. The Wolf took down a second Huntsman with a few quick moves.

At the road's edge, Marnum's arms flailed, spinning like blades on a windmill. For a split second, balanced precariously, his world slowed as he reached for the remaining Huntsman to stop his fall. The Huntsman chuckled, nodding to him encouragingly as he stretched forward to take Marnum's hand.

But Marnum pulled his arms in, committing to the fall. Gravity pulled him downhill into briars and underbrush that snagged his clothing, but couldn't hold him.

Curses followed him as he plunged down a steep embankment, hitting rocks and the lumpy roots of trees. Bruised and panting, he lay at the bottom of the slope, waiting for the blood in his veins to stop throbbing, and letting the normal sounds of the world seep into his battered consciousness. He heard the grunts and shouts of another fight on the road above, and . . . a body hitting the ground?

"Not so jovial now, are you?" he heard the victor ask.

Standing, he decided not to return immediately to the road. As much as he might like to thank the Wolf, he would rather not risk the Huntsmen again. Mentally, he conceded that danger could be found anywhere—on and off the road.

***

Although he believed his next destination to be nearby, the trails had become switchbacks by noon, and deciding which way to go was mind-numbing. He shoved blindly forward, hoping that the paths would converge ahead, and once again he'd be on his way.

The royal guard was suddenly before him, a wall of red wearing a leather and brass wolf's head helmet that hid nearly all his face.

The Wolf had found him.

"Thank you for saving me . . . twice . . . or three times, I guess?"

The eyes hidden deep in the mask were so dark they chilled him. The Wolf cocked his head. And pulled out a knife. "You must come with me. Quickly."

The thick underbrush lining the deer trail rattled with movement and they both jumped back. Something fought through the thicket to get to them. A beast crashed through the briars, snorting, howling, and ripping brambles up by their roots to toss them off its horned snout, sending sprays of dirt like loamy hail in all directions.

Marnum stared, slack-jawed, as the beast drooled over curling tusks and watched him with six glowing, piggy eyes. Caring nothing for the Wolf, it charged Marnum. He swallowed, knowing he was good as dead.

Silent as a shadow, the Wolf slipped between them, slicing into the creature's wrinkled snout and drawing its attention from Marnum. The creature shrieked and swung its heavy tusked and toothy head toward the masked guardsman, sweeping him off his feet and knocking his blade away to tangle in the undergrowth. The creature pawed the ground, digging trenches with its cloven feet as steam billowed from its flared nostrils. The Wolf scrambled back, and Marnum knew this was the perfect time to run—while the beast was distracted.

Instead, he picked up the biggest branch he could, and shouting, whacked the beast on its spiny shoulder.

Grunting, it turned its attention back to him.

Marnum backed up until his shoulders hit the rough bark of a tree trunk. The branch shook in his hands as, out of the corner of his eye, he watched the Wolf roll and retrieve his blade.

When the beast charged Marnum next, the Wolf slid beneath its hanging jowls and drove the blade deep into its stinking flesh, ripping a gash from just below the hinge of its jaw on the right, to the matching bit of bone on the left. Blood poured free, blasting in rhythm to each stuttering beat of the beast's frantic heart. It plowed face-first into the dirt and leaf mold, gouging the earth as momentum carried its body forward until its trembling snout came to rest a hairsbreadth from Marnum's twitching toes.

The Wolf straightened and wiped his dripping blade on his thigh. Crimson blood stained crimson pants, and Marnum pressed his back even harder into the tree. "Thanks."

But suddenly, he was only seeing tree branches and bits of sky from his new position on the ground. The Wolf pushed his helm's snout into Marnum's face. "I am of the Waiting Wolves. And you are whom we have waited for."

"Nice to meet you?"

"You must come with me. Now. And quickly."

"Am I your prisoner? I just saved your life."

"And I yours. Four times now."

Marnum sighed. "Yes. I owe you. I understand. But there's this thing I have to do, and I don't think being your prisoner will allow me to do it."

The Wolf sat on Marnum's chest, knees resting on either side of him. "Explain your mission. I will wait."

"I guess so . . . being a Waiting Wolf and all."

As the guardsman glared into his face—snout to

nose with him—Marnum explained his task. But when he began to sing the lullaby, the Wolf slapped a hand across his mouth. "It is forbidden."

"It is only music."

"You know nothing." The Wolf rose and extended a hand to help Marnum up. "Music must be controlled—leashed like a dog. Otherwise . . ." He nudged the dead beast with his boot. "Things go wrong when music is set free. It is a tool for the most highly educated only. Music is not for your sort. Or mine."

Marnum blinked.

"Come, prisoner." The Wolf grabbed him by the arm. Marnum tried to shake free, but the guardsman's grip was fierce.

"To where?"

"To complete your mission, so I might complete mine."

"But the words I am gathering to shake the Dreamland Tree—they seem to be verses of a song." Hesitantly, he told the guardsman all he knew of his task.

The guardsman shook his head. "Once you see what music makes of men, you will not be so quick to sing—no matter the cause."

When they stopped at the lip of a little valley, the lullaby's words again sang out of Marnum's lips. *"Our cottage vale is deep . . ."*

The Wolf grunted. "Do you remember this place, then?"

"No. Should I?"

"Probably not," the Wolf muttered, passing him on the steep path down. "You were only born here. You did not stay for long. Your birth was . . . an anomaly, of sorts."

It was pastoral, peaceful—sheep grazing and lambs

playing. And then the Wolf strode into their midst. They scattered, bleating over the noise of the burbling stream that cut the vale in half as they crossed the valley's floor.

"Not nearly so mild as a lamb, now, are you?" Marnum asked.

"Meekness gains you nothing."

Marnum finally asked the question that had lodged in his throat the moment he caught sight of one of the white fleeces. "Is my father here, then?"

"Your father guards much different sheep than these," the Wolf said with a snort. The guardsman paused then, looking Marnum up and down. "You do not know who sired you?"

"No." Marnum caught sight of a small cottage not far ahead, nestled amidst wild and roving plant life. "He's a shepherd, though?"

"To quite the flock. And he is quite well-versed with time." They reached the cottage, and the Wolf knocked on the door.

An old man answered. "Ah. And where, oh where, is your sheep's clothing, dear Wolf?"

"Must we always play these same parts?" the Wolf asked with a groan.

"You are the one who is still in the employ of the palace, so yes, I fear we must. But we have another guest, I see. Welcome. Step inside."

Marnum ducked his head to enter. When his eyes adjusted to the small house's dark interior, he saw he was surrounded by things of all sizes, covered by blankets and threadbare tapestries.

"The door," the old man urged. "Close it well and slide the bolt."

The Wolf obeyed, casting Marnum a look that might have been synonymous with "crazy."

"You have finally come home," the old man said. "Just in time, just in time." He clapped his hands together. "You will free the music, and magic will once more be let loose upon the land."

The Wolf coughed. "I cannot let him do that. The royals say that words might be weapons."

The old man's rheumy eyes focused on the Wolf. "And so they might," he conceded.

"If words be weapons, what madness might music make?" the Wolf wondered aloud.

The old man puffed out an exasperated breath. "Take off your mask. In this house, we are all only who we are."

"He does not . . ."

"Then it is time he does."

"Do you know how much harder my job will become once he knows?"

"Off with your head," the old man snapped.

Gloved hands swept beneath the helm's jointed leather jaw, fingers finding buckles and snaps and deftly undoing them. With one last, hesitant look at Marnum, the Wolf tugged free of his mask, and Marnum gasped.

Her hair was long, dark as a raven's wing and bound high on her head, except for a few strands that had slipped free and hung loose around her dark brown eyes. With a grunt, she tucked the helm beneath her arm and gave Marnum a look. Not a smile, but rather a grim glower. She pointed to herself. "Wolf." Then she pointed to Marnum. "Wolf's prisoner."

But he was too busy recovering from his surprise to care how she referred to either one of them. She was beautiful, with high cheekbones and cutting eyes—as lovely as the soothsayer. Far lovelier than the girls back at the workhouse. Perhaps adventuring was not so bad a decision, after all.

She snapped her fingers in his face. "Wolf," she repeated sharply.

He raised an eyebrow. "Bitc—" But before he finished the word, she had him up against the cottage wall.

"Do you see?" she said over her shoulder to the old man. "They never have enough sense not to challenge a woman in a position of power." She mumbled a few choice terms under her breath before releasing him.

Beautiful and strong, he thought, rubbing the spot on his chest where she'd shoved her arm to pin him.

"Get it over with, old man," she demanded. "Tell us what we need to know so I can remind him of his place in the supposed chain of events."

The old man opened his mouth, but the Wolf threw a hand up to stop him. "No. I'll speed up the process. He," she pointed to their host, "was once a very important man, in the employ of the palace. But he became obsessed. With music, and the idea of freeing magic, and so—" She pulled a blanket off one of the strange shapes.

"Guitar," the old man whispered reverently.

"—he began to try and unlock the secret. To assemble the Pieces of Eight. He collected—" She ripped off another sheet, revealing another stringed instrument.

"Balalaika," the old man said.

"—every instrument he could." A tapestry was pulled away, another instrument revealed.

"The armonica—a beautiful device."

"Eventually, his obsession turned dangerous, as his need for anything musical grew too great."

She yanked another tapestry free. The old man gasped.

There, in a cage, was a gilt and jewel-encrusted nightingale.

"They cast him out. He lost everything. His home, his power, his reputation. They sent Huntsmen for both he and his niece, and why?"

"Because of the legend."

"Yes," she snarled. "Because of the legend. Because of the wild idea that by gathering some bits of a song—what is it? Four couplets?—the right man might unlock something infinite. And everyone wants to connect to the Infinite, even if they can't define what the Infinite *is*."

"I do not wish to *unlock* anything," Marnum protested. "Just shake the Dreamland Tree—end the nightmare creatures' attacks . . ."

"But, dear boy, one undoes the other." The old man ran a light and shaking hand across the armonica's globes. "Sit, sit."

They did, and the old man said, "Long ago—"

"I've heard this one before," the Wolf said. "I'll return shortly."

The old man looked at her briefly, then nodded. He began again when the locks slid into place once more. "There were two gods. Twin boys. The eldest was beautiful and loved, and the youngest was ever in his shadow, gifted with clever talents rather than an undeniably handsome face. They both loved the same woman, and set out to win her devotion. The youngest wrote her a song infused with such magic that hearing it felt like falling in love for the first time. He was a god of music and a master of all things magical, and he understood time like no other. But his brother could not have him win his lady love, so he stole the song and presented it as his own. The lady was so impressed she did not heed the other twin's claim that he was the song's author.

"The youngest left, distraught and filled with

worry. He picked up a stone with two pricking ends into which he rubbed all his worries, and when he realized that by forcing them into the stone he could be free of his troubles—of his pain—he withdrew all his worry and angst, his heartache—and some say his conscience—and, placing it all in the glittering, double-terminated stone, set it at the base of the Dreamland Tree. He himself became stone-faced and set. The tree absorbed the worry stone and with it, the young god's trepidation and tribulations. The balance between dream and nightmare shifted, and nightmares seeped out of the stone, poisoning the tree. The young god wandered the lands for many a year, creating things that could either help or harm mankind, depending on how they were treated. He met with his brother once more. They fought. The sky bled at sunrise and sunset for the first time. Mountains were moved and valleys were carved, and to our west are lakes gouged by the fingers of the youngest when his brother threw him down, just before imprisoning him."

Marnum watched him, waiting.

"He's there still, imprisoned in a great lake, master of magic and music, and a tempest of time. If you shake the Dreamland Tree, he will be free again. He *is* music. And music is magic. He is, therefore, what unites us with the Infinite—with true power—and if good music is all about keeping time—well, time has been kept long enough. Look to the stars and the waters to find your way to the tree. You must see things differently now."

The Wolf was at the door again. "We must go."

"So you don't have any of the Pieces of Eight for me?" Marnum asked.

"No, but the song is as old as time, and as powerful as a true heart. You will find the last pieces. In time."

He hurried them to the door, and nearly shoved Marnum out.

They followed the stream in silence for a while. "So," Marnum said to the Wolf, who had once again donned her intimidating helm. "You're a girl."

"Woman. And gender makes no difference in this."

"Gender always . . ."

She stopped on the path and turned to face him. "I am a warrior first and foremost. The rest is secondary."

Marnum put his hands up between them. "I am a prisoner. First and foremost."

She snorted.

"What's your real name, Wolf?"

"Cyrelle."

"I'm Marnum."

"No, you aren't."

He stared at her.

"That isn't the name your father gave you. I remember."

"What?"

"I was five when you were presented and named. It was the first—and the last—court ceremony I attended."

Now Marnum stopped their progress. "What are you talking about?"

"You were born a prince, Marnum. Prince Garendell."

"And you?"

"A common cur." The laugh that followed her description was as sharp as a dog's bark. "But my uncle, he was a powerful man. Once."

"The old man?"

Cyrelle nodded. "Who but a relative would listen to his tales of mad gods?"

"You do not believe in the Dreamland Tree?"

"I believe I have orders to follow. I believe what any good soldier does—I believe my commanding officer. And he said to find you and bring you in."

"Yet you will let me complete my task first."

"I will still obey my orders. We are merely taking the long way back."

"Wait. If you were cast out of the court all those years ago, how are you in the palace's employ now?"

"Given the right papers, anyone can become anything."

"Wait," Marnum said again. "I'm a prince?"

She shrugged. "You are commonly known as the Lost Prince. Your mother stole you and . . ." her eyes focused on his scar as they never had before, ". . . made sure you'd be overlooked. Safe. She learned too late what your father was planning in making you."

"Thy father guards the sheep . . ."

"Baaaa. What else are citizens of our kingdom but *sheep?*"

"Unreal. This is totally unreal . . ."

That was when they were attacked by more Huntsmen.

Cyrelle dispatched them neatly, adjusted her helm, and encouraged Marnum forward.

"Those men were sent by—"

"—your father. The king. You are to be sacrificed."

"What if I'm to *make* a sacrifice of some sort, not *be* sacrificed?" he asked.

"Interesting thought." She shrugged. "Either way, what's life without a little father-son tension? Those men were paid for by *our* tax dollars, and I dealt with them so harshly. That was less than fiscally prudent of me." She clapped her hands together and cleared her throat. "This," she said, spreading her arms wide, "this is where we will find passage to this tree of yours."

Below them, the stream dumped and merged with others to create one wide river to the greatest of lakes, a river filled with boats flying the flags of a hundred different places. It was as if the entire world spread wide below them. Marnum, before little more than a slave, then a hunted sacrifice and lost prince, now felt like something so small there was no word tiny enough to fit the thing he'd become, standing before so grand a place.

***

Cyrelle led the way down into the tangle of drifting and tilting docks as the sun shrugged behind a mountain, and the stars crawled into the indigo sky. "Have a care," she warned, leaping from one wobbling wooden island to another.

"Where are we going?" Marnum asked, trying not to wave his arms to maintain his balance. "Ughh—"

She grabbed his wrist, slipped her hand down to take his, and pulled him across onto the next dock. She dropped his hand and shook her head. "We're there. Now, choose which river rats we ride with."

He blinked. Three broad-bellied ships swayed at the edge of the dock, square sails hoisted to reveal their ship's emblems. One tree, one eagle, and one springing hart. Marnum moved toward the one with the tree's insignia—until he heard a voice say, "This crew is a *nightmare*! I dream of a better ship, a better crew . . ."

Nightmare. Dream.

He swung around to find the voice. On the ship decorated with the eagle stood a man with a mop, swabbing as he grumbled. At the same ship's bow stood a man only a few years Marnum's senior, a telescope in his hands. He addressed the complainer, saying, "Step to me, Tyrell. See things differently."

He—the captain, according to his clothing—exchanged the telescope for the mop and took over for the other man. "Aim high . . . there," the captain said, watching his crewman. "That one not far from the moon—she's a beauty. Brightest star in the heavens."

See things differently . . .

"That one," Marnum said, remembering the old man's words.

After a brief discussion regarding the price of passage and the captain's ignored insistence that Marnum and Cyrelle did not want to accompany them on *their* mission, they were given the right to board.

"And what is this most dangerous mission of yours?" Marnum asked as the boat left the dock.

"We go to destroy the Drowsing Tree. To cut it down and burn out its roots."

"You mean the Dreamland Tree? You can't *destroy* it . . ."

The captain cocked his head, his eyes narrowing to glimmering slits. "That damnable tree endangers our entire world. It must be rooted out."

"It can be *shaken* . . ."

Although Marnum couldn't fathom how the captain's eyes could narrow more, they did, and his gaze fell on the scar on Marnum's cheek, and Cyrelle in her wolf's helm. "Take them!" he shouted, and the crew pounced on them, wrapping them with ropes tied in a half dozen different knots and hitches. To her credit, Cyrelle required four men to drag her down. Marnum rolled his eyes. He had fallen beneath one, but he was large. And quite hairy. That had to count for something.

Watching the land pass by and the men scramble about their duties as they passed into deeper and wider waters, Marnum wondered how he could shake the tree with only four lines of an eight-line song.

"It will never work," Marnum muttered.

"Of course not. One dare not destroy the Dreamland Tree." Cyrelle snorted through her helm. "I might yet believe the tree—all of it—is real . . ."

"Why wouldn't you?"

The Wolf's head faced him, and although he couldn't see her eyebrows, he got the distinct impression one of them was raised. "Is that not the doubter calling the cynic skeptical," she mused. "It sounds a bit crazy," she said, "and you know it."

"You can be quite critical, I think," he pouted. "And for all that, here I am, trying to figure out how to serenade a tree. I don't have all the words. I'm missing lines. No one has given me any new ones."

She blinked at him. "You may be a prince quite removed, but that is most certainly something a prince would say. *No one has given me any new ones.* What if you are only given the beginning and the rest is built from *you*? What if the missing lines are verses you know somehow—words carved into your soul?"

"Your uncle said it's like an ancient love song. I do not have any words of love carved into my soul."

"Perhaps to the left of your soul?"

He knew from her tone she was smirking beneath that helm of hers.

"Try your heart," she said.

He turned away from her. But she had made him think. And see things differently. He whipped back toward her. "What if it's part of *your* heart? What if you know some of these words better than I?"

"If we're speaking of love, I am mute," she assured him.

He groaned, stretched as much as the ropes allowed, and faced forward once more.

"There is a reason *you* must connect the Pieces of Eight. Otherwise, anyone might do it. But a boy born when you were . . . in the region you were . . . this must come from *you*."

The boat slowed and men shouted as an island came into view. On that island, a huge tree sat atop a strangely bulbous hill.

Cyrelle motioned with her snout. "The time has come, Garendell."

"Marnum," he corrected. "I never knew myself as Garendell. I'm just Marnum, a simple man."

He had two couplets—four lines, but a song needed a rhythm and tune. He thought of the rhythms he'd encountered on his journey, the beat of the horse's hooves as he had clung to the belly of the wagon, the spurt of the beast's blood as it had died, the pace of his own feet on the road. His fingers tapped against his thigh, and he began to hum.

Cyrelle looked away, torn.

The crew was divided, some lighting two cannons chained to the deck and aiming for the tree, some scurrying into the shallow water to attack the huge and twisted thing on foot.

If it was what the legends claimed—the source of both dream and nightmare—destroying it completely would cause irrevocable harm. But if Marnum could shake it, free it of the poison . . . He sifted words and tunes and rhythms in his head, testing each on his tongue. He thought of love and he thought of the people he'd met along his way. *"Bridge the distance and heed her call, magic once more will beckon all."*

Cyrelle looked at him, and the Wolf's head bobbed up and down in a nod. "Keep going. You're onto something. I can feel it."

When the sailors began to scream, Marnum focused on the giant tree once more. Broad branches as nimble as arms swept out, stretching and lengthening impossibly, a hundred twiggy fingers grabbing men and hurling them against the shore or into the depths of the lake to drown.

On the hill a fire was lit, flames licking at the tree's thick trunk.

The tree reached down and smothered the blaze with its leafy branches, and the hill at its base writhed, beasts bursting from between its roots and wanting nothing more than to rend and destroy the river rats, to protect the poisoned tree that wished murder and mayhem beneath a stoically peaceful sky.

"Hurry," Cyrelle urged. "You need another couplet." She called to the few remaining men on board. "Set us free—arm us! We will fight beside you!"

She earned only a quick glance before a branch swept out and tossed a man overboard. She tried once more. "Set us loose on it!"

And Marnum found his missing lines at her side.

"A nightmare inside of a dream, Wicked and lovely, though, it seems."

"String it together," Cyrelle urged.

"Infinite ways to test your fate,
O'er the mountains and hills, she waits.
Wise is he, so clever and strong,
He fell from grace, all for a song.
Bridge the distance and heed her call,
Magic once more, will beckon all.
A nightmare inside of a dream,
Wicked and lovely, though, it seems."

The tree shivered, recognizing the song's strain, but in a moment, recovered, and struck out even more cruelly.

"Set us free to fight—there is no honor dying like a pig trussed for dinner!" Cyrelle shouted.

A man raced forward, his cheeks red with exertion, and he looked at them both between frightened glances over his shoulder. "You," he said of Cyrelle. "I will set you free to fight—you look able to brandish a weapon." He slid a doubtful glance at Marnum as he cut through Cyrelle's ropes.

Marnum sang still, twisting the tune.

The sailor handed Cyrelle a blade and swung back around to rejoin the fight.

Shedding her ropes like a snakeskin, Cyrelle grabbed the knot at Marnum's hands and slipped her blade beneath.

"You said you'd fight beside them . . ."

"I will—as soon as I free *you*."

A branch whipped out and swept the front of the deck clear of men.

Cyrelle sawed at the knot faster, the last threads of rope snapping apart as the branch returned and grabbed her, pulling her into the air.

Singing, Marnum shook free of his ropes.

The tree trembled at the song and the power of his newly found voice.

It held Cyrelle high, preparing to fling her into the shimmering depths, and Marnum's voice cracked.

"It's wrong!" Cyrelle shouted. "Not the words—the words are true. Not the tune—the tune is sound." She wrapped her arms around the tree's branch, determined not to be flung into the deep blue. "What said the soothsayer?" she screamed as the tree's branch toyed with her, swinging her from side to side.

"Find the arrangement to reorder your world . . ." he whispered. "The order of the lines . . ."

The branch pulled back, as if weighing Cyrelle, and

Marnum reworked the song and sang it with all that his voice and heart and soul could muster:

> *"Infinite ways to test your fate,*
> *O'er the mountains and hills, she waits.*
> *Wise is he, so clever and strong,*
> *Fell from grace, all for a song.*
> *A nightmare inside of a dream,*
> *Wicked and lovely, though, it seems.*
> *Bridge the distance and heed her call,*
> *And magic once more, will beckon all."*

The tree screamed, shivered, and shook—wood tearing with a sound like thunder cracking as the branches pulled back toward the Dreamland Tree's base, taking Cyrelle to the hill with them. The rioting beasts fell silent and faded to nothing but sand and dust, scattering. The waters around the little island bubbled, and there was a *boom* far louder than thunder, and then the waters settled, leaving nothing but a silence so heavy it rang in Marnum's ears.

Marnum's song ended in a scream when the tree dropped her, and then he was running—across the deck, leaping over the rail and into the water, and bolting up the brief beach to the foot of the hill.

Where Cyrelle lay.

Unmoving.

He stopped beside her, sand and dirt spraying up from his boots as he carefully undid the buckles and snaps at the base of her helm, his fingers fumbling. He tugged the wolf mask free and pushed the stray strands of hair away from her eyes.

She winced and blinked up at him. "Look," she whispered, her eyes focusing on the tree. "It's happening . . ."

The gnarled and twisted branches had shrunk into healthy looking shapes—nearly normal except for their gigantic scale. Something quivered in the tree's trunk, the bark pulsing and undulating. And then, it opened like a knothole had been there all along, and had chosen now to unroll. Something emerged, glittering in the rising moon's light.

"The stone . . ."

The bark split, tugged back, and revealed the more tender part of the tree. A noise like fabric ripping sounded, and wood peeled from the trunk, twisting and turning and becoming something new and strange and separate. Something hollow and sleek, with a long, straight neck and a curving body. Vines snaked out of the hill's base to line the instrument's neck, and the thing slid down the hill to stop at Marnum's feet.

Cyrelle sat up. "You're being granted a gift. It seems you have a new mission, Marnum. Go. Pick it up. It's . . ."

"A guitar?" Marnum asked, taking it into his hands. The god's discarded worry stone shimmered in its head, like a singular eye. Marnum's fingers found their place with an equal sense of wonder and something like instinct, and he ran his fingers down the strings, marveling at the natural tone, until—

Cyrelle winced at the sound of one string. "That didn't sound quite right."

"I just saved the world. Must you be so critical?"

– The End –

WEE WILLIE WINKIE

Wee Willie Winkie
Runs through the town,
Upstairs and downstairs
In his nightgown.
Rapping at the windows,
Crying through the lock,
"Are the children all in bed?
For it's now eight o'clock.

— *Mother Goose*

WEE WILLIE WINKIE
Leigh Fallon

The smell of their breath was the worst part of working in The Nook. The hot acidic tang, thick and potent, made me gag, but it was part of the job.

"Suck it up and smile," is what Seanie had said when I started here last week. "Remember, the key to good tips is big smiles and short skirts."

Swallowing down the bile that crept up my throat, I slapped on pink, crooked lips masquerading as genuine friendliness.

"Another pint of Guinness and a Harp and lime then, John?"

John, one of The Nook's regulars, nodded his head and glanced at his wife, who was busy inspecting the dregs of her warm beer. His sad eyes brightened for a moment as he winked back at me and wheezed, "Ah sure, another won't kill us."

"I wouldn't be quite so sure about that," I mumbled under my breath as I returned to the bar. Feeling John's eyes following me, I tugged down the back of the short black skirt that Seanie insisted I wear.

I stood on the tarnished brass footrest that snaked its way around the dark wood of the ancient bar, and leaned over the counter. "Seanie, the same again for the auld codgers."

Seanie clicked his tongue and winked at me. Something he did to impress the "girls." Well, he called them girls, but really they were forty-somethings, desperate to relive their youth, heaving their saggy boobs onto the bar counter and squeezing their elbows together for maximum impact. "A pint and a half coming up." He flicked the glass in his hands like he was picturing himself as Tom Cruise in Cocktail and not the thick-waisted, balding owner of a gritty old man's bar whose patrons were an aging mish-mash of odd balls from a town left behind during the economic boom of the nineties.

I hated working in the rundown old pub, but jobs were practically nonexistent, and most were taken by all the oldies trying to supplement their crappy, failing pensions. The lounge girl slash waitress position was probably the only one left in the town that the locals didn't mind me taking. Seanie had been gasping to employ the only person in a four mile radius under the age of thirty.

The whole town oozed the stench of age and decay; it didn't even have a school. I had to bus it into the next town over to attend the sparsely populated St. Frances's school for girls, and my parents had to lie about my age to get me into that hellhole. Apparently, the school didn't cater to the under sixteens (whatever that meant). But I was turning sixteen in two weeks, so my parents—desperate to put their financial woes in Dublin behind them—felt justified in a little white lie.

Despite the boredom and funky smells of my evening job, I was happy to have it. It gave me some much needed cash that my parents couldn't give me, and it meant I could spend more time out of the tomb they called a house. Two weeks, that's all it took me, to realize they'd moved me to the deadest, most un-happening town imaginable. Killinamartyle—mecca to the old and lonely and, like my parents, victims of an ailing economy. I dropped off the two drinks to John and Bridie, the only couple in the bar that night.

Bridie acknowledged the drinks with a little smile. "Thank you, Maureen."

Startled by the words from the usually silent Bridie, I corrected her. "Actually, my name's Marie."

John gave the confused Bridie a reassuring smile and covered her quivering hand with his. "Bridie, pet, you know that's not Maureen. This is the new girl, Marie. I told you about her, remember?"

Bridie's face seemed to crumple in confusion. She started nodding her head and dropped her gaze to the table once more.

The only other patron was Smelly Eugene, and his presence was hardly acknowledged. He was like part of the furniture, hunched over his warm pint of ale. His only movements were his hand wiping his constantly running nose, a nod of his chin when he wanted a refill, and the trembling of his lips as he jabbered under his breath about Irene, whoever she was.

I let out a soft sigh. It was going to be a long evening.

***

I stood at the bar, gazing beyond the sea of spirit bottles to the dusty, mottled, mirrored wall. It reflected back the same depressing scene I'd turned my back on. I closed my eyes to block it out, wishing I was back in Dublin. I missed my gorgeous house in the city, surrounded by excitement, life, and my friends. I could feel myself aging as I listened to the sounds of John's wheezing and Smelly Eugene's grunts, constant snorting, and warbling mumbles.

A slight change in the atmosphere made my eyes flick open. The cold, damp evening air flickered by my nose, dulling the smell of stale beer for just long enough to signal the arrival of another customer. Seanie watched as a guy made his way in, shaking off his wet coat before making himself comfortable in the small nook by the window. Seanie's face paled and he stepped back, tripping over a case of Coke on the floor.

Excited by the prospect of a conversation with someone not drawing a pension, I picked up my tray. "I'll go get his order."

"No!" Seanie said, righting himself. "The ladies' needs seeing to."

"But I just clea—"

Seanie continued to stare at the guy. "Go!' he muttered, picking up a towel and twisting it in his hands.

I dropped the tray to the counter with a clatter, biting back the urge to tell Seanie he could stick his job up his arse. I stomped off to the bathrooms as Seanie made his way in the opposite direction, to the nook where the young man had sat down.

"It's been a while, William. What are you doing in these parts?" Seanie said with a slight crack in his voice.

I'd never heard Seanie nervous before. My curiosity got the better of me. As the door closed on me, I put my foot out, leaving it a fraction open, and strained to hear what the two men were saying. I pressed my eye to the narrow gap in the door, wishing Seanie would get out of the way so I could see this William guy. He sounded young, soft-spoken, nothing like anyone I'd met in this festering town.

William's soft, melodic voice rippled through the air in my direction. "There's been no reason for me to be around, Seanie . . . until now." He leaned forward. His dark eyes looked around Seanie's hulking figure and glared in my direction.

I gasped when I caught sight of William. His ashen white skin was set off by the palest of blond hair. But his most striking feature was his youth; he didn't look much older than me.

"No, William, you've got it wrong."

"I never get it wrong."

"She's already sixteen. I swear."

Oh crap! I ducked back, allowing the door to close. Shit. I'd told Seanie I was sixteen so I could get the job in the bar. Someone must have found out. I stamped my foot. Crap, that was my job gone. My heart thumped in my chest. I couldn't let Seanie get in trouble with the authorities. It was my fault. I'd have to come clean. Swallowing down my nerves, I pulled the door open to find Seanie gazing at William's recently vacated seat.

Red heat climbed my face as I approached him slowly. "Seanie, I'm so sorry. I didn't mean to lie, it's just that . . . well, I'm sixteen in a couple of weeks, so it didn't seem to matter so much, you know?"

Seanie stayed staring at the seat with his fingers clasping and unclasping his thinning hair. "You *stupid* child. You shouldn't have lied." His glare swept to the door.

"I'm sorry. Are you going to get in much trouble?"

He spun around and grabbed my wrists. I tried to pull away, not sure what his intentions were. He pulled my hand to his face and glanced at my watch, then dropped my arm. "It's only seven thirty. You still have time. You have to go." He spun me around and started pushing me toward the door.

I struggled for words. "What? Go! You mean I'm fired? I'll be sixteen in two weeks. Can I come back then?"

Smelly Eugene shuffled up behind me. He wiped his nose with the back of his coat, then held out his hand to me. "I'll take her."

"Take me where? I'm not going anywhere with you!"

Seanie ignored me. "Yes, Eugene. Take her, quick. I'll lock up here."

"Look, if I'm fired, I'll go myself. I don't need to be escorted. I live just five minutes down the road."

John and a suddenly alert-looking Bridie abandoned their drinks and stood on either side of me.

Bridie leaned in toward my ear. "You should never lie about yer age round these parts, lovie. We best get ye home, and fast." She looked up at Smelly Eugene. "We'll take her to her house and see she gets in safely. Eugene, you stay close behind, ye hear?"

Eugene grumbled. "I hear ya woman, I don't need telling."

Seanie pulled the curtains. "Enough of the talking and more of the doing. Get her home *now*." He grabbed my coat and shoved it at me as he manhandled me to the door. "I haven't been touched. I want no part of this. Do yourself a favor, Marie. Make sure you're home in bed by eight o'clock round these parts, for the next two weeks, anyhow. Do you hear me? Get yourself to bed by eight."

I struggled to turn around, wiggling my way out of his grip to stare at the four sets of eyes looking back at me. "You're scaring me!"

Bridie hooked her arm through mine as we stepped

out into the mild, damp evening. "And so ye should be, young 'un. And so ye should be." She looked up and down the road. "John, get her other side." John, suddenly spritely for someone in his seventies, grabbed my other arm. I was half-walked, half-dragged toward my house. I glanced back. There, a few paces behind me, was Smelly Eugene, frantically wiping his nose as The Nook fell into darkness.

The unseasonably warm wind whirled around us, mixing uneasily with the light rain, gently lifting my hair and caressing my skin; it curled by my ears, whistling a melodic tune, resembling words.

I spun around, following the sound of the haunting voice that sang among the sounds of fallen leaves and scattered litter swirling on the ground. "What was that?"

Bridie turned me toward her and clasped both hands over my ears. "Don't ye listen to him. Don't ye dare."

I tugged her hands from my head. "Him! Who is 'him'?"

The voice rose above the breeze, much clearer this time. It tickled my ears and induced a dizzying nausea.

"*Wee Willie Winkie runs through the town . . .*"

As we approached my terraced house on the main street, Bridie moved her lips to my ear. "Get yer keys out, have 'em ready. When we get to the door, go in as fast as ye can. Lock the door and get into bed. Cover yer head. Whatever ye do, don't listen to him."

My breath came in short, sharp gasps. Questions lingered, uncomfortable on my tongue. "Why? What did I do wrong?" Bridie didn't answer; she just kept on moving then pulled up when we were nose-to-nose with my front door. "Please, I don't understand, you're scaring me."

Laughter echoed up the deserted street and mingled with the singing wind.

"*Upstairs, downstairs, in his nightgown . . .*"

My eyes darted around, seeking out the owner of the melancholy whispers.

Bridie grabbed my jaw in a shaking, vice grip. "Are your parents in?"

"No." I glanced at my watch. "They won't be in until after eight."

Bridie clutched my wrist. "Look, lovie, ye did noth'en wrong, but young 'uns don't last long around these parts. Yer parents had no business bringing a child into a cursed town. Once it's touched you, ders no leavin'. Just be in yer bed before eight every night until yer sixteen. He'll be watching you. If we'd have known ye was only fifteen we'd never have—"

"Stop yer yacking, woman," Smelly Eugene growled from the shadows. "Let the girl get herself to safety. He's watching."

My head whipped around to them and I stopped dead in my tracks. "Cursed? What curse?"

Bridie's hand clenched my wrist tighter and she whispered frantically. "The fae send the familiar to collect the souls of the children. It was the deal, ye see—the souls of the young in return for the end of famine. The town survived, but the familiar still takes the souls."

A laugh caught in my throat and I tried to shake Bridie's hand from my wrist. "Wait . . . this is about faeries? Seriously, you're saying that William guy is—"

"When the familiar comes to collect, he wears the skin of the first soul he took—wee William Winkie."

John moved onto the step beside us and pried Bridie's hands from my wrists. "We've done all we can, Bridie. Let it be now."

Bridie's blue eyes glistened under the flickering light of the streetlamp. They looked almost translucent. "He's taken them all, ye see. All of them. But there's still hope for ye. Promise me you'll go straight to bed, young 'un. Promise me." She leaned in and put her lips to my ear. "If you see my Maureen, tell her Mammy misses her so."

My eyes flickered to her husband, who was now holding her tenderly in his arms. He nodded at me, then glanced back at his wife.

I pushed the door open and fell into the safety of my home.

"And tell Irene she's always in my heart," Smelly Eugene mumbled, turning his back to me. The three bodies melted into the darkness. The damp, laughing breeze twisted its way around me, pushing against the door as I strained to close it.

My skin was blanketed in tingling goose bumps. Wait until I told Mom and Dad, they'd be sure to move us back to Dublin. So what if we were broke? Anything had to be better than this freak-fest. I raced up three of the steps on the way to my bedroom and then stopped myself. What was I doing? Yes, they'd creeped me out, but it was them, not their stupid stories about having to be in bed by eight o'clock. Ha! What did they think I was, six? Reversing down the stairs, I made for the TV room. I fell back onto the sofa and picked up the remote.

The red digits on the cable box flashed the time at me. Seven forty-five. My heart jumped a little. I laughed at my own stupidity, fought the image of Bridie's pleading eyes, and tried to forget the whispers and the movement of her lips against my ear. I flicked through the channels, but my eyes kept being drawn to the red flashing time on the cable box.

Each flash, another second passing.

Another moment closer to eight.

The flashing seemed to slow, until a second felt like an eternity and mirrored my heart thudding sluggishly in my chest. I glared at the red flashing digit. It pulsated slowly, like time was grinding to a halt. The digital eight faded to darkness, but was not replaced by nine. It stalled. My breath caught in my lungs. My heart ceased beating. A cool breeze ran over my arms and I watched as a fresh onslaught of goose bumps climbed their way up my arms, racing toward me. As they reached my neck, the prickly feeling got softer and crawled to my ear. Whispers, familiar and mocking.

"Looking through the keyhole . . ."

The cool breeze dissipated, my heart dared to beat again, and the number nine slowly illuminated on the cable box. Seven fifty-nine.

I uncurled my legs, feeling for the icy floor beneath them. The cold seized my toes and moved upward, turning my flesh to stone.

Wee Willie Winkie.

I watched the red light pulsate with each passing second. I'd lost track of how many had passed. The desire to run for my bed overwhelmed me as the icy grip of the now familiar voice sang loud and clear from the other side of my front door.

"Crying through the lock . . ."

The sound of a dog barking released my legs from where they had rooted to the cold, tiled floor. First one, then another. A scratching noise at the window nearly made me turn to look, but my eyes were drawn to the red numbers.

Seven fifty-nine flickered to eight.

The front door thudded. Then again and again, growing more persistent. It combined with the voice, now hauntingly clear.

"Are the children in their beds?"

My hands clasped the sides of my head, remembering Bridie's words: "don't listen." The front door was banging now, shaking at its hinges. Rattling like a heavy train was passing just outside. I clamped my eyes shut and drew my breath to scream.

Everything stopped.

Silence chased me up the stairs.

I dove into my bed, burying my head in the soft caress of my blankets, focusing on the sound of my thudding heart and rasping breath.

Footsteps.

Rhythmic beats on the stairs.

The muffled sound of shoes on carpet.

The deafening silence of presence.

Through the flimsy protection of the sheet, I saw his outline as he moved quietly to my bed. His head moved swiftly to mine, the image blurred to darkness as his face pressed against the material in a horrifying mask.

My lungs bowed to the pressure.

My heart grew silent.

I was being siphoned of my very being.

His voice was muffled through the sheet. Words carried on the hot trickle of his breath.

"It's past eight o'clock."

– The End –

COME OUT TO PLAY

Girls and boys, come out to play,
The moon doth shine as bright as day;
Leave your supper, and leave your sleep,
And come with your playfellows into the street.
Come with a whoop, come with a call,
Come with a good will or not at all.
Up the ladder and down the wall,
A half-penny roll will serve us all.
You find milk, and I'll find flour,
And we'll have a pudding in half an hour.
— Mother Goose

COME OUT TO PLAY
Angie Frazier

I stepped into our bedroom and knew something was wrong. The wind from a brewing storm battered the curtains, but I hadn't left the window open.

"Aelwyn?"

My sister didn't move. She sat in the rocking chair and stared into the bleak sky, the wild sea wind toying with tendrils of her hair. She hadn't moved without help, or spoken, for a month, ever since the accident in the bay with Papa. My heart stuttered. Had *she* opened the window? Had she finally come back to me?

I went to her, the sun rising in my chest—but it plummeted, leaving raw twilight in its place. Nothing had changed. Aelwyn's expression was still flat, her eyes the same dead blue. I stared at her pale, parched lips and willed them to twitch. I needed her to look at me, to speak to me. I needed her not to have left me all alone.

The stormy August wind rode low against my back. Our father had perished in the bay and our mother was long dead—so who had opened this window? I crouched before Aelwyn, my hand on her knee. That was when I saw it: a strip of curled birch bark, clutched loosely in Aelwyn's hand.

No.

I slid the curl out and smoothed the edges. My fingers turned to ice. On the tawny underside of the bark were the four words every generation of the village Bleddroth had been taught to fear:

Come out to play.

The witches had been here. They'd left their beckoning for Aelwyn and they wanted her in the forest. Tonight.

***

I found my sister's betrothed at the gristmill. Rhys stood at the loft door, open to where the wheel's paddles slowly rotated, catching the river water on its course toward the sea. His dark brows were furrowed in earnest concentration as he made marks in a ledger.

Rhys was courting my sister, but he'd been my friend first. He'd taken care of us since Papa's accident, and after I found the beckoning that morning I'd immediately thought of him.

He looked up and his fawn-colored eyes landed on me. "Bronwyn? What's wrong?"

He'd always been able to read me like that.

The clatter of machinery screened my voice from the other grist workers. "I needed to see you."

Rhys set the ledger down and slid his pencil behind his ear. "Has Aelwyn taken a turn?"

"No, no." I reached into my pocket. Closed my hand around the thin, curled missive. There were rules. I wasn't supposed to show the beckoning to anyone. But

I could trust Rhys. I didn't want to keep this secret from him.

I held out the bark. He frowned as he took it. The water wheel creaked by, dark water sloshing out of each swaying bucket. He opened his hand—and then closed it, knuckles white.

"*Bronwyn,*" he whispered. His eyes flicked to mine and seared them. "You? But that's impossible. I thought . . . I was certain—" He stopped and came within an inch of my face. I held my breath, aware of him in this awful manner for far too long. It was so wrong. I shouldn't have wanted to kiss my sister's intended the way I did.

"It was left for Aelwyn," I explained.

Rhys practically jumped away. I puzzled over what he'd meant. What had he been '*certain*' about?

"Oh," he breathed, the shock on his face reanimating into something livid. "She can't go. Not when she's . . . the way she is."

No one quite knew what to call it. Aelwyn had come out of the sea with her heart still beating, her lungs still functioning, but I feared she was just as lost as our father.

"I know," I said. My hands shook. "But we can't ignore the beckoning."

Like I said, there were rules. No one ignored the witches in the woods. To do so would invite disaster. Too many children had disappeared from their homes over the years to believe otherwise. Sometimes a birch bark curl would be found in the child's bed, other times, nothing but cold linens. No one knew if the witches punished those who ignored the beckoning, or if the children had gone out to play as ordered and just never returned.

I wasn't going to take any chances with Aelwyn.

Rhys stepped closer. He hitched his chin lower to better pierce my eyes with his. "What are you going to do?"

I closed my eyes, my throat tight. "I'll pretend to be her. I'll go in her place."

Aelwyn and I weren't identical twins, but we shared nearly every feature: fair hair and skin, long legs, and narrow hips. But where Aelwyn's eyes were sea blue, mine were bay green.

"You *can't*," Rhys said.

"I haven't a choice. Someone has to and it can't be Aelwyn."

Frustration corded the muscles along his neck. "You shouldn't have told me about this."

"But—"

"You won't come back!" He latched onto my arms just as his father shouted from across the loft.

"Rhys, a hand here!"

I startled back, relieved for the interruption. Rhys was right. I shouldn't have told him. It had only made leaving more difficult.

I retreated before Rhys could stop me, weaving through the maze of stone wheels and grain basins. I would go into the woods. Tonight, I would be Aelwyn. And I would pray to all that was holy that the witches waiting there wouldn't discover my deception.

***

I glided the comb through my sister's hair. She sat in bed, the quilt gathered around her waist. The air was humid enough to beget thunderstorms but I couldn't leave her uncovered. Pulling the thin, patchwork blanket over her legs had given me a sense of security for her. That she'd be all right when I left.

"And Rhys will take care of you," I told her yet again. My hands trembled as I set down the comb and broke her sheet of blond hair into three sections. The braid was messy, my mind elsewhere.

"They won't know I'm not you," I said. "As long as I go out to play, they won't care."

At least, I hoped they wouldn't.

Aelwyn stared at the wall, eyelids drooping. She'd sleep. She wouldn't even realize I had gone. I eased her down onto her pillow and kissed her cool forehead. I missed my twin more in that moment than in any other during the last month.

There was no point in lingering. I took her lamp and walked to the back door. The forest began just beyond our herb garden. Shivers worked me over. Where was I supposed to go once I entered the woods?

Oddly, my first steps in felt like a release. I was just as curious as I was afraid of the woods and what lingered within them. The trees closed behind me like a curtain. Even with the fanned-out light, I stumbled over the undulating floor, vines and thorns snagging my skirt. I kept a crawling pace until I realized just how lost I'd become. Even if I turned around, I wouldn't know my way home.

"This is a surprise."

I let out a short scream and wheeled toward the voice behind me. Wide arcs of light swayed over the face of a boy. The woodsman's son. He and his father lived on the edge of the woods and kept to themselves.

He stepped over a fallen tree trunk between us. "But you're Bronwyn." His dark eyes gleamed onyx in my lamplight.

"I'm sorry. I don't know your name." How did he know mine?

"Maddox," he said, his manners as rough as his looks. "*You've* come out to play?"

The breath hitched in my throat. A slow smile curved his lips.

"I was certain it would be your sister. Then again, I'm not sorry it's you. Come on," he said, and continued past me.

"What do you mean?" I swung the lantern after him. "You know where you're going?"

Maddox stopped. He pressed one of his thick, dark brows into a downward slant. "You don't?"

I stumbled around a moss-covered boulder. "There were no directions given."

Maddox looked down his nose at me. The shadows from the lamplight cut dark lines along his chiseled face. "You weren't beckoned."

The lantern handle slipped in my sweaty palm. "What? Of course I was."

"If you had been, you wouldn't require *directions*."

Was he saying Aelwyn would have known where to go? But she'd never set foot in these woods. I dug into my pocket and held the curl of birch bark for Maddox to see.

"It wasn't left for you." He didn't even bother to look at it. "If I discovered it this easily, do you think the witches won't? Go back. Tell your sister this is *her* task, not yours."

I let my arm fall to my side. Hadn't he heard?

"She's not well. She can't *move* let alone come out here to do whatever it is the witches want. If I ignored the beckoning . . ." I shook my head. "I have to at least try."

Maddox raked a hand through his hair. The waved, obsidian strands brushed the strong planes of his shoulders, defined, no doubt, from wielding a woodsman's axe.

"Do you have any idea what this is about?" he asked.

I put the birch bark back in my pocket and shook my head. He growled with frustration.

"Follow me," he ordered. I kept close to his heels. "I'll help you—but I can't promise you'll live."

I clutched the rough trunk of a whitebeam. "What?"

Maddox sighed as he stopped yet again and turned back. "The witches only call out those who have the ability to play their games. It's a test, Bronwyn. A test to see who is the best at their craft."

I still couldn't see. "Craft?"

He gave a maddened groan. "*Witch*craft. The one who displays the most skill is admitted into the coven. The others—" he shrugged. "The others don't return."

I dug my nails into the tree. The ground seemed to swell beneath my feet.

"They're going to know you're not a witch," Maddox added.

"But Aelwyn is," I said, my throat hoarse. "My sister is a witch?"

But she couldn't be. I knew my twin and she was just a girl, just a normal girl. I inspected Maddox closer now. His raven coloring and sinuous build spoke of strength and secrets, but magic?

"We need to go," he said, harsh as a Welsh wind curling off the sea.

He cut a path through the woods with confidence. I rushed to follow.

"Your only hope is to show the witches you respected their beckoning enough to come, albeit uninvited. They may spare you."

Maddox drew to a halt. The lamp brightened a thick wall of ivy, vines, and interlocking branches. Craggy stones poked through the gaps of tangled flora. He gripped one with his broad hand. "This is the ladder."

I set the lamp on the ground.

"Climb," he commanded. I didn't have a choice.

I slowly pulled myself up what had to be an ancient wall overrun by the creeping forest. I heard Maddox below me. I was probably holding him up. A burden he'd been saddled with.

I reached for the next stone and my palm came down on a flat surface—we'd reached the top. I crawled away from the ledge and gazed up. The forest had changed.

There was a dreamy, crushed-pearl glow here. It touched the leaves as if the moon had drawn lower and cast everything in its silvery light. I could easily see the little dell of night-blooming flowers before us, surrounded by a crescent of trees. And we weren't alone. Mair and Gwen, two girls I knew from the village school, stood in the clearing. The girls turned toward me, their expressions guarded.

"Bronwyn? I never would have guessed it," Mair said.

"I thought it would be Aelwyn," Gwen said with a note of suspicion.

So had Maddox. How had they known when I hadn't? All I had were questions, but asking them would point to what an imposter I was.

"We might be friends," Gwen said, her voice hardening over. "But the coven only takes one fledgling each year. I intend to be that fledgling."

The trees nearest to us made a rustling noise. A vine lashed out from the clumps of silvery leaves and lassoed Gwen's thin neck. With a violent yank, the vine jerked her off her feet. Gwen's screams were strangled in her throat as the vine reeled back into the canopy, taking her with it.

Maddox's hand closed around my elbow.

"The witches have started to play," he said, and then dragged me toward the opposite line of trees.

"What are you doing?" Mair shouted. "You both have to prove your skill on your own!"

Maddox ignored her, taking me into the strange forest at a near run. The trunks gleamed silver and they trimmed a perfectly manicured path. I heard Mair coming up behind us. What had just happened? That vine had looked alive and it had taken Gwen. Just . . . *taken* her.

Ahead, two yews started to bend at the trunk. They curved toward one another until their branches formed a bough over the path. A cloud of black wings burst from their limbs. Red-eyed blackbirds sprayed toward us, their beaks flashing silver points.

Maddox held something up—a plain brass loop— and shouted, "*Oddi ehedfa at fflam!*"

I screamed as the oncoming blackbirds exploded into a ball of flaming wings. Their tortured caws snuffed out when the fireball struck the path and disintegrated into ash. I stared at the scorched path. Their silver-bladed beaks could have flayed skin from bone.

This was what the witches meant by *come out to play*?

"Off the path!" Maddox shouted, and we dashed into the moon-dusted trees.

Mair veered in front of us. "Banding together isn't allowed!"

Maddox stormed around her. "She's a barren and no threat to you."

Barren. *Without magic.*

Mair gasped as I surged past her. "It *was* Aelwyn then. Stop, Maddox, you can't take a barren to the den!"

Maddox didn't stop.

"The den?" I repeated.

"The witches' den," he replied. "The tests go on until we either reach their den, or until there's only one of us left standing."

Mair shouted, "*Gwraidd byw caethiwo ti!*"

The ground trembled and a tangle of roots erupted from the soil. They looped over my feet and coiled around my ankles. I lost my balance and fell.

"What are you doing?" Maddox asked as Mair ran past us.

"Proving my skill—*I* will be fledgling," she said, and with a whirl of her cape, she was gone.

My fingers scrabbled over the roots sewing me to the forest floor. I looked to Maddox. "Go. You have a chance without me."

He raised his brass loop as if it was a wizard's wand and took aim at the roots. "I have a chance with you, as well."

He murmured something in stilted Old Welsh and the roots unraveled, retreating into the dirt. Maddox pulled me up and kept on through the trees.

"You really had no idea?" he called back. "Aelwyn and Gareth must have hid it well."

Gareth.

"My *father*?" I asked, breathless at our pace.

"It's a family legacy, Bronwyn. Half a dozen Bleddroth families make up the coven. It's odd," he said, peering back at me. "Usually barrens are sent away when they're babies. You weren't."

The thought of that cracked through me like lightning. What kind of lunatics gave away their barren babies and then sent their other children into the woods to play a game of life or death?

And my father had been a part of it.

"Stop," Maddox ordered, and when I did, my toes were hanging over the low banking of a stream.

Ahead, Mair was crossing a staggered set of boulders that acted as a natural bridge across the stream.

"Mair, don't!" Maddox shouted.

Small bubbles popped around the boulder she stood on. The rock started to tremble and Mair windmilled her arms. The boulder pitched violently, slinging her into the stream. She didn't kick or splash. She just disappeared, swallowed by the languid water.

I took a step forward, but Maddox held me back, his loop held before him. "*Gwlybwr at rhew.*"

A fine lace of frost rolled downstream, followed by a hard sheet of sapphire-tinted ice. The flow of water slowed to a shudder, and then froze. Maddox tightened his hand around mine and we went across.

I didn't want to believe that Aelwyn could have done these same spells. She was my *twin*. Why hadn't she told me? And why hadn't my parents sent me away as other barrens had been?

On the other side of the stream, Maddox let out his breath and stared into the trees. He brought me closer to his side. "Whatever you do, don't beg for your life. The witches loathe groveling."

Lights flashed through the trees. Looking, I saw they were the windows of a small cabin. We hadn't moved, and yet the cabin drew closer, sliding through the trees toward us. It looked to be built of stone and laced vines, woven tree branches and twisted tree stumps.

The door swung open.

I wouldn't grovel. I'd meet my fate with courage.

Maddox and I crossed the threshold together. Why had he done all this for me? We'd never even shared a passing greeting, and yet he'd known my name. *"I'm not sorry it's you."*

The door slammed behind us. The low hearth fire suddenly flared, brightening the small room and the people standing before us: three wizened women in bright red shawls and peasant dresses and one young, handsome boy. I lunged forward.

"Rhys!"

Maddox hauled back on my wrist. "Stop, Bronwyn."

Rhys met my confused stare, his eyes filled with fear.

"What's going on? Leave him alone!" I cried to the three old women.

Maddox kept me at his side and hissed, "He's coven."

My blood turned to syrup; my head grew heavy and thick. Rhys. Coven. *Witch.*

"Bronwyn." Rhys whispered my name as he would a plea for forgiveness. "I've told them what you've done."

I stared at the floor, eyes blurring. It didn't matter.

"You and Aelwyn," I said. "You knew about one another?"

Rhys bowed his head. "We know the others who are like us. It's a feeling. A stirring of the blood. It's an energy that makes you see them, and lets them see you."

And I didn't have it. I was the only one who'd been blind.

Rhys stepped toward us. "I don't care that you're a barren, Bronwyn. I only care about *you*. I hoped if I told the witches what you were risking for Aelwyn, they might spare you."

The muscles in Maddox's arm, pressed against mine, tensed. "You weren't the only one to think of that." He faced the three witches to address them. "Bronwyn came out to play not knowing any of this. She feared and respected you enough to risk her life. She doesn't deserve to die."

One of the witches parted her papery lips. "She will not die."

I leaned my forehead against Maddox's arm, a sob of relief lodged in my throat.

But then another witch spoke. "She will stay in the forest as chattel, as recompense for her father's cowardice."

I looked up. "What? No. What cowardice?"

None of the witches looked my way.

"They won't speak to a barren," Rhys murmured before turning to them. "What did Gareth do?"

I thought I could see a touch of the forest's crushed-pearl glow coming from the witches' eyes.

"He wove magic through his daughter's mind."

"To keep her in a waking sleep."

"To excuse her from the beckoning."

Each witch spoke over the next, joining their voices in ringing dissonance.

"He wouldn't," I said, but the witches weren't finished.

"He removed himself from the earth."

"With the counter-curse unknown."

"And the spell will not yield. One of our coven has crossed us. We shall make an example out of the barren."

My head whirled. Maddox snaked his arm around my waist to hold me steady. Papa had cursed Aelwyn and then killed himself. He'd taken her out in the dinghy, into the bay, knowing he wouldn't return.

"If you wish to make an example of someone, do it with me," Rhys said, his voice thick and reckless. "The coven won't care if a barren disappears into these woods, but they will heed *my* disappearance. Please. Let Bronwyn return to Bleddroth."

I started to protest, but Rhys shot out a hand to stay me. My father had done this. It wasn't Rhys's fault and he couldn't suffer my punishment.

"You can't stay here," I persisted. "You're marrying Aelwyn."

He turned to look at me, his jaw tight. "She needs her sister, not a husband." The firelight turned his eyes the color of fine brandy. "And I'd rather save you, if you don't mind."

I sealed my lips, and then his brandy eyes dropped to them. Rhys looked away, but not before I felt warmth in my cheeks, and saw a flush upon his.

The witches bowed their heads in unison. A moment later, all three rose at the same glacial speed.

The one with the papery lips spoke. "We accept the exchange. Maddox Gabriel, you are fledgling. Take the barren and leave."

The cabin door cracked open.

"No!" I reached for Rhys. "You can't!"

He pushed past Maddox and took me by the shoulders. His chest heaved and I knew he was afraid.

"I'm sorry I never told you."

"But Rhys—"

"Bronwyn, you have to go." He tried to peel my hand from his arm.

"I won't."

Rhys wrested my hand free, but instead of pushing me away, he cupped my cheeks and crushed his lips against mine. The kiss was urgent, the press of his mouth desperate, as if trying to make up for lost time. And it was over too fast.

A blast of wind slammed into my chest, knocking me off my feet and tearing my lips from his. The gale shuttled me outside and onto the forest floor, beside Maddox. The door slammed shut and the small cabin sank back into the trees. I stumbled to my feet, but the witches' den was already gone.

"Rhys!" My scream parroted through the silver trees.

Maddox brushed off his trousers as tears scorched my cheeks. What would happen to him? What would the witches do?

"*Rhys!*" I screamed again, my voice rasping.

"It's over. We need to leave their woods." Maddox started across the stream, the water still frozen.

"But what about Aelwyn?" I asked. She hadn't heeded the beckoning. I suddenly realized the witches hadn't promised anything regarding my sister.

Rhys had taken *my* punishment. Not hers.

Maddox thrust his hand out to me, his eyes fierce. "Hurry, Bronwyn."

***

I saw the fire before we cleared the trees.

Savage flames cut a feral dance through the skies above my cottage, a storm of charred orange smoke billowing out over the rest of the village.

I crumbled as soon as I came into the yard. My knees plowed ruts into the herb garden.

"Aelwyn!" I clawed at the ground, trying to stand, my arms and legs numb and boneless. "No! *Aelwyn!*"

Maddox was there, picking me up and holding me back when I thrashed, wanting nothing more than to run straight into the burning cottage. The villagers tossed bucket after bucket of water at the cottage as fire punched through the windows and walls. Their efforts were futile. Aelwyn had been asleep inside, tucked into bed by my own hand, with no one to help her escape.

Our father had thought he'd been saving her. *I* thought I'd been saving her. But we'd both disregarded something crucial. Something we should have always known.

You can't deceive the witches in the wood.

– The End –

HEY, DIDDLE, DIDDLE
Jessie Harrell

Hey, diddle, diddle,
The cat and the fiddle,
The cow jumped over the moon.
The little dog laughed,
To see such sport,
And the dish ran away with the spoon.
— Mother Goose

I COME BEARING SOULS
Jessie Harrell

No one plays cello like my sister. Her dark hair is pinned back from her face, while her bare toes curl into the worn Persian rug. Music flows from Beth, a song so melancholy it makes my heart ache. Or maybe my heart just aches because I know what's coming next. And whether I liked the dearly departed or not, our upcoming trek to the Underworld always sucks.

Down the hall, Addison Clark—cheerleader extraordinaire and Queen Bitch—lies in her casket. I won't miss Addison or having her call me a freak for the seven thousandth time. Like I can help it that my family runs the only funeral home in this town, or that it also happens to be my house? Yeah, maybe I do live upstairs from dead bodies. That's not my fault.

Still, when Addison's glowing orb of a soul starts dancing toward Beth's music, my throat feels raw and it hurts to swallow.

Everyone knows Addison's car plowed into the concrete pillar of an overpass last Sunday, when the roads were thick with ice, but more rumors swirl. Rumors that she'd been sneaking out of her house to cheat on her boyfriend. Rumors that she'd had more than a little alcohol in her bloodstream. And as much as I'd hated Addison while she was alive, if those rumors are true, I'm really going to hate what's coming next.

Addison's soul drifts down the hall, bumping against faded wallpaper and illuminating gold-framed portraits of my grandparents. She picks up speed as she gets closer to Beth. The music *is* entrancing. My eyes grow wide as the pinkish-yellow soul bobs ever closer to Beth's cello.

From behind, my brother nudges me. "Go, Heather. Get her."

He probably doesn't understand why I'm hesitating. It's not like I had a problem plucking old Mr. Lockerby out of the air yesterday, or even cupping the soul of any of the other five car accident victims we've had in the last two months. *Has it really been five? That seems like too many.* But I knew Addison. Something about passing judgment on her doesn't sit right with me.

Still, when Andy shifts his weight behind me, I know I've run out of time. Releasing my black skirt, which I've managed to crush a sweaty handprint into, I reach forward. My fist unclenches and Addison's energy zings just beyond my fingertips. I wonder if she knows me, now that she's passed on. The thought that she might know it's me holding her before her judgment gives me a grim satisfaction.

She hovers, like a painfully slow mosquito, and I snatch her out of the air. Beth immediately sets her cello to the side and scowls at me.

"Took you long enough," she snaps. "I wasn't sure I had another refrain left in me."

Ever the peacekeeper, Andy steps between us. "Let's get a move on, shall we?"

As he pushes through the concealed door in our parlor, it strikes me that I never really think of him as

Anubis. Or Beth as Bast. I'd probably have an aneurism if either one of them suddenly sprouted a dog or cat head, like they were drawn by the ancient Egyptians. And with any luck they don't really think of me as Hathor, because let me tell you how much it pisses me off that I'd look like a cow. A cow? Seriously? I swear the cosmos is still laughing over that one.

Addison's soul grows warm in my cupped hands. Almost like she's trying to burn her way free, and I'm suddenly anxious to get to the Underworld and be done with it. Ducking my head, I step inside the darkened passage and follow my brother. In case you were wondering, yes, there is a light at the end of the tunnel, but you won't find any pearly gates there. And the days of having to cast spells to navigate the Underworld are long since over. The whole passage to death has been condensed to a short walk down a hallway, followed by a simple test.

We cross into the chamber of the Underworld. It's like stepping back into a perfectly preserved, ancient Egypt. The ceilings soar, supported by acanthus scroll columns and massive statues of the gods with their animal heads. Never mind that I'm one of those deities—in some reincarnated form I haven't fully grasped yet. Even so, the room never ceases to impress me. The long shadows thrown by the blazing torches cast the room in patches of darkness that make me wonder if anything is lurking beyond the light.

I march forward to the golden scale occupying the center of the room with its ominous presence. One side of the scale is weighted down by the Feather of Truth. Horus, standing on a raised platform behind the scale, nods at me solemnly, while Thoth clasps his pen, poised to record the official test results. Thankfully, neither of them have bird heads, and look instead like mean college professors.

Stretching my arms forward, I unclasp my hands and release Addison's soul. "Addison Clark, I bid you welcome to the Underworld. May your soul be light and your afterlife long."

Normally, for someone like Addison, I'd rush through the welcoming formalities and earn myself a giant eye roll from Beth, but I'm genuinely worried about Addison's soul. We haven't had one pass the test in almost a month, and I'm tired of the carnage.

Addison's soul bobs forward, alighting on the other side of the scale. The weighted side slowly rises until the Feather and soul are perfectly balanced. I release the breath I've been holding, relieved Addison is going to survive. When I turn to smile at Andy, the crashing scales draw me back, making my head snap around. Addison's soul has toppled the scale, sending the Feather adrift.

As the fluffy, white Feather floats toward the limestone floor, the grinding sound begins. Massive blocks slide open on the far side of the chamber, revealing a dark so black it's consuming. Nails scrape against the limestone, announcing Amemit's arrival. Her nickname—Devourer of the Dead—is well-earned. As she emerges into the light, her leathery crocodile snout appears to be smiling. Once she's cleared her cavern, Amemit rises up onto her hippo haunches, carrying her lioness body like it weighs nothing at all.

"I've been waiting for you, my sweet." Amemit's accent is heavy, thick with the cadence of ancient Egyptian, which I know she still prefers. Lion claws raise Addison's soul off the scale, until it hovers at eye-level with the beast.

"You may materialize," she hisses, and Addison's

soul glows brighter and elongates. The soul takes shape, forming into a translucent image of Addison's old body, complete with confusion and horror etched across that perfect little face. I don't know why Amemit insists on playing with her food instead of swallowing the soul like a pill. I do know that I hate—*hate*—this part of the ceremony, and I step behind Andy to shield myself from it.

His head spins around and a scowl mars his honeyed skin. "She has no power over you unless you give it to her, so stop." He leans in closer and half-hisses in my ear, "Remember who you are. Gods don't cower."

Amemit's teeth click together and her sandpapery hippo feet scrape against the limestone as she advances. Then comes Addison's scream and the crash of bodies as she scrambles backward into Horus and Thoth. If she's looking for protection, she's looking in the wrong place. They'll simply push her back toward her fate. The scales crash again—Addison must be scrambling over them in her effort to flee. Amemit roars, some kind of deranged, guttural wail, and it's then that Addison spots us.

"Andy! Beth!" she shrieks. "Heather! Don't just stand there, help me!" Hearing my name makes my eyes pull open and I peek around from behind my brother just in time to see Amemit's jaws crash around Addison's shoulder. Drops of light—her celestial blood—splatter across the chamber before disintegrating as she's thrown to the floor.

Addison's new scream is gut-wrenching. She must know she's dying all over again. Amemit falls down to all fours, perches above her prey, and smacks her jaws together just above Addison's head. "I've been waiting for something sweet like you," she purrs.

I can't watch. Won't watch. Addison's screams stop as quickly as they came and I know Amemit has finished her off. My stomach clenches and I'm about to be sick. Even though Horus hasn't dismissed us yet, there's no way I can stand in that chamber for another second. Holding back the bile rising in my throat, I tear down our hidden passage, through Beth's music parlor, and straight up the stairs to my bathroom. Amemit may have feasted tonight, but it's clear I won't be keeping down my dinner.

***

I know Beth and Andy will be back soon and I'm not in the mood for their why-the-hell-did-you-freak-out talk.

After pulling on my quilted jacket and wrapping a scarf around my neck, I pluck a set of keys from Andy's room and head out into the night. The door on his rusty Ford pickup squeaks in protest against having to move in the cold. I crank the heater full blast, but know it'll be another ten minutes before I get enough warmth to have feeling in my fingertips, and I'm not waiting around.

As I back out of the driveway, gravel crunches beneath the tires with a popping sound that reminds me of snapping bones. Broken bodies.

I will not think about Addison. I will drive and sing too loud and forget this night ever happened.

Cranking up the volume on my iPod, I shove in the earbuds and blast myself with Snow Patrol. My headlights push against the blackness of the arctic night, exposing the next feet of road just in time for me to drive over them. With my singing, I'm belting out enough hot air to float a blimp, so the windshield immediately fogs over. As I'm wiping the frosty glass with the palm of my hand, a figure steps away from the side of the road.

The headlamps cut across him and I recognize the boy. His face is familiar, and yet different. Jerking the wheel hard to the left, I manage to keep from hitting him, but send the truck into a wild, fishtail spin. My dad's driving advice echoes through my head, and I somehow manage to pump the brakes instead of just slamming my foot into them. Even still, I'm spinning so fast, all I can see is the blur of weeds and trees and pavement as the lights swing around. And I just keep thinking: this is how Addison died. I don't want to die like her.

When the truck comes to rest fifty feet down the road and facing the opposite direction, my heart is hammering hard enough to break out of my ribs. I'm clutching the wheel so tightly it actually hurts to uncurl my fingers. The boy who nearly caused my death is running toward me and I have to know what the hell his problem is.

All but falling out of the truck, my feet crunch into the ice-packed snow and I slam the door shut. "What are you doing?" I yell. "You could've gotten us both killed."

He slows to a trot as he gets closer and it's then that I realize where I know the guy from. He was in our funeral home a month ago.

Because he's already dead.

***

Kyle Reese wasn't the type of guy you brought home to meet your parents. After getting kicked off the baseball team for failing his drug test, he'd barely managed to drag himself to school. And when he did, he was like a red-eyed zombie staggering down the halls.

I don't think anyone was really surprised when he ended up laid out in our mortuary, a victim of his own drunk-driving. And given his track record, it wasn't really surprising that his soul outweighed the Feather, entitling Amemit to another feast. But I sure as hell *am* surprised to see him standing in front of me, a month post-consumption.

His nose looks broken and I wonder whether it was from the accident or Amemit. Maybe both. Did it still hurt? As I study his face, something in his eyes is so sad, I can't tear myself away. There's an ache in my chest, almost physical, that makes me want to protect this guy. To help him, even though he'd just nearly killed me.

"Kyle? Is that you?" I step closer cautiously, not exactly sure how to deal with the resurrected undead, even though I technically do have some power over their souls. He takes another step forward too, bringing himself within the beam of the headlights. It's definitely Kyle. I recognize the pinstripe suit and tacky tie his mom buried him in. Although his silk handkerchief is about to take a nose dive out of his pocket, and I know my dad had dressed him better than that.

Before stopping to think, I reach forward to rearrange his pocket square.

"Don't *you* touch me," he snaps, grabbing my wrist to halt my advancing fingers. Guess he thought I was going for his soul again. Couldn't really blame the guy there, all things considered. But as his hand wraps more tightly around my arm, a blazing pain sears my skin. It feels like we're being welded together, our skins soldered beneath a heat torch. Kyle's panicked eyes tell me he has no idea what's going on either. I can tell he wants to let me go, but he just can't make his fingers release.

The pain makes my head heavy and dark. So dark the road around me vanishes—sinks into darkness, taking my mind with it. Alone with dead Kyle, on the side of a deserted highway in the middle of the coldest January I can remember, I black out.

***

When I come to, Kyle and I are no longer attached. The finger marks branded into my tender wrist are the only proof that I haven't hallucinated the whole episode. That, and the fact I'm not sitting by the road in the snow. No, wherever I am now, it's stifling. What my grandmother would have called "soggy," where the humidity makes you sweat until your clothes plaster to your body.

I sit up, rubbing at my wrist and trying to get my bearings in the pitch dark. I'm in some sort of cave, maybe. It's definitely stone I'm sitting on and there's a dank, cavernous smell assaulting me, but the ground is too smooth to be natural. Straining against the dark, I listen for any sound, any clue to tell me where I've landed after Kyle unwillingly transported me gods-know-where.

Or perhaps more importantly, gods-know-*why*. Why did a dead guy brand me with his touch? Why was he on the side of the road in the first place? Why did he try to make me crash?

As my brain is processing, a noise cuts through the fabric of darkness. It sounds like a rubber-soled shoe scraping against stone. Then the clank of chains. My first instinct is to scramble backward, away from the sound, but a low groan stops me.

"Kyle?" I whisper, hoping I've guessed correctly. Hoping he's not planning on using whatever chains he's got on me.

"Hey, Heather." The chains jangle with more emphasis. "I don't suppose you can get me out of here?"

"Get you—" I start before realizing I'm practically yelling. "Get *you* out of here? I don't even know where *here* is."

Kyle chuckles this dry, ironic laugh that grates on my nerves in a thousand places. "You don't know where we are. Unbelievable."

I scoot closer until my shin butts up against his outstretched shoe. "Look, I'm sorry I had to bring your soul down to the Underworld. Like every other person in the world, I hate my crappy job, okay? But blaming me for not knowing where you brought us when it's pitch-freaking-black isn't helping anything."

"Well then, as you told me a few weeks ago: Heather El Bay, I bid you welcome to the Underworld."

What? This isn't right. This isn't the chamber I'm normally in; there are no torches glowing like miniature suns along the walls. None of this makes sense unless . . .

The distinct click of claws against stone locks everything into place. "Yes, welcome, little goddess," Amemit purrs. I can practically see the dry smile curling her leathery, crocodile lips. "It's so nice of you to come to my house for once."

Without thought, I'm standing, preparing to defend myself against an immortal creature who could eat me for breakfast. But it seems like that has to be against some sort of cosmic rule. At least I hope it is, because

I'm not cowering before Amemit any longer. Not when it's my own soul on the line.

"Mind telling me why I'm here, Amemit? I'm off duty, if you hadn't noticed."

The ground trembles beneath my feet as Amemit advances. Slowly and methodically, each step a heavy death knell. "It seems Kyle here set out to kill the wrong person tonight." She clucks her tongue like an angry hen. "All he had to do was run one, little mortal off the road. Send one more soul to you, so you could deliver it to me. Instead, he brings me you. It's sort of curious, don't you think?"

A million questions all scramble for placement at the front of mouth. "Why am I here?"

Her croak of a laugh sends shudders down my spine. "I can't say, actually. It's a first. Somehow, he must have brought you back with him when his mission was over."

Her answer is unsatisfying, but there are too many other questions that need asking. "So all those accidents; they've been you. Why?"

"I'd like to tell you I'm hungry, but bored is more like it." Amemit's rancid breath seeps down my neck as she circles me. "Besides, your friends are tasty."

"You monster!" I scream. My outrage is just as much for the torture she's been putting me through as for the souls she's devoured. Making me watch her ill-gotten meals. "I'm leaving. Let me out. Now."

"Here's the thing," Amemit taunts. "The doors to my chamber only open when you bring me a soul, but you're in here. Sort of a catch-22, wouldn't you say?"

The wind rushes from my lungs. I can almost hear Amemit telepathically grinding the word "checkmate" into my brain. In a last grasp at hope, I turn to Kyle, who I'd left in forgotten silence once Amemit entered.

"Kyle, is she telling the truth? You need to tell me if there's another way out."

"Why? So you can run away and let her eat me again?"

Sweat trickles down my temples as panic sets in. I'm trapped in a dark cell with an evil goddess and some zombie boy who apparently hates me.

I've heard about adrenaline before, but I can't say I've ever really felt it until right now. Lowering my shoulder like Andy does in football practice, I charge Amenit, hoping to throw her off balance long enough to find a way to escape. If she rolls back on her fat hippo butt, I'm sure I'll get the head start I need. My shoulder connects with her abdomen, but it's me who crashes backward, tripping over Kyle's legs and skidding across the stone floor.

Then Amemit is on me, pinning me beneath her lion claws. "Was that your attempt at an escape?" Her teeth click just above my ear. "I'd tell you to try harder next time, but there won't be a next time for you."

No matter how hard I kick and thrash, I can't shift her off. Her tongue, rough as sandpaper, flicks out of her mouth and licks my cheek.

Disgust and outrage well up into a scream that feels like it could tear out my very soul.

Her teeth, far too blunt and thick but backed by incredible force, rip into my throat, silencing my scream. I gurgle back blood as my body shudders, involuntarily thrashing against the pain of her attack.

Quickly slipping out of consciousness, there's just one thought now, circling my brain: Andy's admonition from earlier that night.

I won't let her do this to me. I'm Hathor.

***

My eyelids are crusted shut with snow. I try to pry them open, but my fingers are so numb and swollen, they barely function. I realize I can't feel my cheek either, or the side of my neck, and I have the sudden image of being a fish laid out on ice at the market. My skin must look blue and dead like scales by now. Although I have no idea when "now" is, or how long I've been packed in my snowy display case.

My brain tells me I have to move. Get up and get help. Find warmth. But my muscles aren't responding. I try to push myself up, but my hands just slip deeper into the crusty slush until my fingertips jam into the frozen ground. Hardly any air is reaching my lungs, and I suddenly realize my neck is probably flayed open. I have no idea how I made it out of Amemit's den, other than sheer force of will, but it's too late. And at this point, I don't even care.

I've never been so cold in all of my life and I silently pray to hear the sound of Beth's cello, calling to me in the distance. I'm ready to let this body go and find warmth in the afterlife. I can no longer stand the exquisite torture of the cold.

I'll follow your music, Beth. Play for me.

The only sound I hear is the crunch of icy snow as my boot struggles uselessly against it, searching for a foothold I'll never find. The best I can do is flip onto my back, get my exposed skin off the ground. Above me, the night sky winks. Stars spin and dance and draw closer. Or maybe it's me that's moving? Yes, I'm floating now, heading toward the stars. My arms spin slowly, like pinwheels in a lazy breeze, but there's nothing to latch onto.

I close my eyes and let myself float. It feels so much better than the cold. I'm sure that if I could turn and look, I'd see my body back on the ground. It was just a vessel for this life, but I miss it more than I should. I wonder what I'll look like next time around.

And if I'll get the cosmic power shaft again.

But even as I think the thought, my bitterness over it is gone.

I close my eyes as the stars grow brighter and the ground dims and it's almost like an invisible lasso is pulling me toward the Milky Way.

When I think of the Milky Way, something clicks. Some legend—or perhaps it was truth— about the Milky Way being milk spilled from Hathor's udders. *My* udders. And in the legend, I feel a connection. A celestial bond with the stars, and I realize I've accepted my role as Hathor. Accepted her power and love, and I can feel all of her other roles flowing into me, too. I wish I'd felt these things earlier—the urge to dance, the feeling of joy.

My soul stretches like the souls of the departed do once judgment is over. My new fingers feel longer than I remember. Thick, black hair hangs in perfect straight-iron form around my shoulders. And my head pulses with a terrible ache just above my temples. It's then I realize I'm sprouting horns. *There are freaking cow horns growing out of my scalp!*

I reach up, running my long, new fingers over the spikes, and feel a metal disk sharing space between them. My brain is racing, even though my ascent has slowed to a crawl. Something familiar tugs at the corner of my mind. Something about the sun.

And then I know: the circle between my horns is the sun-disk. I've fully transformed back into Hathor as the ancients knew her. Knew *me*. As I'm allowing my aching head to relax, cradled by the weightlessness of space, the faintest of sounds weave their chords around my heart. I tilt my head, straining to listen. The notes grow more distinct now that I'm focusing: a song I'd never mistake anywhere.

Beth is playing for me.

Her death lullaby confirms what I already know: my time with the El Bay family is over. I can almost picture my human shell laid out in a satin-lined coffin. Beth would be clutching her cello to her chest, while Andy chuckles as he recalls some long-ago antic of mine from when we were kids.

It was a beautiful life—crappy job, unexplained goddess role, and all.

Turning my new body to Earth, I pass over the moon. Bathed in its reflective glow and awash in soft light and peace, it feels good to be back to being me.

– The End –

THE LION AND THE UNICORN

The Lion and the Unicorn
Were fighting for the crown;
The Lion beat the Unicorn
All about the town.
Some gave them white bread
And some gave them brown;
Some gave them plum cake
And drummed them out of town!
                    – Mother Goose

THE LION AND THE UNICORN: PART THE FIRST
Nancy Holder

London, 1603

Susana trembled in the darkness, one hand gripping the flickering torch, the other balancing a goblet of wine and a single slice of plain brown bread on a silver tray. She was to take it to the King, to break his fast. He would partake only after his ghastly work was done.

Screams rose from below the winding staircase, echoing against the stone, and pummeled Susana's heart, and her soul. She would have given a year of her life for permission to refuse her task.

She was sixteen, nearly a woman grown, but she was dressed to pass as a page in trousers and fine hose, and a brown velvet doublet so rich that whenever her hand brushed against it, she caught her breath. She wore a jeweled dagger on her belt, a warning that she would cut any man down who would dare to attack her master.

She jerked as another scream shot up from the hell beneath her feet, spilling wine on the stair. In the firelight it looked like blood.

Above her, thunder rumbled. The air was sodden. Like a wet woolen cloak draped about her shoulders, her duty weighed heavy and hard to bear. Not for the world did she wish to go down to that hellish place.

Six months before, King James I, the Unicorn, had come to London town. Susana had thought he would bring happy fortune to his united kingdoms. But it seemed that in the never-ending battle against the Devil, war had been declared upon England.

Queen Elizabeth—Good Queen Bess, the cub of Henry VIII, the Lion of England—was dead but half a year. She had reigned for forty-four years, good years. But the last months of her reign had been troubled. Her Majesty's ailing mind had not been clear—her orders bewildering, her commands impossible to fulfill. Plots and schemes grew like fungus as rivals vied for her throne. There was talk of civil war.

Then God had roused her from her confusion long enough to name her nephew, King James of Scotland—as her successor. England was saved from violence and strife.

In haste, the royal coat of arms—two English lions—had been redesigned so that the English Lion and the Scottish Unicorn together reared proudly. King James's new arms had been carried before him on a beautiful July day as he had entered London town for the first time. Rising on tiptoe in a cacophony of drumbeats, trumpets, and cheers, Susana had hoped to glimpse his royal presence as he headed for the church to be crowned. Surrounded by a glittering retinue of courtiers and soldiers, the king himself had ridden a fantastic warhorse, and his armor had gleamed as if it were made of gold. Sunbeams had poured down on his head, making a circle that shimmered like a halo. And so the people said, "God's blessings are upon James."

"Long live the king!" she had cried so loudly that others around her had chuckled, then taken up the cheer.

Then on that day, in that moment, someone had tapped Susana on the shoulder. She'd glanced left and right. But all eyes had been on the king, and as she'd looked back at King James, the tapping seemed to be coming from *inside* her.

Inside her *heart.*

And a voice that whispered deep within her mind, *Fear not.*

Susana had caught her breath. That was the greeting angels uttered when they approached mere mortals. But an angel wouldn't speak to *her.* She was just a girl, and a commoner. Just a laundress.

Fear not, the voice repeated.

As if it were already happening, Susana had seen herself dressed in male clothing. A goblet was in her hands and she was lifting it up to King James. His face was glowing, his smile saintly.

Then the image had faded, and she'd been back in the street. And at that very moment, King James had turned his head and seemed to look straight at her, that same blessed smile on his face.

She had caught her breath and staggered backwards. God Himself wanted her to serve this king. God *Himself.*

***

Fear not, an angel had told Susana, but she had been afraid. She had cut her hair and stolen nobleman's clothing from the laundry—a hanging offense. She had taken the name "Robin Fletcher," and asked to be seen by the chamberlain for a position in the palace. Her answers were pleasing, her manner respectful, and she had been brought into the happy circle of the king's company, to personally serve the king his food.

She had brought him plum pudding and wine at the very meeting where he had informed his new privy council that a great war was being waged against the person of the king. Good Queen Bess had spared England by naming him her successor, but he had become a target of evil. Great numbers of witches in Scotland had confessed that they and their sister witches in England cursed him night and day. They hexed him and plotted his doom. They didn't want a man—much less a pious, God-fearing man—upon the throne. They did not want a woman, either.

They wanted Satan to rule their lands.

The king knew much about the matters of good and evil. He had written a book on the subject, called *Daemonologie*. He knew how to detect the presence of witchcraft, and how to make the guilty confess. In no time at all, scores of accused Englishwomen—and a few men too, had been flung into dungeons, tortured, convicted. Susana had been shocked by the filth of the cells, and the brutality of the tortures, but more astonished to see just how many Brides of Satan polluted the land.

Like the evil harridan now down below, alone with the king.

"I am afraid," Susana whispered aloud to the angel she had not sensed since that day at the procession. "Please, can you make me not so fearful?"

But the tapping and the voice were silent, as they had been ever since the king's triumphal march into London. And over time, Susana had begun to suspect that she had imagined the vision. In the heat of the day and the excitement, perhaps she had had a sort of mad fit.

Now, stepping off the stairs onto the mossy, stony floor, she heard the screaming and pleading—the denials—and she bit back a wave of nausea. As she began the dreary walk down the dank corridor that led to the torture chamber, the accused witch shrieked that she was guilty, through and through. Eagerly guilty. Susana reeled at the revolting secrets the old woman revealed in a tumble of half-intelligible words to the king. Yes, she was a witch; and yes, she had consorted with Satan in all manner of unspeakable ways; and yes and yes again, she was glad the truth was finally out. The witch knew this was her only chance at redemption, and she would kiss the king's boots in gratitude, if only he would untie her from the rack... and if her arms and legs could be put back in their sockets.

"You are the king. Please heal me," the old witch said, weeping. Her words slurred together. She had had very few teeth at the beginning of the questioning. Susana supposed she had fewer, if any, now.

"You *are* healed. God Himself has done so," the king replied graciously.

The witch kept crying. "My arms..."

"The body is but a dwelling place for the soul. When you are burned, your soul shall not perish, but have everlasting life with our saviour," James said.

"*Burned?*" the witch shrieked. "But I-I confessed!"

"And now, the cleansing fire will purify your sin," King James informed her, and Susana shut her eyes at the thought of the torment to come. It was the worst way to die that she could imagine.

The wretch moaned, and then cried out, and then screamed so hard it rattled Susana's very bones.

She was nearly at the end of the corridor, about to turn left, when an eerie green light emanated from the torture chamber. She froze in horror. Like a glowing mist, it glazed the stone walls and ceiling. Then she heard the king heaving loudly, as if in mortal peril.

"My lord!" Susana cried as she broke into a run.

She flew around the corridor. The king's back was to her, and the tall, stately monarch stood with his legs wide apart and his arms flung open. His head was thrown back, and his moans were frightful. The green light was rising from the bruised and bloody old woman wrapped in rags, stretched tight on the rack. It billowed toward the ceiling, then draped down over the king like a shroud.

"Sire!" Susana shouted in a high-pitched voice, dropping the tray and the torch. The goblet clanked and rolled. The king jerked and staggered, looking over his shoulder in her direction. His Majesty's eyes—nearly black—were rolling back in his head.

"He steals it," the hag hissed through broken teeth.

The noxious light played over King James's body, as if caressing him. He shook from head to foot like a foaming dog. Quaking, Susana forced herself to go to him.

Before she reached him, the light flickered out. The king swayed, his head drooping, and shuddered hard. A hiss rose like steam from the rack. Susana gasped. God's blood, what had just happened?

The king raised his head and looked at Susana. He was clear-eyed, and he smiled gently at his "page."

"Robin. I had begun to wonder if you'd fallen down the stairs and broken your neck," the king said.

"Forgive me, Your Majesty," Susana managed to grind out, careful to her voice low and gruff. She knelt on one knee and picked up the cup, the tray, and the bread. Then she collected the torch and awkwardly rose. "Pray, sir, what was that horrible green light?"

"One last attempt to kill me," James replied,

sneering at the hag he had tortured. "Did you hear the abomination confess?" Avoiding the sight of the rack, keeping her eyes on the torch, and thinking of flames; Susana nodded. "Confess, and beg for mercy, then seek to murder me after I had assured her that Christ had forgiven her?"

So is she dead? Susana trembled.

"Did you see?" the king bellowed at her. Susana jumped.

"Yes, Your Highness, I s-saw," she assured him. "'Twas fearsome."

"Say nothing of it," the king said quickly.

She looked up at him in surprise. "Sire?"

"If my chaplain heard that she had tried to kill me, he would refuse to absolve her of her sins before her burial. But I know that in her deepest of hearts, there was goodness." He looked over at the rack. Susana did not.

"Shall I fetch help, Your Majesty?" she asked.

"No. Fetch more wine," the king said, sounding a bit merry. "My faith in our Savior protected me from the evil she sought to inflict. All is well."

"Come with me, sir, please," Susana begged. "What more is to be done here?"

"Much is to be done," the king replied, his cheeriness evaporating. "Witches do not act alone. Where there is one, there are many. And they are waiting in their cells for their last chance at salvation."

She quaked. The green light had covered him. What if the others tried to enshroud him with their black magic as well?

Reading her hesitation, the great man tousled Susana's short, mannish locks and said, "Fear not. Is that not what the angels tell us? Fear not, lad. I am the Lord's good servant, and this is what I must do."

Susana stared at him. Surely, these words uttered from his mouth were a sign that her angel was nearby. That she was on the right path.

"Yes, Your Majesty," she said, bowing low. She saw witchblood on the stem of the goblet and quickly moved her fingers away. She began to leave when the king took the torch from her.

"Make haste to return," he told her. "I thirst."

"Yes, Your Majesty," Susana replied.

"And, Robin? Call out to me in the passageway upon your return. I will tell you when it is safe to approach. I would not want one of these witches to inflict their attacks on you. I am protected by the divine right of my kingship, but *you* are only a page."

Protected by an angel, mayhap, Susana thought. But she said nothing. She feared for the king, but she was grateful that he would protect her from evil.

As she re-climbed the stairs in darkness, she heard more screams, terrible ones, and smelled smoke and burning flesh.

"God's wounds, does he burn one of them here? Now?" she whispered, and tears of horror trailed down her face. Her heart thundered in her chest and she paused, feeling sick and faint. She shut her eyes tightly and bit her lower lip, struggling not to retch.

Then guilt prickled her cheeks as she made haste to fetch the wine. It was the very least she could do, when he braved such terrors on the behalf of all his subjects, including her.

When Susana reached the ground floor of the castle, the jailers and guards made sport of Robin Fletcher's obvious distress. The men had become hardened to the pleas of the wicked. They mocked "the blood-boltered old whores" the king put to the question. When Susana poured more wine for her master, they laughed at how "his" delicate hands trembled.

More rude comments followed as Susana stumbled back down the stairs, deep down into the pit. Her foot touched the floor and she minced slowly back down the passageway.

Ragged screams buffeted her ears, these ripped from a different throat. Susan's hand clenched the torch as she crept forward. Her heart pounded, and she was dizzy from holding her breath.

Then the same strange green glow spilled down the passageway. It was stronger and brighter than before, reaching farther into the corridor as if to seek her. Susana trotted backwards like a child escaping the tide on the beach.

"We know what you're doing, warlock!" a woman shrieked. "And we'll stop you!"

Then her words became a wail, and a cry, and then there was nothing but nonsensical gibbering and green light that threatened to wash over Susana's shoes.

She started to retreat; then something knocked against her heart, as if asking entrance. Then it felt as if someone wrapped their hand around her wrist and urged her forwards. She struggled, but the pull was insistent. She tried to cry out to the king for help, but she found that she couldn't utter a word. Whether mute from fear or an enchantment, she didn't know.

Inside her mind, she heard the words *Fear not.* As distinctly as the first time, as clearly as if someone spoke them directly to her. But she was still afraid as she began to move toward the green light. Then as quickly as she came forward, it receded, until it winked out and she stood in the circle of her torch's fire.

"You thought to thwart me." King James's tone was low and angry. The malevolence in his tone gave Susana pause. He sounded not like himself at all. "But I took it."

Susana was pulled forward again, until she could see into the torture chamber. An old woman had been manacled by each wrist, and hung from chains bolted into the ceiling. She was covered in blood, and her head rested on her chest. But the king . . .

All she saw was black on blackness; then she made out his silhouette. From the head of his shadow, two horns protruded. Horns like the Devil's own.

Stunned, she covered her mouth and darted back around the corner. She pressed her back against the stones and bit her lip to keep from screaming.

I did not see that. It is not as it seems, she told herself.

"Robin?" the king called in a loud voice. "Have you come?"

She was paralyzed with terror. She had to clear her throat twice before she could speak. "I am here, Your Majesty," she called. "I have your wine, sire. May I approach?"

"You may," he said grandly.

Her heart stuttered; she laid it down to a miracle that she had the ability to move. She saw the king with his back to her as he lifted the woman's head by the hair and stared into the glassy eyes. He let the head drop and turned around.

For one moment, his eyes seemed to be completely black. But no, they were his normal, deep-chestnut brown.

"Wine. Good," said the king.

He reached out a hand to take the cup, and Susana, overcome, sank to one knee in a chivalrous gesture to mask her fear. His fingertips brushed her knuckles and sharp, ice-cold pain burrowed into her bones. Her head lowered, tears welled, and she listened to the thunder banging like drums against the castle walls.

"Did you overhear her confession?" the king asked.

He attempted to sound neutral, but she detected an edge of suspicion in his voice. As if, perhaps, Master Robin had seen and heard what he should not.

"No, sire," she said. "Ought I have?"

"No. It is well with you. I alone must bear that burden. I heard it before she died."

"That is good, then, Your Majesty," Susana forced herself to say.

His reply was a mean chuckle, nearly a snigger, like that of a small boy who had committed an offense, and reveled in not having gotten caught.

God strike me dead for thinking poorly of the king, but there is something amiss, she thought, as the king drank down the wine. *Something very wrong.*

The room spun. She felt her heart hammering in her chest, followed by a frisson of awful, life-threatening fear that skittered up her spine.

There is nothing here for me to do, she told herself, *but to obey the commands of my king. That is where my duty ends.*

"Take this cup from me," King James ordered her. He sighed with mournful weariness as he held it out to her. "Ah, would that you could take it all from me."

As she took the cup, words poured into her mind: *It will be taken from him, and you shall help.*

As if to stifle her from crying out, a kiss brushed upon her cheek, bestowed by one invisible.

Fear not, said the voice. But she was more afraid than she had ever been in her entire life.

Like a dirge, like a march to the scaffold, thunder beat against the castle as Susana and King James left the torture chamber. But Susana had the worst feeling that she would be back there soon, in a very horrible way.

- Here Endeth Part the First -

THERE WAS AN OLD WOMAN

"There was an old woman who lived in a shoe,
Who had so many children she didn't know what to do,
So she gave them some broth without any bread
And whipped them all soundly and put them to bed."
– Mother Goose

LIFE IN A SHOE
Heidi R. Kling

She wasn't always like this.

Before the New Rule, when it was just Zeb and me, she'd take us outside and push us on the swings higher, higher! And we'd lean back so far my hair would breeze the sand and Zeb would jump off and we'd all laugh like pure happiness in the sun and the wind.

But since the New Rule, since choice was a thing of the past, she'd had one baby after another after another, turning our two to four, our six to eight, until there were ten of us (and counting) living in one shoe-box apartment south of a town no one cared about.

The twelve of us shared two bedrooms and one bathroom.

She shared her room with the youngest of us: the baby and the toddlers, too young to sleep alone. The rest of us piled into the second room. Four boys sharing a double mattress on the floor—one Zeb found behind the dumpster, stained with urine and other stuff I tried not to think about. They slept Charlie Bucket style, while the girls—my two younger sisters and myself— shared one lone twin.

When our father was on leave from the military he

shared the room with her, and I took care of the babies in the living room, in front of the wall TV. It was constantly left on, blasting segments of news footage from the wars around the world: Iran and Israel the most recent and, apparently, the most popular of the five.

Father's visits were a mixed blessing.

We liked his regulation pockets, lined with lint-covered candy. Oh, we'd line up like it was the best thing since sliced bread (which it was). He'd pat our heads and let the boys count his new scars, and then look over at mom and, in a voice not unlike the war reporters', say, "Now it's your turn for a treat, old lady."

The last time he came home, her dress was clean, clear from milk stains on the breast. Her dark hair was combed, her lips shining with gloss she must've stolen, because no way could we afford that. She'd smiled and let him drag her into the bedroom like he was the best thing since sliced bread (which was arguable) and I'd turned up the volume of the limbless soldiers and rotting crop news until Mom banged a warning on the wall.

Why must the little ones be exposed to their noises? That was the real warning: a shrill sound, an alarm, a warning that in a few months, long after he'd gone, we'd see the result of his visit.

The stomach swell of another mouth we couldn't feed.

After Dad left, her smile lasted only until the sickness began. Her groaning was replaced with hurls of vomit into the toilet, or sometimes the kitchen sink if she couldn't make it in time.

"You okay, Mom?" I asked. She slapped my hand off her shoulder with the growl of a rabid dog. My eyes stung more than my hand. But I was used to this. And as her stomach grew, so did her anger.

"Warm up the broth!" she shouted on a day she was particularly agitated.

"Don't we have any bread? The cupboards are bare."

"Of course we have no bread. If we did, don't you think I'd give it to you?"

I wasn't sure. Maybe she stuffed it under her mattress to eat after she whipped us into bed.

Father wasn't due back for another six months.

They came home. Planted their seed. Flew away.

"I'm so hungry, Mommy," Frankie, one of the little ones, whined from the ground next to her. The evening was particularly hot; there was particularly bad news on the TV.

"Shush, you," Mother said, shooing him away.

"Me too, Mommy," Julip said.

"Shh!" Mom snapped.

That one got a slap.

I scooped Julip up and soothed her tears and placed her in the middle of the double mattress. I gave her a ball of pink string to play with. The pink matched the harsh mark on her little cheek.

"Mom." I re-entered the room. "The little ones are hungry. They need to eat."

"We're all hungry," she said, her eyes glued to the screen.

I stepped between the screen and her eyes.

"You need to stop this."

"Stop what?"

"These kids. You need to stop having them."

"Stop having them?" She looked at me like I was crazy.

"Yes. We can't afford them. They are starving."

"There's nothing we can do to stop them from coming."

"You have to stop visiting Father. Letting *him* visit *us*."

"Have you gone mad? That would never be allowed."

"Then we need to figure out a way around it."

"Hush," she said, pointing at the screen. "They'll hear you."

"I don't care."

She sat quietly for a second, smoothing the faded fabric of her dress over the swell of her stomach. "You *should* care. This will be your life soon."

My stomach lurched. "What?"

"On his last visit, Father told me you are being recruited as a wife, by someone in his unit. He will bring him the next time he comes." She looked me over with a scrutinizing frown. "And he told him you were pretty, so we have some work to do."

"There is *no way* this is going to be my life."

For a second, she almost looked sad, human. But then her mouth froze into that same thin line. "You have no choice," she said. "Move out of the way now. Shoo, shoo, little lamb."

***

She was sitting up sound asleep on the patchwork couch, like she was dead and didn't even know it.

As carefully as if I were holding the last spoonful of broth, I lifted her sleeping arm off the chest of the youngest baby, a chubby redhead I'd named Freedom (because she was done with naming babies). Freedom twitched and we froze.

All ten of us.

Two babies were on Zeb's back, one on my hip, and now this one, which I gently swung over my shoulder. The others, wide-eyed and willow thin, were holding small hands like a line of ducks.

I supposed I should cry, leaving her alone like this in her shoebox. But that was before I'd found the bread she'd hidden from her babies. The babies she hit because they were hungry. All we had were the clothes on our backs and the last three slices of bread I'd found under Mother's mattress. It was enough.

I didn't hate her. I couldn't.

She didn't know.

She was too stupid to protest then, and too destroyed to care now.

She was wrong about me, though. This wasn't going to be my life, not without a fight. It wouldn't be my brothers' and sisters', either. "You know why they do it," Zeb whispered to me once. "We're like crops to them, raised to fight in their never-ending wars."

"You'd think if they wanted decent crops, they'd figure out a way to feed us better," I'd said wryly.

Today I said something different as my eyes ran over my mother's swollen belly for the last time. "Maybe if she just has the one baby, she'll take care of her? Like she used to do us?"

"If she doesn't," he said as we slipped out the front door, "we'll come back for that one, too."

Over the border, swing sets still flew with laughing children, ripe strawberries grew on farms, and parents weren't forced to have more children than they could afford.

Some couples couldn't even have children, we'd heard. And they weren't even punished for it.

I was hoping we could find some of them, loving and generous, who might help us. Maybe even take a few of us in.

And if we couldn't, well, then Zeb and me, we'd figure something else out.

Anything was better than her life in this shoe.

– The End –

INTERLUDE: HUMPTY DUMPTY

Humpty Dumpty sat on a wall.
Humpty Dumpty knew he would fall.
None of his counselors and none of the doctors could
fix Humpty Dumpty after all.
Humpty was lonely, and teased by the kids.
He'd run away crying, and often he hid,
From bullies and intolerant kids and adults,
They kicked him, and beat him to quite bloody pulps.
One day poor Humpty had had quite enough,
Of crying, and hiding, and daily rebuffs.
"Stop it, you'll be sorry," were Humpty's last words.
Before climbing the tower in search of the bird,
Who told him he'd be free, be able to fly,
If only he'd listen, and jump from up high.
So Humpty willed courage and strength from inside.
He wrote one last letter, and posted online.
I'm nothing, and no one, and now you will see,
As I jump from this wall, totally free.
I'm clear now, it's fine here, I'm finally happy.
You can't touch me or tease me, or call me a fatty.
Good night to you losers, still walking around.
My name is Humpty, splat on the ground.

BABYLON

How many miles to Babylon?
Three score and ten.
Can I get there by candlelight?
Aye, and back again.
If your feet are nimble and light,
You'll get there by candlelight.
– Mother Goose

CANDLELIGHT
Suzanne Lazear

"But I have to go. *Everyone's* going," Juliet huffed as she stood toe to toe with her mom in the hallway.

"No, you're not going to that party; you're too young," Mom's voice ricocheted off the walls. "This conversation is over." She marched toward the kitchen.

"I hate you." It tumbled out of Juliet's mouth as she ran in the opposite direction. She slammed her bedroom door so hard that the corner of one of Melody's sketches on the wall became untaped.

Melody, lounging on her bed, looked up from her homework, short red hair hanging in her eyes in a curtain so thick Juliet wasn't sure how she could see the book at all.

"That went well." Melody blew the hair out of her face, revealing green eyes.

"Shut up." Juliet flopped onto her own bed and hugged her pillow to her chest. "She doesn't get it. It'll be social suicide not to go to the party."

"You could sneak out." Melody glanced at her book, then wrote something down.

"But that's temporary—it's *always* something. She pitched her voice to mimic her mother's. "Juliet, your skirt is too short; you're not going out with that much makeup on; no, you can't stay out until midnight.' It's *so* unfair."

"Will you turn the TV on?" Melody made another mark on her paper.

Juliet blinked. She was pouring out her heart and Melody wanted to watch *TV*?

"Turn it on yourself," she huffed.

"Can't, remember?" Melody scrunched her freckled nose in distaste. "No TV, no computer, no cell phone *for three months*. But I *can* be in the same room when the TV's on. And right now, my show's on. *Please?*"

Oh, yeah. Her younger sister wasn't exempt from their mom's wrath, either.

"Sure." Juliet grabbed the remote off the nightstand between their twin beds and pointed it at the TV. "Why won't she let us do *anything*? No one else's mom is like this. Ugh!"

Melody nodded. "Seriously. Talk about social suicide—no phone for three months? I might as well die."

"And in the news, another heartbreaking teen suicide," the TV reporter said.

Click. Next channel.

"Tune into tonight's special: Runaways in America —a sudden problem, or is it just finally coming to light?" someone else said.

Click. Next channel.

"Is this the right channel?" Juliet asked.

"Yup."

"Are your parents unfair?" A sympathetic female voice asked them on screen as a commercial played.

The girls looked at each other and nodded.

"Do they just not understand?"

"Yep," Juliet sighed. "Ugh, and Todd Wilkins was going to be there, too."

"He's pretty cute," Melody agreed.

"Well," the commercial continued, "come to Candlelight Center, where we understand. Where we can help." An address flashed across the screen.

Melody cocked her head. "Candlelight Center? I've never heard of it."

Juliet jumped off the bed; this was just what she needed. "We should go." Excitement bubbled inside her. "Don't you see? They can help us. Not only will I be able to go to the party, and you'll get your phone and laptop back, but we'll *never* have to go through this again."

She did a little dance as she ran a brush through her long, red hair.

"Aren't you coming?" Juliet pulled on her shoes, glaring at Melody who'd yet to move, green eyes affixed on the TV.

"After my show. Please?" Melody pleaded, still lounging on her bed. "I *really* want my phone back, but if I don't watch this, I won't be able to keep up at lunch tomorrow."

"Well . . ." Juliet twisted her body back and forth, as if that would help her decide. "I suppose it can wait half an hour."

***

"Oh, that's so unfair," clucked the blonde counselor, Pamela, as they sat across from her in a curtained cubicle in the bright and clean Candlelight Center.

"Right?" Juliet replied. "Please, help us. I have to go to my party."

"And I want my phone back," Melody added.

"I'm sure you do." Pamela looked their age, but that was a thing with peer counselors, right?

Juliet practically leapt out of the plastic chair in excitement. "So you can help us?"

"There is a place . . ." Pamela opened a drawer.

"A place?" Juliet's heart fell. "Oh, I thought you could bring Mom here and tell her how stupid she's being."

Melody's eyes lit up. "Wait—what place?"

"It's called Babylon." Her voice hushed. "Imagine a place with no parents, where you can do anything you want, whenever you want."

Juliet twisted in her chair, suddenly unsure. "I don't know if I want to leave, I just want to go to the party."

"She'll *never* understand," Pamela warned. "No, if you're to have the freedom you want, then you need to get out before she totally ruins your life. Just think of all the friends you'll make, all the parties you'll go to— and no one will tell you what to wear or when to come home." Her eyes danced as if she was imagining being there, too.

Melody slapped her hand on the desk. "I'm in."

"Wait—you *are*?" Juliet's heart skipped a beat.

"She's already making my life miserable. Imagine when I'm your age." Melody shuddered. "Do you know what it's like to have no phone? To not even be able to use the computer for schoolwork?"

For a moment, Juliet just sat there, thinking. "Where is this place? Is it like foster care?"

"Not at all. You'll be independent, yet taken care of—and most importantly, no one will boss you around." Pamela smiled knowingly.

It didn't actually sound bad. But . . .

"We should go," Melody hissed. "Show Mom *we're* in control. We can always go for a little while, and then come back." She looked at the counselor. "We *can* come back, right?"

"Of course." She waved it off with her hand. "But you probably won't want to."

"Well . . ." Juliet considered this. If they disappeared and then returned, Mom would be so grateful that she'd never punish them again—and if she did, they'd just leave. She looked at Melody, who flashed her puppy eyes. "I'm in—but just for a little bit. How do we get there?"

The counselor set a little bundle on the desk. "The only way to get to Babylon is by candlelight."

"Candlelight? Is that a train?" Juliet stared at the lump of fabric.

The counselor leaned in, voice daring. "You *do* believe in magic, don't you?"

"Magic?" Okay, this was getting weird.

Melody snatched the bundle and shoved it in the pocket of her hoodie. "I do." She bounced in her seat. "Wait, I know this poem. Babylon is real?"

"Very. It's been a refuge to misunderstood children for thousands of years, and you can't expect a place like that to be here, right?" Pamela's look made Juliet feel stupid for even considering disbelieving in magic.

"Right . . ." An unsure feeling spread through Juliet. "But I just want to go to my party."

"In Babylon, you can go to parties every night—or even in the day," the counselor added. "You don't even have to go to school."

Melody stood. "We're so in. So what do we do?"

"Just follow the instructions. Believe me, it'll be so much better for you."

Would it? Juliet stood. "Thank you."

"Come on, let's go."

Melody dragged her home.

When they got there, their mother met them at the door, hands on her hips.

"Where have you two been?" she demanded. "You're not supposed to leave without telling me."

The early uneasiness Juliet felt at the idea of leaving their mom melted away. "We're not babies. It's not even dark," she snapped.

Her mother's mouth formed a hard line. "Juliet, you're grounded. Melody, you're grounded even more."

"What?" Melody shrieked. "We just went for a walk!"

"Girls." Their mom's hands pressed against her temples. "I'm not trying to ruin your lives. There's some bad stuff going on out there and I'm just—"

"I don't want to hear it," Juliet snapped, tired of being bossed around. "I hate you."

Grabbing Melody's arm, she ran toward their room, not stopping when their mom yelled that rudeness was unacceptable and to go to their room.

Like they'd go anywhere else.

Juliet locked the door. Anger whirred inside her. "Unbelievable."

Melody stood there, frozen. "She took the TV."

"What?" Juliet looked—the TV shelf sat empty.

"I can't believe she took the TV," Melody wailed, flopping onto her bed. "Wait . . ." She pulled the bundle from her hoodie pocket. "Tonight after she goes to bed?"

For a long moment, Juliet gazed at the bundle. Then she looked at the empty TV shelf, and thought of all the things she'd missed because of Mom.

A smile spread across Juliet's face, and for the first time all day, her heart felt lighter. "Yes, tonight after she goes to bed."

***

"That is so gross." Juliet made a face at the instructions. "How do we know this will work?"

They sat on the floor of their room, the only light coming from the old nightlight they kept because it gave them enough light to do things without alerting Mom.

Melody held out a pocket knife. "If it doesn't work, what have we lost, other than a little blood?" The nightlight cast eerie shadows over her face. "I'll go first."

Flicking open the knife, she grimaced as she sliced her palm. Blood dripping from the cut, she wrapped her hand around the white candle, smearing it with crimson.

Melody held out both the knife and the bloody candle to her. "Here."

Juliet hesitated.

"Are you afraid?" Melody teased, voice soft so Mom wouldn't hear.

"Of course not," Juliet hissed. What *did* they have to lose? If nothing happened, they'd just put their pajamas back on and return to bed. She grabbed the knife, sliced her palm, and then coated the candle with her own blood, making it look as if it was red, not white.

"Ow." Juliet stanched the flow of blood with a tissue. "Now we light it?" Her heart thumped. What if it *did* work?

"Yep."

Juliet held the candle while Melody struck a match and lit it. Then Melody wrapped her hand around the bloody candle. "Now, we recite the poem. Remember, we have to say it three times."

Juliet's belly quivered, but Melody looked so sure,

so calm—and she was the *younger* sister. "Let's do it."

How many miles to Babylon?
Three score miles and ten.
Can I get there by candlelight?
Yes, and back again.

Three times they whispered the verse, clutching the candle. The whole time, Juliet felt sick and dizzy. As they uttered the last word for the third time, the flame went out. The floor fell away and they found themselves tumbling through darkness, both shrieking.

Juliet hit the ground with a thud and looked around. They were in the middle of a lush garden, the sun was up, and she could hear the sounds of running water and voices. "Shit." She sucked in a breath.

"It worked." Melody's eyes widened as she tucked the candle into her hoodie pocket. "We're in Babylon."

"Juliet, Melody, you came. I'm so glad." A blonde walked into the clearing. Pamela, the girl from Candlelight Center. She offered Juliet a hand up.

Juliet did a double-take. "Wait—you're here?"

"Well, yes. Babylon is my home. I go into your world to bring others here, so they can be safe and happy." She smiled and helped Melody up, who didn't seem nearly as hesitant as she leapt to her feet, green eyes dancing.

Home. That meant it *was* possible to go back and forth between the worlds. Relief flowed through her.

Juliet took Pamela's offered hand and stood. "What now?"

Brushing the dirt off her jeans, she looked around the lush paradise.

"Why don't I show you around?" Pamela no longer wore jeans and a t-shirt like she had at the center. Her pretty pink dress looked of an old style, but not outdated.

Juliet looked at Melody, who nodded. "Why not?"

Pamela led them out of the garden and to a little town of dirt roads, little buildings with painted signs, and cottages with thatched roofs.

"Welcome to Babylon." She gestured to the street. "This is Main Street, where you can get food or clothes from the shops, or go into a pub or restaurant for something to eat." She pointed to a place with a dancing sheep on the sign. "Juliet, that's the best club in all of Babylon. I'll take you to the party there tonight myself."

Juliet didn't answer. Everywhere she looked, children and teens were dressed in everything from modern clothes to stuff out of historical movies. A few kids played a game with a ball. Some girls walked into a building with a teacup-shaped sign. Across the street, a really hot guy disappeared into a building with a book painted on it.

"Yeah, he'll be at the party," Pamela told her.

Well then.

"But how do you pay for things?" Melody frowned. "We didn't bring any money."

Pamela laughed. Money? You don't need money in Babylon. People work, but it's because they want to, not because they have to. Everything is free and plentiful. You never grow up, never grow old. Truly, this is paradise."

"Really?" Juliet tried to figure that out. "How?"

A wide grin lit up Pamela's face. "Magic."

"Yeah, Juliet. *Magic*," Melody teased as they walked.

Right. After all, they were *here*.

They passed a candy store. Melody's eyes widened

as she practically pressed her face to the glass.

"Go get whatever you want," Pamela urged. "Then I'll show you to a cottage of your very own."

***

Music pulsed around them as Pamela led Juliet through the dark club. A very European-looking guy in a two-toned coat played the pipes along with a band as teens danced with abandon. Melody waved from a table filled with girls her age as they gossiped about . . . something. She'd made friends almost immediately.

"He's been watching you ever since you walked inside," Pamela whispered, nodding towards a tall, cute guy with brown hair and tanned skin. The same guy she'd seen earlier.

Wow. Much hotter than Todd Wilkins.

"Let's have something to drink." Pamela dragged her to the bar and ordered a drink. It was free, just like everything else. Even the dress she wore. She could get used to this.

"Hi." Hot, tanned guy sat down next to her. Juliet tried not to giggle. "New here?"

"Um, yeah." Her cheeks burned, how stupid she sounded. "I'm Juliet."

"Hi, Juliet. I'm Marc." He smiled, revealing dimples. "Want to dance?"

She looked to Pamela, who shrugged.

"Sure." After all, who was here to tell her no?

No one.

***

Juliet lost track of time. Every night she went out dancing until the sun rose, sometimes with Pamela, nearly always with Marc and his friends. Marc worked in the bookshop and she often helped him. He had been here since something called the Children's Crusades. Children aged a little, but no one completely grew up—certainly, no one grew old. She could deal with that—to be young and have fun forever.

Nearly everyone she'd met had some sort of horrible story, fleeing from forced marriage, abuse, starvation, or in the case of one girl, the lion pit. Everyone's stories made not being allowed to go to a party feel trivial. Like she and Melody weren't really worthy of the refuge offered by such a wondrous place. But she wasn't ready to go.

"Juliet, is that you?" Melody whispered as Juliet tiptoed past her door in their little two-bedroom cottage. Finally, they had bedrooms of their own.

"Guess what? Marc held my hand as he walked me home." She giggled, yawning. Dawn was rising. Time for bed.

Melody, still dressed, stood in the doorway. "I . . . I think I'm ready to go home. We've been here a long time. Mom's probably getting worried."

"But I'm not ready to go." Juliet blinked. "Marc still hasn't kissed me."

"I like it here, but I miss my friends, and well . . ." Melody fidgeted. "I miss Mom—compared to some of the stories girls here have told me, our mom's a saint."

"True . . ." She took a deep breath, not quite willing to believe she was about to admit this. "I miss Mom, too. Yeah, she's mean sometimes, but you're right, she could be so much worse."

"So can we go home? Please?" Melody pleaded. "I want my bed and my TV and my phone. And Mom." She traced the wooden floor with her bare toe. "I want Mom."

As much as Juliet loved the freedom, she actually sort of missed having someone there. Sure, Mom punished them, but she did a million little things Juliet had always taken for granted, and now missed.

"How *do* we get home?" Juliet asked. "Should we ask Pamela?"

Melody shook her head. "Noooo."

"What?" She blinked. Pamela was always so nice; like the de facto mom of Babylon.

"I've talked to other girls. Pamela is great, as long as you're happy and having fun, but the moment someone wants to go home . . ." Melody shuddered and a chill shot up Juliet's spine.

"Maybe we shouldn't risk it?" Homesickness stabbed her heart, especially when Melody's face fell. "Okay, we'll go home. What should we do? Should I ask Marc?" Now him . . . him she'd miss.

"I saved this." Melody held up the bloody, half-used candle that had brought them here. "When Pamela asked me for it, I told her it was gone."

"Wait—do you think there's something sinister about this place? Like children die to keep up the magic?" She shivered.

Cocking her head, Melody thought for a moment. "No, nothing like that. Unless you leave—my friends say those who leave don't return."

"Well of course not, because they've left," Juliet teased. Okay, so Babylon was just a magic haven for children who'd led horrible lives. All the more reason to leave—so someone else could have their place.

Melody waved the candle. "So?"

"Now?" She thought of Marc and how he made her heart flutter.

"Please?" Tears glinted in her eyes. "I miss home."

Juliet wanted to stay for one more night, but the

expression on Melody's face broke her heart. "Hey, don't cry." She wrapped her arms around her sister. "If you want to go home, then let's light the candle and go. It's been fun, but you're right, we've been gone, what, weeks? Months? Mom's probably worried sick."

They sat on the floor of Melody's room.

"What do we do?" Juliet's belly fluttered with mixed emotions.

"The same." Melody had a knife and matches. "The poem says we can get there, *and back again.*"

"Makes sense to me." Juliet cut her palm, fresh blood mixing with the dried blood already on the candle stub. "Here." She handed it to Melody. Something opened and closed in another part of the cottage. "Wait—was that a door?"

Melody smeared her blood on it. "I didn't hear anything. Light the match."

Taking a deep breath, Juliet lit the match. They both held the candle and chanted. Footsteps echoed down the hall, but she didn't stop.

As they started the last line of the last verse, Marc entered the room.

His dark eyes widened. "Wait—Juliet, no!"

They uttered the final word and like before, the floor disappeared from under them and they plunged through a pit. A scream ripped from her throat as she landed on the ground with a *thump.*

"Wait—where are we?" Juliet looked around at blue walls and bunk beds. This wasn't their room.

Melody stood and frowned. "We used the whole candle. Where *are* we?"

They walked through the house, the layout similar to theirs, but filled with things that clearly weren't.

Juliet tore out the front door and stared at the house numbers. "Shit."

"There's been a mistake." Melody's voice shook.

Juliet's heart raced. What was going on?

She ran to the corner, and Melody followed. Everything looked different—the cars, the houses, like something out of a movie that took place a little bit in the future.

She peered up at the street sign. "This is our street. This is our house."

"It's not ours." Melody sniffed. "Where's Mom? I want Mom."

"Let's go to the center and get some answers." They took off running and Juliet just couldn't shake the thought that something wasn't right.

When they got there, a coffee shop stood in place of the center. Her heart sank all the way to her feet.

"It's gone," Melody wailed.

Juliet hugged her sister. "Why don't we use their phone to call Mom?"

How long *had* they been gone?

They walked into the shop and the barista eyed them curiously. So did the other customers. Dread balled in her belly.

"Um, excuse me; can we use your phone? I lost mine and I need to call my mom. Please?" Juliet asked. Melody wrapped her arms around herself and sniffed.

"Sure," he wiped his hands on his apron. "Is everything okay? Should I call the police?"

She shook her head. "Really, it's okay."

He led them to the back and showed them to the phone.

Melody slumped against the wall, nose red.

She dialed her mom's familiar cell number. It rang and her heart skipped a beat. "Pick up, pick up," Juliet whispered.

"Hello?" The voice sounded . . . old, but at the same time, familiar.

"Mom?"

Melody's eyes widened.

"Who's this?" the voice demanded.

"Mom, it's me—Juliet—and Melody. We're sorry, we're so sorry." Tears streamed from her eyes. "Where are you? We just want to come home."

The party, being in trouble, none of that mattered anymore.

"I don't know who you think you are, but don't think I won't call the police," she snapped.

"But Mom, it's me, Juliet." Could she really be that mad?

"No it's not. My girls died thirty years ago. Now leave me alone."

The line went dead.

Her blood turned to ice as she turned to Melody.

Melody's green eyes widened. "Is she mad? How long were we gone?"

Juliet sunk to the ground as her world crashed down on her. It all made sense—the house, everything being future-like. Why should time in a magic world run the same? After all, it never did in the stories.

She buried her face in her hands. "Thirty years." The words barely made it past her lips. "We've been gone for thirty years."

– The End –

ONE FOR SORROW

One for sorrow,
Two for joy,
Three for a girl,
Four for a boy,
Five for silver,
Six for gold,
Seven for a secret,
Never to be told.

– Mother Goose

ONE FOR SORROW
Karen Mahoney

The first night the crow raps on my window with its hard beak, I have only just climbed into bed.

Tap-tap-tap.

Three times and then it waits, politely, staring in at me with hooded eyes.

Blink. *Tap-tap-tap.*

I don't open the window that first night, but it returns the next. And then again the next.

On the third night, I relent.

I slide open the window, just enough for the crow to slip beneath, and it hops inside. The cold air freezes my breath into ghosts as I struggle to close the window again, while my visitor watches from the cracked wooden sill beside me.

Claws click as it shuffles to the edge and scans my room with those beady eyes.

Shivering, I jump back into bed and pull the comforter right up to my chin. The crow spreads its inky wings and flutters onto one of the carved bedposts by my feet.

We regard each other, the crow and I.

What does it want? If this was a dream it would be able to speak, and I could find out why it was here. We could have a conversation, and maybe it would even teach me the language of crows.

But the crow is just a bird and it doesn't speak. It doesn't even squawk. It only perches at the end of my bed, blinking occasionally, watching me until I fall asleep.

***

The next morning, the crow has disappeared.

It was a dream, after all. The window is shut fast, and my bedroom door is closed. There is no way in or out for a creature without human hands.

Disappointment nips at my heart. Something magical has been taken away from me. If it was just a dream, then maybe that means magic doesn't exist—despite what my mother used to say.

But no matter the stories of my childhood, I know the truth: you can dream about magic, but dreams themselves aren't *real* magic.

That's when I find the black feather on the floor by the window.

So . . . *not* a dream, then.

My heart soars. I hold the feather reverently and twirl it between my fingers. I sniff it and it smells of licorice and the night sky. Winter sunlight from the window gleams cobalt blue along its fine edges, and I find myself wondering about the crow. Where did it come from? How could it leave my bedroom before I'd woken up? Where did it go, when it wasn't tapping at my window or perched at the foot of my bed?

It was a mystery.

It was magic.

I wait for the crow to come back the next night, but I fall asleep despite the strong coffee I forced myself to drink before going to bed. I wake suddenly in the morning, still bone tired and dying to use the bathroom. I search the window ledge outside my frosty window, hoping for signs of the crow. Clues. Another feather, perhaps, or a four-taloned footprint. *Anything.*

But nothing disturbs the smooth ice outside.

The next night I don't go to bed at all. I pull my small chair close to the window, curl up with a blanket and a book of poems by Edgar Allan Poe, and wait. The single black feather serves as my bookmark. Or a talisman.

Just before dawn, my vigil is rewarded. I hear the rush of wings as a silhouette passes the window, first one way and then the other. The shadow returns and settles on the narrow ledge. I can hear the scuffling clicks as the crow struggles for purchase in the thick layer of ice.

I fling off the blanket, run to the window, and open it. I take care not to spook my guest, and I can't help my secret smile when he hops inside.

He? Yes, I decide. *He.* It looks like a boy crow to me, though I can't say why.

He shakes out his fine wings and then glides to my dresser, landing on top of the mirror so that he can clean his frost-damp feathers. I glance down at the carpet, hoping he might have left me another gift, but the floor remains clear of his fine plumage. I pull my blanket back around my shoulders, shivering in the frigid air that hangs like mist in the room. I'd closed the window quickly, but the early morning air still lingers.

The crow watches me, his head cocked to one side, eyes unblinking. I take a tentative step forward, and then another. I glance at the photographs of my sister and me, and then back at my visitor. He shows no sign of fear, so I take heart and edge a little closer. I am afraid he will leave before I manage to unravel this mystery.

When I stand directly in front of the dresser, I look up at the top of the mirror and meet the bird's serious gaze.

I say, "Hello." I only feel slightly ridiculous.

The crow nods its head once, as though acknowledging my greeting.

"What do you want with me?" I ask.

He blinks.

"Can I help you at all?"

The crow flicks out his wings with a sharp *snap* that startles me. I take a quick step back.

He settles again, watching and waiting, eyes steady and bright, like two drops of polished coal.

I glance at his wicked claws and frown. *What is that?* There, on his left ankle . . .

Keeping my gaze on his I move forward again, hoping for a better view of the glint of metal I'd just seen. I wonder what might happen if I try to touch the crow? Would he fly away? Try to escape? Flap around my room, squawking and shedding feathers until I open the window and set him free?

I don't want him to be scared of me, so I resist the temptation to reach out.

He might attack me. Peck out my eyes, like in a movie I'd seen once upon a time.

Chills sprinkle along my spine. What a thought! The crow wouldn't hurt me.

My crow is a friend.

I get as close as I dare, so close that the dresser draws are pressed against my pajama-clad legs, and I look at the crow's left ankle. His gray, scaly skin reminds me of the many colorful pictures of dinosaurs that used to fascinate me when I was a child.

The metal winks as the crow stirs, and I gasp. I don't quite know what I had been expecting. Something romantic. A ring of finest gold, perhaps. Something out of a fairy tale or a nursery rhyme. Like the stories Mom used to tell us when we were very small.

Before the accident. Before she and Alice died.

Silver circles the crow's leg. It presses tight against the flesh, like a noose. There is no easy way to remove it. Not that I can see. There is a tiny loop of metal attached to the smooth edge, and threaded through that loop are three chain links. The final link is bent and partly open at one end.

It is as though my crow has broken the chain attached to the silver cuff around his ankle. Had he been a prisoner? And if he was a prisoner, who, then, had been his jailer?

Questions flutter around my mind, making me dizzy.

I glance up and meet those intelligent eyes. This time, he doesn't blink.

But *why* would someone keep a crow chained by its ankle? What's the point? Crows are hardly the sort of bird people would want to keep as pets. At least, not out here.

I try to imagine this crow—my crow—in a cage, attached to a little perch by that cruel manacle. Like a songbird, only with no song that most human ears would want to hear.

Before I realize quite what I am doing (or so I like to tell myself), I rest my finger against the tip of one of the crow's wings. His head whips around, sharp like his beak. Sharp like a claw. He makes a crow-sound, deep in his throat.

Caw! Caw!

A warning.

I pull back, ashamed rather than afraid. I hope the noise hasn't woken Stella. My father is away, which is a small comfort.

The crow shakes himself, ruffling those beautiful feathers for a moment before they settle again.

"I'm sorry," I say. "I didn't mean to offend you."

Who am *I* to touch this beautiful creature? Here I am, already thinking of him—it—as *my* crow. What's wrong with me? I have clearly lost my mind.

The crow closes his eyes, ignoring me.

I fold my blanket and lay it across the armchair by the window, then crawl into bed. The sun is just coming up and I don't think I will be able to sleep, no matter how tired I am, not with the crow sleeping in the room. I am too aware of him. I imagine I can hear his breathing, the beating of his tiny heart. The faint rustle of his wings.

But eventually, I do sleep. I fall into a nightmare that spirals down and down into darkness, like a narrow staircase. I dream of blood and decay and death. I dream of crows, too many to count, swarming around me like a black cloud.

A murder of crows.

***

Four hours later, my father's wife knocks at the door and pokes her head around it, tugging me from the lingering threads of the nightmare.

"Are you getting up today, Rose?"

My gaze immediately darts to the dresser, but there is no sign of the crow.

Stella leans against the door. "I know you don't have school, but you shouldn't keep staying up so late at night."

"I'm awake," I say, burrowing deeper under the covers.

"It looks like it," she replies, smiling. Stella's all right, considering. "I'll bring you a cup of tea. I just made a pot and it's still hot. That might help."

"Thanks." I stifle a yawn.

"I heard from your dad this morning."

"Good."

Her smile fades. "He sent his love."

Yeah, right, I think. "That's nice," I say.

She finally pulls the door shut, and I poke my head out from beneath the comforter. There is no sign of last night's visitor. No way could he have gotten out alone, not unless he can open a window with his beak.

I slide out of bed, shivering as my feet hit cold carpet, and pull the purple curtains aside. The fields stretch out for miles beneath the blue-white sky. Not for the first time, I wonder whatever possessed Stella to marry my father. She isn't cut out for farm life.

But then, neither am I.

I grab the blanket from the chair and shake it out. I stop as something flutters to the floor.

Another feather.

I scoop it up and cradle it in my hands. I know it must be my imagination, but I can almost swear it is still warm against my chilled fingers. This feather is even more handsome than the first, long and smooth and so black it shines ebony-bright.

I place it next to its twin between the pages of my book.

What does it mean? I try to figure out how the crow manages to escape my room. It's like one of those classic "locked room" mysteries that Poe himself was so fond of.

The only possible explanation is that my crow can disappear into thin air. In a puff of smoke, like magic. And, really, what kind of an explanation is that?

I think about it all day. I worry at it like one of our neighbor's dogs with a bone, trying to untangle *The Case of the Disappearing Crow.* While I help Stella with lunch, I imagine all kinds of wild scenarios. My favorite is the one where the crow turns into mist—like a vampire—and floats from my room through the tiny cracks along the window frame. Or perhaps beneath my door.

If it weren't for those two feathers, I would be convinced I had been dreaming all along.

But the feathers were *there.* I even ran upstairs to check.

I could hardly wait for night to fall.

That night, however, my crow doesn't return.

I wait and wait in the chair by the window. It is bitterly cold and I can't stop myself from worrying about the crow. Perhaps he is freezing somewhere. Alone and injured.

Perhaps whoever chained him in the first place has somehow recaptured him. He might be in a cage, unable to free himself this time.

He might be under a spell. A curse.

Maybe he's dead.

"No," I whisper, as I watch the window and pray. I haven't prayed since the day of the accident, seven years ago.

He will come tomorrow, I tell myself.

But he doesn't. Nor the next night, nor even the next.

The crow does not return, not even on Christmas night. Not on New Year's Eve.

"Everybody leaves," I say, as I study the fields and the sky, searching for a dark speck that will give me hope. I see something dart and flit wildly across the setting sun, and my heart soars—

Until I realize that it is just a lone bat, and I swallow disappointment sharp as a razor.

Another week passes, and school starts up again. The vacation with its magical visitor feels more and more dreamlike. A distant memory. It is as though my crow has flown away forever, and taken my hopes along with him.

Life falls back into familiar patterns. My father returns from the farming conference, so I spend more and more time in my room. I wish, not for the first time, that there is a lock on my door, but he removed it after Mom and Alice died all those years ago.

The thought crosses my mind that my life is not unlike the crow's. We are each, in our own way, prisoners—even though we come from very different worlds.

***

My heart is heavy when I take the bus along plowed roads, dirty snow piled like miniature mountains on either side as we rumble toward school. I press my forehead against the damp glass and watch my reflection. I try not to think about the crow. My gaze catches on a sign by the side of the railroad crossing: *Mind the Gap.* I touch my chest, where a new space has opened. This new fracture has settled alongside the others, one for my mother and one for Alice, my twin. My other self. And now, strangely—perhaps, inexplicably—for a crow.

I wrap my arms around my backpack and hold on as hard as I dare.

Inside it I have the book of poetry, with my two feathers tucked between the pages like secret love letters.

Throughout the day, Michelle keeps asking me how I am. I say "fine" so many times she gets annoyed. It's not like we're all that close, anyway. We just don't have any other friends, so we sort of got stuck with each other as freshmen. Three years later, we are still stuck. Neither of us fits in—at least not here, in our little community of farming families. I am like a walking wound, someone to be avoided at all costs. Michelle Okorafor, on the other hand, holds her head too high for someone who looks so different, and Nigeria might as well be on another planet. Together, we are like an old married couple who don't know what we would do if we didn't have each other.

It turns out Michelle is still upset that I didn't make it to her seventeenth-birthday dinner, the one she had with her family. At the time, I'd told her that Stella needed me to help out on the farm, what with my father being away. That usually keeps her quiet, although missing her birthday was probably a step too far—even for me. This time she was hurt. I should have felt guilty, but I had been numb for so long it was difficult for something as banal as guilt to register.

I just hadn't wanted to do anything during the vacation. The snow had fallen heavily, and I had a lot of homework.

And then there was the crow. At least his visits had made me feel *something*.

Michelle and I walk into last period together, that first day back at school, and all I can feel is relief that it's almost over. I got through the day. I wonder how I will make it through another day like this, and then another. What about the whole week? A month. A semester. Graduation seems so far away. How could I travel that far without wings? I sit in my usual seat by the window at the back. Michelle flops down next to me and immediately pulls out her cell phone, her quick fingers dancing across the keys. I rest my chin on my hand and gaze outside. It is already getting dark, so all I can really see is my own reflection: long brown hair falling in thick waves around my pale face and my serious grey eyes staring back at me.

I look beyond myself, watching the reflected classroom as my fellow students settle themselves at desks and pull books from their bags. I can see Richard Poole in the far corner, sitting with one of his regular cronies. I see Hanna Skarsgård take off her woolen hat and fluff out her flattened blonde curls.

My gaze shifts once more . . . and my eyes meet those of a stranger.

I stifle a gasp, instinct kicking in and saving me from more of Michelle's questions. Turning my head away from the black mirror that the window has become, I look across the classroom.

A new boy sits across the aisle from Michelle, but she is too busy texting with her little sister to notice. He is looking right back at me.

His scruffy hair is so black it shines cobalt blue beneath the lights. His eyes are dark and his face is almost as pale as mine.

He smiles at me.

My gaze flicks to Michelle, but she is still engrossed in her virtual conversation. I look at the strange boy again, wondering why my smile won't work. I must look sullen and stupid. I try to swallow away whatever is stuck in my throat, but even that doesn't help.

Mrs. Brennan strides into the classroom and bangs the door behind her.

"Sorry I'm late," she says, holding up a sheaf of papers. "It seems we have a new student with us today."

All the muttered and not-so-muttered conversations stop. Even Michelle puts down her phone and glances around the room, finally realizing she is sitting across the aisle from the new kid.

The scruffy-haired boy is now the center of attention. He doesn't look too happy about this, but he leans back in his chair and accepts our assessment of him.

"Let's welcome—" Here, Mrs. Brennan stops to adjust her glasses and consult her paperwork. "James Vanderveer."

We all watch James Vanderveer like he belongs to a fascinating new species.

All except me. I watch him for an entirely different reason. I can't take my eyes off him, not even for a second. Not because I think he is beautiful—which I do—and not even because he is new and different, someone to brighten up an ordinary, dull day at school. Which he is.

I cannot take my eyes off him because I know who he is. I know it, deep inside me, even as my logical brain tells my crazy heart to get a grip. This is . . . impossible. Crows don't turn into boys so they can attend high school. That's not how real life works.

But perhaps my life has become something else. Perhaps magic *is* real in a world where lonely crows visit human girls at home on winter mornings.

James tilts his chair back, and I see that he is wearing black jeans and heavy boots. He looks tough, like he can take care of himself. The leather of his jacket is cracked and comfortable-looking. He seems a little wild, a little bit *Rebel Without a Cause*, and my heart beats faster than it has in a long time. He tilts his head to one side and meets my eyes. His are so black they are like two pieces of coal. I know I should be afraid of the intense expression on his face, and yet I am not. Maybe it's for the same reason he wasn't afraid of *me* after I let him into my bedroom. When he had been nothing more than a bird.

Mrs. Brennan's voice drones on. Something about how Mr. Vanderveer's application got mixed up, and his family thought he was starting the next day. That's why he was so late to school today. But after that explanation, my mind drifts away from the class and all I can do is wait for the lesson to end. Not long, I tell myself. Not long.

I watch the clock. I tap my foot. I sneak glances at the boy-crow and hope Michelle hasn't noticed how weird I am acting. I chew the end of my pencil and pretend to focus on world history, while instead I am focusing on James Vanderveer's hands as he turns the pages of the textbook somebody gave him.

A flash of light catches my attention and I stare. Even though I already knew, this confirmation makes my stomach clench. I blink and look again.

He is wearing a silver ring, like a miniature cuff, on the little finger of his left hand.

There is a noise in my ears, like the *whoosh* of the train as the school bus waits by the tracks. I think I might faint, even though I am sitting down. My head feels all tingly.

"Miss Crawford, are you unwell?"

Mrs. Brennan is leaning over my desk, and Michelle is watching me with genuine concern.

James is standing behind our teacher, and I wonder

when he appeared there because I don't remember him moving. I cannot read the expression on his face.

"I'm fine," I say. "I think I didn't eat enough, that's all."

There is more clucking and mother-hen behavior from Mrs. Brennan, and in the end I have to accept a slip from her so I can visit the nurse, just to stop her fussing.

"Michelle," our teacher says, "if you could go with—"

"I'll go," James Vanderveer says. He speaks in such a way as to make it clear there will be no argument. The decision has been made.

Michelle stares at him, open-mouthed, and I wonder if she will dare to contradict him.

James stares back, his eyes like a storm in the calm planes of his face.

My friend closes her mouth.

Mrs. Brennan frowns, but that is the extent of her dissent. "Very well. Off you go then."

I grab my bag and cram books and pencils inside with shaking hands. My fingers touch one of the feathers and I shiver. I don't look at Michelle as I leave the room. I don't look at anybody. I watch my feet on the floor, and the only thing I am aware of is James as he walks beside me and opens the door.

He gestures me out into the corridor ahead of him, but he stands so that I have no choice but to brush against him.

When our arms touch, an image flashes into my mind, clear as a winter sky over the fields: *the room is small and bare, apart from a cage swinging gently from a hook in the stone ceiling. The cage is made from dull metal, curved into claws that grip the base. I cannot see a door, but there must be one somewhere, for otherwise how would the cage's occupant get in— or out? There is a narrow perch welded between the bars of the cage, with a silver chain attached to it. And attached to that is a crow—*

My crow—the boy who, even now, is looking down at me with an animal's eyes in a human face.

I stumble into the corridor, disoriented, my heart pounding a rhythm that threatens to drive me to my knees. I lean against the wall and breathe, in and out, trying to figure out what just happened.

James regards me from a distance. He doesn't try to touch me again—perhaps he knows better. I am relieved and disappointed all once. And then I am irritated with myself for wanting his touch when I don't even know him and am not even sure I'd like him if I did. I'm not sure of anything. He might not even be *real*. Perhaps I have lost my mind at last, and this is some kind of super-delayed PTSD.

Without needing to discuss it, we leave the school. I crumple the permission slip and drop it into a bin outside. The cold air hits my face, makes my eyes water, and I immediately feel better. I don't need a nurse. I don't know what I *do* need, but it's nothing they can offer me here.

I slide behind the bicycle rack and push my way along one of the many utility blocks at the edge of the school grounds. James follows me, walking quickly and quietly as we move through the jagged bushes that have grown in the narrow space. I stop and turn to face him, alone with this boy who is strangely familiar and utterly alien.

"You're . . . I . . ." I can't even get the words out. What are you supposed to say to someone who shouldn't exist in the world we know? Our safe, familiar world.

Safe? I can't help laughing at that. What's so harmless about a world that takes away the people you love the most? What is so damn safe about a world that rips you into pieces and then expects you to get through life with only half a heart?

James touches my face with his hand, the hand with the pinky ring that might once have been a shackle. I feel the cool silver kiss my cheek and wish it was this untamed boy's lips instead.

I feel the blush spread all the way from my neck to my forehead. What am I thinking? This is surreal, crazy, messed *up*. Wrong?

I don't want it to be wrong. I gaze into his eyes and see a kindred spirit hiding in those shadowy pools.

"Wait," I say. I push his hand down and step back. "Just . . . wait a minute."

He nods. He waits.

I take a deep breath, trembling as I let it out. "James Vanderveer. That's really your name?"

"It's the name she gave me." His voice is low and husky, almost as though he doesn't use it often. He sounds older than seventeen.

"Who do you mean? Your mother?"

"Nah," he says. He kicks a stone by his boot. "The witch."

He talks differently from the others around these parts. He doesn't belong any more than I do, but for reasons I don't quite understand. Not yet.

But I intend to.

I reach out and rest my fingers against the back of his left hand. I make sure not to touch the ring, but I want to. I want to know what it is, who put it there, what power it holds over James Vanderveer.

He watches me, but doesn't move away. Something in his expression dares me to do more, so I run my fingers across his hand until they stop at the cuff of his leather jacket. I imagine sparks where our skin comes into contact.

James grabs me with his other hand, too fast for me to stop him. I hardly see the movement, just a blur and then his fist is gripping my hip, and he drags me toward him until our bodies touch. His fingers curl into one of the belt loops on my jeans, twisting until I have to press myself against him.

There are no visions in my head this time, just a delicious blankness that makes me feel like an untethered balloon.

All this time, his left hand doesn't move, and I've wrapped my fingers around his wrist without even realizing it. I am looking directly into his face, pale and savage, with strong features that make him look more *other* than I know what to do with. He dips his head to mine slowly, so slow, giving me plenty of time to push him away. He is testing me, challenging me to be the one to say no.

Well then, I think with a secret smile. He doesn't know me. Maybe nobody does, not anymore. Not since Alice.

I tug his left hand forward and place it firmly on my other hip. Now I am trapped in the circle of his arms, and I wrap mine around his neck, reaching up on tiptoe and swaying against his chest.

I catch a glimpse of a feral smile as his lips clamp down on mine, and the world stops turning as I take him in.

This boy I don't even know, is holding me against his lean body and running his tongue along the seam of my mouth, encouraging me to kiss him back. I freeze, just for a moment, not because I don't want this, but because I am *savoring* it. Enjoying the warmth of him, the smell of him. He tastes of licorice and the night sky, and I don't want him to stop. Not ever.

Mind the gap, I think, before stepping over the edge. I kiss him with everything I've got: all of my loneliness and rage and pain. I pour it all into James as he meets my passion with his own. I let him touch me in places I've never been touched before. I am dizzy, drunk. I feel as though I am flying as he moves his mouth against mine in a kiss that lasts a thousand years. My toes curl inside my heavy winter boots.

When he finally comes up for air, I'm still clinging to him because my legs are as mushy as horse feed. My lips tingle, and I imagine I can still feel his fingers beneath my shirt. I want him to kiss me again, to touch me again. I grab his face between my hands and pull him toward me.

He laughs and nuzzles my neck. I sigh, content.

He pulls away, and this time I let him. We leave the school and run across a nearby field just as the sun goes down. James follows me without question, his intelligent eyes darting around and taking everything in. He's a fascinating combination of hyper-aware and laid back.

We creep into Mr. Forester's barn, climb the tall wooden ladder, and hide ourselves in the hayloft. I don't want to go home. I'll be in trouble as it is, what with how late I'll be and how I didn't call Stella. I try to tell myself she won't be worried about me, but I know that's not true. She cares, in her own way, but it can never be enough for me. How can she possibly fill the holes in my heart? Nobody can.

I look at James and wonder if that could change. I never used to think of myself as a romantic, but this . . . this is something else. If magic is real, then maybe there really *can* be a magical connection between people. Especially when one of them can change his shape and fly.

Anything is possible, I tell myself. You just have to hold on and believe.

So that's what I do. I hold on to James's hand and we talk, sharing our lives and our scars. When two lonely people connect, the sun shines even at night. I feel warm all the way through, despite the winter air creeping into the barn like a secret—like the secrets we exchange in low tones. We pass them back and forth between us, each tentatively revealed truth like a piece of brightly colored glass.

I tell James about Mom and Alice. I tell him, my voice barely above a whisper, about the accident on the old railroad, seven years before the new crossing was finally built last summer. Too late for my family. *Mind the gap*, I think, before showing him the empty spaces in my heart. I like him even more when he doesn't suggest ways of fixing me.

He just listens and holds my hand until it is his turn to share.

James tells me about how he was born different from most people. His clan originates from the mountains, but now they try to live among human beings and pass for "normal." There aren't many of them left—the Crow People, he calls them. Men and women who can change their shape, grow feathers and wings, who can take to the sky and soar above the world.

Even though I believe him, it still makes me shiver to hear him say it in that straightforward way he has.

And then he tells me about the witch and the curse, and I am shivering for an entirely different reason. He puts his arm around me, pulls me close, and we listen to the night calls of the farm beyond our perch.

I glance at the silver ring on his little finger, the

ring that holds the key to his freedom. He sees what I'm staring at and clenches his hand into a fist, hiding it from me.

I remember the rawness in his voice when he told me about the death of his own family—a bad death at the hands of an ambitious witch. *A murder of crows.* I want to help this strange boy so very much. Maybe one of us can find a happy ending.

"Tell me more about this curse."

"I told you all of it. I can't take the ring off. Believe me, I've tried."

"Let *me* try," I say, stubborn.

He shakes his head. "Nobody can help me, Rose."

"You've given up?" I can't help the note of anger that creeps into my voice.

"There's nothing or nobody can get this ring off a me," he says. "No how. No way."

I meet his black eyes. "Nevermore?"

His lips twist into something resembling a smile. "Something like that, yeah."

"Wait," I say. I push up onto my knees, ignoring the scratchy hay as I lean toward him. "There is always a way."

"There ain't. What's done is done."

The witch took him home with her, kept him in a cage, treated him like a pet. The silver manacle around his crow-form's ankle was attached to a chain, and it was charmed to keep him trapped as a bird. Sometimes she would let him out, force him to change into a boy, watching feathers give way to flesh, until he stood naked before her. She made him take her name— Vanderveer—and told him he could be her son.

"Only," he says, looking down at the ground, "I don't think a mother should touch her son the way she touched me."

I dig my nails into my palms, wanting to use them against *her*. The woman who enslaved this boy. Who treated him like he was nothing. Used him.

He escaped, though. Eventually. The witch, it seems, is a busy woman, with other schemes to concoct. While she was away—on a business trip to Europe—James managed to peck through his chains, pick the lock of the cage door with his beak, and fly to freedom. But the cuff was still around his ankle, and that was why a crow had come tapping at my window one cold winter night.

The witch found him and caught him again, though. That explained his disappearance after those first nights we shared.

"She punished me," he says. "Fixed it so I'm stuck in one shape. And the worst part of it . . ." His voice trails off and he shakes his head.

I bury my face in his neck, snuggle as close as I can. "What?" I ask him. "Tell me what she did to you."

"She made me choose," he says, softly.

I breathe in his warm scent. "I don't understand."

"Said I can stay human or crow, but can't be both. Not ever again."

"You chose human," I whisper, pulling back to look into his eyes.

He strokes my cheek. "Yeah, I guess I did."

"And then you escaped again?"

"Nah, she's keeping tabs on me." He holds up his hand and the ring flashes.

"What would happen if we *could* get it off?" My mind is racing again, looking for possibilities.

He sighs. "I don't know. Not sure I *want* to know."

I'm suddenly not sure whether I want to find out, either. This way, at least he can be human—with me. I shake my head at how selfish I can be. I want to be a better person, so I listen to what he says next.

"In this shape, like *this*," he continues, "I'm only half a person."

I nod, thinking of Alice. My other half.

He leans his head against a bale of hay, stares up at the roof. "My heart . . . it don't feel right, you know?"

"I know," I say.

"Sometimes, it feels like I'm dyin' inside."

"Yes," I whisper.

We sit, holding each other for a long time. I still want to kiss him, but it's just a passing thought now. A feeling that comes and goes, like watching fireflies in the fields at night. There is more at stake here than kisses. More, even, than love.

Later, he reaches inside one of his boots and pulls out a pocketknife. I'm not scared of him. I know the knife is not for me.

"You asked me earlier how I tried to get the ring off."

I swallow. I know what's coming.

James pulls out the blade. It is long and sharp.

"I cut off my finger," he says, conversationally. "But even then, the ring stayed on."

Nausea churns in my stomach. I can't say anything, but I don't need to.

"An' then my finger grew back and the ring was just . . . *there*."

He stares at his finger in disbelief, almost as though he is reliving the moment when his severed limb regenerated before his eyes. He put himself through all that fear—all that pain—for nothing. Could I do that? *Would* I do that? Losing a little finger would be bad, but maybe not as awful as a thumb. I try to imagine what it must have been like, to feel the blade biting into skin and bone.

I push those thoughts away and find my voice. "What did *she* do? The witch, I mean. When she found out what you'd done."

He laughs, a terrible sound that reminds me of a crow's call. "She made me clean up the mess I'd made. I even had to put my own finger in the trash."

I think I might vomit, but I hold it in by taking deep breaths. Slow breaths.

"I was thinking," he says without looking at me, "that maybe there *is* something we can do, after all. Maybe it didn't work before because it needs to be someone else who does the cutting."

"I . . . what?" I am almost more surprised by the fact that he has actually strung two full sentences together, rather than shocked at *what* he's suggesting.

Although of course, that does shock me. I try to pretend that I don't understand him, but he is not fooled.

"You heard me, Rose." Now he looks at me with something close to desperation on his face. "Meeting you is a sign of . . . something. You could take the knife and—"

"You have no way of knowing that will work!" I am standing over him, and I don't remember how I got there.

He pushes himself to his feet, towering over me in turn. "And you don't know that it won't."

I shake my head, trying to think of a decent argument. I come up with nothing.

James holds my shoulders, makes me look at him. "A while ago, you was tellin' me how there's always a way. Well, maybe this is the way."

"I can't do that. I just . . . can't."

"The curse is on me—or maybe just the ring. Might be that it takes another person, someone *apart* from the magic, to break it."

It is a good theory, but that's all it is. I can't cut off his *finger!* How do you do something like that to another person?

But he is pressing the knife into my hand. "Take it, Rose. All my family are gone, so I ain't got nothin' else to lose." His eyes glitter. "You're my only friend. I'm beggin' you to do this for me."

"James, I—"

"Don't tell me you can't. Don't you do that," he says, almost shouting.

"Shhh!" I look around guiltily, suddenly aware that it is late and we are alone in my neighbor's barn. "You'll wake the dogs."

He folds my fingers around the cool handle of the pocketknife. "Just do it fast. It's sharp as talons, I made sure of that."

I glare at him, trying to hide behind anger. "You planned this all along! You knew you were going to ask me to do this; that's why you followed me to my school."

"Nah, that was her. The witch. She made me enroll so I can graduate. She wants me *educated.*" He snorts.

"I don't want to do it," I say.

"I know you don't," he replies. Now his voice is gentle, and his eyes have returned to their familiar blackness. "But I'm askin' you, all the same."

I bite the inside of my cheek, tasting copper. I wonder how much blood will flow from his finger when I slice it off.

That's when I know I'm going to do it. I pull back my shoulders and meet his eyes. He looks scared, like he saw my decision on my face the very moment I made it, but he crouches down and lays his hand on the wooden floorboards of the loft. The silver ring gloats at me as it shimmers in the shadows cast by his body.

I squat beside him, touch his feathery hair quickly with my free hand, before setting to work with the knife.

The second before I sever his pinky, James touches my shoulder. My heart slams into my ribs, and I just stop myself from cutting in time.

"What?" I hiss.

"I'm sorry," he says.

"*You're* sorry?" I shake my head. "You're crazy."

His lips quirk. "Yeah. Been told that before."

I choose that moment to slice all the way down, through the base of his finger just behind the cursed ring. I have to press both hands on the knife's handle and lean all of my weight on it to break the bone.

I try to pretend I can't hear the sound it makes.

The ring falls and rolls toward a gap in the floorboards. There is no time to think about the bloody finger, or to remember James's shout of pain. I drop the pocketknife and throw myself after the ring. I manage to grab it before it disappears.

I sob with relief when my fingers close around it. The silver is warm, and I wonder if it is because of the magic or because James was wearing it until moments ago. I open my hand and stare at the smooth silver resting in the center of my palm. It is speckled, like an egg. Fresh blood rubs off on my skin.

Another cry brings me back around, but James has disappeared in a rush of feathers. He flaps his wings and lands on my shoulder. I look down at his crow feet, and am not surprised to see that one talon is missing.

We've broken the curse, but at what cost?

"You're a crow," I manage to say.

He cocks his head, listening. If he was human right now, I think he would be smiling at my ability to state the obvious.

My lip trembles and I try hard not to cry. When I feel hot tears running down my cheeks, I know I have not been successful. He's a crow again. It didn't work, not in the way we hoped.

He cannot turn back into human; I know this without needing to be told. The curse is broken and he is free of the witch, but now he is trapped in his *other* form. The one he didn't choose.

And I am alone again.

I feel my crow settle onto my shoulder.. His talons dig into my collarbone, but I don't mind. He presses his sleek feathers against my cheek, as though trying to offer comfort. For some reason this makes me cry harder.

Perhaps I could try melting the ring in a furnace. I shake my head. I know it's hopeless. I have visions of it magically reforming before my eyes.

And then I have another thought. A crazy thought.

The ring grows cool in my hand as I think it through. More time passes, and I can make out the first slivers of dawn sliding through the cracks in the barn roof. What do I have to lose? There is Stella, but she is my father's wife. She's not my mother. And Michelle. But she'll be graduating this year, anyway. She can finally get out of this small-minded community, travel, see the world. I think of my father.

Nobody would miss me.

I close my eyes and slide the ring onto the middle finger of my left hand. Intuitively, I know that it will fit.

Crow-James cries out, but he cannot stop me.

Caw! Caw!

Bet you didn't see that coming, I think, smiling to myself.

Flesh melts away. Bones reshape themselves and shrink. Feathers, blue-black and shining, flow across my body as I change into something new and wonderful for the first time in my life.

My last human thought is: *Alice.*

My first crow thought is: *Two for joy.*

We spread our wings, and fly.

– The End –

THE GIRLS AND THE BIRDS

When I was a little girl, about seven years old,
I hadn't got a petticoat, to cover me from the cold.

So I went into Darlington, that pretty little town,
And there I bought a petticoat, a cloak, and a gown.

I went into the woods and built me a kirk,
And all the birds of the air, they helped me to work.

The hawk with his long claws pulled down the stone,
The dove with her rough bill brought me them home.

The parrot was the clergyman, the peacock was the
clerk,
The bullfinch played the organ, we made merry work.
– Mother Goose

THOSE WHO WHISPER
Lisa Mantchev

They cast me out of the village the day my mother died. When they tore me from her body, I fought, kicking and scratching, fierce in my grief. A stinging slap to the face startled me. The second left my ears ringing.

The rough hands belonged to the blacksmith. He drank wine all day and punished his wife by night. That's what the birds told me, anyway.

"We'll have no more o' that now," he said.

The raven on the windowsill didn't approve of such rough manners. She took to the sky with a loud "caw!" that echoed off the stones around us. My hand reached for Mama but only managed to grasp one of the pennies weighing down her eyelids.

"Give her t' other coin as well." That was the woman who spent her early morning hours baking pies for the school children. When the birds spoke of her wares, they told tales of cat meat and sawdust. "It's all she has in the world."

"More than she deserves." The storekeeper shoved the second penny into my hand. The birds didn't have to tell me that he sneaked his thumb on the scales whenever he weighed out flour and salt; I'd seen that for myself.

"The second death in as many days," the pie woman mused as we exited the cottage. She wore her discomfort like the prickles on the blackberry vines. Yesterday, the miller's daughter had been found, drowned in the pond. "There's something at work here."

"Devil's child." A chorus of spitting followed that one, a ward against evil, but no one would meet my gaze save the blacksmith's son, Ayden. A ragged urchin of a child a few years older than I, he had the greenest eyes I'd ever seen. When he caught me looking at him, he turned tail and ran back to the forge.

The two largest of the villagers wasted no time after that, carrying me to the outskirts of the town. The others had rope and rocks and harsh words, though they were nothing I hadn't heard before. I let it flow over me like the water in the creek bed.

Mama was gone, never to come back. We'd no other family save each other, and for seven years, that had been more than enough. She sold one set of herbs by sunlight at the market and the other by moonlight out the back door of our cottage, enough to put food on the table. Our arms were never empty, wrapped about each other at night. That morning, I'd gone to pick what berries I could reach from the hedge. Returning, I'd found her pale and lifeless, as stiff as a fallen bird, her skin as soft as feathers ruffled by a wind.

Our presence was barely tolerated as it was; now that Mama was gone, I was to be rooted out, a weed from a flower garden. At the stone mile marker, the blacksmith set me down in the dust. The birds watched from the trees overhead.

"Go quietly," the meat pie woman advised, "and

don't come back. It'll go worse for you if you come back." As one, they left. No one glanced over their shoulder; to do so would bring grave misfortune upon them.

I stood there, a rock digging into my bare foot, until I was quite alone on the road. My hands opened like two flowers in the sun, and two pennies winked at me in the light. The pearl-plumed dove alighted on my shoulder and offered a soft coo of comfort in my ear.

"Of course," she said next, "you'll need something warm to wear, Little One."

I looked down at my dress. It was threadbare with washing, but it had been clean when I'd put it on that morning. Darned in a dozen places, but with such skill that you'd have to be told to know it. It had been Mama's, the last of her scent clinging to it like a mother's arms.

"Right then," I said, turning my nose north. "To Darlington."

It took the better part of a day to reach the town. It was leaps and bounds larger than our village, the roads paved with stone, the buildings of brick and wood. It wasn't for me; I knew that before I smelled the coal fires or saw the brightly clothed children heading for the schoolhouse. Skirting a low rock wall, I chanced upon an untended laundry line. There was a plain petticoat that fit. A cloak hanging next to it was the darkest of greens, far too long for me, but heavy and warm. I left the coins pinned to the line as payment.

It was easy to disappear into the forest. Almost at once, I felt I was merely another leaf growing on the trees. When I sat, I was no more than a clump of moss on the shaggy log. When hunger found me, there were berries and nuts and mushrooms enough to turn it back. The dove helped, flitting from branch to branch, showing me the best path through the brambles.

When we came into the clearing, I reached for the first stone.

***

The hawk rode my wrist, preening over her kills. As well she should; the fat brace of rabbits I carried in the other hand would fill all our bellies that night and beyond. Though the leaves had not yet turned, the number of nuts the squirrels had stored promised the leanest of winters. The stone building where the birds and I had sheltered these ten years held up against the fiercest storms, but I'd learned the starving way to lay in enough food and wood in the autumn months.

Luckily enough, I had my mother's trick with herbs. I pulled them from their wild beds and sold them in Darlington during the summer. Copper pennies accumulated in an old leather bag I kept hidden in the owl's tree, and the rest of my hours were spent berrying and hunting, drying food over small, smoky fires, and waiting for the snow to arrive. Weeks would pass in which I didn't speak to a living soul that wasn't feathered. I had little use for the pale town's creatures who requested my wares in whispers, the ones who scuttled away from my stall like black beetles. I sometimes imagined the birds scooping them up and gobbling them down, crunching through their gaily colored carapaces.

As for myself, I dressed in gray, but the woolen cloak I'd taken years ago off the laundry line was still the darkest of greens. Mossy embroidery grew along the hem now. I'd lined it with tiny down feathers donated by my friends. When I walked, it rustled like wings. Reason enough for the villagers to whisper.

Reason enough to cross the road when they saw me coming.

"That's the Wild One," mothers would whisper to their children. "She's more animal than child."

And perhaps I was. Perhaps one day I would step back into the forest and my feet would take root in the dirt and my arms would reach up to the heavens and leaves would sprout from my fingertips. It wouldn't be a bad way to spend a few hundred years. At least then, I'd have a bit of rest. But that wasn't to be my lot today. The moment I got back, I needed to skin these small sacrifices, prepare the meat, clean my hunting knife—

I drew up short the moment I entered the clearing. There was an odd bundle collapsed upon the gray flagstone threshold. A filthy arm reached for the door, but several inches separated fingertips from wood. The birds sat atop the roof of my sanctuary, unnaturally silent witnesses to this strange scene.

There is nothing quite as unsettling as a large gathering of very quiet birds.

In agreement and in warning, the hawk dug her claws into my leather glove. "Take care, my pet."

"Tsh." Though I soothed her, I set down the rabbits and pulled out my knife as I approached.

The stranger saved me the trouble of jabbing it in the backside. With a groan, the heap of rags rolled over, revealing its owner: a young man who'd come up on the wrong side of some coin. Both his eyes were swollen shut and encrusted with blood. His mouth was a ragged gash in his face. I could have ended his misery, slit his throat from ear to ear, but I only ever killed what I was going to eat.

"What are you doing here?"

The raven on the roof echoed my query in his raspy, black-feathered voice.

Filthy hands sought out the hem of my cloak. "Water?"

Loathe to let him enter my sanctuary, I wavered a moment. When the dove trilled a plea for mercy, it reminded me of a day long past, a day in which a friendly hand might have been welcome. Stepping over the rag-man, I retrieved the bucket by the hearth and dipped up a tin cup. Returning to my guest, I pressed the cup to his cracked lips.

He drank greedily, water sluicing down either side of his face like two muddy creek beds. When he was done, he managed a lopsided smile. "My thanks."

Uncertain what to do with his unexpectedly charming manners, I retreated a step and repeated my question. "What are you doing here?"

"Escaping hell," was his quiet answer. "My dad's beaten me for the last time."

"Ah." Dipping the oldest scrap of linen I owned into the bucket, I approached with caution. "Your father did this?"

"And more." He winced when I pressed the rag to his face, but didn't protest. The worst of it cleared away, the boy managed to open his eyes; they were the vivid green of lichen in unexpected sunshine.

The dove cooed in recognition. "That's the blacksmith's son."

The other birds nodded and dipped their heads. "The blacksmith's son."

"His son—" It sounded like the bullfinch wanted to say more, but the peacock stopped her with a nip of her beak.

The lad looked up at me and blinked. "Sida?"

It had been ten years since someone had last called me by name. I had to remember the way of answering to it. "Yes. And you're Ayden."

A long moment passed between us, and it was as though cottages popped up around us like wild mushrooms, the memory of smoke and pig slops and shit drifting through the clearing. I cast it all away from me as I would the guts from the rabbits. "Where will you go?"

"To the water." When he ducked his head, grubby locks of hair fell into his swollen eyes. "I'll find a ship and sail for the islands. You can gather the gold dust off the beaches by the handfuls."

"You've never been on the water before." I don't know why I offered the argument. It's not like I wanted him to stay. If an animal wasn't going to hunt for me or scavenge seeds for me or tell me where the ripest of the blueberries were to be found, I had no use for it whatsoever.

"I'll learn," Ayden said with a fierce scowl. "And I'm strong enough to lift whatever they like."

That bit was at least true. The muscles of his arms couldn't have belonged to anyone except a man who hammered metal into subservience. "You've been doing your father's work."

"For the last three years. When he hasn't been sleeping, he's been piss-drunk, not fit for anything but raging and rutting."

"What will he do without you?"

"Starve, most likely." When Ayden shrugged, though, he winced again.

"What's wrong?" My concern surprised me; I should have been showing him to the road by now.

"My wrist. I think he broke it."

Reaching for the rabbits, I made my mind up about something without consulting the birds. "You can't lift-and-carry on a ship with a broken wrist. You'll have to stay here until it mends."

"I can't do that." He looked about. Reflected in his eyes, I could see the rough way I'd been scratching out a living. "You're barely keeping yourself alive out here."

The birds laughed at him then, filling the clearing with raucous jeers.

"We manage better than you think," I said. "And you can earn your keep, never fear. Even with only one good arm, I think we'll find use for you."

***

Ayden proved his worth within the first week, chopping wood and fetching water and dragging fallen limbs into the clearing while I was out hunting with the hawk. The birds kept a wary eye on him as he cleared out the cotes and spread clean, dry grass on the floors and brought back blackberries by the bucketful and caught a string of fish with only a hook and a prayer; in seven days, he'd earned their respect and my own. Evenings were spent outdoors in the pleasant, late-summer twilight. I used my voice more then than I had in all the years since leaving the village.

Never reminiscing, though. Neither of us wasted words on the past.

Thinking he would need it aboard a ship, I taught him the constellations. I had my own names for them, my own stories: an egg sitting upon a wall; a brother and sister traipsing up a hill; the mouse running down the face of a grandfather clock.

We decided he couldn't leave until he could climb a tree as he would the rigging on a merchant vessel. Sooner than expected, the day arrived when I woke to hear him patching the roof of my sanctuary. I knew his wrist must be nearly healed. The autumn was gone;

winter decorated everything with hoarfrost. I lay abed far longer than I ought, listening to the sound of Ayden's merry whistling.

I didn't cry, whatever else the birds might tell you.

Over our breakfast of thick porridge and nuts, I kept my gaze to the table. "It's the last market day of the season."

"Aye?" Mouth full, that's all he could manage.

It will be better when he's gone. He eats enough for three.

Though he works more than six.

I sighed into my water cup. "Will you come with me or stay here?"

"Better to stay," he said, shifting upon his rough seat. "Someone might recognize me there and carry word back."

I nodded. Burdened by something more than the straw packs full of herbs, I found the walk to Darlington longer than usual. Thorns reached out to claw at my ankles. Plagued by errant winds, the trees murmured their unease. I set up my stall with less care than usual. When I wished myself home, I followed that with inward curses.

You'll be sorrier still when he leaves.

The thought was as heavy as a stone sitting upon my heart. I watched them pass by: the baker who over-salted the porridge so his children would eat less of it; the schoolmaster who cried o' nights, taking the whipping switch to his own back. My next customer was the magistrate's wife. The birds had little to say about her, other than she spent money she could ill-afford upon hats decorated with the feathers of their fallen comrades. I counted out her change and wrapped her rosemary in brown paper. I couldn't manage a smile or thanks, and she marched off in a huff.

"Ungrateful girl," she cast over her shoulder, grand plumes waving in a sudden wind.

And I was. Sullen and eyes downcast, I was unprepared for the flapping of frantic wings. The hawk and the dove circled the marketplace, crying out to me.

"Stranger! There's a stranger headed for the clearing!"

I abandoned the herbs and money upon the table and ran for home. My heart pounded, a hammer upon an anvil, and my cloak streaming out behind me almost lifted me from my feet. Without thinking, I pulled my hunting knife from its sheath. Though I wanted to fly in, claws outstretched, I forced myself to approach with stealth.

The blacksmith was a ragged excuse of a man, but he still had strength and fury enough to choke the life from his son. Ayden was on his knees before him, red-faced and struggling to breathe.

"Ingrate," his father spat. "Snot-nosed toerag. You'll not run away from me again—"

My knife found the soft spot alongside of the blacksmith's neck before he could finish the next ugly accusation. "Let him go."

It took longer than I would have liked. When Ayden fell forward into the leaves, he didn't move. So very still. I was reminded of my mother, dead on the hearth.

The blacksmith slowly turned to face me. He narrowed his eyes—the color of mud, not moss—and snorted. "Who do you think you are?"

I didn't owe him my name. "Leave this place and don't look back. It's bad luck to look back."

"This is the king's forest," he said with all the bluster and blow of a spring storm. "You're trespassing here." His gaze drifted to the drying racks. "And poaching, by the looks of it."

"Everything here is mine." I never let my knife waver. "Given to me by tree and bird."

"Mad talk!" The blacksmith looked into the trees, noting the presence of the hawk and the dove, the peacock and the bullfinch. "You . . . you're the herb woman's whelp. The one we put out of the village all those years ago."

The hawk landed on my shoulder. "He killed his wife."

The dove trilled in agreement. "She was going to leave him."

Before the peacock could silence her again, the bullfinch screeched out, "He killed the miller's daughter all those years ago! Drowned her in the pond! We told your mother . . . she knew. She knew."

She knew. The birds had told her. And the blacksmith had killed her for it.

The blacksmith somehow knew that I now possessed the darkest of his secrets. "So they've told you. Nattering pests. I should have wrung their necks."

And yours. He didn't have to say it; I saw it in his eyes.

I loosed the hawk upon him, let him take those murderous eyes with her claws. He went down with a scream, and I followed the noise to the ground, my cloak rustling like wings. The whispers had been right; I was more animal than child when I cast aside my knife and tore open his softest parts and pulled flesh from bones. My claws shone with blood and soft sunlight. His cries were like music, fading like a violin after a long, last note.

A glance at Ayden revealed that his chest yet moved with the shallowest of breaths. Before he could wake, I dragged the blacksmith's body into the tiny stone sanctuary. Without caw or comment, the birds helped me pull the stones down upon him. When the cairn was done, I pulled the leather pouch of coins from the owl's tree. Ayden groaned and rolled over as I approached him, his eyes yet closed but his mouth twisted into a grimace. Kneeling in the leaves, my bloodstained fingers pressed the money into his open palm. One step back, and then another. Only a few more and I'd step out of the clearing, never to return . . .

"Don't fly away without me, little bird." Though Ayden's voice was no more than a rasp, he staggered to his feet.

"I'm no fit companion for you," I said hoarsely. "For anyone. Your father is dead by my hands." I jerked my chin at the cairn.

Not a glance did Ayden spare for the heap of stones that had played hearth and home to us these last few weeks. When he took my hand, he didn't flinch away from the blood crusted under my nails. "No daughter of the village need fear him now."

I let my fingers twine through his, thinking them like jesses put upon a hunting bird. I might fly far and fast, but I'd return to him, wherever that might be. "To the golden sands, then."

We quit the clearing with the birds flying ahead as the first flakes of snow started to fall.

– The End –

LITTLE MISS MUFFET

Little Miss Muffet, sat on a tuffet,
Eating her curds and whey;
Along came a spider,
Who sat down beside her,
And frightened Miss Muffet away.
– Mother Goose

LITTLE MISS MUFFET
Georgia McBride

Secrets were hard to come by in Clemente. Our town was small enough that we had only one school, and Delia Redhood's grandmother catered all the events, whether wedding, funeral, or graduation party. Mrs. Oladen, who ran the foster home up the street, knew each of the students at Clemente Day School by name. After all, she was also its kindergarten teacher, and taught each of us at one time or another.

Then there was Dad. Considered a widower by the townspeople since Mom disappeared nine years ago, he took over Kingsmen pharmacy to keep busy. Believe me when I tell you, it's pretty hard to keep secrets from a pharmacist. When Humphrey Dumwooley climbed to the top of the clock tower and jumped, neither Dad nor EMS could help him. It was Dad who'd tried to intervene at first when he learned the troubled boy hadn't filled his prescription for anti-depression medicine in months. And that's just the kind of town Clemente was: everyone knew almost everything there was to know about everybody else. Almost.

What we really and truly wanted to remain hidden, we hid and hid well. Secrets that were old, dark, and horrible stayed buried under lies, half-truths, myths, and old wives' tales. That is, until Taylor Sayers showed up.

Very little was known about Taylor Sayers, except that he was new to town. No one knew where he'd come from, or how he'd ended up in Clemente, of all places. All anyone knew was that we knew nothing about him, and it seems that's the way he liked it. He kept to himself and didn't bother choosing sides in the geeks vs. goths war that raged at Clemente Day School. But for those of us who couldn't get enough of his startlingly blue eyes and jet black hair, there was only one place to be after school: track team practice.

I tried not to be obvious like those other girls, the ones who drooled over him and tried desperately to get his attention; cherry-colored lips and push-up bras were so juvenile. I took a vastly different approach. I simply ignored him.

Headphones in and oatmeal bar in hand, I ate my favorite afternoon snack and watched him brood. I reluctantly took a seat near Jessica Sparks, Eliza Teardown, and Tiara Knowles: the Fearsome Threesome, as they stupidly called themselves. I was the only one of us who didn't have a boyfriend on the team. Therefore, I was branded a loser, a nobody, a less than nothing wannabe reject. The words I used to describe them weren't nearly as nice.

Someone bumped me from behind, harder than I'm sure was necessary. My oatmeal bar flew out of my hand, landing two rows down the bleachers. I watched helplessly as chunks of yummy goodness settled on a splat of bird poop. Flies nearby were interested in a green lollipop that had been left behind. My mouth watered.

I turned to see who was behind the cruel gesture.

Luanne Limey, former head cheerleader turned plus-sized teen model.

I removed my headphones. I could still hear the music blaring through the earbuds, but now it was partially drowned out by giggles and howls from the Fearsome Threesome and their lackey, Luanne.

"Real mature. Real freaking mature." With a shake of my head and a hard shove of my music player into my bag, I huffed at the girls before removing and then throwing an open plastic bag their way. When the screams started, I turned to see Jessica covered in black spiders, making their way up and into her hair. The other girls screamed and squealed and cried as they watched their friend and self-professed leader writhe in pain from the spider bites. It wasn't like any of them would ever apologize. So I did the only thing I could. Sometimes, getting even is a whole lot more satisfying than a half-hearted apology.

On my way down the bleachers, I caught a glimpse of Taylor, who was looking right at me. All I could do was run, away from Taylor and his accusatory stare and the damage I'd done. I ran to the only place I could think to go. I didn't expect anyone to be there.

I sat under the cherry blossom tree on the far, east side of campus where I usually ate lunch. I didn't mean to overhear. But sometimes, I see and hear too much. They were arguing. That much was clear. Her flame-red hair and onyx eyes worked together to vex him. I saw everything, despite being frozen by equal amounts horror and intrigue.

Kristen, my sister, had long suspected her boyfriend Evan of cheating. Three months ago Tiara Knowles, her best friend since the first grade and knower of all things romance-related, had advised her to wait until after prom to confront him. I know, because I'd overheard them talking about it. "You can't possibly break up with Evan now," Tiara had whined. "Prom is in eight weeks. Why give up the chance to be prom queen for that loser?"

"I know, but I just can't do it. Everyone knows. Why was I so stupid? How could this happen . . . to *me*?" Kristen fell in a ball of sobs into Tiara's waiting arms. At least, that's how it had looked from the other side of the keyhole.

"It's gonna be all right," Tiara had soothed. "Lucky for you, you received all the good looks in your family. You can have anyone you want. All you have to do is spin your little web. Do you know how many guys would love to go out with you? If it wasn't for your freak of a sister, you would have had ten dates for prom by now."

"Paige can't help . . . how she is." Kristen had looked up at Tiara. "You really think this is her fault?"

"I know so. If you weren't related to that pathetic little nothing, you would have won the head cheerleader position this year. No one likes a freak who dresses like she's going to a funeral and is always playing with bugs. Gross! I'm itching just thinking about it."

That was all I'd heard. I could have listened more, but there was no point. My sister blamed her horrible life on me.

Tiara Knowles. Who asked her, anyway? And why Kristen listened to a word she said was anyone's guess. Evan had been Tiara's boyfriend before Kristen sunk her teeth into him. Tiara was probably telling her all of that just so she could steal him back! And yet, watching them argue just a few short feet from my tree, my sister seemed genuinely hurt by what Evan had done. Her face was almost as red as her hair, and her eyes were dark and wet with the pain of betrayal. I felt bad for her. She didn't deserve to be humiliated like that. Sure, she ignored me when others were around, and pretended I wasn't her "real" sister whenever anyone asked, but still. She was all I had.

"You're gonna pay for this, Evan Sugarback." Kristen removed her hands from size-two hips. Evan's eyes were wide in amusement. Kristen spun on her heel, then turned back to add, "I hope you and your little girlfriend choke on your stupid crowns!" With a flip of her hair, she disappeared into the afternoon haze, faster than any person had a right to depart. I don't think he knew she had merely shrunk to her real size. I watched her scamper away on eight tiny legs and up into her favorite hiding spot—the old willow tree. It wasn't like her to show her other side in public, but I supposed today she didn't much care about the consequences. I started to run to her, to try to talk sense into her or offer comforting words, but a web grew up around me, pinning my feet to the ground.

Evan tensed his shoulders, then walked briskly away, as if something had spooked him.

"Please, I need to . . ."

My voice was lost in the intricate, constricting web. Looking up, I saw a spider dangling overhead.

"Let her go. She'll calm down soon enough. Then she'll see that a human boy will never be the right choice."

"But Mother," I protested. "Why should she have to suffer like that? She doesn't embrace our lifestyle. She wants to be with humans."

I settled back into the web, gave up resisting it. She cradled me in the soft, elastic silk of her making. I hated not being able to do anything for her. I couldn't spin webs. All I could do was hunt insects, small birds, and tiny lizards. Useless.

"When she's calm, she'll see she's made the right

choice. As for you, a little birdy told me about your stunt this afternoon."

"What?" I pushed at the web, but it hardly budged.

Mom lowered her spider body alongside me. It was kind of intimidating, watching her up close and knowing she could never take on a human form again. That she gave it all up for us girls, so that we could live as humans whenever we wanted. It was intimidating, and sad.

I wanted to cry, to scream and kick something, but caught in the comfort of her loving restriction, I only managed a single tear.

"Since when do you consort with birds?"

"Paige Muffet, I didn't raise you to be selfish. And I certainly didn't teach you to seek revenge on those who do you harm. I allow you to change easily from spider to human because I think it will keep you safe. If you decide to use your powers for evil, I may decide otherwise."

"All of this is your fault!"

Kristen appeared in front of me, eyes angry, challenging. She grabbed at my neck with her hands, now human along with the rest of her five foot eight inch frame. I gasped, unable to do much else, as Mom slowly unwrapped me.

"Kristen, what's the matter with you?" Mom asked, struggling to release me quickly as Kristen tightened her hold around my neck.

"What's the matter with me? *You* are what's the matter with me."

"You can't be serious, Kristen. You let that stuck-up, two-faced tramp, Tiara Knowles turn you against your own family!" I struggled to speak, but I was certain Kristen understood me. I think I made her even madder.

Mom scurried up to the top of a high branch.

"And your fault, too!" Kristen grabbed at Mom with her other hand. She must have been truly out of her mind. She could crush Mom.

"What's the matter with you?" I said. "Are you nuts? You would attack your own mother?"

Mom must have thought so. She jumped to a higher branch.

"Once I'm rid of both of you, everything will be perfect. No one will bother Dad and me, and I won't have to spend my time being a loser, looking for bugs and birds to eat. Look at what you've turned me into! Now Evan Sugarback thinks I'm a freak like the two of you!"

Mom used to think Kristen wouldn't go through the change. And she didn't, until she turned seventeen. She had only lived like this for a few months. I've been this way since I was five, so I've had some time to get used to it. Still, I don't recall going ape-shit nuts over it.

"Kristen, you've gotta calm down," I said, finally free of Mom's protective web. I grabbed her hand, still around my neck. "You haven't thought this through. Killing me or Mom won't make you any different than you are. And it certainly won't protect Dad. How will it look when his daughter goes missing a few years after his wife did? He's never really gotten over the suspicion, you know."

"I can't live like this. I won't." Kristen grabbed feverishly at the branch where Mom sat, eyes wide.

"Kristen, please."

Then Kristen did something totally unexpected. She opened her mouth, grabbed Mom off the branch, and shoved the spider into her mouth. The entire track team probably heard my screams. Kristen fell to the ground and began frothing at the mouth, her body convulsing. Then it stopped. I fell on top of her and slapped her face.

"Kristen, Mom, please. Kristen, wake up. Kristen."

I opened my sister's mouth and moved her tongue aside. My poor, dead mother lay limp at the back of Kristen's throat.

Sobs overtook me. After a while, a tap on the shoulder brought me out of my stupor.

I looked around, but saw no one. I pulled Mom out of Kristen's mouth, then closed it. Poor Mom had lost three legs to Kristen's venom. I slumped in defeat, just as another tap touched my right shoulder.

I turned to find Taylor, his eyes still accusing, only now they had proof.

"I . . . I didn't do it. I swear!"

Stumbling away from the spider and my sister, I noticed something strange about him. Something I'd never noticed before. He looked kind of like a . . . bug.

"Run. If you run now, no one will know you were even here. I'll take care of it. I'll take care of everything. Just go."

Just then Taylor's right arm extended so that it touched the ground. Then his left did the same. I screamed as I watched six more shoot out from his back. Hairy, hairy arms that now touched the floor as legs. His eyes bulged out from his head, which became dome-shaped. His nose was almost invisible by the time his body dropped to the ground, looking less like a boy and very much like a spider of the same size as his former, human self.

I struggled to my feet and did as Taylor advised. As I started running, I heard the wet, crunchy sounds of a large spider devouring its prey, and I knew he had done it for me.

– The End –

WINKIN', BLINKIN', AND NOD

*Winkin', Blinkin', and Nod, one night sailed off in a
wooden shoe;
Sailed off on a river of crystal light into a sea of dew.
"Where are you going and what do you wish?" the old
moon asked the three.
"We've come to fish for the herring fish that live in this
beautiful sea.
Nets of silver and gold have we," said Winkin', Blinkin',
and Nod.*

*The old moon laughed and sang a song as they rocked
in the wooden shoe.
And the wind that sped them all night long ruffled the
waves of dew.
Now the little stars are the herring fish that live in that
beautiful sea;
"Cast your nets wherever you wish never afraid are
we!"
So cried the stars to the fishermen three—Winkin', and
Blinkin', and Nod.*

So all night long their nets they threw to the stars in the twinkling foam.
'Til down from the skies came the wooden shoe bringing the fisherman home.
'Twas all so pretty a sail it seemed as if it could not be.
Some folks say 'twas a dream they dreamed of sailing that misty sea.
But I shall name you the fisherman three—Winkin', Blinkin', and Nod.

Now Winkin' and Blinkin' are two little eyes and Nod is a little head.
And the wooden shoe that sailed the skies is a wee one's trundle bed.
So close your eyes while mother sings of the wonderful sights that be.
And you shall see those beautiful things as you sail on the misty sea,
Where the old shoe rocked the fishermen three—Winkin', Blinkin', and Nod.

– Mother Goose

SEA OF DEW
C. Lee McKenzie

In the week before the moon found them beneath the bloated bellies of storm clouds, they drifted in the lifeboat without sight of land. The boys, the stowaways, the survivors.

And Miranda.

She hunkered under the tarp and a soggy blanket, peering out at them with worry and a sizable dose of fear. She was adrift in a foreign sea among strangers. Yet one of those three had hauled her from the water and saved her life.

Which one? Maybe Winker. He was skinny and had some kind of tic in his cheek that made his left eye twitch, especially when he looked in her direction. Or was it the guy whose name started with B? What was it? Blandy? Blakie? He had a vacant look and his lips were always moving, like he was telling himself secrets.

Or could it have been Nodfarker? That guy had one creepy name. He was always telling them when to eat, if they could have water, or how much. Miranda had fantasized about tying his leg to an anchor while he slept, then pushing him over the side of the dinky lifeboat.

Only there was no anchor. Besides, he was the one who netted the fish that they ate raw to stay alive now that the supplies were almost gone, so offing him wasn't her best idea.

The worst one, however, was easy to pinpoint. She kept asking herself why she had let that tour guide talk her and her friends into joining the cheap cruise from the mainland to the tropical island of Milaou. His tiny-toothed grin flashed through her mind. She wondered if he was still smiling in that death trap of a ferry.

Miranda sat up as Nodfarker leaned over the side of the boat and dragged the net through the water. Soon he had two lively, silver herring. He dropped them on top of the supply box and slit them open before their tails stopped flipping.

She turned her head. *Whoever mentions sashimi to me when this is over, dies.*

"Here. Your share." Nodfarker held out a chunk of grayish fish.

The smell churned her stomach, but she took the piece between her thumb and forefinger. She held her breath, and swallowed it whole.

He nibbled at the edges of his portion, taking his time as if he had a juicy Big Mac.

Her stomach growled, demanding more food, at the same time bile rose into her throat. Lurching over the side, she cast the chunk of herring back into the sea.

When she turned around, no one seemed to have noticed she'd hurled precious food. Winker averted his gaze. The guy whose name began with a B had his eyes rolled to Heaven, mumbling. Nodfarker was chewing with his eyes closed.

"Where did the name Nodfarker come from?" she asked.

"Say what?" He opened his eyes and fixed them on her.

"Nodfarker. Your name."

Winker doubled over in laughter, and the other one stopped mumbling long enough to manage a pale smile.

"It's Ned Parker," he said, slicing the second herring into fours. "Your ears must've been plugged with saltwater when I pulled you into the boat and said 'hi.'"

Miranda flinched, remembering her plunge into the sea. She'd felt queasy and left her friends below to go on deck. As she'd stood looking over the railing, the ferry had suddenly rolled, pitching her headfirst into the water. She'd kicked frantically, but it was as though thousands of fingers clutched at her, dragging her deeper. That's when a single hand descended from above, grasped hers, and pulled her out of the water. Ned had saved her life.

He passed her another sliver of fish.

She took it, but this time she didn't put it in her mouth. She studied him, doling out the herring to the others, making the portions equal.

He wasn't really that creepy. He was about her age, maybe a couple of years older. Nineteen? His dark hair had a boyish way of curling across his forehead and his chestnut-colored eyes were steady when he looked at her. Maybe it had been that wretched name that had made him seem so disagreeable.

"So how'd you get on that ferry?" Miranda asked.

"We wanted to see Milaou before heading home." Ned shrugged. "We were down to our last few bucks, so we stowed away in this lifeboat."

"Bad decision." Miranda bit off a small bite of fish. She'd try nibbling and hope she could keep it down this time.

"No," Ned said, tossing fish entrails overboard. "We got away. I don't think anybody else escaped being sucked under when the ferry capsized."

He held out the bottle of water and the cap. "Three capfuls each, okay? That gives us four more days, and then we do a rain dance."

For almost a week they'd huddled under the tarp, wishing the rain would stop, bailing fresh water into the salty sea to stay afloat, and drinking from the sky. They'd filled their one container, and now they already needed to ration every drop.

She sipped her last capful, handed it to Winker, and closed her eyes. It was too hard to stare over the endless water knowing only four days' supply was between them and thirsty death.

"We'll head south." Ned held up the compass. "Try to find a shipping lane."

"Why south?" Miranda asked, opening her eyes and focusing on his face.

"Warmer weather. More chance for a cruise ship." He shrugged. "I'm guessing." He reached for the oars and dug them into the choppy sea. "Time to work out."

Miranda slowly gnawed at the herring and distracted herself by admiring the way his biceps rippled under his skin. After about twenty minutes, he stood, unzipped his fly, and sent an arc of pee over the side before he zipped up and leaned back against the side of the boat, resting.

Until now, she'd managed bathroom privacy at night when the others were asleep. But now she couldn't wait that long.

When the other two turned their backs and followed Ned's example, she clenched her jaw, then asked. "How do I pee on this pleasure cruise?"

Ned grinned. "Guess it's over the side for you." He faced away. "Yell when you want us to pull you in."

They kept their backs to her as she stripped from

the waist down and slipped into the water. She clung to the side, peeing and feeling lonely on the outside of the boat while they sat inside waiting, smug in their maleness.

"I'm finished," she yelled, and Ned and Winker hauled her in. They went to their places, still keeping their eyes averted as she dried and dressed.

Once she'd sat in her usual spot, Ned nudged Blakie. "Hey, entertain us." He looked at Miranda. "Give him any math problem and he'll solve it in his head. He does it all day."

"And Blakie?" She cocked her head so he'd know how dumb the name was to her.

"That's how his mom called him for dinner when we were kids."

"What about Winker? That's unusual, as names go." She hadn't meant to say that.

They stared at her, and she had no way to cover her embarrassment at being so rude. She shifted her gaze, but Winker broke the tension and pointed to his jumpy cheek. "Obvious, right?"

Ned smiled and Miranda felt grateful for being forgiven so easily. "Winker's my word guy," he said. "So I got things covered. One solves my math problems; the other one gets me through English."

It became the routine, then, that each morning Ned portioned out the fish and the remaining rations from the wretched box of stale supplies. Blakie amazed them by doing high-level math problems. They'd spend hours trying to prove him wrong, but he never was. He gave answers to problems like ten to the square root of 675.444 the way Miranda solved "two plus two."

"Blakie does it again," Ned said, returning their pencil to the supply box for safekeeping. "Damned kid was always a genius."

A genius maybe, Miranda thought, but as remarkable as the inside of his head had to be, he was one hundred percent unremarkable on the outside. His brown hair hung limp to his shoulders and matched his eyes in color and texture. Miranda pictured him as he would look in clothes other than the Santa Cruz Slugs tee he'd chosen to wear the day of the ferry disaster. She imagined him with a wrinkled shirt, not quite white, with a flip phone in one pocket and pens in the other. One pen would, of course, have leaked blue, but he wouldn't have noticed.

He had a gentleness to him. Some girl might want to save him from that not-quite-white and wrinkled shirt. She might find his exterior appealing because she loved his genius and wanted to free him from common concerns like fashion. She hoped Blakie would find a companion, but he had to get rid of that nickname.

On the fourth day, when Ned passed the bottle to her, she said she'd wait. They all voted to wait. Without saying so, they'd agreed to give the heavens more time to send fresh water. But that night, thirst overcame them, and they drank their portions under the clear sky and full moon. There was no rain the next day either, and the moon flooded the ocean with brightness, taunting them day and night with water they couldn't drink.

"Eskimos wish on the moon to bring them back to life." Winker, who never said much, sat and stared up, his cheek still for a change.

Miranda drew in her knees. "Eskimos make wishes like that?"

"Prayers maybe," Winker said. "I can't remember. I read about it when I did a report on Alaska in eighth grade."

"What happens when it's dark of the moon? How do they . . . wish for it to bring them back then?"

Winker's tic kicked into high gear. "Uh . . . don't . . . know. But when it's not up there," he pointed skyward, "it's . . . supposed to be . . . gathering souls . . . taking them to earth again."

She pulled the blanket over her head, shutting out the moon and trying not to listen to the ruffling waves against the boat. When she felt a tug on her blanket, she stuck her head out and stared at Winker.

"S . . . sorry I said . . . that."

His eyes, shaped like teardrops, made him look as if he suffered from perpetual melancholy, and Miranda had an urge to touch his cheek. She thought maybe she could smooth the nervous tic away, but she held back. Touching seemed too intimate for someone she barely knew; besides, he didn't invite it. This was their first real talk.

"I'm not hiding because of what you said." But that wasn't true. The minute he'd told her the myth, something caught inside her, and she didn't want to see the moon. She didn't want the temptation to wish on it to bring her back from death. If she did, she'd be giving up on the hope of rescue and life. She couldn't do that. Ever.

She shivered in the sudden wind that seemed colder than the nights before.

Ned took out the compass, then dug the oars into the sea with more force than usual. When he pulled them into the boat, he didn't look in their direction, even though all eyes were on him, asking if there was a problem.

"Look," he said, "it's getting colder, so we should move closer together, especially at night." He scooted next to Miranda and Winker. "Come on Blakie, let's sleep in a pile like Wild Things." His laugh had a dryness to it.

So they huddled under the tarp, sharing their body heat and their fear. During the night, Ned's arm encircled Miranda's shoulder and pulled her into him. At first she held back, but she was tired and cold and the sound of his heart comforted her with its steady beat.

When the sun found them, she pushed the tarp away, blinking into the brightness of morning. Ned sat across from her, drawing the oars in steady strokes through the water.

After an hour, he traded off with Blakie, then Blakie traded off with Winker. Miranda took her turn, too.

Then Ned checked his compass. "Stop now," he told her, and she leaned back to stare at the cloudless sky.

Blakie moved his lips, solving math problems, hiding in a place where numbers added up to perfection and the messy reality of being stranded in a lifeboat didn't exist. Miranda wished she had an inner place like that to distract herself.

"We better cover up." Ned looked at Blakie and Winker, who sat together. "Less sun, less water loss." Ned tried for a smile. "You'll have to wait for that suntan until you get back home, Miranda."

Back Home. The place she'd wanted to escape for the past two years because her mother had turned into such a bitch. Her father had simply turned and run. The divorce was going to be ugly, and she didn't want any part of it. She'd already had enough of the nightly fights. This trip with her senior class had come at exactly the right time. She'd withdrawn enough money from her college savings to make it, and she'd relished every moment away from Back Home. Every moment until she'd landed in the sea and all her friends had been sucked underwater . . . forever.

"Where's Back Home for you?" she asked, directing the question to any of the three, trying to erase the images of her drowned classmates.

Ned answered. "Northern California. A beach town. We've surfed together since we could hop on a board. You?"

"Iowa. Corn-fed and Midwestern, through and through." For a moment, the taste of hot-buttered corn on the cob filled her mouth, but it vanished almost as quickly as it had come. She licked her lips and found they were sore. Her head ached, too, so she burrowed under the tarp and dreamt of water, of butter and corn and the farm—the real Back Home. When she'd been little, it had been a perfect place. A tire swing at the side of the house. Mom pushing her high into the air. Dad in the kitchen every midday for dinner, his face streaked by sweat and plowed earth, earth that had belonged to the Langlies for three generations. That lifestyle had vanished along with the farm. Poor crops for three years running. Dad sold the land before he lost it to the bank. Then they'd moved to the city where none of them—

"Blakie!" Ned's voice shattered her restless sleep, and she scooted from under the tarp.

Ned knelt over Blakie, pressing Blakie's wrist between his hands, then shaking his shoulder. He pushed hard on his chest. Again. Again. "Wake up, damn you!"

Winker looked at Ned, then down at Blakie and the knife lying next to his body. Then Winker fell back and buried his face in his arms.

A thin, red line trickled from Blakie's wrist to where Miranda sat. She threw the blanket over it and watched as the red soaked through.

Ned pulled Blakie onto his lap, swaying back and forth. "You idiot. You effin' idiot."

As the sun settled low, hovering just above the line between sky and sea, Ned released Blakie's body and began to wrap him in the blanket.

"Where are you going . . . and what do you wish?" Winker whispered. "The old moon asked the three. Never . . . afraid are we. As we sail into the sea of dew."

So whether it was a wish or a prayer or just a conversation between human beings and the ancient moon, as Blakie's body slipped into the choppy water Winker knelt and Ned knelt with him. "Please," Winker said, "find Blakie. Bring him home."

Miranda sought out the darkness under the tarp to avoid the cool white light from overhead, to avoid hearing the entreaties for the dead Blakie, to avoid giving up on life.

That night, as the air chilled, the pile of three slept under the tarp, but not well. Winker bolted upright, screaming about the moon. Ned curled around her back, and Miranda found his hand and held it. This hand had saved her once; she prayed it would save her again. Before the sun arrived, she slept, believing that it would.

Rain didn't come the next day, but a thick mist did. They made a catch basin from the tarp, spreading it across the end of the boat and funneling one end into the empty container. By noon they had half a cup of water, and they each took one small capful onto their tongues, holding it in their mouths, not wanting to swallow.

It wasn't enough to stop Miranda's head from throbbing or her lips from cracking. When she looked at Winker, he looked back at her with sunken eyes. His cheek hadn't twitched since the day they'd sent Blakie into the sea, but now it began again.

"When did this start?" Miranda stroked his cheek as if it were something she'd always done. Now, touching him seemed right. The way he looked at her with his teardrop-shaped eyes invited her to do it.

Winker didn't pull back, but took his time before answering. "After my mom died." He drew his tongue over his teeth. "My dad took it hard. Spent lots of days drunk." He swiped his hand over his face. "I read and surfed . . . the rest of the time." Winker looked at Ned. "He and Blakie . . . got me through."

The rest of that day they slept. Woke with starts. Slept again.

After that, Miranda lost count of the days. Now, she only counted the drops of water Ned placed on her tongue. It gave her comfort to watch how he held the cap. How he measured water, then presented it to her, and then to Winker before recapping the container and returning it to the supply box. This ritual helped her forget the half cup of water was nearly gone.

Miranda thought about those first days together here and realized she missed them because of all those rituals Ned didn't perform anymore. He didn't paddle or check the compass or talk about keeping them headed south. He didn't net herring and serve her small slivers. Since Blakie had gone, there was nothing to distract them from the slowness of time, and it was as if Winker was sinking into himself a bit more each time she looked at him. All any of them did was sleep, and hopelessness spread like a contagion.

Then one night, when the sky had cast a silver net of stars overhead, after they'd taken water and after the sun had disappeared, Ned didn't roll over and sleep. "We should set up a watch," he said.

Miranda felt a surge of renewed hope, and when she looked at Winker, his eyes were focused on Ned and her as if he really saw them.

Winker raised a hand. "I'll take . . . early watch. Sunrise to mid . . . morning."

"Midmorning to when the sun passes overhead— about two. Okay, Miranda?" Ned asked.

She nodded.

"I'll take it until sunset," he said.

"We're not catching a southern current, are we?" Winker asked, but it sounded more like a statement of fact.

Ned shook his head. "No. It's getting colder," he swallowed, "and dryer every day."

He was having trouble talking. Miranda was, too. Her tongue didn't fit inside her mouth like it should. It had thickened, and rubbed against the roof and the sides like a rasp.

The next day she lay under the tarp, shivering because the sun seemed to have lost its heat. When she felt a tug on her foot, she struggled to sit.

"Your turn," Winker said. He stretched out and slept before she could get to the side of the boat.

Before noon, Miranda couldn't stay awake. Her head jerked forward or lolled back, bringing her again to her watch. If any ship passed, she knew she'd miss it. She couldn't do that. She was desperate to yell, "Throw us a line. Give us water."

She no longer needed to pee. That humiliation of going over the side of the boat half-naked had ended some days ago, but she knew what that meant. She remembered the humiliation with some longing.

Ned relieved her from her watch, but she sat at his side and didn't return to the tarp.

"If a ship . . ." She tried to swallow, but she had no saliva. "How do we signal?"

He pointed to the supply box. "Flare gun."

They were using few words, saving energy, avoiding the pain of cracked lips.

The supplies in that box had to be years old. The crackers had been stale, the tins slightly bulging and filled with odd-tasting fruit. She let her eyelids scrape across her irises and slept, sitting there next to Ned, hoping that her first thoughts about the flare gun were not the right ones. It would work. It had to.

Then one day, Winker didn't wake her for her midmorning watch, and she knew it was because he'd fallen asleep. She crawled to him, shook him, and took her place.

Even though she struggled to stay awake and scan the horizon, she must have dozed because the sudden and harsh rocking of the lifeboat brought her out of dark dreams. She blinked and looked around, thinking that if she didn't hold to the side she might be washed overboard. A wake flip-flopped them in the water. Her mind was slow from dehydration, but she tried to piece together what this meant. Then she got it. There had to be something big making those choppy waves. She looked ahead and to both sides. Only emptiness. Then she looked to the stern, and there it was. Looming like a great white mirage. A ship.

Miranda stood, shouted, waved her arms. She grabbed up a blanket and flapped it in the air.

Winker and Ned scrambled to her side. Ned opened the supply box. He held the flare gun so it pointed at the sky and pulled the trigger. It fired, sending a red streak into the air. He stared after the ship, gritting his teeth. "Come around." He fired again, but this time the flare didn't discharge. Again he pulled the trigger, but nothing happened.

Ned hurled the gun into the supply box, sank back against the boat, and buried his head in his arms.

Miranda and Winker watched the great ship become smaller until they could no longer see it.

That night they slept apart, shivering. In the morning, Miranda stayed under her blanket, waiting for Winker to call her and dreading another day on watch. It wasn't until the sun dipped low in the West that she sat up and realized Winker had never awakened her.

She crawled to his blanket and pulled it back. He wasn't there. She nudged Ned awake. "Winker's gone."

It took a moment for him to understand what she meant, and then he said, "He left us." Ned curled his knees to his chest and pulled the blanket over his face.

Loneliness swallowed her in one gulp, sending her into a pit of hopelessness unlike anything she'd ever experienced. She'd thought the day strangers carted off their farmhouse furniture would be her worst. Then her dad left with a grim goodbye, and that was even more miserable. She'd never expected to face something worse than that. She longed to cry. She longed to drink the sea dry, but when she licked her lips, the saltiness reminded her how terrible even one sip would be.

Sleep was her only escape, so she lay down next to Ned's bundled form and closed her eyes. She set her mind free and—as if from a great distance, maybe as far away as the moon—looked down on the two of them, the tiny boat and the vast sea. She dreamed of Iowa where the sea only existed in movies and cool water in tall glasses was taken for granted. At first light she stared into another clear day, surprised and not a little disappointed to find herself adrift on a sea and not standing on the Iowa soil of her dreams.

Ned hadn't moved since last night. She placed her hand on his chest, then snatched it back when she couldn't feel his heartbeat. Her quick movement made her dizzy, and for a moment, she thought he'd stirred.

When her head cleared, she touched him again, feeling for some spark of life. There was none, and a rush of terror shot through her.

Missing the closeness of another, she put her ear against his chest, and stayed pressed to Ned's stillness, her eyes closed, their pile of two growing colder with each beat of her lonely heart.

When day slipped into night, she rolled onto her back and found herself in a world of two moons—one in the sky and one drenched in the sea. Ready at last, she prayed. "Please bring me—all of us—home."

She laid down again and returned to thinking about beautiful things like sweet water. Soon, the boat stopped being a boat and became a cradle, the cradle that had rocked her. The cradle that used to be tucked into the back corner of the attic in the Iowa farmhouse, waiting for the next generation. Sold, she remembered. There would be no cradle for her children, so she shouldn't be worried about not having children. Blakie would see the logic in that. She'd tell him.

When the darkness came for her, the cradle rocked her to sleep and the misty sea slapped along the sides. Out of that darkness, Ned's hand reached for hers. He hadn't deserted her. Trusting him again, she let herself be pulled to the side of the lifeboat.

And then she tumbled into the dewy sea, where the moon watched from above and waited below. Where starry herring nibbled her toes and fanned their silver against her skin. Where Blakie mumbled his perfect math solutions, Winker recited the moon prayers of Eskimos, and Ned Parker offered drops of clear, cool water for her tongue.

– The End –

THE CLOCK

There's a neat little clock,
In the schoolroom it stands,
And it points to the time
With its two little hands.

And may we, like the clock,
Keep a face clean and bright,
With hands ever ready
. . . To do what is right.

— Mother Goose

TICK TOCK
Gretchen McNeil

"This can't be right."

Shannon eased her car to a halt at the top of the hill and flipped on the interior light. She held the torn corner of her mom's newest celebrity magazine in front of her eyes. It had been the only scratch paper within arm's reach when Shannon answered the call from the Mommy's Happy Helpers babysitting service for whom she occasionally gigged, and as she squinted to read her mostly illegible handwriting scrawled across a photo of Nicole Kidman's Golden Globes dress, she secretly hoped her mom would blame the destruction of her favorite bedtime reading material on Dad.

"2201 Hillcrest Road," she read aloud. Shannon glanced up at the street sign dully illuminated by her headlights. It clearly indicated that the dark, windy road which quickly disappeared up the side of the canyon was, in fact, Hillcrest Road.

Shannon drummed her fingers against the steering wheel. It had been only fifteen minutes since she'd turned off Pacific Coast Highway into one of the older Malibu neighborhoods and started winding up into the hills, but it felt like she'd left Los Angeles's most exclusive beach community behind her. The modern estates with security gates and twenty-foot-tall hedge rows had at first thinned, then disappeared altogether as she climbed farther up the hill. As the road opened up onto a plateau overlooking the Pacific Ocean, Shannon thought her Garmin had guided her to a dead end. But, no. The green and white street sign clearly indicated that the dismal, abandoned Hillcrest Road continued, and since the last house she'd passed at least a half mile back had been numbered 2190, her destination must lie farther up the hill.

Shannon lifted her foot from the break and maneuvered her car into the narrow, winding lane, trying to fight back the uneasiness growing in her mind.

It had been a weird, last minute assignment. Her parents were at the Metzgers' for bridge night, and Shannon had just changed into her PJs and settled in for a marathon of bad reality television when she saw Mommy's Happy Helpers pop up on her cell phone. She'd almost let it go to voicemail. The lure of Snooki and J Wow was strong, and besides, between work and studying for finals, it had been weeks since she had a night all to herself.

But Debbie, her boss and the owner of MHH, always gave Shannon first crack at the best assignments, which usually meant a big fat tip at the end of the night. She thought of her college fund, which needed a serious shot in the arm if she was going to afford anything other than a JC, and so with a stoic sigh, Shannon had picked up Debbie's call.

"Shannon, thank God you're home." Debbie sounded out of breath.

"What's up, Deb?"

"Annie didn't show for an assignment."

"What? I don't believe it." Shannon had a hard time believing that her best friend had bailed on a job. "She didn't call or anything?"

Debbie clicked her tongue. "I got a garbled call about five minutes ago. I could barely understand a word she said."

"Is she okay?"

"I don't know!" Debbie snapped.

Shannon flinched. Debbie wasn't usually this wound up. More cool, everything-happens-for-a-reason hippie than Type A control freak.

She heard Debbie take a deep breath, then after a few seconds, she exhaled slowly. "Look, this is a brand new client. A biggie. Heads a huge film production company out of Australia and just moved to Malibu last month. I needed five referrals just to land him so Annie not showing up is a mess for me."

Shannon pursed her lips. She'd known Annie since they were in preschool. Always on time, reliable to the point of an obsessive compulsive disorder, Annie wasn't usually a flake. But ever since she'd started dating Cam Hunter, she'd pretty much lost track of everything else in her life. Grades, soccer practice, even Shannon had fallen by the wayside as Annie paraded around school in Cam's white Hollister sweatshirt as if she'd been branded by her new relationship.

And now her flakiness was going to ruin Shannon's TV night.

"I know, I should have called you first," Debbie said, clearly trying to butter Shannon up. "But Annie begged me for some extra gigs and . . . well . . ."

"It's fine," Shannon said. Whatever. Debbie would make it up to her later. For now, she sensed time was of the essence.

"Good," Debbie said quickly. "Thanks. The house is way up in Malibu. Can you make it there in thirty minutes?"

Shannon glanced down at her cotton pajama bottoms and threadbare tank top. Thirty minutes to change and haul her ass from Topanga to Malibu? It was a stretch to be sure, but she could just make it. Assuring Debbie she'd be there by eight o'clock, Shannon hastily wrote down the address on the nearest paper she could find, then scribbled a note to her parents and hustled out of the house.

Thirty minutes later, Shannon found herself on a road right out of a horror novel. The scraggly foliage crouched over the narrow roadway, practically squeezing it out of existence. The single paved lane of Hillcrest Road seemed to cling to its independence, maintaining its domain from the encroachment of nature. The surrounding trees were dense, but held at bay by recently resurfaced asphalt, and though Shannon was half-convinced she was going to drop off the face of the earth at any moment, there was something comforting in the fact that the road, however remote, was meticulously maintained.

Hillcrest Road took a precarious ninety degree turn and suddenly the trees thinned, giving way to an expansive front yard. The sweet smell of newly mowed grass wafted in through her open windows as Shannon pulled her car into a quadruple-wide driveway.

"Whoa." Whatever Shannon's horror movie influenced subconscious expected to see at the end of Hillcrest Road, the house before her certainly wasn't it. She *should* have been staring at a dilapidated mansion, complete with spiky iron fence, broken windows, and a family graveyard conveniently built on an old Indian burial ground.

This? Not so much.

2201 Hillcrest Road was a sleek, modern estate. Austere in its glass and steel façade, the house was brilliantly lit, flooding a soft yellow glow down onto a meticulously manicured lawn. Beyond the house, Shannon could see the glittering lights of the Santa Monica Pier far in the distance. She could even make out the slowly rotating lights of the Ferris wheel, flickering in and out as the massive wheel hauled tourists around for iconic views of the southern California coast.

As she climbed out of her car, Shannon caught movement in one of the second-floor windows. The silhouette of a head and shoulders standing at the pane. Must be her charge for the night. Shannon started up the walkway, then paused. There were two silhouettes in the window now, both the same height and the same build.

Then, multiplying like amoebas, the two became four.

Shannon blinked a few times. Had her eyes gone completely *schizo* or was she actually staring at four kids in the window? Four bodies who stood shoulder-to-shoulder like conjoined paper dolls in almost perfect symmetry. Same height, same build, same age.

Quadruplets?

Cha-ching! Four kids meant double her rate, plus with a house like this way up on a private Malibu road, the family must be swimming in cash. An Australian film producer? Dude must be loaded to have moved his whole family out here. Shannon smiled to herself, picturing a fat, hundred-dollar tip in her hands at the end of the night. *Thank you, Annie, for bailing tonight to make out with your boyfriend. Your loss, my gain.*

With an expectant grin, Shannon rang the doorbell.

She waited for the sound of rambunctious kids careening down the stairs, each desperate to be the first to open the door. But instead, the house was oddly quiet. Disturbingly so. Not a voice, not a yell, not even the sound of a television or radio cranked up to max volume.

Nothing.

Shannon took a step back and gazed up to the second-story window. The silhouetted children were gone. She *had* seen four of them up there, hadn't she? In Shannon's babysitting experience, four kids in one house are rarely quiet at the same time unless they're all sound asleep. Maybe they didn't hear her ring the bell? Huh, weird, since all four of them had watched her walk up to the house. Maybe they were just shy?

A light ocean breeze gusted across the front yard, whipping strands of dark blonde hair across Shannon's face. Despite the warmth of the evening, a chill crept up the back of her neck. She shook her shoulders with unnecessary force, as if attempting to extricate herself from an unwanted embrace.

Don't be stupid. Shannon reached her finger toward the doorbell.

Before she touched it, the front door swung open.

Shannon gasped. She couldn't help it. The whole evening had an air of the surreal and the sight before her was no exception. A child stood in the doorway. He was eight or nine years old with thick, black hair worn long over the ears in an outdated style that reminded Shannon of early photos of The Beatles. His outfit also felt anachronistic, though from a different era: a bright red polo shirt tucked into belted khaki shorts that came just to the knee, and a pair of unnaturally white socks and sneakers.

The boy kept one hand on the doorknob, while the

other hung lank at his side. His face was oddly devoid of expression, and Shannon couldn't tell if he was scared, bored, or confused at the prospect of a stranger at the door. He just stared at her, silent and still, until Shannon shifted her feet, uneasy at the way the kid looked right through her.

After what seemed like an eternity, Shannon cleared her throat. She was being stupid. He was just a kid.

"Hi," she said, in a light, airy, I'm-your-new-favorite-babysitter voice.

Silence. The boy just stared.

"Um, I'm from Mommy's Happy Helpers," she continued. Was there something wrong with this kid? "I'm the replacement babysitter."

Nothing.

Great. This gig was going to be more work than she thought. "Are your mom and dad home?" Shannon took a step toward the door. "Maybe you can tell them—"

Without a word, the boy stepped aside, swinging the door wide open. Clearly, it was an invitation to enter the house, but Shannon hesitated. Why was she so nervous? She'd babysat for dozens of families, many of whom had large houses tucked away in the hills. She'd always been safe. One of the reasons she liked working for Debbie was that all the clients were vetted in advance. So why was she suddenly apprehensive about this one?

She was just tired. That had to be it. She was letting her imagination get the better of her.

Shannon forced the muscles of her face into one of her brightest, most inviting smiles, and stepped inside the house.

The entryway was practically as large as the entire home Shannon and her parents rented in Topanga

Canyon. It was two stories high and ran the entire length of the house, stretching fifty feet in each direction. The hardwood floor was a geometrical mosaic of dark and light triangles, waxed and polished with an almost painful glean. Sconces blazed along the walls, and three enormous chrome chandeliers hung from the rafters of the ceiling, illuminating the space in such dazzling light that Shannon had to blink a few times until her eyes adjusted to the brightness.

And yet the room felt cold—intimidating and uninviting. Twin staircases curved up the wall directly opposite the front door, but with the exception of the red-shirted boy who stood like a sentry at the door, there wasn't a single piece of furniture in the space.

Except one.

Tick. Tick. Tick.

Directly opposite the front door, centered on a wall between the staircases, stood an enormous grandfather clock.

Tick. Tick. Tick.

"Wow," Shannon said. Not "wow" as in "awesome!" but "wow" as in "what the hell is that?"

The clock was grotesque. Eight feet tall and wide enough for two adults to stand comfortably inside the body, the clock was an imposing presence in the room. The exterior was a mix of dark and light inlaid wood that, while matching the pattern of the parquet floor, seemed out of place in the sleek, modern home. Two massive pillars flanked either side, and the square face that housed the actual clock mechanism was decorated with curved flourishes that looked almost like devil horns. The face itself was a gothic mish mash of twisted wrought iron and Roman numerals, complete with a barometer and a dial which showed the current phase of the moon.

She took a few steps toward the clock. "That's bizarre."

Shannon felt a rush of air behind her, then the door slammed shut. She spun around. Red Shirt still stood beside the door, but a second child—a girl—stood by his side. Like her brother, she had jet black hair, close cropped around her face but longer in the back. She wore the same belted, khaki shorts, but her polo shirt was lemon yellow.

"Hi," she said, trying to sound casual. "I'm Shannon."

No answer.

Tick. Tick. Tick.

Shannon glanced back at the clock. It was ridiculously loud, its rhythmic tick echoing off the high ceiling and wood floor. As she stared at the face, she noticed the second hand was frozen in place. The clock wasn't moving.

"Hey," she said, walking up to the clock. "Did you know this clock doesn't work?"

"There's a neat little clock,
In the school room it stands."

Shannon spun around. There were three of them now. Another child had appeared as if out of thin air. Another boy. Same haircut and uniform as his brother, but he wore a blue shirt.

Where the hell were they coming from?

"And it points to the time,
With its two little hands."

They recited it together—Red Shirt, Yellow Shirt, and Blue Shirt—in perfect unison.

Clearly, this was some kind of joke the kids were playing on her. Hazing the babysitter. Sure, they outnumbered her, but Shannon was the closest thing to an adult in the room. She could handle it.

"Cute," she said with a wink. "Now, where are your parents?"

Slowly, from left to right and back again, the three children shook their heads.

"Okay," Shannon said slowly. No parents? What the hell were they doing leaving eight-year-olds alone in the house? Maybe that was normal in Australia, but Shannon was pretty sure it was illegal in California.

This made things significantly more awkward. Without the parents, she had no idea what to feed the kids, when to put them to bed. Most parents wanted to interrogate the new babysitter for at least twenty minutes to assuage their fears. Not these guys. Apparently, they had no problem abandoning their kids to an unknown, unproven babysitter.

Shannon felt the hairs on the back of her neck stand at attention, the same creepy-crawly sensation she'd felt on the walkway when she saw the four silhouettes in the window. *So stupid.* This was Malibu, after all. Playground of the rich and entitled. It probably never occurred to the parents that bailing before the babysitter arrived was at all unusual. Maybe they were used to leaving the kids with a housekeeper or something . . . .

"Oh!" Shannon said. "Do you have a housekeeper?"

Again, the kids just shook their heads.

"Er, okay. A cook? Au pair?"

Same slow shake of heads.

"So there are no other adults in the house right now?"

Together, all three kids raised their right arms and pointed a finger at the clock.

The clock? Why the hell were they so fixated on the clock?

"Funny, guys," she said. "That's a clock." She noticed the time said three o'clock when it must have been near eight. "And it doesn't even work."

> *"There's a neat little clock,*
> *In the school room it stands.*
> *And it points to the time,*
> *With its two little hands."*

Shannon was starting to lose her patience. She stormed up to the clock. "No, it doesn't point to the time. It doesn't work. Its eight o'clock and this thing says three. Get it?"

Tick. Tick. Tick.

The noise of the clock's mechanics upbraided her. Why wasn't it showing the right time? For some reason, it bugged the hell out of her. She needed to fix it.

Shannon peered into the clock's face, looking for a latch for the glass cover, but the casement seemed to be attached at all points. Maybe there was something in the back? She stepped to the side of the monstrous clock and froze.

Sticking out from behind the clock was a bright-white piece of fabric. It looked vaguely like a shirt sleeve.

Shannon reached out and pulled. A white sweatshirt unfurled from where it had been shoved behind the clock. "What's this?"

> *"There's a neat little clock,*
> *In the school room it stands.*
> *And it points to the time,*
> *With its two little hands."*

There were four of them now. Four kids. A second girl had joined her siblings. Same hair, same clothes, with the exception of an emerald-green shirt.

They recited the verse together, adding another line.

"And may we like the clock
Keep a face clean and bright—"

"Enough with the clock," Shannon snapped. She was tired of the weirdness, a house in the middle of nowhere without parents, kids appearing out of thin air, a ticking clock that couldn't tell time. This place was freaky. Shannon silently cursed Annie for not showing up.

Annie.

Shannon looked down at the sweatshirt she'd pulled from behind the clock. A white Hollister sweatshirt. Just like the one Annie had borrowed from her boyfriend.

Using both hands, Shannon held the unzipped sweatshirt up in front of her. A dark red stain marred the front.

Shannon dropped the sweatshirt as if it was on fire. Annie's sweatshirt soaked in blood? With a shaky hand, she fished her cell phone out of her pocket and dialed her best friend's number.

Tick. Tick. Tick.

Brrrrrrrrrrring!

A muffled phone rang out. It sounded as if it came from inside the clock.

Without a second thought, Shannon yanked open the front of the grandfather clock. Instead of the clicking mechanics of a well-kept timepiece, Shannon saw a face staring back at her. Blue eyes wide open, jaw slack in a silent scream, blood soaked blonde hair hanging lank and heavy across her shoulders.

Shannon knew that face.

Annie.

Her right hand had been crossed awkwardly in front of her as she had been shoved inside the clock, and blood trickled down her hand, gathering at the tip of her index finger in large, sticky drops before falling, one-by-one, onto the floor of the clock.

Drip. Drip. Drip.

> *"There's a neat little clock,*
> *In the school room it stands.*
> *And it points to the time,*
> *With its two little hands."*

Annie's phone lay discarded next to the pool of coagulating blood. It stopped ringing as Shannon's call when to voicemail.

"Oh my God," Shannon said. She fumbled with her phone. She could barely even think straight as she pressed 9-1-1.

> *"And may we like the clock*
> *Keep a face clean and bright,*
> *With hands ever ready . . ."*

Shannon turned back to the kids, phone to her ear. "What did you—"

The words froze on her tongue. The kids were right in front of her. Faces devoid of expression and staring straight ahead of themselves. Each child held a large carving knife which glistened in the brilliant light of the chandeliers.

They opened their mouths and raised their knives in unison.

"To do what is right."

Shannon never heard her own scream.

– The End –

RING AROUND THE ROSES

Ring a-round the roses,
A pocket full of posies,
Ashes! Ashes!
We all fall down!

– Mother Goose

A POCKET FULL OF POSY
Pamela van Hylckama Vlieg

I have blood on my hands.

I don't remember anything, and have no idea why I woke up on a park bench blocks from my house. I stand and shove my hands in my pockets. I have to remember what happened last night. I need to get home and wash my hands. The blood is dry. It flakes when I rub my hands together, but not all of it is coming off. It's under my nails and embedded in the cracks on my hands.

What did you do last night, Jake?

My jeans are filthy. I hope that's mud on the knees and not more blood. "One more block," I murmur. My house is locked but I find my keys in the front right pocket of my jeans. I head straight for the bathroom. I just want to take a shower.

I let the water get warmer than I usually like it. I feel the need to scald the red from my hands. The water in the sink turns pink and my stomach turns sour. I feel sickness fighting its way up my throat, but I hold it down. I sit on the floor of the bathroom and think. The last thing I remember is picking my girlfriend, Rose, up at her house after dinner. *What happened after that?*

My memory is coming back in short bursts. I remember a field; it was after dark and full of wildflowers. I made Rose a posy of the purple and white flowers. Reaching into my pocket, I find the small bundle of flowers still tied together with a long blade of grass. *I must have never given it to her.* I remember the field. It's on the edge of town. Maybe my car is there.

I grab some money from the dresser in my bedroom and walk the block to catch a bus heading north. I haven't ridden the bus since I got my car last year, but the schedule is still embedded in my mind. I'll probably never forget it. I have fifteen minutes to wait. I text my mom that I'm feeling ill and don't want to go to school today and that I'll see her when she gets home from her shift. She works nights at the hospital in the maternity ward. I like that she's gone four nights a week. I can skip curfew and she has no idea that I even did it.

The bus rolls past the park and I get off at the next stop. Sure enough, my car is in the small, five-car parking lot in front of the park. I start there and try to retrace my steps to where we sat down last night. I keep walking straight through the flowers. I walk in a straight line through the field. The weeds and flowers reach my knees, and I find nothing. I walk in a circle this time and see a ring of flowers mashed to the ground, as if someone had been sitting on them. I rush forward to see if there are any clues, and that's when I find her.

If it wasn't for the fact that her throat was open, I could have believed that she was sleeping there with the flowers surrounding her. *She's dead. Rose is dead.* An accusing voice reminds me that I woke up with blood on my hands. *Did I do this? Did I rip my girlfriend's throat out?*

I have to call the police. Someone has to come get Rose and someone has to tell her parents. But what if I did this? How long do you go to jail for killing your girlfriend? No. There's no way I would ever hurt Ro. Something is going on here, something I can't remember. I want to know why this happened, and I want to know why I didn't help her. I drag the bundle of flowers out of my jeans pocket and place them in her cold hands. *Beautiful dead flowers for a beautiful dead girl.*

I turn and run back to my car. My nerves are completely shot and I drop my keys. I stand up and see a police officer on a motorcycle drive by. He makes a u-turn and comes back to the park.

"Hey, son," he says in his official business voice. "Everything all right?"

"Yes, sir," I say. "I was just getting ready to drive to school." I force myself to smile at him, feigning innocence. I could be innocent. I don't remember killing Ro.

"Get a move on," he says, donning his helmet again.

I nod and open my car door. I wait until I see which direction he is going before flicking my turn indicator on and committing myself. I thank the stars that he went the opposite direction from home.

Parking my car, I head into the house and change into different clothes. I stuff my jeans in the bottom of the hamper, telling myself I will deal with them later.

Mom will have no trouble believing I am sick. I look as pale as death, as white as Rose looked in the field. A sheen of cold sweat covers my body, making me feel gross. I hop into bed just as she comes through the door.

"Jake?" she calls.

"In here, Mom," I answer, not bothering to tame the quiver in my voice.

She comes into my room and puts her hand on my head. "Do you want some Tylenol?"

"No, I just need to rest," I say.

"Well . . ." I can see that she doesn't like it that I don't want the pills. "Okay, I'm going to get some sleep but wake me up if you need anything."

I nod, not trusting myself to answer. My mom is great, I love her so much. I feel the need to blurt out everything that happened to me this morning, but I'm not ready to talk. And I really don't want to stress her out. She takes a lot of crap at the hospital and she's been raising me all by herself since Dad died. I tighten my lips and hold it all in. She goes to bed and I sink deeper into my despair.

***

I spend a week at home. I can't face my friends. I can't face anyone, really. I ignore texts and calls. Mom thinks I have the flu.

On the sixth day, they find Rose.

I want to stay home forever. The only reason I am going to school today is to avoid going to the doctor. I have overstayed my welcome and Mom is ready to get me well and back out of the nest.

I decide not to breathe a word to anyone about any of this until my memory comes back. Going to school is a great way to rest my brain from the constant question marks of trying so hard to remember. Also, I need to keep up appearances. I don't think I am guilty, but that doesn't mean others won't.

The fall morning has a chill to it. Cold weather always makes my car a little hard to start, but the third time I try the engine, she turns over. It is a short drive to the school. When it's warm, but not too hot, I leave a half hour earlier and walk. It clears my head.

The parking lot is full and I end up having to park on the street. I barley make it to my first class before the bell rings.

Fifty minutes are up before I notice it. English has never been my favorite subject. Still, I usually don't zone out for long periods of time in class.

The hallway is teeming with students fighting their way to their next class. I fight a path upstream to my locker. I input my combination slowly; I want to let the hall thin out a bit before shutting my locker and facing the world again. I grab my history book and close the door. As I turn around, I see two men in suits coming toward me. Their pace is brisk and my fight or flight senses are begging to kick in. I stand my ground and wait. They know I've seen them already, there is no use trying to play nonchalant.

"Jake Garrus?" The bigger of the two asks.

"Yeah," I say. I am dying to add a "who wants to know?" to the conversation.

"I'm Detective Benton and this is my partner, Detective Shepard," he says, nodding to the smaller of the two. "We'd like to talk to you, son. The principal has given us the use of the teacher's lounge. Would you mind following us?"

I nod. I can't trust my voice not to betray fear, or worse yet, guilt. I follow them silently. If I hadn't been scared out of my wits, I might have been a little excited to go into this room. No one is allowed in there except for staff, and I have always been a little curious about what goes on behind the closed doors.

Benton opens the door and I walk in. Curiosity makes me look around and I am a bit disappointed with what I see. For a moment, I think about what I would tell Ro about being in here. She would have loved to hear that there was no disco ball, no martini bar—just the same tables and chairs we have in the cafeteria. I would give anything to tell her all about it.

"Have a seat, Mr. Garrus," Shepard says, smiling.

Oh, I see. It's going to be good cop, bad cop, with Shepard playing the nice guy. I decide to play along. "You can call me Jake."

"Well, Jake," Benton says. "Where's your girlfriend?"

I try to look stunned; they can't know I was anywhere near that field. I have to think fast. "I don't know, officer. I haven't seen her since our date the other night."

"When was that, son?" Shepard asks nicely.

"Monday last. I picked her up after dinner and we went out. I drove her home before her curfew at midnight," I say.

"You haven't been to school since then," Benton says, glaring at me.

"No, I had a stomach bug. My mom came home from work and pronounced me too ill to go to school. You know how moms are," I say, smiling brightly. "What's this all about?"

Benton stands and slams his hands down on the table. "Are you going to keep playing coy with me?"

"Now, Benton," Shepard says. "What he means is, do you know what happened to Rose?"

"No, I haven't been answering my calls or texts. I've . . . I've been too sick."

"You really don't know?" Benton asks. I see pity in his expression. Good, that means he's buying it. I shake my head at him.

"We found Rose in a field, son," Shepard says. "She's dead."

I shudder and push myself back from the table. The image of Rose lying in that field, pale and white except for the angry gash at her throat, threatens to do me in. I run to the back of the room and heave into the trashcan. I don't usually have a weak stomach, but guilt, nerves, and unidentifiable emotions are warring with each other and causing me to be sick. When I finish, Shepard hands me a glass of water. I return to the table and sit down.

"She's gone?" I ask. I already know this, but I still feel the need to have it confirmed.

"Yes," Benton says. His angry sails seem to have lost wind and he is being nicer to me. "You were the last person seen with her."

"I can't . . ." I start. I have to play this right; I need to find out what happened to Ro, so I need the cops not to suspect me. "I don't know what happened after I left her at home. We were going to watch a movie, but decided to hang out up near Pregnant Hill instead. We didn't do anything, if that's what you're thinking. Rose wasn't like that. I took her home and she kissed me goodnight and went inside." I look up at the detectives. They seem to buy my story. "That's the last time I saw her."

"Here's my card," Shepard says, handing me a white slip of cardstock with a number on it. "Call us if you hear anything. You can go back to class. There's a number for a grief counselor on the back."

I nod and stand up. I look at both of them one last time, then grab my history book from the table and leave. When I get to class, the teacher doesn't ask any questions. He must have been informed I would be late.

At lunch, I go through the motions. I grab a slice of pizza and sit at my normal seat. There's no way I am going to be able to eat. Especially here, with Rose's empty seat beside me. I see Elijah and Addie coming toward me. They look sad. I'm not sure I am ready for this conversation of loss between friends. They sat with Ro and me every day, we had all four been friends forever. It's kind of funny how we had evolved into couples.

When they get to the table, Elijah looks more pissed than sad. "What the fuck are you doing here?"

"What?" I ask.

"You heard him," Addie says. Her face scrunches up in disgust.

"What's going on, guys?" I am at a loss.

"Are you seriously looking me in my face and pretending you didn't do anything wrong?" Elijah asks. "You killed our best friend, and right now I am feeling pretty murderous myself. You better find somewhere else to sit."

"I didn't kill anyone," I say. I'm not sure I sound too convincing. I'm not convinced of my innocence, either.

"Just. Get. Out." Addie says.

So I do. I stand, leave my tray, and walk out of the cafeteria. Everyone stares at me. One kid even throws potatoes at me and misses. Walking through the hall isn't any better. People outright stare at me. They all think I am a murderer. Maybe I am. Something inside of me tells me otherwise. I would never hurt Ro. I loved her. I have to find out what really happened that night.

No one says anything as I leave. No faculty tries to stop me as I leave the school through the main entrance and head to my car. When I get home, I closet myself in my room and lie down on my bed. Sleep seems to be the only thing I can handle right now.

***

When I wake, it is dark. I fumble around for my phone

to get the time. Five a.m. I have slept another day away. I wonder if I will ever be able to stay awake for more than four hours. I can't go back to school today. I have to remember. I have to go back to where Rose died.

***

There are few cars on the road and I get to the field of flowers in record time. I walk to where her body had been laying when I stumbled upon her Tuesday morning. The flowers lay trampled and broken all over the field; the police had no time to protect Mother Nature as they made their way to Rose. Using my phone as a flashlight, I find where she died. Police tape is still strung in a makeshift barricade the cops had erected when they were investigating her murder. It looks crass in the dim light. I sit at the edge of the ring of flowers and begin to cry. Coming back here has done nothing for my memory. I am no closer to finding the truth than I had been when I woke up with bloody hands and posy in my pocket.

"I told you to forget." The voice is hard and sinister. It is deep and has the timbre of someone who smoked way too many cigarettes. I turn around, fighting my phone for light.

"Who's there?" I ask, fear obvious in my voice.

"You don't remember me?" The man asks, stepping into the vague stream of light.

"No," I say. "I don't remember anything."

"This poses a problem," he says. "I told you to forget and you should have forgotten everything. The fact that you have been back here at least twice shows me that my coercion didn't fully work. I'm not hungry. But I could eat."

"Coercion?" I ask. "What do you mean?"

"You are young," he says in way of an answer. "And handsome. Perhaps we could come to an agreement. I have been alone for such a very long time."

"How do you know me?" I ask. "How do you know how many times I've been back here?"

"I could smell you, on her body," he says.

"What?" I ask. Then it hits me. Her throat was torn out. I remember everything.

We had decided to go all the way. I had bought her a fifty-cent ring as a joke at the supermarket. We were going to be married after college; we had both been accepted to UNC. She wanted to go to the field; she thought the flowers made it more romantic. I had to go back to the car; I had forgotten my lone condom there. On the way, I picked flowers and fashioned the posy I left with her.

When I got back, this man was leaning over her. He heard me approach and stood. There was blood all over his mouth and the collar of his old-fashioned shirt. He walked toward me and whispered one word. *Forget.* I remembered nothing else.

"I see you remember me after all," he says, smiling. "How would you like to live forever?"

I turn and run. I want to get to my car, but in the dark I become lost easily, and I'm sure I'm headed in the wrong direction. I hear him laugh.

"All right then," he says. "A hunt it is. I hope you are fast. I like a challenge."

I stumble. Every horror movie I have ever seen flashes through my head. I am making all the wrong decisions. All I need is blonde hair and a huge set of boobs; I am acting like the girl who runs upstairs instead of out the door. I resolve to make a smart decision. I have to think about everything that has happened. My brain doesn't want to believe what my heart has already seen. Vampires exist and I have about a nanosecond before one is on top of me.

There are no trees in the field, so grabbing wood for a stake is out. I have to wonder if you even need wood. Wouldn't any sharp, pointy thing through the heart do the job?

He hits me from behind and I fall to the ground. I feel as if I can't get air, my vision is blurring and my back arches in pain. He stands, looking at me as if he doesn't know what to do with me. I check my phone. Five-fifty. He must think I am trying to call for help, because he kicks the phone out of my hand. But I don't require the light anymore. The sky is already turning orange.

He grabs my shoulders and smiles. I watch his teeth shift over, making room for fat, wide fangs that elongate before my eyes. I want to scream, but his eyes challenge me to do so. Like it would make killing me so much better for him if I did. Instead, I feel around on the ground. I almost let out a whoop of joy when I find a heavy rock. He is leaning toward my neck. I bring the rock to his temple. He rolls off of me, groaning, and I stand. Then I run again. This time, I know I'm going in the right direction.

I can see my car. I am almost home free, when something grabs my ankle, pulling me roughly to the ground for the second time. I turn over and kick out with my other leg, but the beast keeps his hold.

"No, no, little human. No more games. But since I like you, I will ask you again. Die or become like me?" he says, smiling victoriously.

"Neither," I say. I feel brave enough to smile back at him. If I am going to die, I want it to be on my terms.

I wait for him to bend down. When he does, I stick both of my thumbs in his eyes. I feel some squishy resistance but then something gives and the vampire is screaming, but it doesn't sound human at all. It sounds more like a banshee wail. He grabs my wrists and I pull my fingers out of his sockets and roll him over easily. He is too distracted by the pain to fight me. I'm right beside my car when I see the tree. I race to it and break a good sized branch off at an angle. This monster will hurt no one else.

When I get back to where I'd left him, he isn't there anymore. I look around and see him standing a few feet in front of me, still holding his hands over his eyes. The vulnerability in his stance makes me reconsider my murderous plans for a moment. Then I remember that he is a murderer of many with no remorse. My resolve hardens. I walk toward him.

"Don't come any closer human, I can still kill you," he says, but his voice shows that he isn't sure that he can still win.

I say nothing. When I am two feet in front of him, I kick out, connecting with his knee. He falls to the ground, landing on his knees and he pulls his hands away from his face. The sight of his eyes and what I did to them makes me want to run away, but I have to end this.

Pulling my arm back, I aim for the middle of his chest and bring the stick down, hard.

His ashes fly all around me in the morning wind.

I turn and head back to my car. No one will believe me. I wouldn't believe me, either. The one good thing is now I know I can weather anything. I know for sure.

I didn't kill Rose.

– The End –

JACK AND JILL

Jack and Jill
Went up the hill
To fetch a pail of water.
Jack fell down
And broke his crown
And Jill came tumbling after.
Up Jack got
And home did trot
As fast as he could caper.
Went to bed
And plastered his head
With vinegar and brown paper.
– Mother Goose

THE WELL
K.M. Walton

I do not like my brother Jack. With crossed arms, I stand over him, watching him sleep. I study the rise and fall of his chest. He sleeps soundly, always has. Jealousy and worry don't stick to Jack. How could they when they've fastened themselves around my waist, poised and ready to pull me under at any given moment.

Jack readjusts underneath the blanket and his black curls fall into his eyes. The amount of female attention he used to get—the constant visits, filled with giggling and hair tossing and touching—did nothing but get in the way of keeping things running around here. And further build my resentment.

The sound he makes when he licks his lips reminds me of a sloppy yard dog. He grunts in his sleep. I clench my teeth and leave my brother snoring on the sofa. There is work to be done. Like always.

I grab a fresh candle from the box and check our reserves. "Damn it," I grumble. We'll have to figure something else out. Before lighting the candle and unlocking our front door, I peek through our front window. I count the flies on the glass. Eleven today. Three less than yesterday.

This was my grandmother's routine, what she taught me to do. It has been a few months since she died peacefully in her sleep, but a dark morning hasn't come that I haven't looked through the window first, before stepping foot outside. When she was alive, we usually checked for strangers or sick people. Now, I check for flies.

The more flies, the more death.

My Nan and Jack and I watched a lot of death last year. The nightly news ran story after story of entire towns dying in a week. Thousands of people. Gone. Birds fell dead from the sky. Major cities placed under martial law. The human death toll was in the hundreds of millions before modern living stopped.

My Nan took her last breath by candlelight, tucked underneath her treasured quilt. There was no blood, no gasping for air. Nan had just closed her eyes, and that was that. A plain old, regular death.

All of our town had died. My brother and I had no idea why the virus hadn't affected us. But it hadn't.

The Shiver Rash swept across continents in just under a year. The government named the fast-moving virus after William Shiver, the first known victim. But sickness and death took a long time to reach Porcupine Creek, and for a few months we Alaskans thought we'd been spared. A benefit of living the clean life up here. We thought nature would protect us.

When my trig teacher was found dead in her driveway, face down in a pool of her own blood and pus and covered in black flies, Alaska lost its mind.

Everything kicked into hyper-speed. People ping-ponged around—clearing out stores, emptying gas stations, crying their eyes out. It only took Porcupine Creek forty-eight hours to go into lockdown. Families holed up in their houses, their windows covered in thick plastic tarp. Fireplaces sealed.

People were able to keep in touch for a little while—giving reports of who'd died or who was infected. Then the emergency generators stopped humming. No one wanted to leave the safety of their sealed homes to fill their generators with fuel. I will never forget the day our generator went quiet. I felt the void in my skin. The quiet made me itch.

We all thought I'd contracted The Shiver.

I even texted Courtney that I'd finally gotten sick. My last text from her read: Mom died last night. My mouth is bleeding now. It sucks we'll never go to prom.

I cried into my pillow until the sun came up.

Courtney and I had been best friends since third grade. Her father had moved their family up here from Florida to mine for gold. My parents had done the same thing before my brother and I were born. Neither of our fathers had ever struck it big, but we used to say it didn't matter, because we'd struck it rich when we became friends. Corny and dorky, but true.

Sometimes, I lie in the dark and hold entire conversations with Courtney in my head. We make plans, we laugh, we talk about our crushes, homework, shopping, and our annoying older brothers. In these imaginary moments, we never talk virus. Dying at sixteen doesn't come up. Ever.

I'm still here. Jack is still here.

I hear the sofa cushions squeak. My brother is up. "We're low on firewood, Jack," I shout over my shoulder. If I had to go climb that steep hill to gather the crowberries, then he was going to do *something* to help.

"We're low on water," he mumbles as he comes into the entryway. We'd been sleeping in the living room to stay warm, to be close to our makeshift fire pit. Before we sealed ourselves off, Jack had rolled a rusty steel drum up from the garage. It sits in the center of the living room.

I stare at my brother. Did he think I didn't know we were low on water? I'm shocked *he* noticed. "Yeah, I know."

"Do you have to sound like you hate me every second of every day, Jill? What the hell? God, I just woke up." He rakes his hand through his hair. "Don't you think I'm as miserable as you are? I didn't kill everyone. The virus did."

I laugh in his face.

"You're a bitch," Jack says. He turns on his heel and heads into the kitchen.

It's in these moments that I crave my evil wish: that Courtney had been immune instead of Jack.

The fact that Jack was three and a half minutes older than me has everything to do with how I feel about him. He clawed his way from my mother's womb, leaving her bleeding to death in the tub. Her body had gone still. Or so I've been told.

Despite the fact that not a single soul knew I was still inside of my dead mother—the silent and mysterious fraternal twin—I'd wanted to be born as well. My entry into the world was far less violent than Jack's. I simply slid out on my own into the warm bathtub water. Slick and bloody and new. Well, that's the story Nan always told me as she tucked me in with her icy hands and warm brown eyes.

When Jack and I were only two days old, the grief of losing his beloved wife had caused my father to dive headfirst into the old, dried-up well at the top of our hill—the hill I was about to climb. For months, no one knew my father's fate. Everyone, including Nan, believed he'd simply run away. The talk in town was that the stress of infant twins mixed with the sudden death of his wife sent him over the edge.

The irony of how my father actually died, falling over the edge of a well, plummeting to his death, hadn't been lost on Nan. She told me so on my tenth birthday, along with the haunting fact that my father's bones were still at the bottom of the well.

His crumpled body had decomposed. No one knew he was down there. By the time our neighbor accidentally discovered my father's remains, my Nan thought it better to leave him undisturbed. The rain and the flies had stripped dad's flesh and muscle, leaving only his bones.

Jack is slamming kitchen cabinets. That's usually my job. I'm the miserable twin. He tells me so every day. *He* seems angry today, which makes me angry. *What the hell does he have to be angry about?* I do almost everything around here, while he locks himself in the bathroom for hours, crying like a damn baby.

I stomp into the kitchen. "Hey, you know what?" My sudden yelling startles him. "The fact that I am forced to spend the rest of my days on this empty planet, alone with you, makes me want to join Daddy at the bottom of that well!"

"I'll push you in," Jack deadpans. "It'll be a win-win." He glares at me and then pops a handful of crowberries into his mouth. "You know what? You make me sick."

I slam the front door on my way out. *I* make *him* sick? I wasn't the golden child, the one everyone loved, the one showered with compliments and adoring looks. He was the one every teacher gushed over. The one Nan adored, always making his favorite moose stew with crowberry pie for dessert. I don't even think Nan realized I didn't like meat until I was twelve.

Nan. I tromp past her grave. The wood of the cross has yet to darken, its sandy color a reminder of the day we were forced to unseal the house. Nan's body needed to be buried. At that point, Jack and I were pretty confident in our immunity to the virus, but we weren't one hundred percent sure. We agreed that giving Nan a proper burial was worth the risk of dying.

When the sun rose the morning after putting Nan in the ground and neither of us felt sick, we opened up the house.

I look over my shoulder as I trudge up the steep hill. Jack doesn't follow me. The thick summer grass makes no sound underneath my boots. What fills the air is the clank of the metal pail hitting against my thigh with every step I take. The solitary sound is thick and absolute. There are no animals or rustling leaves. No planes or birds overhead. The road just beyond our property line has been empty since spring.

I dig my boot into the ground to steady my footing, and I look out over the valley. I swat away the flies circling my head. The beauty of the landscape—the snow-capped mountains off in the distance, the bright blue sky—saddens me deeply. Why did we survive? Why us? Why couldn't Courtney have survived instead of Jack?

I reach up to bat another fly. The pail falls from my grasp and tumbles down the hill. "Crap." Without thinking, I lunge for it. I need it to hold the crowberries. I lose my footing and land hard on my butt. Then I slide a few feet before coming to a stop. "Ahhh. Ow." I exhale and slowly stand up.

My sweatpants have ripped. I can feel the crisp morning breeze hit the back of my thigh. I reach back to assess the damage. The hole is huge. I switch the pail to my other hand and notice the blood on the wooden handle. I must've cut my leg.

Like sharks to crum, the flies show up. They love blood. My Nan used to call them mini-vampires.

I look down at the house and wince. I'd rather continue up the hill with a bloody leg and flies trailing behind me like rats than go spend unnecessary time with my brother.

I limp my way to the top. I lean on the cold stones of the well to catch my breath. I'm lightheaded. The flies tickle the back of my thigh. I swish them away. It's no use. My knees give a little and I grasp the well to steady myself. My hand is covered in blood.

I scream my brother's name.

The sun shines directly overhead. A bright light illuminates the depths of the well, lighting up my father's remains. I blink and stare down at his white skull for what feels like forever. The sun inches across the sky.

"Jack!" I shout again. Random thoughts torture me as I hopelessly swat the flies and do my best not to pass out. I wonder what my father's voice would've sounded like. How his hug would've felt.

Where is my brother?

I drop the pail and hear it bounce down the hill. I turn to watch. There is the top of Jack's head.

My brother goes white when he sees the blood. "You're infected?"

Little white spots twinkle when I shake my head. "I fell." I don't think I can stand anymore. Jack runs to my side and catches me before I hit the ground. I go limp in his arms, my legs no longer able to hold me up. Jack stumbles a bit and we both slam into the side of the well.

I let out a scream. My wound took the brunt of the

impact. Jack reaches up and puts his hand over my mouth. "Shhhhh. You're too loud," he whispers. "Be quiet. Shhhhh."

I nod.

He slowly takes his hand away, but continues to grasp me tightly with his other. "It looks like you've lost a lot of blood, Jill."

I nod.

"I don't know how to fix your leg," he says flatly.

I nod.

He exhales into my face and nods along with me. I can smell the sweet crowberries on his breath. "You know what I have to do right?" He smiles and gently moves the hair out of my eyes.

I stop in mid-nod. I *didn't* know. Why was I nodding? "Help me back to the house."

His lips tighten and his nostrils flare. He shakes his head. Slowly.

"Jack, I can make it."

He leans down and whispers in my ear, "I don't want you to make it."

My eyebrows pinch together. "What are you talking about? Help me down."

"You won't . . ." his voice trails off. He looks over at the well. "Dad. You can be with Dad. You always visit him anyway."

My brother has broken with reality. Lost his mind. Snapped.

I twist from his grip and hang my head over the lip of the well. A loose stone breaks free and lands at my feet. My father's skull stares up at me. I don't want to die.

Jack yanks me back by my hair, and I cry out in pain. We land in a tangled heap. My blood is now smeared up and down his arms.

"Jack! Stop! What are you doing?" I shriek. His grip on me is firm. I can't break free. "You're hurting me."

My brother has madness in his eyes.

"Help!" As soon as the word leaves my lips, he laughs.

Through clenched teeth he says, "There is no one to help us, Jill. No. One."

"You want to live alone? Be by yourself? That's crazy, Jack." My chest heaves, yet I'm breathless. "What about Nan?" I didn't even know what my question meant. What *about* Nan? What did our dead grandmother have to do with anything right now?

But this gives my brother pause, and he releases his hold on me just a little. "Nan? Nan?" he murmurs. With every ounce of energy I have left, I roll out from underneath him and scurry away on my hands and knees. Jack is on his back, his arms crossed over his face, and he's sobbing.

"I was g-going to be an architect, Nan," Jack chokes. "You told me I was your prince. Everything's ruined, Nan. It's over."

Bile shoots up my throat. I gag and vomit into the grass. The flies descend. I watch them crawl through my pile of goo, and I retch again. My leg throbs. I just want to get off of this hill and lie down on the sofa. "Jack, I have to stop the bleeding. I need your help. I can't make it down without you."

He uses the heels of his hands to wipe away his tears, and he sits up. We watch each other. Tears roll down my cheeks. I'm in agony. "Please," I say. Jack shows no reaction to my tears or my begging. Instead, he tilts his head and stares through me.

"I don't want to die up here, Jack. You have to help me down."

Like a spring, he hops to his feet, and he gets me standing without saying a word.

"I'm sorry," I say. He wraps his arm around my waist and leads me to the lip of the hill. "Go slow, okay?"

Jack ignores me.

I look up at him, but he continues staring down toward the bottom of the hill. "Jack?" I tug on his shirt. "Go slow."

"I know you blame me for our parents' deaths," he says. "You are a bad person, Jill. A very bad person. You're twisted and . . . and . . ." He goes quiet.

My heart should be pounding and thudding, but it's not. Most of my blood has left my body, sliding down my thigh and saturating my sock. My knees fail and I take hold of my brother's shirt. Jack grabs my shoulders and squeezes me so hard that I feel his fingernails pierce my skin. "You have always hated me!" he shouts in my face.

My eyes cloud over and I can feel myself collapsing. I must get him off me. If he loses his footing, he'll drag me down with him.

I smash my head into his chest to surprise him. He lets me go. And with all of my might, I push my brother backward.

His body folds in half as he reaches for something to grab onto.

I instinctively take a step back.

I watch him bounce and smash down the hill. His head takes the brunt of his landing. Blood shoots from his skull in slow motion.

"Jaaaaaack!" I cry out. Oh my God, what have I done? What have I done? What have I done?

I suspect that Jack is dead. The unnatural angle of his leg makes me cringe. His body is as still as stone.

"Jack. Jack. Jack." I moan.

I stumble to the well. My blood is everywhere. How *I'm* not dead already is a miracle.

"Daddy, I-I've killed Jack," I whisper down to his bones. "What do I do?"

I have the clawing urge to dive into the well. To crush *my* skull. To land in a tangled heap on top of my father's remains. Pain on top of pain.

I try to lift myself over, and my legs give way. I slide to my knees. "I'm sorry, Jack. Daddy, please help me." Pleading to my dead father feels right, so I repeat myself.

The flies have reached a swarming level, and I don't have the energy to swat them away anymore. They crawl over my eyes, buzz in my ears.

I need to see if Jack is alive. Maybe he didn't die. Maybe he needs my help down there. Since I'm unable to stand, I roll, as if I'm on fire, and make it to the edge. I lift my head to try and spot my brother. The hill is too steep, and I'm too low to the ground to see down to the bottom. "Jack?" I shout. Well, I'm shouting it in my mind, anyway. There is no volume to my voice. My throat is only able to produce a low groan.

I turn over onto my back. Tears slide down my temples and into my hairline. I choke on my sobs. The sky looks fake, too perfect. The clouds too fluffy. The blue too blue.

I push off with my hand and set myself in motion. Downhill.

– The End –

STAR LIGHT, STAR BRIGHT

Star light, star bright,
The first star I see tonight,
I wish I may, I wish I might,
Have the wish I wish tonight.
                              – Mother Goose

THE WISH
Suzanne Young

I lean my elbows on the railing of the deck, the sound of the party loud on the other side of the sliding glass doors. I stare up at the sky, navy blue streaked with the dark gray of hidden clouds. It's serene out here: the soft wind, the half-moon hanging low. If I could forget that I'm at a party with my boyfriend—sorry, ex-boyfriend—and the new girl he's dating, life would seem almost peaceful.

But that would be a lie.

Aaron has been gone for two weeks. Not truly. No, I can turn and see him through the glass doors if I want. He'll still be slow dancing in the middle of a rowdy party, holding Rachel close, murmuring in her ear. But witnessing that would tear me apart—expose every last inch of my pain, fear, and loneliness. So I came outside to the quiet night. Just me, the sky, and one lone star.

I smile sadly, remembering the rhyme from when I was a child. "Star light, star bright, the first star I see tonight," I whisper. "I wish I may, I wish I might, have the wish I wish tonight." I debate a minute, trying to narrow down all of my hopes and dreams to just one thought. But I'm still broken with heartache. Heartache that will never heal.

"I wish I were dead," I say, and lower my head into my hands. It's all so hopeless, even if I know that sounds trivial. But Aaron is only one of the pieces of my shattered life—albeit the biggest and most jagged shard.

The tears have barely escaped my eyes when I hear a soft laugh.

"Wow. That was pathetic."

I gasp and turn to see a stranger leaning against the house. His eyes are bright green even in the shadows, his skin pale and smooth. My first reaction is to cuss him out, embarrassed that he heard me reciting a stupid nursery rhyme. But I try my best to hold on to any appearance of sanity.

"Not as pathetic as creeping up on unsuspecting victims," I reply.

"Ouch," he says, touching his chest. "You make me sound like a serial killer." When he smiles his dimples deepen, and in that instant I think he's possibly the most attractive guy I've ever seen. Then again, I once thought the same thing about Aaron.

"Until you ruined it," the stranger continues, "this was a really good night. But now you've made me so sad, *I* might just leap from this deck."

I laugh, his morbid humor fitting my mood exactly. "I won't stop you." I step aside, giving him a clear path to the railing. He shakes his head, refusing my offer, and walks out from the shadows.

"I'd rather not," he says, taking a spot next to me on the deck.

"I'm Lauren," I tell him. "And you are?"

"Peter."

"Really? Not something trendy or cool?"

"Nope. Just Peter."

We grow quiet, staring toward the glass doors leading into the party. I notice Aaron in the crowd, his blond hair damp from sweat, his arms draped over Rachel's shoulders. The familiar sense of loss overwhelms me, and I lower my eyes.

"I don't do this every day," I tell Peter.

"Talk to handsome strangers?"

I look sideways. "Well, that. And wish myself dead. It's just been that sort of night."

Peter nods. "I know those nights well."

Somehow, I doubt that. With his looks and his apparent charm, I find it hard to believe that Peter has found himself on the short end of the dumping stick very often. I, on the other hand, have been whacked with it.

Aaron and I had dated for two years, even though the last three months had grown a little cold—at least on his end. To deal with the breakup, I tried to convince myself that I never really loved him at all; that maybe I just liked having a boyfriend. Other times, I thought I'd die if I never heard him whisper that he loved me again. My confusion was only solidified when he started dating Rachel in the open—a sophomore. A cheerleader. A goddamn stranger to him.

It's only been two weeks and he brought her here— to Rex Lively's graduation party. Flaunting her in front of everyone. In front of me.

I think again, *I wish I were dead.*

"Are you hungry?" Peter asks, brushing his fingers across the bare skin of my arm as he tries to get my attention. His touch is ice-cold, but at the same time, completely refreshing. Maybe it's just been too long since I've let anyone get this close to me.

"Not really," I respond. "I don't think I have much of an appetite right now."

Peter nods at this and then slips his hands into the pockets of his jeans. I take a moment to glance over him, his dark hair, his plaid button-down shirt, and the black string he has tied around his wrist. I wonder what it means, and I think to ask him, but he lifts his gaze to meet mine.

"We could just go talk," he says. "After all, you've ruined my night. At least entertain me."

I laugh. "And why would I want to do that? I don't owe you anything."

His easy expression slips away. "No, you really don't. But I won't leave a suicidal girl at the railing of a third-story deck all alone. This just seemed like the easier way to get you inside."

At the thought of going back into the party, my stomach twists. "I can't do that," I say. "There are people in there I don't want to see."

"I could raid the linen closet and knot some bed sheets together so we can shimmy down."

I peer over the railing, but then shake my head. "Maybe we'll just rush the front door." I slip off my heels to let him know I'm serious. He looks more than a little entertained.

"We could make him jealous," he offers.

I freeze. "What?"

"Your ex-boyfriend." He points toward the house. "That's who we're fleeing, right?"

"How did you know that?" I can't keep the humiliation out of my voice.

"I just did." He shrugs. "So how about it? One slow dance to rule them all." He grins, the darkness behind it mischievous, even a little sexy. It's petty and stupid to try and make Aaron jealous, especially when he doesn't care.

So I'm surprised when I say yes and slip my shoes back on before taking Peter's hand to pull him forward.

***

A new song starts to play the minute we get inside. The beat is fast, the thumping of the bass drowning out most of the words. It's hardly a slow song, but Peter takes my arm and spins me until I'm pressed against him. I can feel the stares of the people around us, even hear a girl murmur, "Who's Lauren with?" Just being noticed is enough to make me smile. I've felt invisible at school—as if Aaron had taken more than my heart when he broke up with me. As if he'd taken my entire existence.

Now I'm real. Here with Peter, I'm someone to see. And when he leans forward to whisper, his breath cool on my ear, a shiver runs down my back and I think that I don't have to be so sad anymore. That maybe tonight I can start over and let go of Aaron. Let go of my past before it crushes me.

"Now dance," Peter murmurs. I close my eyes as he wraps one arm around my waist, his other hand sliding into my hair to rest protectively on the back of my neck. We're so close—not even really dancing, just . . . being.

The song drifts away, the people drift away. For a moment, there's peace. Peter is a sense of calm that I haven't felt in so long. It's like I'm finally safe with him, whoever he is.

"My parents are getting divorced," I say softly, keeping my eyes closed so I don't shatter the illusion of us being alone. "And they're so angry all the time. They're so angry at each other that they don't even see me anymore."

"Shh . . ." Peter soothes, his fingers gliding over the skin of my collarbone. When I open my eyes to look at him, he's there—beautiful, even in this crowded, sweaty mass of people. His dimples deepen. "Do you have a car?" he asks.

***

Peter asks if he can drive, and since I'm still feeling slightly heady after our dance, I toss him the keys. A soft smile plays on his lips the entire trip down the freeway, and it isn't until we pull onto the city street that he looks over at me.

"I'm a good dancer," he says with a smirk.

"So good."

"If that party hadn't been horrible, I would have kept you there all night. Maybe until they kicked us out. You were being sweet."

"I can be sweet," I tell him, slapping his shoulder.

He feigns shock. "This from the girl who said she wouldn't stop me from taking a dive off the balcony?"

"I do believe you called me pathetic."

His expression falters slightly, and he turns back to the road. "I didn't mean that. I just get sick of hearing people complain sometimes. I don't think you're pathetic now." He rubs absently at the black string tied around his wrist, and I furrow my brow.

"What's that bracelet for?" I ask.

He glances at it, as if surprised it's there. "To remind me of something I have to do later. I'm forgetful sometimes." He turns to me and smiles. "Get caught up in the moment."

"Am I distracting you?"

"Oh, Lauren." His voice is low and gravelly. "You have no idea."

Tingles spread over my body, and I almost lean over and kiss him. But before I even notice we've stopped, he's unhooking his seatbelt. "Let's go dance some more," he says, and gets out of the car.

I'm laughing as I climb out of the passenger side to meet up with him, but I freeze when I see where we are. "The cemetery?" I ask in disbelief.

Peter turns back to look at me, standing under the iron archway of the historic cemetery in Old Town. Most of the headstones have been reduced to unreadable stumps of marble, weeping willows bent and crying over the graves. It isn't scary, not really. I've been coming here for years—actually sat under the tree by the mausoleum to write my college admittance essay. I'm just stunned that Peter would bring me here. This place was my secret.

"Are you afraid?" he asks, putting his hands on his hips like he's challenging me. "I swear they won't bother us. They're a pretty quiet group." He grins, and I roll my eyes in return.

"How are we going to dance without music?" I ask, walking toward him. "Unless you plan to hum the entire time?"

Peter widens his eyes. "Now that would be weird." He pulls his phone from his pocket and clicks through his song selections until one starts to play. He waits to see if I'll argue, and when I don't, he holds out his arm for me to take.

We walk under the archway of the cemetery to the curved tree near the mausoleum. Peter sets his phone on a nearby grave and once again sweeps me into his arms, more playful than he'd been at the party.

"I love it here," he says. He twirls me around, and then puts his hand on my back to dip me low. "I come here sometimes to write."

"No way," I tell him as we settle into a gentle sway. "You don't strike me as a writer."

"I am. Depressing stuff, mostly. I tend to fall in love with tragic things." He smiles. "Go figure."

I tilt my head, meeting his vulnerable gaze. So he has experienced heartbreak before. Maybe we have more in common than I thought. When the song finishes, Peter takes his arms from around me to scroll again through his phone, finding something with a faster beat.

"It was more than an ex-boyfriend," I say to his turned back. "Aaron by himself isn't a reason for anything, let alone death."

At the word, Peter turns to face me. "Then why?" he asks.

I shrug. "My parent's divorce—the fear of how it will change things. They're different people now, and my childhood, it's as if they're saying it was all a mistake. Sometimes I wonder if I was the mistake." I shut my eyes, the feelings tight and heavy in my chest. "Then there's college," I continue. "I worked my ass off to get into Albany." I look at Peter again. "The same school as Aaron. And now . . . I don't even want to go. It would be awful. Nothing's going right. Nothing is working out the way it was supposed to."

"What about tonight?" Peter steps closer and I instinctively reach for him, my arms around his neck as he runs his eyes over my face, pausing at my lips.

"I would say my night has definitely improved," I tell him. "And you? How did you end up all alone on the deck of a party?"

"I was looking for someone. But I found you instead." He sweeps a lock of my hair behind my ear. "I think I've been searching for you for a long time— only I didn't know it. In case you've never noticed, Lauren," he says, dropping his voice to a whisper. "Most people suck."

I laugh. "But not us?"

"No," he says with conviction. "We're the awesome ones. We're the few who leave ourselves vulnerable—never faking our feelings, always trusting even though we shouldn't." He rests his cheek against mine, moving us slowly with the rhythm. "People like us deserve love, only we never find it," he whispers. "Because, like I said: Most. People. Suck."

He turns, and his lips brush against mine. They're as cool as the night air, but inviting. My heart begins to race, and suddenly I want him to devour me. I knot my fingers in his hair as he kisses me harder. The world around us seems to spin and I think something so crazy, so impossible, that I have to pull away from him, stumbling over the uneven earth.

Peter's cheeks are flush, his green eyes darkened with desire. He licks his lips, a slow smile pulling at the corners of his mouth. And I realize . . . this is love at first sight. This is that stupid, never-actually-happens feeling they base movies on.

Dear God, I'm in love with him. The relief breaks through my chest as I realize that I never loved Aaron; he never made me feel so wanted. So normal. So perfect.

Peter steps forward, grabbing my hips to pull me close. He buries his face in my hair, his lips grazing my ear, my neck. "My soul mate," he whispers. Then he laughs and pulls back. "I'm doing it again. You must think I'm a total freak."

"I would," I say, tracing my finger down the collar of his shirt, pausing to play with the top button. "Except I feel entirely the same way. So either we've got some serious chemistry, or one of us is a figment of the other's imagination."

Peter leans in to kiss me, soft and sweet. Then he takes my hand and twirls me around. On the third pass, he stops to kiss me again—holding me close as our tongues meet, his fingers sliding over the bare skin just under the hem of my shirt. Soon it's like I'm on fire—I want to give him everything at once. Want to be with him forever.

A glint of light catches my eyes, and I look away to see the sun on the horizon. "It's morning," I whisper. Peter doesn't answer, and instead, wraps his arms around me as he turns toward it, kissing the top of my head. As he runs his hand down my arm, I notice the bracelet again. I guess I have been distracting.

"Peter," I say, tugging on his hand. "What did you have to do tonight? Did you forget?"

He stills, glancing down at me with an expression so sorrowful, it's like the earth drops out from under my feet. "No," he whispers. "I didn't forget, Lauren."

I'm alarmed at how brokenhearted he looks, how his eyes turn glassy as he watches me. "What?" I ask. "What do you have to do?"

Peter smiles sadly. "Your wish," he says. "You made that stupid wish on the star."

For a moment, I don't even remember what he's talking about. I back away and he lets me, his features pulled down with the weight of his despair.

"But I . . ." I stop, not wanting to say the words. Peter nods and all at once, I'm so regretful that I can't even cry. I can't even scream. "Who are you?" I ask, still sure that I'm in love with him. That he's in love with me.

"We could have been so good together," Peter murmurs, closing his eyes. When he opens them again, they are no longer green. He's still beautiful, but the mischievous green is swapped out for an ominous black. I gasp and cover my mouth, backing up until I'm against the stone wall of the mausoleum.

The bracelet on Peter's wrist begins to dissolve, falling away as ash. He apologizes, his voice low and dark as he reaches a shaky hand in my direction.

And tells me that he is Death.

– The End –

A BUNCH OF BLUE RIBBONS

A Bunch of Blue Ribbons
Oh, dear, what can the matter be?
Johnny's so long at the fair.
He promised he'd buy me a bunch of blue ribbons,
To tie up my bonny brown hair.
– Mother Goose

A RIBBON OF BLUE
Michelle Zink

Ruby Monahan looked at the clock, willing the minute hand forward. College Trig had never been her favorite subject, but today the thirty-nine minute class was almost unbearable. It wasn't that Mr. Cohen spoke in a monotone, his words running together like one big, run-on sentence. It wasn't even Trevor and Brad, sitting in the back, guffawing quietly like the jackasses they were.

It was because today, the carnival flyers would be posted.

She knew today was the day because it was the first Monday in June, and the flyers always went up the first Monday in June. The carnival wouldn't start until Thursday night, but the posters were a milestone, proof that the fair was coming, that for a few short days, Ruby's gray world would be full of color and life and sound.

She was so busy imagining it—the striped tents and canopies, the smell of sugar spun in the cotton candy machines, the flashing lights of the Ferris wheel and tilt-a-whirl—that she jumped when the bell finally rang.

She stayed in her seat while everyone filed past, even though she wanted to run for the door like everyone else. She'd learned the hard way that it was better to let everyone go ahead so she could take her time without their eyes on her back, the shuffling of their impatient feet behind her.

She put her notebook in her backpack. Then, when everyone had reached the door, she maneuvered her way out of the chair, got her balance, and moved slowly forward.

"Goodbye, Ruby," Mr. Cohen said on her way out the door.

"Bye, Mr. Cohen."

She continued forward, grateful it was the last class of the day. Sometimes she moved so slowly that the next class would already be entering the room while she was still making her way through the doorway. In the best of cases, it resulted in an awkward dance, the nicer kids moving aside, trying not to seem annoyed while they waited for her to move out of the way.

But that was only if someone like Trevor or Brad wasn't around to make fun of her. Only if someone like Melanie Curtis wasn't there, smirking and flipping her curly black hair like some kind of beauty queen, rolling her eyes like Ruby was keeping her from a date with Channing Tatum or something.

Then it was excruciating, and Ruby would try to hurry out the door, keeping her head up on principle but avoiding their eyes, hoping they'd just let her pass, leave her alone.

The end of the day was always better, and she made her way through the halls, already clear, the majority of students gone right after the bell, anxious to be free.

She didn't bother to stop at her locker. She'd made a point to get her books together at lunch, knowing she'd want to hurry to the light post on the corner right after school. Her left foot was bothering her more than usual. The cerebral palsy had twisted it at an odd angle, forcing her to drag it behind her a little as she walked. Most of the time, she didn't think about it. She'd been born with CP. She didn't know anything else.

But every now and then her bones hurt, a dull, throbbing ache that seemed to spring from the core of her body. Sometimes it came from her foot. Other times it came from her wrist, bent slightly backward, or the curled fingers of her left hand.

Still, today was one of her favorite days of the year, and she was determined not to let anything spoil it. She made her way laboriously through the big metal doors and out into the sunshine.

It was warm, the kind of day just before summer, when the heat is gentle, the breeze a soft embrace. Ruby waited at the corner, looking both ways and making sure there weren't any cars coming before she crossed the street. When she was safely on the sidewalk, she stopped, looking at the piece of paper stapled to the light post.

20TH ANNUAL BUCKLAND BROTHERS
TRAVELING CARNIVAL

There was other information, too. A list of acts and rides, dates and starting times, fine print that absolved the carnival organizers of responsibility in case of injury or death.

But the important thing was that they were coming.

In just three days, Ruby would be walking the grounds, listening to the beautiful, clunky mix of accordion and organ that was piped through the speakers, hearing the carnies call out to people passing by, trying to get them to play the games that were always slanted to give the carnival an advantage.

None of which was the reason for her excitement.

As she turned around and started for home, avoiding the cracks in the sidewalk that might cause a fall, she only had one thing on her mind, the same thing she thought about every year when the carnival came to town; here was another chance to look for the old woman and the boy.

***

It had started when she was thirteen. Grandma had taken her to the carnival as a reward for a particularly grueling few weeks in which Ruby had been forced to endure a fresh round of tests and blood work, not to mention an MRI that had given her such awful claustrophobia that they'd had to pull Ruby out of the machine, forcing the doctors to start all over again three separate times.

Ruby had never seen anything like the carnival. She was captivated by the sights (the tall man in the striped hat on stilts, the cymbal-clanging monkey), smells (peanuts and dirt and copper and the faint scent of manure), and sounds (bells ringing as people won the games, shrieking from kids on the rides). There were things Grandma wouldn't let her do. There always were. But it was still the most exciting thing Ruby had ever seen, and she'd dragged her bad foot through the dirt, stopping at every single booth and not feeling an ounce of pain.

But the highlight had been the fortune-teller. Ruby had to beg—her grandmother wasn't one for "malarkey"—but in the end, Grandma had taken a big drag on her cigarette and handed Ruby a dollar. Then she'd sat on a picnic bench outside the tent, making it clear that she had no intention of accompanying Ruby inside.

Ruby had only hesitated a second before parting the curtains and stepped into the tent, fear and excitement mixing in her blood until she felt dizzy with them both.

The old woman sat at a table draped with rich, purple velvet, an array of mismatched candles flickering at its center. Ruby had been momentarily disappointed. The tent was sparse, the mystical decor—other than the table and candles—nonexistent. Nothing at all like on TV.

The woman had waved her forward. "Come, child! Sit, and let me tell tales of your future."

Ruby had moved forward, feeling self-conscious about her halting gait. But the woman had only smiled, her eyes moist and warm. Silver hair escaped from a scarf around her head, and her rings reflected off the ceiling of the tent, a kaleidoscope of color.

"Take that chair there, child." The woman gestured to the chair across from her. "It's been waiting just for you, as have I."

Ruby sat and placed the dollar on the table.

The woman shoved it aside. "Your hands?" she asked.

Ruby lifted her hands, looking at them in question, and a second later, the old woman took them in her own. Ruby was surprised to find the woman's flesh warm and dry, comforting, like her grandmother's.

She turned Ruby's hands over so that her palms faced the ceiling. Then she peered at them, her forehead wrinkled, her brow knit together in concentration.

"Hmmm . . . I see," she murmured. "Just as I thought."

Ruby sat up straighter, staring at her own hands. "What? What do you see?"

"You're imprisoned," the woman said softly. "A beautiful bird with clipped wings."

Ruby felt her face flush, tried to pull her hands away. But the woman wouldn't let them go.

"Nothing to be ashamed of, child. No fault of your own. You have a purpose here, just like anyone else." She clucked her tongue. "Besides, better times are ahead."

"Better times?" Ruby repeated.

"Freedom . . . light . . . love," the woman said, meeting her eyes. "They will all come with the boy."

"The boy? What boy?" It wasn't at all what she'd expected the old woman to say.

"Why, the boy from the carnival, of course."

Ruby looked around, as if the boy would step from the shadows. "I don't see anyone."

"Never you mind." She set Ruby's hands on the table and patted them gently. "You'll know him when he comes. He'll come bearing a whistle, a ticket, and a ribbon of blue. And everything will be just fine." She patted Ruby's hands again. "You'll see."

Ruby had sat there a minute more, wondering if the woman would say anything else. When she didn't, Ruby had thanked her and left.

When her grandmother had asked what the fortune-teller said, Ruby just told her that she would have freedom, light, and love. Those were the important things in the message anyway. The things she wanted most.

But her grandmother had snorted, her unspoken cynicism hanging heavy in the air as they made their way home.

***

That was four years ago. Ruby had never spoken to her grandmother about it again, but every year she went to the carnival, hoping against all rational thought to meet the boy. Hoping, even, for another chance to talk to the old woman, to see if "freedom, light, and love" was just a line she fed everyone willing to part with a dollar.

But the woman had never been there again. In fact, the carnival had never had another fortune-teller. Ruby knew it was irrational to keep hoping, but she couldn't help it.

Hope was in short supply. She'd take it where she could get it.

***

That night, Ruby made dinner and did the dishes. Her grandmother tried to help, but the emphysema had gotten worse in recent years, the oxygen tank she was forced to drag around at least as cumbersome as Ruby's twisted limbs.

Ruby tried not to think about what would happen if her grandmother passed on. Ruby's mother had died giving birth, her father gone long before that. Ruby was somewhat functional, more functional than a lot of people with CP, but it still scared her, the thought of being all alone in the world. What would she do for work? How would she support herself? Babysitting Conner, the seven-year-old next door, wouldn't even cover her medications. Besides, he'd grow up eventually. Then what?

She put water on for the peppermint tea that settled her stomach. Almost constant nausea was one of the things she hated most about the new anti-seizure medication the doctor was trying her on. Even when she was hungry, she could rarely eat, and she'd shrunk from 120 pounds to 105 in the six months she'd been taking it, proof that while there might not be such a thing as being too rich, you could definitely be too thin.

"Take it you're going to that fair again," her grandmother rasped from the kitchen table.

Ruby took a deep breath, bracing herself for the criticism she knew would come. "Probably."

Her grandma put out the cigarette she was holding in her hand. "Waste of money, if you ask me."

Ruby had to bite back the words she really wanted to say: *I didn't.*

She shrugged instead. She had her own money. Not much of it, but enough for an occasional movie, a coveted book she couldn't get at the library. She would have taken more babysitting jobs if she could get them, but looking after infants and toddlers was out of the question with her useless hand and even parents of older children sometimes looked skeptically at her when she inquired about babysitting, like her mind was as messed up and twisted as her limbs.

Her grandmother broke into a fit of coughing. Ruby limped over, adjusting the controls on her tank so that it would deliver a little more oxygen to her lungs. Ruby hated that she still smoked—especially so close to the oxygen that could ignite, blowing them all to kingdom come—but she knew her grandmother was suffering, too. She carried it differently than Ruby, a chip on her shoulder instead of a pail of water balanced carefully atop her head, but Ruby was certain they weren't very different underneath it all.

Her grandmother took a deep breath, sucking in the oxygen, her eyes losing the spark of panic Ruby had come to recognize when she had trouble breathing. Ruby squeezed her shoulder gently. Her grandmother looked away, unable to meet her eyes.

***

School was excruciating on Thursday. When the bell finally rang, Ruby didn't wait for everyone else to leave before she got out of her desk. Her eagerness earned her a few muttered remarks from Trevor as she blocked the aisle, but she was too excited to care.

She went home, took a shower, and dried her hair. She considered her clothes carefully, finally settling on an old floral skirt she'd bought at the thrift store. She paired it with a simple white t-shirt and the French blue ballet flats she'd saved to buy last summer. Then she waited for the sun to begin its descent, because the carnival was always better at night. Once her grandmother was settled, Ruby left the house.

She walked the short distance to the fairgrounds alone, the sidewalks becoming more crowded as she got closer to the carnival. She was half a block away when she heard the *clack-clack-roar* of the mini-coaster rising up over the music.

Stepping across the threshold was like entering another world. The moment her feet crossed from the sidewalk onto the dirt and matted grass of the fairground, everything else fell away.

She took a deep breath, soaking in the atmosphere as she strolled the aisles, taking her time, gazing into each booth and stopping to talk to some of the carnies along the way. They smiled and laughed, and her eyes were drawn to the trailers and motor homes that lurked in the shadows behind the tents and canopies. What would it be like to be one of them? To travel from place to place, every week a new adventure? To meet new people all the time and to be surrounded by others who surely had their own secrets, their own burdens?

She had just bought a cloud of pink cotton candy and was reveling in the fizzy feel of it dissolving on her tongue, when she saw the boy walking toward her. He looked out of place, his pants too loose, old-fashioned suspenders holding them up over a white shirt. He didn't wear sneakers, but dress shoes, like the kind Mr. Cohen wore with his frumpy suits, though the boy's were scuffed and dirty while Mr. Cohen's were always super shiny.

Ruby ducked her head, meaning to pass him without drawing attention to herself, but he stopped in front of her so that she was forced to stop, too.

"Hello," he said, brushing a lock of dark hair from his eyes.

She resisted the urge to look behind her, to make sure he was actually talking to her. "Hello."

"I'm Sam."

She looked down at his hand, held out for her to shake. She couldn't remember the last time someone had tried to shake her hand. Usually people looked at her twisted wrist, her clenched fingers, and didn't know what to do.

She took his hand with her good one. His skin was clean and soft. "Ruby."

He nodded knowingly, like he'd known her name all along. "Would you like to walk, Ruby? I have a few minutes before my break is up."

She thought about it, wondering if there was some kind of catch, and deciding there wasn't. "Okay. Do you work here?" she asked as they started walking.

"When they need me." He stuffed his hands in his pockets. "What about you? What do you do?"

"Me?" She laughed. "Nothing, really. Just . . . you know, go to school and stuff."

He tipped his head at her, like he'd caught her lying, and she found herself speaking again, saying things she didn't plan on saying.

"I read. And . . . I listen to music and . . . well, I think a lot, I guess."

"And you come to the fair," he said.

"Yes."

He bent down and picked something up as they came to the end of the aisle. She was surprised when he took her hand and placed the object in her palm without even looking at it.

She opened her fingers and saw that it was a whistle, the tin polished to a high shine despite the fact that he had found it in the dirt.

"For me?" she asked softly.

"For you."

He'll come bearing a whistle, a ticket, and a ribbon of blue.

"It was nice talking to you, Ruby." He turned to go, looking back over his shoulder. "See you tomorrow."

She watched him go, his stride confident but not cocky. It was only later that she realized there hadn't been a question mark in his final words.

***

She spent the better part of the next day thinking about Sam. About the dark eyes that seemed to be telling her something precious and important. About the way he'd said he'd see her tonight, not just like he wanted her to come, but like he knew that she would.

She'd carried the whistle carefully in her pocket, taking it out once or twice, staring at it like it held the answer to all of life's mysteries. After dinner, she'd cleaned up and gotten Grandma settled into bed. She was having more trouble breathing than usual. Ruby wondered if they would have to make an unexpected trip to the doctor for new meds.

And all the while Sam was there, hovering at the periphery of her mind, a promise in the night still to come.

By the time she arrived at the fair, her heart was thudding in her chest. She had no idea where Sam worked, if he ran one of the games or food kiosks or if he just helped set up and tear down.

She started down the first aisle, stopping when she saw Trevor trying to win a stuffed animal for Melanie, who looked surly and annoyed. It made Ruby wonder at the strange component of human nature that allowed someone like Melanie to be elected Prom Queen. She wasn't nice. No one even really *liked* her. But it was like she was so sure of her own superiority that everyone else thought they must be missing something, like Melanie really must be amazing if she was so sure of it, even though if they'd stopped to think about it, they would have realized she was just a stuck-up bitch.

Just once, Ruby wanted to see someone worthy get some attention. It didn't have to be her. Just someone— anyone—*good.* Someone like Amelie Cavanaugh, who always held doors for Ruby and walked with her to class, talking about books and movies and music like Ruby was normal, like she was one of them. No one ever made fun of her when she was with Amelie, because Amelie had been nice to all of them at one time or another when they really needed it.

But still, Amelie hadn't won Prom Queen, because the truth was, she was just *too* nice.

She'd reached the end of the first aisle, a wave of

disappointment washing over her with the possibility that maybe she wouldn't see Sam at all, when he stepped from the shadows.

"Hello, Ruby." His voice was intimate, familiar, like they'd known each other longer than one day. Like they'd spent hours and hours talking instead of just a few minutes.

"Hi. I wondered if you'd be here tonight." Normally, she would have regretted the words, cursed herself for sounding pathetic. But she found she had no regrets. Nothing with Sam was ruled by normal boundaries, unspoken rules. It just was.

"I've been waiting for you," he said simply.

"You have?"

"Of course." He held up two paper tickets. "Want to go on the Ferris wheel?"

Her heart caught in her throat. She'd never been on the Ferris wheel. Going alone wasn't an option, and her grandmother wouldn't have gone with her in a million years.

"It's okay," he said, gently. "I'll be right there. I know the guy who runs it. He'll wait as long as you need."

Like she'd voiced all her fears aloud. Like he could see the scene playing out in her mind, the long shuffle to the Ferris wheel seat, everyone staring and whispering.

She nodded. "Okay."

They walked to the center of the carnival. The Ferris wheel rose from the ground like a many-lighted beacon, and Sam put a hand on her back as he guided her into line. It was strange, that touch. Foreign and exciting and the most natural thing in the world.

When it was their turn to board, the bearded man who ran the ride reached for the bar, lifting it so Ruby could get in. He smiled right into her eyes as she moved past him, Sam's arm on her elbow to steady her.

It wasn't as difficult as she'd expected. Sam's guidance helped, and she realized then how much easier life was with someone by your side, someone just to *be* there, to steady you when you were unsure.

She settled next to him on the red vinyl seat and the bearded man clicked the safety bar into place. The wheel started to turn, and Ruby felt her stomach drop as they rose into the night sky. They weren't moving fast, but it was the most exhilarating feeling she'd ever had. The town stretched before them, lights twinkling in the distance. She could see the school and the market and even, she was sure of it, the house she shared with her grandmother. But from this vantage point, everything looked beautiful, magical.

She laughed out loud, unable to contain her delight. When she looked over at Sam, he was smiling, his eyes tender. He reached for her hand and didn't let go, the wheel turning and turning, making graceful circles in the sky while Ruby tried to remember every moment. Maybe this is what the old woman had meant. There was the whistle yesterday, and now, the Ferris wheel and freedom.

She wanted the ride to go on and on, but eventually, the wheel slowed down, moving in increments as the bearded man stopped it to empty each seat of its passengers. When it was their turn, Sam got out first and reached for her hand, helping her to her feet and guiding her off the platform.

They walked down the ramp, and this time when Ruby stumbled, she laughed, because the other Ferris wheel riders were doing the same thing, trying to get their legs back under them after being in the sky.

"Well, I guess I better get back to work," Sam said reluctantly.

She nodded. "Thanks for the ride. It was amazing."

He smiled into her eyes. "It was."

For the first time, Ruby felt awkward, embarrassed. She didn't know what to do in situations like this, She didn't have a cell phone, didn't use the computer much. Was it too forward to ask for his phone number? Would he ask for hers?

Her face got hot as the seconds ticked by, Sam's eyes on hers.

"Oh!" he said suddenly. "I almost forgot!" He reached into his pocket, pulling out a piece of paper and handing it to her.

She looked down at it, folded over in her palm. "What . . . what is this?"

"It's a pass." He shuffled his feet a little. "Tomorrow's the last night. I was hoping to see you, but I didn't want you to have to pay."

She heard the old woman's voice in her head: . . . *a whistle, a ticket, and a ribbon of blue.*

"Thank you," she whispered.

He reached over and gave her hand one last squeeze. He paused, like he wanted to say something, but in the end he just turned away.

She stood there, watching him go, the ticket warm in her hand.

* * *

Her grandmother was worse the next day, the coughing so bad she could hardly breathe. After a phone call to the doctor, the home nurse came by and made some adjustments to the oxygen tank. Ruby cooked them all grilled cheese sandwiches while the nurse made

Grandma comfortable. They ate in the living room, Grandma propped up on the couch, her eyes glassy with fatigue.

Nibbling at her sandwich, Ruby was torn. She knew the nurse planned to stay until ten. Knew her grandmother would be looked after. But Ruby felt bad leaving anyway, like she was abandoning her when she most needed comfort.

But there was Sam. She saw his dark eyes in her mind, felt his hand, strong and gentle on her own when they'd ridden the Ferris wheel. He was expecting her, and she had no way to reach him, to tell him she couldn't make it. Tomorrow, the carnival would be gone, and Sam with it.

She felt guilty for the relief that flooded her body when her grandmother nodded off on the couch, a soft snore coming from her mouth. She would just go for an hour, no more. The nurse could keep an eye on Grandma for that long. She wouldn't even know Ruby was gone.

She changed into a peasant skirt that swished around her legs, trying not to be embarrassed at the realization that she wanted to look pretty for Sam. Then she said goodbye to the nurse with a promise to return by ten.

This time, Sam was waiting for her just inside the gate. His face lit up when he saw her, and he walked toward her with a smile.

"You made it."

She smiled. "Yes."

His eyes were like a ray of sunlight on her face. It was like he saw only her, and under his gaze she blossomed like a flower. She felt herself opening. Opening and opening and opening. All of her body and soul turning inside out, revealing all the best, most pure, most peaceful parts of herself. All the pieces that were hidden by the drudgery and monotony of her days.

"Let's walk." He held out his hand.

She took it, and they moved down the aisle.

"What do you want to do?" he asked.

No one had ever asked her that before. "I don't know."

He stopped, turning to look at her. "Think about it, Ruby. What do you want to do? What have you always wanted to do?"

She only had to think about it a minute. "Everything," she admitted.

He grinned. "Everything it is."

They played the ping-pong game, Ruby turning down the prize of a goldfish because, really, she couldn't take care of one more thing. They threw darts at balloons tacked to a plywood wall, Sam handing her a stuffed bear when he won. They ate cotton candy until their tongues turned blue, funnel cake until their fingers were sticky. Ruby wished the old woman was there so they could both pay to have their fortunes read, so she could tell Ruby if this was the boy she'd mentioned all those years ago.

Finally, they came to the end of the last row. Ruby's stomach hurt from laughing so hard, her cheeks sore from smiling. It was the happiest day of her life.

Sam pulled her into the shadows, one arm around her waist. "I have something for you."

"You do?" She was whispering and she didn't know why, except that maybe she was afraid to break the spell of their last night together.

He nodded and reached into his pocket, pulling from it a bright, blue ribbon. It trailed, silky and shimmering, from his hand.

"I thought it would look nice in your hair," he explained. "May I?"

She nodded shyly, turning her back to him, resisting the urge to lean into him as he tied it around the ponytail at the back of her head.

He turned her gently around and ran a finger across her cheekbone. "What are you afraid of?"

The question took her by surprise. "What do you mean?"

"What is your biggest fear?"

She swallowed, thinking. "I don't have one anymore."

"Why is that?"

"I was afraid of never being happy, of never being normal, of never *feeling* the way other people seem to feel every single day."

"And you're not afraid of that anymore," he said. "Why?"

Her cheeks grew hot with embarrassment. "Because I've felt that with you. I've laughed. I've been happy."

He lowered his face to hers, touching his lips softly against her own. "This is just the beginning, Ruby."

And then, something strange happened. A subtle buzzing in her head gave way to total release. She looked down, trying to figure out how she could be standing, and on the ground, seizing, at the same time. How she could feel whole and healthy and well while her body was wracked with seizures, her limbs flailing against the hard-packed ground, the teddy bear lying in the dirt beside her.

Others rushed over from the carnival. An older woman knelt on the ground beside Ruby's other-body, tipping her head back, yelling at someone to get something to put between other-Ruby's teeth so she didn't bite her tongue.

And all the while Ruby stood by, healthy and whole. She finally looked up, surprised to see Sam still standing there next to her.

"It will be okay, Ruby. There's nothing to be afraid of." He held out his hand. "Are you ready?"

She nodded and took his hand, understanding now that it had always been about this moment. She sent one last look to her other-self, her body still jerking, the people around her frantic, barking instructions to each other. Her skirt billowed on the ground around her, the blue ribbon trailing from her hair.

Sam started walking, leading her toward something bright and beautiful up ahead—not too far, just a little bit farther. There was a lightening within her, an easing of a burden she hadn't known she carried. As the light enveloped her, the rest of her world faded into the background, into nothing—a pinprick compared to the fullness that waited in the light.

She didn't hesitate as she took the final step, Sam's hand in hers, his eyes soft and warm on her face.

The old woman had been right. There was freedom, light . . . and so very much love.

– The End –

SEA OF DEW

*Winkin', Blinkin', and Nod, one night sailed off in a
wooden shoe;
Sailed off on a river of crystal light into a sea of dew.
"Where are you going and what do you wish?" the old
moon asked the three.
"We've come to fish for the herring fish that live in this
beautiful sea.
Nets of silver and gold have we," said Winkin', Blinkin',
and Nod.*

*The old moon laughed and sang a song as they rocked
in the wooden shoe.
And the wind that sped them all night long ruffled the
waves of dew.
Now the little stars are the herring fish that live in that
beautiful sea;
"Cast your nets wherever you wish never afraid are
we!"
So cried the stars to the fishermen three—Winkin', and
Blinkin', and Nod.*

So all night long their nets they threw to the stars in the twinkling foam.
'Til down from the skies came the wooden shoe bringing the fisherman home.
'Twas all so pretty a sail it seemed as if it could not be.
Some folks say 'twas a dream they dreamed of sailing that misty sea.
But I shall name you the fisherman three—Winkin', Blinkin', and Nod.

Now Winkin' and Blinkin' are two little eyes and Nod is a little head.
And the wooden shoe that sailed the skies is a wee one's trundle bed.
So close your eyes while mother sings of the wonderful sights that be.
And you shall see those beautiful things as you sail on the misty sea,
Where the old shoe rocked the fishermen three—Winkin', Blinkin', and Nod.

– Mother Goose

SEA OF DEW (Extended version)
By C. Lee McKenzie

In the week before the moon found them beneath the bloated bellies of storm clouds, they drifted in the lifeboat without any sight of land. The boys, the stowaways, the survivors.

And Miranda.

She hunkered under the tarp and a soggy blanket, peering out at them with worry and a sizable dose of fear. She was adrift in a foreign sea among strangers. Yet one of those three had hauled her from the water and saved her life.

Which one? Maybe the skinny one named Winker. He had some kind of tic in his cheek that made his left eye twitch, especially when he looked in her direction. Or could it be the guy whose name started with a B? What was it? Blandy? Blindy? Blakie? He had a vacant look and his lips were always moving, like he was telling himself secrets.

Or could it have been Nodfarker? What a creepy name. And he was bossy, always telling them when to eat, if they could have water, or how much. She'd fantasized about tying his leg to an anchor while he slept, then pushing him over the side of the dinky lifeboat.

Just a couple of problems. No anchor. And then she didn't have the stomach for that kind of thing. Besides, he was the one who netted the fishthat they ate raw to stay alive now that the supplies were almost gone, so offing him was not her best idea.

Her worst one, however, was easy to pinpoint. She kept asking herself why she'd let that tour guide talk her and her friends into joining the cheap cruise from the mainland to the tropical island paradise of Milaou. His tiny-toothed grin flashed through her mind. She wondered if he was still smiling down there in that death trap of a ferry.

Miranda sat up as Nodfarker leaned over the side of the boat and dragged the net through the water. In minutes he had two lively, silver herring on board where he dropped them on top of the supply box and slit them open before their tails stopped flipping.

She turned her head. I can't eat one more piece of herring. And if anyone even mentions sashimi to me when this is over, he dies.

"Here's your share." Nodfarker held out a chunk of grayish fish.

The smell churned her stomach, but she took the piece between her thumb and forefinger, then looking away and holding her breath, she swallowed it whole.

"You're welcome," he said, nibbling at the edges of his portion, taking his time as if he had a juicy Big Mac in his mouth.

Her stomach growled, demanding more food, at the same time bile rose into her throat. Lurching over the side, she cast the chunk of herring back into the sea.

When she turned around, none of them seemed to have noticed she'd hurled precious food. Winker averted his gaze. The guy whose name began with a B had his eyes rolled to Heaven, mumbling something she couldn't hear. Nodfarker was chewing with his eyes closed.

She swiped her mouth with the back of her hand and swallowed saliva to wash down the bitter taste. She had to keep from thinking about her hunger and that revolting meal on top of the supply box.

"Where did the name Nodfarker come from?" she asked.

"Say what?" He opened his eyes and fixed them on her.

"Nodfarker. Your name."

Winker doubled over in laughter, and the other one stopped mumbling long enough to manage a pale smile.

"It's Ned Parker," he said and sliced the second herring into fours. "Your ears must have been plugged with saltwater when I pulled you into the boat and said hi."

Miranda flinched, remembering her plunge into the sea. She'd felt queasy and left her friends below to go on deck for some air. As she'd stood looking over the railing, the ferry had suddenly rolled, pitching her headfirst into the water. She'd kicked frantically, but it was as though thousands of fingers clutched at her, dragging her deeper. That's when a single hand descended from above, grasped hers, and pulled her out of the water. Now she knew it had been Ned's hand that had found hers. He'd saved her life.

He passed her another sliver of fish.

She took it, but this time she didn't put it in her mouth. Instead, she studied him, doling out the herring to the others, making the portions equal. He moved deliberately, and she flashed on Communion and the way the priest presented the wafer and the cup. There was ceremony when Ned served their one meal.

On closer inspection, he wasn't really that creepy.

He was about her age, maybe a couple of years older. Nineteen? His dark hair had a boyish way of curling across his forehead and his chestnut-colored eyes were steady when he looked at her. Maybe it had been that wretched name that had made him seem so disagreeable. Maybe it had been the terror of falling into the sea and the dark, drenching rain that hadn't eased until now.

"So how'd you get on that ferry?" Miranda asked.

"We wanted to see Milaou before heading home." Ned shrugged. "We were down to our last few bucks, so we stowed away in this lifeboat for a free ride."

"Bad decision." Miranda bit off a small bite of fish. She'd try nibbling and hope she could keep it down this time.

"Better than some," Ned said, tossing the scales and bones and entrails of the fish overboard.

"We got away. I don't think anybody else escaped being sucked under when that ferry capsized."

Ned held out the bottle of water and the cap. "Three capfuls each, okay? That gives us about four more days, and then we do a rain dance."

The irony wasn't lost on her. For almost a week they'd huddled under the tarp, wishing the rain would stop, bailing fresh water into the salty sea to stay afloat, and drinking from the sky. They'd filled the one container they had, and now they already needed to ration every drop.

She sipped her last capful of water, handed it to Winker, and closed her eyes. It was too hard to stare out over the endless water while knowing that in that plastic bottle only four days' supply was between them and slow, thirsty death. She looked up, hoping to see clouds again.

"We'll head south." Ned held up the compass. "Try

to find a shipping lane and pray a ship comes along."

"Why south?" Miranda asked as she opened her eyes and focusing on his face, so all that ocean became a blue backdrop.

"Warmer weather. More chance for a cruise ship." He shrugged. "I'm guessing." He reached for the oars. "Time for my work out," he said as he dug the oars into the choppy sea, then stopped, checked the compass, and rowed onward.

He was used to exercising. Miranda could tell, and as she slowly gnawed at the herring, she distracted herself by admiring the way his biceps rippled under his skin. After about twenty minutes, he stood, unzipped his fly, and sent an arc of pee over the side before he zipped up and leaned back against the side of the boat, resting.

Miranda felt her cheeks flame with embarrassment, then with anxiety. Peeing during the daylight hours and the problems it presented for her hadn't occurred to her until that moment, and until that moment she hadn't needed to pee. Until now, she'd managed bathroom privacy at night when the others were asleep, but today she couldn't wait that long.

When the other two turned their backs on her and followed Ned's example, she clenched her jaw then asked, "How do I pee on this pleasure cruise?"

Ned grinned. "Guess it's over the side for you, mate." He faced away. Winker and the other guy did as well. "You better strip from your waist down, hang over the side, and yell when you want us to pull you in."

She grumbled under her breath about the injustice and the indignity and the downright crappiness of having to take off her pants, hang over the side of this . . . this rubberized excuse for a—

"Done?" Ned asked.

"No!"

"All right. Just asking."

They kept their backs to her as she slipped into the water, clinging to the side, peeing and feeling lonely on the outside of the boat while they sat inside waiting, smug in their maleness.

"I'm finished," she yelled, and Ned and Winker hauled her in with their heads turned away, then went to their places, keeping their eyes averted as she dried and dressed. The other guy leaned back, mumbling at the sky.

Once she'd finished and sat in her usual spot, Ned nudged the mumbler in the leg. "Hey, Blakie. Entertain us." Ned answered Miranda's next question before she asked it. "He's a math whiz. Give him any math problem and he'll solve it in his head. He does it all day."

"And Blakie?" She cocked her head so he'd know how dumb that name was to her.

"That's how his mom called him in for dinner when we were kids."

They were longtime friends. She was the outsider in two ways: a female and a new acquaintance. "What about Winker? That'sunusual, as names go." She hadn't meant to say that. It had slipped out.

They stared at her, and she had no way to cover her embarrassment at being so rude. She shifted her gaze, but Winker broke the tension and pointed to his jumpy cheek. "Obvious, right?"

Ned smiled and Miranda felt grateful for being forgiven so easily. "Winker's my word guy," he said. "So I got things covered, right? One solves my math problems; the other one gets me through English Lit."

It became the routine, then, that each morning Ned

portioned out the fish and the few remaining rations from the wretched box of stale supplies. Blakie amazed them by doing high-level math problems without paper and pencil. They'd spend hours trying to prove him wrong, but he never was, and he never seemed to think he'd done anything especially brilliant. He gave answers to problems like ten to the square root of 675.444 the way Miranda would say, "Two plus two equals four."

"Blakie does it again," Ned said, returning their pencil to the supply box for safekeeping. "Damned kid was always a genius."

He might be a genius, Miranda thought, but as remarkable as the inside of his head had to be, he was one hundred percent unremarkable in any way on the outside. His brown hair hung limp to his shoulders and his eyes matched in color and texture. Miranda pictured him as he would look in clothes other than the Santa Cruz Slugs tee he'd chosen to wear the day of the ferry disaster. She imagined him with a wrinkled shirt—not quite white—a flip phone in one pocket and pens stuck in the other. One pen would, of course, have leaked blue, but he wouldn't notice that. He wouldn't notice the mustard or catsup stains on the leg of his jeans, either, or think that his sandals and socks were the biggest anti-fashion statement anyone could make.

Still, he had a gentleness to him. Some girl might want to save him from that not-quite-white and wrinkled shirt. She might find his exterior appealing because she loved his genius and wanted to free him from common concerns like fashion. Geniuses ought to have companions with average IQs and tons of common sense. She hoped Blakie would find one, but he had to get rid of that nickname. No girl would sleep with someone named Blakie.

On the fourth day, when Ned passed the bottle to her, she said she'd wait. They all voted to wait after that. Without saying so, they'd agreed to give themselves one extra day; they'd give the heavens more time to send them fresh water. But that night, thirst overcame them, and they drank their portions under the clear sky and the full moon. There was no rain the next day, either, and the moon flooded the ocean with brightness, taunting them day and night with water they couldn't drink.

"Eskimos wish on the moon to bring them back to life." Winker, who never said much of anything, sat and stared up, his cheek still for a change.

Miranda drew in her knees and rested her chin on them. "Eskimos make wishes like that?"   "Prayers, maybe," Winker said. "I can't remember exactly. I read about it when I did an eighth grade social studies report on Alaska."

"What happens when it's dark of the moon? How do they wish . . . pray for it to bring them back then?"

Winker's tic kicked into high gear, and he stammered, "Uh . . . don't . . . know. But when it's not up there," he pointed skyward, "it's . . . supposed to be . . . gathering the dead souls . . . taking them to earth again."

She pulled the blanket over her head, shutting out the moon and trying not to listen to the ruffling of the waves against the boat. When she felt a tug on her blanket, she stuck her head out and stared at Winker.

"S . . . sorry I said . . . that."

His eyes, shaped like teardrops, made him look as if he suffered from perpetual melancholy, and Miranda had an urge to touch his cheek. She thought maybe she could smooth the nervous tic away with her fingers, but she held back. Touching seemed too intimate for someone she barely knew; besides, he didn't invite it. He was distant, tucked inside his quiet sadness. This was their first real talk.

"I'm not hiding because of what you said, Winker." But that wasn't true. The minute he'd told her the myth, something caught inside her chest, and she didn't want to see the moon. She didn't want the temptation to wish on it or pray to it to bring her back from death. If she did, she was afraid it would be like she was giving up on any hope of rescue and life. She couldn't do that. Ever.

She shivered in the sudden wind that seemed colder than what they'd had since they'd started this survival journey.

Ned took out the compass, then dug the oars into the sea with more force than usual. When he pulled them into the boat after half an hour, he didn't look in their direction, even though all eyes were on him, asking if there was a problem.

"Look," he finally said, "it's getting colder, so we should move closer together, especially at night." He scooted next to Miranda and Winker. "Come on Blakie, let's sleep in a pile like Wild Things." He laughed, but it had a dryness to it.

So that night they huddled under the tarp, combining their blankets, their body heat, and not a little fear. During the night, Miranda felt Ned's arm come around her shoulder and pull her into him. At first she held back, but she was tired and cold and the sound of his heart comforted her with its steady beat. She liked the feel of his hand in hers.

When the sun found them, her head rested on the bottom of the boat. She pushed the tarp away, blinking into the brightness of morning and staring at Ned across from her, drawing the oars in steady strokes through the water.

After an hour, he traded off with Blakie, then Blakie traded off with Winker. Miranda took her turn, too.

After another hour, Ned checked his compass, then told her to stop, and she leaned back to stare at the cloudless sky.

Blakie still moved his lips, solving math problems in his head, hiding in a place where numbers added up to perfection and the messy reality of being stranded in a lifeboat didn't exist. This aimlessly floating island had nothing to do with the logical beauty of math. Miranda wished she had an inner place like that to distract herself. She was sick of huddling under that tarp to escape.

"We all better cover up." Ned looked around at Blakie and Winker, who sat together. "Less sun, less water loss." Ned tried for a smile. "You'll have to wait for that suntan until you get back home, Miranda."

Back Home. The place she'd wanted to escape for the past two years because her mother had turned into such a bitch. Her father had simply turned and run. The divorce was definitely going to be ugly and she didn't want any part of it. She'd already had enough of the nightly fights with the screaming and breakage of family glass. This trip with her senior class had come at exactly the right time. She'd withdrawn enough money from her college savings to make it, and she'd relished every moment away from Back Home. Every moment until she'd landed in the sea and all of her friends, along with hundreds of others on that overcrowded ferry, had been sucked underwater . . . forever.

"Where's Back Home for you?" she asked, directing the question to any of the three, trying to erase the images of her drowned classmates.

Ned answered. "Northern California. A beach town.

We've surfed together since we could hop on a board. You?"

"Iowa. Corn-fed and Midwestern, through and through." For a moment, the taste of hot-buttered corn on the cob filled her mouth, but it vanished almost as quickly as it had come. She licked her lips and found they were sore. Her head ached too, so she burrowed under the tarp and slept, dreaming of water, dreaming of butter and corn and the farm—the real Back Home.

When she'd been little it had been a perfect place. A tire swing at the side of the house. Mom pushing her high, so she could tap the tree branches with her toes. Dad in the kitchen every midday for dinner, his face streaked by sweat and plowed earth, earth that had belonged to the Langlies for three generations. That lifestyle had vanished along with the farm. Poor crops for three years running. Dad sold the land before he lost it to the bank. Then they'd moved to the city where none of them—

"Blakie!" Ned's voice shattered her restless sleep, and she scooted from under the tarp.

Ned knelt over Blakie, first pressing Blakie's wrist between his hands, then shaking his shoulder, then pushing hard on his chest. Again. Again. "Wake up, damn you!"

Winker looked at Ned, then down at Blakie and the knife lying next to his body. Then Winker fell back against the side of the boat and buried his face in his arms.

A thin red line trickled from Blakie's wrist and across to where Miranda sat. She threw the blanket over it and watched as the red soaked through.

Ned pulled Blakie onto his lap, holding him against his chest, swaying back and forth. "You idiot. You effin' idiot."

As the sun settled low, hovering just above the line between sky and sea, Ned finally released the body of his friend and set him on the bottom of the boat. "Give me that blanket." Ned held out his hand to Miranda, and she pushed the blanket toward him with her foot, not wanting to touch it with all of Blakie's life soaked into its fibers.

"Winker, help me." Ned was taking charge again, giving orders.

Winker spread the blanket and Ned rolled Blakie inside. "Miranda, take one leg. Winker, take the other one."

"Wait!" Miranda stayed where she was. "You have to say something. I mean, you have to say some words."

When her grandmother died, the priest had said lots of words. Long life. Going to a better place. Take time for grieving, but move on to rejoice and celebrate your loved one.

"Okay. Say something." Ned let Blakie rest on the bottom of the boat again and waited.

She didn't have any words. Her mouth was sticky, and when she tried to focus on Ned, he blurred.

"Where are you going . . . and what do you wish?" Winker whispered, but his words took to the wind and sounded as if they'd been said loudly, maybe in a church sepulcher. His cheek twitched and he brushed at his eyes, but they were dry. He had no tears to wipe away. "The old moon asked the three."

"What in the hell is that?" Ned snapped.

"Something my mom used to read to me," Winker said. "It's all I can think . . . think to say."

The only sound was the slapping of water against the side of the boat. Then Ned lifted Blakie by his arms. Winker took one leg and Miranda the other, and they laid the body along the thick band of rubber that separated them from the sea. It was Winker who pushed Blakie over the edge. He slipped away without a splash and disappeared beneath the surface.

Winker stared at the spot as if he didn't want to lose sight of the place that had swallowed Blakie. "Never . . . afraid are we. As we sail into the sea of dew." He cleared his throat. "I'm talking to the moon tonight, Blakie. I'm asking for it to bring you back."

So whether it was a wish or a prayer or just a conversation between human beings and the ancient moon, that night Winker knelt and Ned knelt with him. "Please," Winker said, "find Blakie. Bring him home."

Miranda sought out the darkness under the tarp to avoid the cool white light from overhead, to avoid hearing the entreaties for the dead Blakie, to avoid giving up on life.

That night, as the air chilled, the pile of three slept under the tarp, but not well. Winker bolted upright two times, screaming about the moon. Ned turned first to face away from her, and then to curl around her back. When he pulled her close to him, Miranda found his hand again and held it. This hand had saved her once; she prayed it would save her again. And finally, before the sun arrived, she slept, believing that it would. Believing that Ned Parker would find that shipping lane and that the three of them would soon be on a ship, safe.

Rain didn't come the next day, but a thick mist did. Together they made a catch basin from the tarp, spreading it across the end of the boat and funneling one end into the empty plastic container. By noon they had half a cup of water and they each took one small capful onto their tongues, holding it in their mouths, not wanting to swallow.

It wasn't enough to stop Miranda's head from throbbing or her lips from cracking and bleeding. When she looked at Winker, he looked back at her with sunken eyes that didn't seem to register her presence. His cheek hadn't twitched since the day he'd sent Blakie into the sea, but now it began again.

"When did this start?" Miranda stroked his cheek as if it were something she had always done. Now, touching him seemed okay. It seemed right. The way he looked at her with his teardrop-shaped eyes, he seemed to invite her to do it.

Winker didn't pull back, but he took his time before answering. "After my mom died." He drew his tongue over his teeth. "My dad took it hard. Spent lots of days drunk." He tried to swallow, then swiped his hand over his face. "I read and surfed . . . the rest of the time." Winker looked at Ned. "He and Blakie . . . they got me through."

The rest of that day they slept. Woke with starts. Slept again.

After that, Miranda lost count of the days. Now, she only counted the drops of water that Ned placed on her tongue with the exactness of a priest. It gave her comfort to watch how he held the cap. How he measured the water, then presented it to her and then to Winker before recapping the plastic container and returning it to the supply box. This ritual helped her forget that the half cup of water was nearly gone.

Miranda thought about those first days together on the boat and realized she missed them because of all those rituals that Ned didn't perform anymore. He didn't paddle or check the compass or talk about keeping them headed south. He didn't net herring and serve her small slivers of them. She realized that she didn't miss eating anymore. Her focus was on drinking.

Since Blakie had gone, there was nothing to distract them from the slowness of time, and it was as if Winker was sinking into himself a bit more each time she looked at him. All any of them did was sleep, and hopelessness spread like a contagion.

Then, on one of the days after they'd taken water and the sun had disappeared, Ned didn't roll over, cover his head, and sleep. "We should set up a watch," he said that night when the sky had cast a silver net of stars overhead. "We're sleeping at the same time, and if a ship comes near we won't see it."

Miranda felt relieved to have Ned making plans again. She felt a surge of renewed hope, and when she looked at Winker, his eyes were focused on Ned and her as if he really saw them.

Winker raised a hand. "I'll take . . . early watch. Sunrise to mid . . . morning."

Ned said, "Midmorning to when the sun passes overhead—about two. Okay, Miranda?"

She nodded.

"I'll take it from two until sunset," he said.

"We're not catching a southern current, are we?" Winker asked, but it sounded more like a statement of fact.

Ned shook his head. "I don't think so. It's getting colder and drier every day." He waited, as if he didn't want to say the rest.

Or maybe, Miranda thought, he was having trouble talking. She was. Her tongue didn't fit inside her mouth like it should. It had thickened, and it rubbed against the roof and the sides like a rasp.

The next day she lay under the tarp, feeling the light but shivering because the sun seemed to have lost all its heat. When she felt a tug on her foot, she struggled to sit.

"Your turn," Winker said, and he stretched out and slept before she could get to the side of the boat.

Before noon, Miranda couldn't stay awake. Her head would jerk forward or loll back, setting off an alarm and bringing her again to her watch, but if any ship passed quickly she knew she'd miss it unless it bore down on them. Oh, and she really wished it would bear down on them, make huge troughs next to them that would raise them up into the air so they could shout, "We're here. Throw us a line. Give us water."

She no longer needed to pee. That humiliation of going over the side of the boat half-naked had ended some days ago, but she knew what not peeing meant. She remembered the humiliation with some longing.

Ned relieved her from her watch, but she sat at his side and didn't return to the tarp.

"If a ship passes . . ." She tried to swallow, but she had almost no saliva. "How do we signal?"

He pointed to the supply box. "Flare gun."

They were all using few words, saving energy, avoiding the pain of cracked lips and thick tongues.

The supplies in that box had to be years old. The crackers had been stale, the tins slightly bulging and filled with odd-tasting fruit. She let her eyelids scrape across her irises and slept, sitting there next to Ned, hoping that her first thoughts about the flare gun were not the right ones. It would work. It had to.

Then one day, Winker didn't wake her for her midmorning watch, and she knew it was because he'd fallen asleep. Before the sun arrived at its highest point in the sky, she crawled to him, shook him, and took her place.

Even though she struggled to stay awake and scan the horizon, she must have dozed because the sudden and harsh rocking of the lifeboat brought her out of dark dreams. She blinked and looked around her, thinking that if she didn't hold to the side she might be washed overboard. A wake flip-flopped them in the water. Her mind was slow from dehydration, but she tried to piece together what this meant. Then she got it. There had to be something big that was making those choppy waves. She looked ahead and to both sides. Only emptiness. The same as she'd seen for days. Then she looked to the stern, and there it was. Looming like a great white mirage. A ship.

Miranda stood, shouted, waved her arms. She grabbed up a blanket and flapped it in the air.

Winker and Ned scrambled to her side. Ned opened the supply box. He held the flare gun so it pointed at the sky and pulled the trigger. It fired, sending a red streak into the air. He waited. Staring after the ship, he gritted his teeth. "Come around, damn you." He fired again, but this time the flare didn't discharge. Again he pulled the trigger, but nothing happened.

Ned hurled the gun back into the supply box, sank back against the boat, and buried his head in his arms.

Miranda and Winker watched the great white ship become smaller and smaller, until they could no longer see it.

That night they slept apart, shivering in despair. In the morning, Miranda stayed under her blanket, waiting for Winker to call her to her watch and dreading another day of seeing nothing—not a speck of land, not anything resembling a ship. It wasn't until the sun dipped low in the West that she sat up and realized Winker had never awakened her.

"Winker!" She crawled to his blanket and pulled it back. He wasn't there. She nudged Ned awake. "Where is he?" she asked when he opened his eyes and looked up at her.

It took a moment for him to understand what she was asking, then he pushed himself up and looked around, as if he expected to find Winker at any moment. "He left us," he said before lying down, curling his knees to his chest and pulling the blanket over his face.

Loneliness swallowed her, sending her into a pit of hopelessness like nothing she'd ever experienced. She'd thought the day their farmhouse furniture was carted off by strangers would always be her worst one. Then she'd thought the day her dad left with one suitcase and a grim goodbye would be her worst one. She'd never expected to have something more terrible to face. She longed to cry, but she had no tears. She longed to drink the sea dry, but when she tasted her lips with the tip of her tongue, the saltiness reminded her just how terrible even one sip would be.

Sleep was her only escape, so she lay down next to Ned's bundled form and closed her eyes. She set her mind free and—as if from a great distance, maybe as far away as the moon—looked down on the two of them, the tiny boat and the vast sea. Then she dreamed of Iowa, where the sea only existed in the movies and hot-buttered corn and cool water in tall glasses were taken for granted. At first light, she stared into another cold, clear day, surprised and not a little disappointed to find herself adrift on a sea again and not standing on the Iowa soil of her dreams.

Ned hadn't moved since last night. She placed her hand on his chest, then snatched it back when she couldn't feel the beat of his heart. Her quick movement made her dizzy, and for a moment she thought he'd stirred. When her head cleared, she touched him again, feeling for some spark of life. There was none, and a rush of terror shot through her.

Missing the closeness of another, she put her ear against his chest, and that was how she stayed—pressed to Ned's stillness, her eyes closed, their pile of two growing colder with each beat of her lonely heart.

When she felt the day slip into night, she rolled onto her back and found the moon. She struggled to sit, and when she looked around her she found herself in a world of two moons—one in the sky and one drenched in the sea. Now she was ready to pray to be taken back to the land of the living, and she had to do that before she could no longer form the words.

She said it once, her tongue sticking to the roof of her mouth. "Please bring me home. Please bring all of us home."

Had either of the moons heard her? If one had, would it find her when it left the night sky or when it left the sea in search of souls? Would at least one of them gather Blakie and Winker and Ned, too?

She prayed one of them would, and then lay down again and went back to thinking about beautiful things, like sweet water. After a while, the boat stopped being a boat and became a cradle, the cradle that had rocked her and her mother and her grandmother. The cradle that used to be tucked into the back corner of the attic in the Iowa farmhouse, waiting for the next generation. Sold, she remembered. Sold at auction. There would be no cradle for her children, so she shouldn't be worried about not having children. Blakie would see the logic in that. She'd have to tell him.

When the darkness came for her, the cradle rocked her to sleep and the misty sea slapped along the sides. Out of that darkness, she felt Ned's hand reach for hers. She'd known he wouldn't desert her. He'd saved her once, hadn't he? Trusting him again, she let herself be pulled to her knees, a place of prayer. Or was she simply too shaky to stand? She clutched the side of the lifeboat, and, with a smile, said the word as if it was two.

"Life. Boat."

And then she tumbled into the dewy sea, where the moon watched from above and waited below. Where starry herring nibbled her toes and fanned their silver against her skin. Where Blakie mumbled his perfect math solutions, Winker recited the moon prayers of Eskimos, and Ned Parker offered drops of clear, cool water for her tongue.

– The End –

THE LION AND THE UNICORN

The Lion and the Unicorn
Were fighting for the crown;
The Lion beat the Unicorn
All about the town.
Some gave them white bread
And some gave them brown;
Some gave them plum cake
And drummed them out of town!
                    – Mother Goose

THE LION AND THE UNICORN: PART THE SECOND

By Nancy Holder

On the eve of Susana's seventeenth birthday, a shooting star appeared in the sky and hung there like a candle. Some called it an auspicious omen. Others said it foretold the death of someone important. Susana knew there were some who meant wished on that star for the king to die.

The people longed for an end to the burning times. It seemed that the more witches the king tortured and killed, the more witches he found. The sheer numbers were beginning to alarm his subjects, but how could one speak against their sovereign lord in such matters? James himself had written much on the divine right of kings. God Himself had anointed him and placed him to rule over his subjects.

For Susana, the star was not a star at all. It was her angel, and she was terrified to see it. She knew very well what its appearance signified: the time had come.

She was to kill the king.

No one else had seen the things that "Robin Fletcher" had seen. No one else knew that most of the accused witches the king ordered thrown into the dungeons were innocents. Nor did anyone know that His Majesty took real pleasure in forcing them to tell lies in order to spare themselves further torment. He liked to hurt them. The pleasure he found in crushing bones and searing flesh was inhuman.

As far as she could tell, the king was himself inhuman.

She remembered the first time she had seen the green mist rise from an old hag in the dungeon. She knew it now for the glow of magic. How some came by it, she was not sure, but it was powerful, and capable of fearsome things. She had spied on the witches in their dungeons, and watched them heal each other's wounds, and summon vermin to bring little bits of food. Of a dark night, she had seen a witch swear to her cellmates that she would gather the coven to curse the king's soul to hell, then disappear forever.

Susana had tried to deny what she had heard and seen in the torture chamber, and what she had seen in the king's black eyes. She tried to tell herself that the streams of green light were attacks on the king, and he was risking his life each time he put a witch to the rack.

But she had to admit what she knew: The king was stealing the magic from the witches, and not for the sake of his people.

King James I, the Unicorn, was a warlock, and he had boasted to his most recent victim that soon he would have amassed enough power as to be unstoppable.

"And then shall my master come forth, and I shall give him my crown, and bow down in triumph before him," he had told the tormented woman. "And no army on this earth will stop us."

Fear not, the knock upon Susana's heart now called

out as she looked up at the star. For while no army on earth could stop the king, "Robin Fletcher" could.

She and she alone served him his wine and bread.

***

"Robin?" the king called impatiently.

Near the entrance to the torture chamber, Susana held the tiny vial of poison over the goblet of wine. She had been promised that it would be quick. Quick for the king, yes. But the punishment for traitors was horrible. Her body would be pulled apart, and all her organs yanked out, and burned. And she would then be beheaded, and she would not lie in hallowed ground.

Fear not, said the voice. It came from inside her. She felt the tapping inside her heart, and shut her eyes tightly. Then she poured the poison into the goblet and placed it on the tray with two slices of bread, one brown, and one white. She put the vial into her doublet and picked up the tray, and her torch.

The pressure inside her heart seemed to grow, expanding until a warm glow hummed through all her veins. But it couldn't thaw the icy terror that made her shake as she headed down stairs and into the passageway toward the torture chamber. She stopped once, then was urged on. Stopped a second time. Moved forward.

She saw the green light and heard the screams of an old woman. She heard low laughter—the king's—and clutched the goblet tightly. She was so afraid that she considered drinking it herself.

"Robin?" the king called.

Her angel must have moved her limbs, for Susana was paralyzed with fright. Forward, then. Slowly.

"I'm here, Your Majesty," she said, facing him.

Green mist was soaking into his skin. His victim was lying in a pile on the floor.

He held out his hand for the cup. Her angel put her hand around the goblet and held it out to him.

"Is it good wine?" he asked her.

"The best, sire," her angel made her say.

He took the cup and raised it to his lips. Looked at her steadily over the rim. She opened her mouth to speak, but no sound came out.

Then he threw it in her face, grabbed her, and dragged her to the empty rack. She was so stunned, she didn't fight back—or couldn't—as he put a manacle around one wrist, then the other. She could only gasp as he fastened the restraints around her ankles.

"Murderer!" he screamed. "Did you think I wouldn't *know*?"

He snapped his fingers, and an image appeared in Susana's line of vision. She saw herself putting the poison in the wine. She wanted to deny it, or to lie— say it was an elixir for his health—but she didn't have time as he hit her, hard, across the face.

"You've known," he said. "For months, you've known, and you never told a soul. No one will miss you. No one will come to help you now."

She felt something *hot* against her leg, and then it burned with unimaginable pain. She screamed.

It happened again.

She screamed again.

He laughed, and bent over her. His eyes were black, and she saw the horns rising up on his head. Writhing, she tried to look away, but he clasped her under the chin and forced her to look at him.

"Such a pious man he was," the king said. "On his knees every dawn, praying for Scotland, and then for England. But we knew we could take him. And we have."

She gasped. "Sire, help me," she managed to grind out. "My king."

"We've buried him deep," said the king—or the spirits, or demons, pretending to be the king. "He's nearly gone."

More pain surrounded her. She couldn't even scream this time.

It is not the king. It never was, she thought hazily, although the ability to think was leaving her. Everything seared and burned and *hurt*.

"You're the only one who knows," said the demons inside the king.

And more pain.

And more.

Where are you? she cried out to her angel. *How can you let this happen?*

Then there was a knocking in her heart; and the voice whispering, *"Fear not."* And as her eyes fluttered, barely open, she was enveloped in a haze of white light.

She heard the king scream, and saw the white light rise from her body and hover above his. He threw his head back at the sight of it and began to scream.

"No!"

He batted at it with hands that turned into claws. His nose stretched to a point and huge teeth pushed out from his lips. His skin turned scarlet. He looked like Satan.

"No!" he cried again.

The light shimmered around him and he raced to the rack, giving the wheel a hard twist that threatened to pull Susan's arms and legs from their sockets.

"Make it stop!" he ordered her. "Stop now!"

She could do nothing but groan. The pain was unendurable. As he gazed down on her, turning the wheel again, the mist curled around him, brushing against his crimson skin. His eyes like coals, he hissed like a serpent.

"Then I'll stop it with your death," he said.

A sword appeared in his hand and he raised it over his head. She welcomed death if it would stop the agony; but she was bitterly sorry that she had waited so long to do something about him.

"He is inside us," said the demon that had hold of King James. "He is trying to stop us. He has always tried. He has always failed."

Hearing that, Susana grieved for the king as well. If she had moved sooner…

The sword came flying down in an arc. Susana was too injured to move, but she had time for one word, *"Father—"*

And then something came between her and the sword. It was a luminous hand, connected to a figure of shimmering white. Wings unfurled from its shoulders. Her angel. Her stuttering, slowing heart registered astonishment, and hope, and she whimpered—for that was the only sound she could make.

The angel turned its head toward Susana. It said, "Fear not."

Then angel and demon-possessed king wrestled. The angel would grab hold of the king's body and throw him to the floor. Then the king swept his leg beneath the angel's feet and it crashed beside him. The angel struck the king hard across the face. The king made a double fist and brought it down on the angel's back, where its wings were attached.

And Susana continued to die. She could feel her strength ebbing, so that it took all of her concentration to force air into and out of her lungs. Her heart skipped beats, then did not beat, then beat too fast. Her blurry vision caught flashes of white and scarlet; and shrieks like the demons of hell buffeted her bleeding ears.

The two fought all over the torture chamber, their shadows thrown against the wall. The possessed king called for guards, but none came. The angel tossed him to the floor again and again, but each time, the king rose and dealt the angel a terrible blow.

Beneath the punishment of the king's pummeling fists, the figure of light began to fade. Fists cross in an attempt to ward off the blows, it shakily turned its head toward Susana, and for the first time, she saw its face.

He was a young man near her age. His eyes were wide and heavily lashed with silver; his nose was long and straight; his generous lips pulled back in a grimace of defeat. Two tears like diamonds rolled down the hollows of his cheeks.

"I am sorry," he whispered.

"He is losing hope," said the monsters inside the king. "And when hope is lost, we swoop in."

***

The king raised the sword over his head and brought it down on the angel's head. With a cry, the angel crumpled to his knees and his light grew so dim that Susana could see through him.

The demons are going to win, Susana thought, horrified.

But then her heart—not something in it, but her heart—forced her eyes to stay open. She whispered to the angel, "Fear not."

He blinked at her and his lips parted in astonishment. And then his light grew a little brighter once again.

"Fear not," she murmured.

His wings unfurled as he got to one knee. But the king was rushing him again, ready to pummel him.

And then she looked past his shoulder and yelled at the king himself. "Fear not!"

"He is terrified," the demons informed her, laughing. "He gave up hope long ago." He kicked at the angel, who darted just out of reach. The king charged after him.

"Fear not, sire, fear not!" she cried.

The king staggered backward as if something had struck him; as he staggered, the angel flapped his wings back, forth, in a slow, deliberate manner. Then white light burst from him, blazing like the star that had hung in the sky, and the king opened his mouth to scream. The light poured into the king's mouth, and the angel moved his wings again. White light filled the room, surrounding the king, filling him, lifting him up into the air as he struggled and fought.

Susana's manacles and ankle bolts fell away. As she sat up, she felt no pain. She leaped off the rack and fell to her knees, crying, "I fear not! I fear not!" Then everything became an aurora of brilliance, and she fainted.

***

When she came to, she was seated in a small chamber. One window was open, and she saw the sunshine, and many trees, and heard merrymaking.

She had been placed into an overstuffed chair, wrapped in an ermine robe. She gasped. It was the king's coronation robe. And to her right was a golden tray; upon it, a jeweled goblet of wine and a filigreed dish of plum pudding.

Across the chamber, the king was kneeling at a

prayer desk; a large illuminated Bible was opened before him. He was murmuring the Lord's Prayer.

He lifted his head. "Ah, you're awake," he said raising his head. He turned to look at her. "Once named Robin and now…?"

She took a shuddering breath. "Forgive me, Your Majesty. Let me tell you how I came to disguise myself. I had a vision—"

"And I thank God that you did," he said, rising. He walked to her and picked up the cup. "I must beg forgiveness of you, and of all my people. Henceforth, my new reign has begin. One of peace, and tranquility." He gestured to the window. "Word has spread among those who should be told that I was not myself. I can only hope their curses will turn to blessings."

He handed her the cup. She was too shy to drink it, and he smiled.

"Fear not," he told her. "Mistress…?"

"Susana, Your Majesty." She snaked her hand from beneath the ermine robe and took the goblet from him.

And as she drank, she thought she heard the pounding of her heart, or the booming of the thunder, or the thumping of drums; but the sound she heard was none of these:

It was the rushing of wings as the angel—her angel—hovered in the window, the sun behind him, gazing at her with a heavenly smile. His wings moved, and he touched his fingertips to his lips and blew her a kiss. She felt it in her heart, and her eyes welled with tears.

"'Tis not farewell," the angel said. "For I am yours."

Then the light blazed so bright that she had to shield her eyes. When she lowered her hand, the king was on his knees, and he was surrounded by a hundred—a thousand—baskets of bread. He looked up at Susana, and they began to laugh. Then they each grabbed up handfuls of bread and tossed it out the window. She saw a towering may pole, and fiddlers, and mummers and jesters. She saw happiness as the bread rained down like manna from heaven.

Drummers played, and the people cried, "God save the King!"

And Susana knew that God had.

Through His angel and his servant, He had.

– The End –

Author Acknowledgements

The following contributors have chosen to include the below acknowledgements.

Leigh Fallon
Huge thanks to Georgia and the team for all their amazing work and support. It was a pleasure working with you guys. Also, to my wonderful critique partner, Morgan Shamy, and the gorgeous Kim Harrington who ran her spookometer over Wee Willie Winkie for me, you guys rock. Lastly, thanks to Tina Wexler, my agent, who is the epitome of awesome.

Nancy Holder
My sincere thanks to Glenda Jackson, my first Elizabeth.

Heidi R. Kling
For victims of child abuse, please know that there's a brighter life waiting for you to find it.

Karen Mahoney
For Mum, who read it first.
Georgia McBride
Thank you to Mother Goose for creating a world of

Shannon Delany and Max Scialdone
Both Shannon and Max would like to thank the staff at Month 9 who made this process easy, and their joint beta readers: Jen McHugh, Steven Blaze, Patty Locatelli, Melissa Murray, and Karl Gee. Shannon also thanks her family and friends and gives special thanks

to Max Scialdone who taught her a lot about music and musicians during this process. Without Max's friendship and expertise Marnum and Cyrelle's world wouldn't sing. In addition, Max would like to thank his mother for her unwavering support.

Pamela van Hylckama Vlieg
I would never be able to write such dark things without the imaginative childhood I had. I would like to thank my mother Barbara Herzig for that. My Agent Laurie McLean for helping me brainstorm, and my blogger BFF Shanyn from Chick Loves Lit for beta reading. To my husband Marco, and my children Addie, and Elijah - I would be nowhere without you.

K.M. Walton
Acknowledgements: Thank you to Georgia McBride for asking me to participate in this anthology and for believing in my writing before I even had an agent. Thank you *to* my agent, Sarah LaPolla, for everything. And to my husband and sons, thank you for allowing me the time to get lost in my stories.

Gabriel Stone and the Divinity of Valta

Available in print and eBook from Month9Books in
January 2013
www.month9books.com

A Shimmer of Angels

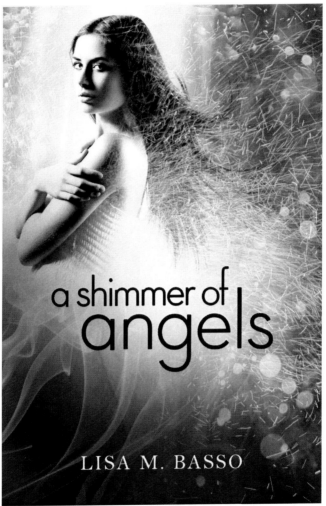

a shimmer of
angels

LISA M. BASSO

Available in print and eBook from Month9Books in
January 2013
www.month9books.com

Sidekick: The Misadventures of the New Scarlet Knight

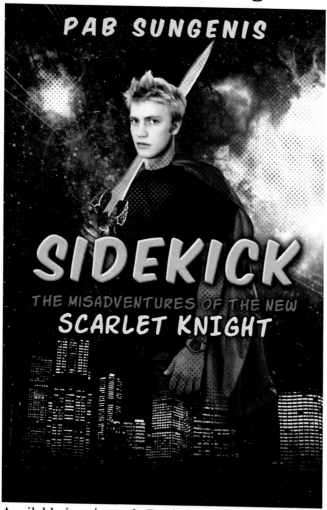

Available in print and eBook from Month9Books in March 2013

www.month9books.com

Pretty Dark Nothing

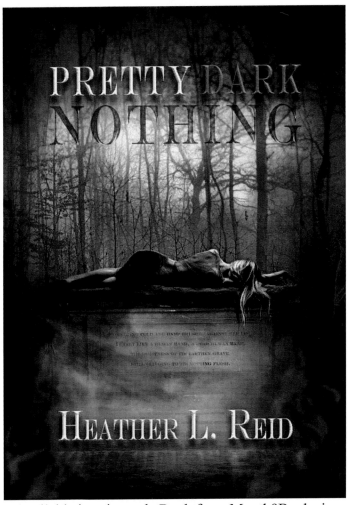

Available in print and eBook from Month9Books in
April 2013
www.month9books.com

My Sister's Reaper

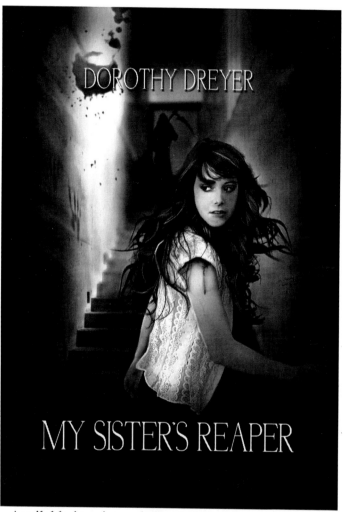

Available in print and eBook from Month9Books in
May 2013
www.month9books.com